The Annunaki Enigma: Armageddon 2015

Authors

E. Gaylon McCollough, M.D.
and
Symm H. McCord, M.D.

Philip Reed Moran - Editor

A-Argus Better Book Publishers, LLC
North Carolina***New Jersey

The Annunaki Enigma: Armageddon 2015 © *2013*
All rights reserved by E. Gaylon
McCollough and Symm H. McCord

A-Argus Better Book Publishers, LLC

For information:
A-Argus Better Book Publishers, LLC
9001 Ridge Hill Street
Kernersville, North Carolina 27285
www.a-argusbooks.com

ISBN: 978-0-6157885-6-2
ISBN: 0-6157885-6-4

Book Cover designed by Dubya

Printed in the United States of America

"...for the words are closed and sealed up to the time of the end. Many must be tested, and tried with fire; the transgressors shall transgress; and none of the transgressors will understand; but the wise shall understand."   Daniel 12:9-10

Introduction

In the fall of 2007 E. Gaylon McCollough, M.D., a facial plastic surgeon in Gulf Shores, Alabama, released his latest book, *Let Us Make Man.* In this book, the doctor set out to intellectually search the scriptures and to use all of the knowledge that we have attained to answer a question that has had very little scholarly scrutiny. Many of us have wondered as we read the Bible exactly how God actually went about "making man".

Dr. McCollough began to wonder if there was an overlooked revelation hidden in Genesis 1:26 which reads: "And God said let us make man in our image, after our likeness; and let them have dominion over the fishes of the sea, and over the fowl of the air, and over the cattle, and over all the earth, and over every creeping thing that creepeth upon the earth."

There are so many questions and Dr. McCollough did a masterful job of searching the Bibles and scriptures of many of the world's religions and the minds of many very knowledgeable people in his quest for the answers to these and many other questions. In his treatise, *Let Us Make Man,* he calls on the archangel Metatron with whom he engages in an interactive conversation. During the poetic encounter, the archangel reveals untold mysteries and answers to many of the questions that are asked. The links between creation and evolution and between science and theology are at long last revealed in a manner that is comprehensible to modern man.

Within three months of the publication of Dr. McCollough's book, another book, a science fiction novel, written by Dr. Symm H. McCord, a retired family physician in Waynesville, North Carolina, was released.

Seeking the same answers and having considered almost exactly the same questions for years, Dr. McCord, in *The Annunaki Enigma: Creation,* presents a story of an Above-Top-

Secret group working out of the United States Naval Observatory in Washington, D.C., and the efforts of one of its members to protect the sixty-year-old secret of the truth behind the crash at Roswell, New Mexico, in 1947, and the innumerable current sightings of unidentified flying objects in the skies around the world.

The member, Zach Donovan, is charged with the duty to guard this mystery, but the introduction of a female journalist dedicated to uncovering the information causes serious problems within the group. During this time the story of Jhowah and the challenge he made 38,000 years ago (to create and populate a distant planet with a newly created species of beings) is presented and the amazing tale of the Challenge is told.

For anyone who has doubted the existence of intelligent life beyond earth, *The Annunaki Enigma: Creation* could provide a bridge to reconsideration.

Doctors McCord and McCollough's research revealed that no one had ever fully explained who "us" is and who is being referred to as "our". If it is the angels, who are they and where did they come from? Did all of the angels help, or were there only a few or maybe just one other. How was man made? Was it from dust? What does the Bible mean by "dust"? Does it mean dirt or could it be a metaphor for some primordial mixture of genes or organics that found its way through the cosmos to the third planet from our sun? Was "making man" an impulsive thought and action by God, or was it a well-thought-out idea that required planning and much scientific thought and endeavor? Who is God and where did He live? We know He is a "supreme being," and if he created the earth, he is, necessarily, from some other place and rules over other civilizations in the universe.

The authors hope that you will use their merger of fact and fiction woven throughout the pages of *The Annunaki Enigma: Armageddon* to arrive at your own conclusions. Their wish is that you would incorporate the knowledge contained herein to stimulate your curiosity and help you see the world from a more enlightened point of view. They invite you to join in the quest for answers that the people of earth will someday learn. One thing is for certain, you will see God and "us" (our Creators) in a newfound light.

All who read this book will view "the news of the day" with insight that might have otherwise escaped them and will better understand what kind of world the people of this generation are in the process of creating. What will the "One World Order" truly become?

Acknowledgements

But for the foresight of U.S. Army Major General David Bockel, Washington, D.C., this novel would not have been written. As a military leader the general was trained to believe that there are no coincidences and when he read books written by two separate long-time friends, both being physicians and strangers to each other, General Bockel was driven to bring the two of them together, pointing out the commonalities between them. The introduction and virtually everything that followed can best be described as a cyberspace collaboration to write a sequel to the two books. The authors wish to express our thanks to our mutual friend, Major General David Bockel.

We would also like to express our thanks to our editor, Philip Reed Moran, who did the tedious work of going through our each and every word and punctuation in order to correct all grammatical errors. As usual, he did much more for us in using his ability to almost read our minds, to make excellent suggestions in revising some of the parts that needed improvement.

Preface

The world has begun to change from a, hopefully, cooperative group of individual nations into a global society ruled by a "one-world government" which governs out of the United Nations in New York. It is led predominantly by Muslim nations. The United States has become no more than a geographical branch of this government, and is rapidly transforming into a Marxist society and away from its original capitalist beginnings. There is a great unrest within the United States from conservative political groups who have become disenfranchised from their constitutional form of government. The new state controlled medical community is in rebellion and disarray. A global banking system is charged with the stability of a weak and failing economy. The domestic army that has evolved from AmeriCorps, using fear as a weapon, has gained complete control of the American populace which has cowed to it much like the populations in Europe during the early and mid-1900s.

Energy continues to be an international problem. The early attempts to replace carbon-based fuels with alternative fuel sources are not adequate. Even though there is a global society, the Muslim dominated United Nations has maintained a monopolistic control of this energy source within the Middle East nations. Billions of dollars have been invested around the world in an attempt to discover a clean and inexpensive form of energy to replace oil. To date no adequate replacement has been found.

Israel, since its repudiation earlier by the American president, has become the target of many nations, but the age old threats of annihilation from Tehran have increased in intensity. The common consent of the other nations with regards to Iran's verbal assaults and threats to launch their evolving nuclear arsenal—along with the lack of condemnation of the same from the

Dr. Gaylon McCollough
And
Dr. Symm Hawes McCord

United States—have emboldened the Iranians as if to add fuel to a fire.

The world has changed dramatically within the past few years and the citizens of the world are unable to do anything to change the direction of government. Global unrest is mounting. For reasons not yetdisclosed to them, the leaders of the world's most technologically advanced nations are suddenly summoned to the remote island of North Bimini by the United Nation's Secretary General. What they find there reveals long-awaited secrets to the creation of man and this planet, and fulfills many predictions from the past coming out of numerous cultures and religions.

Erich von Däniken's theory of ancient astronauts is shown to be true but the power and demands of these alien "visitors" are more than Earth's leaders are willing to accept. What happens after this encounter is the basis of predicted events given to us in the Book of Revelation. The second coming of the beings that Genesis 6:4 identified as: "the sons of God" (the Annunaki) sparked a chain of events that will alter the course of humanity forever.

The words and events portrayed in this book are inspired by the geopolitical happenings taking place today. The events and characters are fictional and are from the imaginations of the authors but, based on the actual global occurrences at this time, we could very well see such a scenario take place unless the leaders of this planet heed the lessons of history and the warnings of our Creators and make changes now.

The Annunaki Enigma
Armageddon 2015

Table of Contents:

CHAPTER ONE

THE INITIAL CONTACT

December 22, 2015
Washington, D.C.
White House, Oval Office

The U.S. president looked up from his desk and noted the intent look on the face of his chief of staff.

"What is it, Dick? You look distressed."

"Sir, United Nations Secretary-General Amano is on the phone. He says it is urgent and he must speak to you now."

The president lifted the phone, pushed the appropriate button, and put it to his ear. "Mister Secretary-General, what is so pressing?"

"Mister President, we have a situation developing in the Caribbean in the vicinity of the island of North Bimini. We are about to have extra-terrestrial visitors. What I must tell you about them at this time is that this contact will be of universal importance; so, I am ordering the heads of states of all superpowers and several other important nations to immediately go to Alice Town on that Island. I cannot tell you anymore about them now, but you'll understand why when they arrive. You will be met there and transported to the planned landing site. Sir, it is imperative that this all be done with utmost secrecy. Your secret service can work out the logistics with my people."

"Mister Secretary-General, I have a nation to run here. I can't be flying around to little island countries looking for UFOs."

"I cannot impress upon you the importance of this meeting and the need for representation from the highest level of leadership in your country. It is important that you attend in person. We need the United States president, and not a lower level staff member. Please, I cannot say more without risking a leak. Even secured phone lines such as these can be monitored. You must come!"

As the president lowered the phone his face was stern. "Dick, something significant is happening on North Bimini. I don't know the extent. Amano wouldn't say, but he was very upset. I've never heard him sound like that. Make immediate plans for me to get to Alice Town.

* * *

Moments Later In The Kremlin
Moscow, Russia

"But I have to meet with the heads of state of two nations today. I can't make it down there for some fantasy."

The president listened as the secretary-general explained. There was no way that he could avoid this visitation. He placed the phone into its cradle and looked up at his aide. "Get me the fastest transportation we have to the island of North Bimini in the Caribbean, and do it immediately. I really wish I knew what this was all about."

* * *

Ten Minutes Later
Beijing, China
Office Of The President

"I'm most sorry Mister Secretary-General. I am too important to the stability and guidance of my country to make this secret meeting that you have planned for us."

"You must change your mind, Mister President," Amano urged. "This is an event of historical importance that may have immense consequences if handled improperly."

"Sir, I'll leave the handling up to you," the Chinese president responded. "You represent the world."

The Chinese president handed the phone to an aide and stood up from behind his desk. He stretched his arms in a relaxing motion and looked at the members from his staff who were sitting across from him and shrugged.

"I'll let the United Nations take care of this. All they'll do is talk, as usual. I have no time to waste on this."

* * *

6:00 PM, December 23, 2015
On A Bimini Beach To The West Of Alice Town
In A Temporary Meeting Structure

"Your attention, please," begged Amano, the secretary-general, as the volume of chatter in the structure began to drown out his request.

Many of the leaders were milling about talking with others and speculating on the reason for the developing situation. They were concerned about the urgent and top-secret orders that the secretary-general had given each of them.

In the audience were two members of an elite U.S. group that was unknown to the populace except for those investigating UFOs. Doug Bradley and his superior, Hank McConnell, were members of Aquarius, a branch of the Majestic-12 group based in the U.S. Naval Observatory that had been actively working the UFO scene since 1947. They were the only people there, other than the secretary-general, who knew the extent of this quickly organized meeting.

Doug McConnell watched as Amano brought down the gavel on the makeshift podium, silencing the room. The U.N. leader looked about the room, his jaw was clinched and concern echoed in his voice.

Amano pounded the gavel as the chatter subsided. "Thank you for coming here today and doing it in such a timely manner. I have noted that there are some leaders have chosen not to come and I believe that they will regret that decision.

"Yesterday we received word through credible sources that the UFOs which we have been observing for many years will be arriving here tonight." He paused as the room filled with an eerie silence. "They have requested our presence, or more accurately, they have told us to be here tonight when they arrive. They also declared that they are the reason that we and this planet exist."

"Are we saying that these beings are our Creators? They are God and the angels?" the Mexican president asked.

Amano stared at him, waited for a moment and answered.

"Yes."

The room exploded as those attending expressed amazement and disbelief at what they had just heard. They had all wondered about the large vehicles which were being seen in the skies around the world. It was said that they could maneuver in ways not possible in any airplane, jets, or even rocket powered vehicles that were controlled by current earth technology, but God, angels -- how could this be?

"Gentlemen and ladies, silence, please. As you now realize, this will be the most epic event in the history of our planet. In the past, some of you have had communications with UFOs, especially the United States which has maintained long term communication. Their communication has been rather one-sided, with very little information given to us as to their origin or the purpose of their constant surveillance of our world."

"Why should we believe them? What are we to do when they arrive?" the Russian president asked.

"We honestly do not know," Amano answered shaking his head. "We just have to wait. We've had ongoing speculation for years as to who they are and what they want with us. Tonight we may find the answers to, at least, some of our questions. I wish I could tell you more but we are truly in the dark. We have representatives here who have had contact and know more about them than I do, but they have been warned many times by these extraterrestrials to not reveal any of their knowledge."

"So they *are* extraterrestrial?" someone in the audience shouted.

"Our intermediaries have advised us," Amano continued, "that they should be arriving here on the beach within the hour. We don't have a definite time frame but I believe we should gather there now. Let me stress the necessity of being orderly, and I also feel compelled to say that, from what our advisors tell us, we have no reason for fear."

With that the group rose out of their seats and began moving toward the door to the beach which was only seventy or seventy-five yards away from the building.

As he exited the building, Doug Bradley could see several battleships and an aircraft carrier a half-mile or so out on the water. There were F-15 and F-16 jets patrolling the sky around the assembly area that were from the Nimitz class carrier which happened to be the USS Ronald Reagan.

Several hundred yards up the beach in both directions, he could see the blue helmeted units of United Nations troops that Amano had ordered in to guard the meeting.

The winter skies over Bimini were darkening as evening approached and the black horizon became fainter as Venus began its traverse through the sky. As the first visible celestial body of the evening her glow was comforting. The rhythm of the waves and the slow dance of the palm fronds helped to soothe the anxieties of the approaching world leaders as they began to gather near the edge of the water.

The serenity of the moment was suddenly broken as five F16s screamed across the coast line in perfect formation as they guarded the most important meeting of beings in the history of the planet.

"I wonder how these leaders will react when they see a starship descending from the sky." Doug said in a low voice as he leaned his head toward Hank. "Most of have never seen a UFO and have based most of their understanding on the words and descriptions of witnesses to form their images. The real thing will be quite different."

"Agreed," Hank responded. "Let's hope no one panics."

When they reached the beach Doug saw Amano, the UN leader. He was speaking into a walkie-talkie and nodding his head, apparently in agreement with whoever was on the other end. As he lowered the walkie-talkie he looked up, scanning the sky above.

"I'm in contact with one of our ships off the coast," he said in a loud voice and looked back at the large group of leaders. "They are monitoring the skies with radar. The captain tells me that they have locked onto a very large vessel heading this way. We should soon have visual contact."

"There, there it is," the United States president shouted and pointed toward a region of the sky.

The members all began looking upwards in that direction and soon a loud hum of excitement could be heard up and down the beach."

"I don't see it." The French president complained in his native tongue.

"I think I do," said an excited British prime minister pointing upward. "Yes, I do. It's just a small speck with a light on it."

The conversation and speculation picked up as the object came closer.

"It has more than one light," the Brit added after a short lull in the talk.

"It looks like a triangle with lights on each corner," the Australian leader exclaimed, as it came even closer.

The discourse was becoming louder and louder as the vessel approached. They were just beginning to realize the enormity of the ship.

"Look at that," Doug said touching Hank on the shoulders. "The size and configuration are growing larger and larger. It's thicker on the front angle than in the back, and now you can get an idea of the height and length of that thing. My God, it must be ten stories high out front, and the length is unbelievable. Hank, that thing is long enough to land one of our jets on top of it."

"No wonder some of our witnesses have had such contempt when we've tried to play down the size of these vessels they described to us."

As the gigantic starship began to settle above the beach, quietness engulfed the crowd that was awed by the sight above them. The view of the sky was blocked by the profile of the massive machine. The underside was lit by lights that came on as it hung three or four hundred feet above the beach. The details of the under surface could be seen with great clarity and exhaust vents, piping, and the many formations of that visible part of the ship were in plain view. The three large bright lights on each corner of the vessel shined downward, lighting up the beach for many yards past its borders and out over the waves that were rolling in. The light was so bright that some of the leaders were shielding their eyes.

"Look at the details on the belly of that ship," Hank noted. "What the hell powers it? How can it travel such distances so fast? Maybe we'll find answers to some of our questions when we talk to the beings that control it."

"Aye mates, I see a door or gate or something opening in the back," the Aussie leader informed them as he looked toward the rear of the ship.

As he spoke several shuttles began to exit from the opening doors. They appeared small, maybe ten feet wide and twenty or thirty feet long. The fronts of these flying matchboxes were sloped downward like a wedge, and as they exited the mammoth starship they moved slowly toward the beach. One by one seven shuttles settled side by side on the white sands of the beach that were reflecting the light shining from the base of the starship. All but one were a gray color. The seventh vehicle parked between the other six was a luminous-bright white. On the side of each ship was the profile of a snake coiled on its tail with the upper third of its body standing erect. A forked tongue was protruding from its mouth.

Doug stood transfixed looking at the sight above and exclaimed in a low voice. "I can feel my heart racing, Hank. It's been a long time since we've been so close to them. The circumstances were different; then, there wasn't as many of them. I recall only small shuttles and nothing like that behemoth floating above us now."

"When our visitors come out of the shuttles, these worldly leaders are going to be stunned," he continued. "I'll never forget the first time I saw them."

Just as Doug finished his sentence, the doors on each side of the shuttles began to slowly rise upward like the wings of a bird as it begins flight.

As the onlookers gasped, the first beings from the gray shuttles exited and gathered around the white one. There appeared to be three species, one of which was obviously the gray of Roswell fame with its large almond shaped eyes. The second species was a bit larger than the grays and appeared more closely related to the human species of earth. Its skin had a yellowish hue, and the black hair on its scalp was coarse. Most noticeable was the small solid black eyes. The third group that exited the gray shuttles was made up of a very large and warrior-like species. Their skin covering was a mahogany color. They had large amounts of body hair, and eyes that appeared totally human with an iris and pupil, surrounded by white.

"God, look at them," the U.S. president gasped.

Momentarily, a single-taller figure emerged from the white shuttle. The grace of its movement was noticeable. It was a gray, but this creature was much taller than the other grays. He and the other beings from the white shuttle were dressed in long Toga-like apparel and appeared to be the leaders of the group. The dress of the remainder of the group coming from the six gray shuttles was also in the manner of a fabric wrap but was limited to the pelvic region, with a shoulder wrap for use when needed by the males, and a wrap which concealed the chest and breasts for the females.

The large gray approached Amano. The secretary-general's personnel gathered closer to him as if protecting him from the unknown. Standing erect in front of Amano, the gray spoke to him. "My name is Jhowah. We have much to discuss. Please take us inside?"

"Yes," Amano answered after a short pause. He turned to the assembled group of leaders and spoke. "Let us return to the temporary facility and hear the words of these beings."

With that they all turned and he led the entire gathering into the building.

Doug Bradley was in his sixties, stood tall and erect, and was bald with the perimeter of his scalp showing a growing amount of gray hair.

Doug's superior, Hank McConnell, was the chief of the Aquarius group, a clandestine unit of the federal government that had been responsible for crash retrieval and cover-up of the UFO phenomenon. Hank was a short but muscular guy in his forties who had a full head of hair, but had kept a flat-top haircut since his teen years. He handled the Aquarian group with a stern no-nonsense demeanor, having been a top sergeant earlier in his career before being assigned to the unit. When a UFO crashed his team would come together like a well-oiled machine and complete the clean up in rapid time.

When an obviously legitimate sighting of a UFO occurred, they would get into the mix and usually be successful in debunking it with well-placed remarks which might often lay ridicule on the witnesses. Ridicule was the main tool used by Aquarius and other branches of the government until recent efforts to desensitize the public. It was an effective method to keep down the assumed public anxiety over the idea of extra-terrestrial intelligent life. A report by the Brookings Institute in the early 1960s suggested the use of such precautions for fear of the effects such a revelation might do to world societies and religions.

As Doug and Hank entered the building, they could sense the electricity in the air coming from the anticipation of those present. There was constant chattering in the room as they found a seat.

"Hank, I know we have been working with these beings from a distance for all these years, but doesn't this all overwhelm you sometimes? I mean now that we are face to face with them and their vehicle, as large as it is, floating above us. The enormity of space and the fact that we were created by these beings from other worlds and from other star systems is something that those people, who haven't been privy to what we've known for years, are going to have a hard time digesting. The Bible speaks of 'false prophets.' Theologians will have a field day with this. They will surely try to say that this is the work of the devil. I wonder what miracle Jhowah will use to prove that He is who He says He is."

"It does make more sense than the way I have always wondered about God," Hank admitted. "After all, we've always been told that we are made in His image."

"In their image," Doug corrected him.

"Exactly," Hank consented, "and you and I certainly don't look like the image we saw tonight. I've always pictured Him somewhat like Moses with a staff in one hand and with open arms standing on a cloud high above us. Perhaps he will address some of these questions today.

"By the way, I have discussed your question about the general acceptance of Jhowah with our chief, Majic-1, on several occasions," Hank continued, "and his opinion and the opinion of those in the know is that there have been over sixty years of viewing unidentifiable, unworldly craft or UFOs, alien abductions, the Star Trek and Stargate television series, the Star Wars movies, Planet of The Apes and Superman movies. Beside the science fiction books and video exposure, the crash of the shuttles at Roswell, New Mexico, during the lightning storms in forty-seven has been thoroughly investigated and it has been shown that there is little doubt that the crash was of a spaceship and that there were several humanoid beings aboard, beings that were not of this planet. There has been a host of witnesses to the event that have come forward, including a general and a Colonel who were a part of the cover up.

"They feel that the populations of the earth have been desensitized and are not only ready to accept this revelation but are eagerly waiting for it to occur. After all, our Bibles began preparing us for this event thousands of years ago. If you are a believer it's not very difficult to fit this all into the stories from the Bible. They were handed down through the ages by people who were obviously not very high tech and unable to comprehend some of what they saw."

"I see where Majic-1 is coming from," Doug replied. "I just didn't think that it would happen in my lifetime."

As Doug finished talking he noticed a hush come over the assembled group and all began looking forward where Jhowah was approaching the podium.

Jhowah was an intimidating site and as Doug looked about he saw the expressions on the faces of the others. This alien being was not exactly like the pictures of the gray extraterrestrial species that they had all seen in magazines and on TV documentaries over the years. This gray's features were stronger and His large black eyes seemed to bore into their very minds which, in reality, He was doing. He wore a long white covering reminiscent of the togas of ancient Rome which, in retrospect, may very well have been originally designed from such dress.

Doug noticed the human individual standing at his right who also was draped in the toga-like material. He was taller than Jhowah and a very handsome man with long, flowing, and uncut brown hair. The two stood soldierly erect and looked at each other; never really speaking a word, but it was obvious that they were in communication.

"Hank, do you think the human could be Jesus?"

"I don't know, Doug. Aren't we taught that they are one and the same, as well as the Holy Spirit?"

"Yes," Doug answered with a bit of confusion on his face.

"I guess we'll just have to wait and see," Hank concluded.

Soon Jhowah turned and held his arms out wide in an effort to let the audience know that he was about to speak. When He brought his arms back down and placed his long gray spindly fingers on the speaker's podium not a sound could be heard.

His voice was not loud nor was it unusual from any that the audience had heard before. All representatives in the audience heard every word he spoke. No translation was required for anyone among the many national representatives present, a point Doug noticed with amazement.

"I bring you a message of welcome into the new and modern age that you are about to enter. The beings you are being exposed to from our mothership, the SSV Command, are the very beings who worked so diligently many millennia ago to create this beautiful world that you have been given. They also created your original ancestors and, as well, initially helped them to adapt to this planet using a simulated surface environment on our starship. They later moved them down to their colony site to carry out their lives."

He paused and looked about, his eyes scanning the group and, as Doug realized, his mind was assessing the thoughts of all.

"I know you have many questions," he continued. "I know many of you are wondering where we were before we came here. It is time that you know. We have all come from an area in this galaxy known to you as the Reticulum Constellation. Zeta-1 Reticuli, the furthest star system of our home planets from here, is about thirty-five light years based on your system of chronology and linear measurement.

"It took many years to prepare your planet for human inhabitance. The evolutionary process to prepare your planet for intelligent life occurred well before we came and created animal and plant life. It was a slow and tedious process of a number of alternating cycles, some of which came very close to destroying even the microscopic forms of life that first evolved here. Each cycle, however, resulted in an infrastructure needed by the human species to exist here. When your kind was created, we imbedded a code in your genetic makeup so that each subsequent generation could evolve in mind and body. We also knew that it would become beneficial for you and the other life forms that would inhabit the planet with you, and for them to evolve with you. Each cycle created resources that you would eventually need to sustain life and prosper as a species.

"Once the atmosphere and surface conditions of Soleus-3 successfully evolved to support a pleasant climate, a menagerie of life forms was compiled and strategically seeded over the lands and waters among those that had spontaneously evolved. One creature in particular was created with both the ability and responsibility to have dominion over all the rest. That creature was the one I instructed Moses, when he synopsized the events of creation, to call 'Adam'.

"Creating this uniquely suited outpost on Earth or Soleus-3 was the pivotal point in a genetically engineered experiment that originated a long time ago in the star systems that I previously mentioned known to you as the Reticulum Constellation.

"The team that was assembled created a garden paradise that you call Earth; though, as I have previously indicated, in our systems your planet is known as Soleus-3. The name we gave it is based on your positioning in relation to your star, which you have named *the sun* but which we refer to as Soleus.

"At long last, your species has evolved to the point that it can grasp what is happening to you and around you. For reasons that you will come to see, we have intentionally revealed ourselves to you in small doses. The pilot program of which you have been a part, is a complex and challenging one that involved dimensions that you are not yet, prepared to comprehend. However, today I thought that it might help if I addressed some of the questions that have perplexed your kind for thousands of years. By doing so, it might help you to understand why you are here. More importantly, it will show you why I am here. For those of you who are not scientists, what I am about to reveal may seem a bit confusing. I know that you are recording my words, so you can refer to them as often as necessary to help with your understanding.

"Those of us who participated in the creation of your planet and the human race come from four different planetary systems. We are three different species and we based your races on our species. It was the idea of one of our top scientists and we made it a part of our plan as we began to create humanity.

"The first cloned creation was created on Hivania, the mother planet of our scientific institute, since our genetic labs are located there. Strategically selected chromosomes were gathered from the three participating species. Once compiled, the prescribed genetic materials were extracted from the pool and scientifically engineered into a never-before constructed genome; the one that came to be known throughout the Reticulum Alliance as the human genome.

"As expected, the new being was a composite of physical and intellectual features possessed by its gene donors, and, like each of us, possessed the ability to be the master of its thoughts and actions and to communicate thoughts to us and to each other by both verbal and non-verbal means. Inbred into our creation's intricately designed body was the capability to reproduce others of like kind, giving the species, when we were ready for you to do so, the capacity to evolve physically and intellectually as well as individually and as groups. The Reticulum Experiment of Jhowah was devised to see if, given the ability to create a world of its own choosing, what kind of a colony would the mortalized version of god like beings choose?

"This challenge was conceived by myself and developed and refined by the geneticists in our Hivanian labs. All of the scientists we gathered to create the human genome are members of a group which is known as the Society of Reticulum Genetic Engineers, or SORGE for abbreviated reference. Once developed, the pilot program was assigned to the individual specialty that who had been trained and given experience in previous similar projects.

Up until the time of this experiment, each of the planets within our kingdom was colonized by relocating selected individuals from existing species. But, we saw an opportunity to create an entirely new species, a dream of all SORGE members, capable of sharing the traits of each of us who were committed to creating Reticulum-like colonies on planets throughout the galaxy.

"Initially, the Solean project seemed to show great promise, but the intervention of one our former allies, turned adversary, created confusion in the minds of the new species.

"Human beings were forced to choose between our ways and those represented by the traitorous outcast, Sezan, who became obsessed with envy and set out to derail the project as it was intended. Very quickly, Soleans learned that serving two masters was impossible. Sezan had long been aware of this truism and used it to convince many of your fellow Soleans that, with him, they could build up great treasures, giving *them* power over other men and the privilege to enjoy many immoral and enjoyable acts of the flesh.

"Despite repeated admonitions from messengers of the Reticulum task force, including the exemplary mission carried out when Metatron lived on your planet as Enoch, and then by my only son, known on your planet as Jesus of Nazareth, Soleans seemed bent on a course of defiance and self-destruction.

"It was our hope to use your races to heal the distrust between our three species. What we did, however, was to stand by and allow you to exercise free will, a trait that we instilled in you, and a decision that led to your dividing into competing societies. Rather than looking upon each other as co-inhabitants and protectors of your planet, you looked upon your fellow man as an adversary. Too many of you followed leaders who sought power over you and others. As a result, all kinds of racism and cults developed here. As greed, envy, and hatred took root, they began to eat away at your societies. The ways of Sezan interfered with how we hoped the experiment would play out.

"When human creation occurred we instilled in you all of the things that a civilization needs to survive and prosper. The greatest gift was free will, the ability to choose your own destiny as a species and to create a world of your own choosing."

Doug leaned toward Hank and spoke softly. "I never expected that he would take so much time to explain all of this."

"I'm glad he has," Hank said.

Jhowah continued with his revelation.

"Our hope was that you would choose 'good' over 'evil' and evolve into an advanced civilization, much like our own. We gave you the best genes and characteristics of each of the three races who were involved in the experiment. SORGE chose to call our challenge the 'Jhowah Experiment' or 'The Challenge of Jhowah' because I had made the challenge a year before it was begun. Our objective was to see if we could begin with a raw totally underdeveloped planet and create a Reticulum-like world in this star system.

"As I referenced earlier, there was one of your Creators who made unauthorized changes in our plans. You have referred to him as Satan or Lucifer but we all know him as Sezan Lucefed, a Dromedan who was originally from the planet Dromedos. He was incarcerated for his heinous act which caused many problems in our work and in your history, and almost caused the destruction of your original ancestors. He was sentenced to spend eternity on the penal planet of Sheolos, but while in transit to the planet he escaped from his captors and returned secretly to Soleus-3 to collect a following of those who were loyal to him. He has been able to evade capture, and continues in his efforts to thwart our plans and take control of all that you are.

"Our hopes also have been for a civilization here on Soleus-3 from which we could study and learn, to see what beings derived from the three gene pools we used to create the human genome could become. We had great hopes of going on to another world in another star system and using this accumulated knowledge to create other beings, probably human like you, and add more life to our beautiful universe. We have halted such an effort as we have observed you in these most recent days."

Hank and Doug both turned to each other wondering what was ahead that would cause this change in Jhowah's plans.

"Technology has the potential to enhance your lives and beautify what you already have," he continued, "but as you look more and more into the secrets of the universe and experiment with your learned technology, you have made some very bad decisions. We realize the influence that Sezan has had on humanity that opened the way for these poor decisions. It comes from all of the continents and their subdivisions. The different governments you have created show a complete lack of trust among you, leading to chaos and wars designed to rule over your fellow man and make him subservient to you. The wars that occur and the complete corruption of the great code of law which I gave to Moses and were reiterated by Jesus of Nazareth are unacceptable. I will not allow this to continue.

"Some of the religions that have been created by humankind are not based on love of me or your fellow man. They are the clever work of Sezan and his minions. Hiding behind religious doctrine, you hate in my name. You enslave in my name. You follow leaders who are beholding to the ways of Sezan or Satan, as you call him. You are deceived by great orators who advocate class and racial warfare and the ultimate annihilation of those who try to follow my commandments. You kill in my name. You have made a mockery of me and the greatest project ever conceived. We have tried to create a society here on Soleus-3, but what has evolved is something quite different."

Doug looked about. He could see apprehension in the eyes of the leaders. It was evident that Jhowah had come to inform mankind of his displeasure, face to face, and offer it one last opportunity to change the distrusting patterns that it had embraced. Not one individual there, from journalist to world leader, could deny these admonitions of Jhowah.

He continued, "In order for all of us, Creators and created alike, to continue with our lives and the dreams that we have in place for our futures, you must put aside your petty differences of politics and the agendas you have for national or global domination. I will not allow my Son to continue to bear a burden that you should carry. You were created with free will, the capacity to know right from wrong, and the ability to choose between the two."

Jhowah paused. Doug knew that he was assessing the thoughts of the Earth leaders. The Hivanian sensed apprehension and even thoughts of deception that he could not allow. There were a few who knew there could be no other course, but their resolve was not shared by the majority of the representatives seated before him.

"No!" the leader exclaimed with a determined sound to his voice. "We will not be duped by those of you with plans to deceive. Those who do so, will regret your actions if you attempt to do."

It was a shock but the representatives of Earth were beginning to realize the powers of this supreme being who stood before them. They had not been aware of course; of his acquired ability of telempathism and that it was a gift occurring when Sezan, whom earthlings called Satan, had discovered the enzymatic cause of aging while working as a member of SORGE on their home planets.

Sezan's genetic manipulations to neutralize the enzymatic anomalies of aging had unexpectedly accelerated the evolutionary process of the communicative centers of their brains and created an incidental side effect that gave them the ability to sense the thoughts and the emotions of others. They were both telepathic and empathic. This event had occurred before the beginning of this project on Soleus-3 and before Sezan's failed incarceration for attempting to control the creations by instilling an unauthorized genetic change.

Through experimental manipulations of the genetic code of the creations in the project, and without authorization by the specialists in SORGE, Sezan had attempted to augment their sexual urge, explaining that he was doing so to reduce sexual apathy which would eventually reduce the population of the creations. It was then that his effort was discovered and he was expelled from the project and incarcerated only to escape later while being transported to the penal planet of Sheolos.

Jhowah became angry as He looked about and sensed the desire of the earthlings in His presence to undermine His efforts. His anger was reflected in His large black eyes as they emanated a noticeable reddish hue which intensified as His anger increased. It was quite obvious that Metatron sensed Jhowah's anger.

"As I stand before you I have made a decision," Jhowah explained, controlling his anger. "We cannot afford to waste time with our planned efforts and let those of you who might try to deceive to continue their wrongful ways. Because there are those among you who have been loyal to my laws, I will delay judgment. There will be a period of probation and monitoring among the nations of this planet in which we will observe the actions and emotions of its leaders.

"Be forewarned, we will not tolerate any further deceit or acts of war, overt or covert. As we return to Paradon, the city where our science labs are located on my home planet of Hivania, I will leave in my place, the most trusted of my leaders, Metatron, who stands here beside me, and whom you have known through Biblical teachings as Enoch, the son of Jared in the early days of your human civilization.

"Metatron will remain here on or near Soleus-3 to see that our covenant with you is consummated. You will learn more

about him and the covenant. For some among you, his presence will serve as a comforter. For others, he will represent
the one *true* all-seeing eye. He will be returning at intervals to
assess your progress at maintaining peace. Now that you have
seen me and heard my words of admonition with your own
ears, he will assess you as you create a society of love not distrust, chaos, and war and report his findings to me when needed.

"When we are assured that you are committed to applying
yourselves to a common goal such as I have now repeated to
those of this generation, we have plans to go forth into the universe to other planets where we will work towards the creation
of newer and even greater civilizations. There are planets that
we have already identified as capable of sustaining and nurtur-
ing life as we know it and similar to what you have here on So-
leus-3.

"Ready your minds and ambitions toward preparations for
such things. Look about you and determine who among you is
with me and who is with Sezan? If there are those whom you
know to be Sezan's disciples, cast them aside and remove them
from positions of leadership. Those who are beholden to me
must prove that you are willing to do what is necessary to
change what has been happening on this planet since our first
creations defied my instructions. This is the first step in saving
the earth and its inhabitants.

"The hopes of the populations of the Reticulum planets
are with you as I now depart. My hope is that you will heed
these admonitions. You are our children, the creations of our
minds from our hearts; however, the time will come when we
will have to decide if you are with us or against us. Metatron
will be here or nearby and will come to you if you need him.
Goodbye until I return."

With those words Jhowah stepped back from the podium,
stared at Metatron, and then made his way to the front of the
stage, his toga-like dress swirling as he moved about. He stood
erect and bowed his head and, as the onlookers watched in

awe, raised his arms and faded slowly from their sight. Metatron, who had stood beside him, departed in less dramatic fashion using the same dimensional transfer technique. Although many of those present had seen the science fiction television series and movies in which mortal beings were "beamed" to other locations; this was the first time they had witnessed or even realized such a mode of transport was possible.

In their manner of departure, Jhowah had certainly shown that He and Metatron were capable of a miracle. The chatter of those present rose slowly. The great leader had left an indelible impression on them and had convinced many of the unbelievers of the supremacy of his being.

But the seeds of discontent were also present in the room. Samael Amazad, a Dromedan agent of Sezan Lucefed, hoping that Jhowah wouldn't see him, had successfully slipped into the meeting before it had begun. He was seated near the entrance to the temporary facility. His ability to mask his thoughts and emotions from the extraterrestrial creators had been developed and refined for millennia and he would be taking the information, which he had learned, back to Sezan. His disguise as a third-world journalist had served him and Sezan well. His Dromedan facial characteristics were easily covered by make-up and dark glasses. If possible, and if events allowed, his knowledge would add significantly to Sezan's ability to interfere with Jhowah's plans and would assist him in his desire to, one day, control the project and the earthly creations.

Onboard Sezan's starship

Seated in his private quarters aboard the armed starship which he had commandeered many millennia ago, Sezan Lucefed awaited the arrival of Samael. Sezan, being a Dromedan, was not the same gray-type extraterrestrial as Jhowah. His eyes, unlike the large almond-shaped eyes of the gray Hivanians, were small steel-black organs and protected somewhat by a prominent epicanthal fold near his nose. He had hair which was of a coarse texture and jet black with no curl. His skin carried a slightly yellow hue, features that were the same as those of Samael.

Anger at his expulsion from the Project of Jhowah still simmered inside of him over the millennia, and his plight to avoid detection by the security forces of the Reticulum Alliance caused a constant need for alertness. He realized that if he should ever be apprehended he would spend the remainder of eternity on the penal planet of Sheolos in the Zeta-1 Reticuli star system. The age-arresting therapy, which he had devised, would cause him endless suffering through eternity in the torrid climate of that planet.

He had often pondered his options as to how he would avenge his pride by taking control of the project from Jhowah, or if that became impossible, to destroy him as well as the creations which he had so skillfully designed and nurtured when he was in charge of human cloning in the project. Yes, he had also nurtured their development and maturation until Jhowah discovered his deceptive ways and the injurious amino acid sequence that he had caused to be entered into the architectural plans for the basic DNA of the three races. This sequence was developed to enhance the sexual appetite of the creations which Sezan had described as being done to prevent sexual apathy, but which, as Jhowah had pointed out, he had planned to use as a tool to control their lives, as well as the rate of development of the creation's populations.

Now, Jhowah had revealed himself to the leaders of Earth and had told of his plans to cull the numbers of the creations. He had divulged the projects plans to go on to more and greater ideas with those loyal and obedient creations and Creators that remained. Sezan would soon find from Samael that matters were being complicated by Jhowah who had assigned Metatron to remain on Soleus-3 to remind its inhabitants of Jhowah's continued presence among them. The events of the day would make it more difficult for Sezan to influence the colonization plan throughout the Reticulum Alliance planet group and other worlds not yet chosen.

The Reticulum Alliance was created by the governments of planets from four star systems. Hivania, a planet in the Zeta-1 star system, was the first of the group to develop faster-than-light travel and they went on to spread their culture, science and technology to two others: Janos in the Tau Ceti system and Dromedos in the Zeta-2 Reticuli system. Zeta Reticuli was a binary star system but set far enough apart for each to have developed its own planetary families.

After development of the Alliances an overpopulation problem developed among these worlds. This anomaly was caused by the development of the age-arrest therapy on Dromedos by Sezan Lucefed himself. There came a point at which, out of necessity, more room was needed in order to protect the ecology and environments of all of the worlds of the Alliance. The Alpha-Mensae star system was explored and its fifth planet was found to be ideal for the creation of a fourth world to receive voluntary colonists to relieve the overpopulation from the other three worlds.

Considerable work was completed on Mensae-5 to prepare it for the colonization. It was here that the scientists of SORGE practiced and refined their skills and expertise in the cloning of new species of both the plant and animal kingdoms. Their technology was honed to a fine edge with the development of instruments to easily create amino acids, to properly sequence these into functional units, and to combine the units of the genes with a gene paste media that was accepted at a cellular level.

When he was still a part of the project, the labs of Sezan were more active than they had ever been as they cloned the new species. Considerable knowledge was gathered and learned by these designers of life as they created the new animals and plants to occupy Mensae-5 along with the future interplanetary pioneers from the other three worlds.

After the completion of the Mensae-5 colonization, the knowledge gained was applied to the general populace and a cloned organ program was begun in which internal organs, limbs, skin and bony joints, among other things, were produced on a daily basis. As life expectancy increased because of the age-arrest therapy developed, so did injuries and infirmities. When they occurred there was usually a solution at the Cloned Organ Institute (COI) managed by Sezan on his home planet of Dromedos. Stem-cell implantation or specific cloning procedures were perfected to replace aging brain cells and to advance cognitive and telempathic skills.

Being a very energetic and brilliant group who constantly sought ways to use their knowledge and expertise to improve their own kind, the members of SORGE enthusiastically went about creating a new species of beings, one that would reflect the appearance and intelligence of those who accepted the challenge presented to them by Jhowah. He was the Hivanian leader of SORGE, and the architect of, and creative influence behind this magnificent interstellar project. The challenge he made was: *"To go into the universe, find a suitable planet, create from it a new world, design and develop human, animal and plant life forms and nurture the created society to its maturity."*

As reflected in the revelation of the Hebrew mystics, and at Jhowah's direction, Soleus-3 was created to reflect the lower dimensions on the Tree of Life. Because it was a new world, the species created to colonize it had to begin their quest to reach the archetypal world that existed on Hivania from the lower dimensions.

Sezan was wise enough to know that, although the capacity for balance had been reached on Soleus-3, a growing number of Soleans were exercising the choice of evil over good. And, Jhowah was not happy with the end results of this matured society. In fact, His dislike was so profound that He would be making changes in the plans they had all originated eons ago for the joining of the creations of Soleus-3 with the societies of the Reticulum. He might exercise the option of selective harvesting and do away with those creations that were corrupt. Executing this option could mean the end of Sezan's shadowy army. Throughout the Reticulum Alliance, the answers to this question would be forthcoming, and sooner than anticipated.

Samael Amazad was among the individuals disloyal to Jhowah, but loyal to Sezan whom he followed when the Dromedan leader escaped from incarceration when being transferred to prison. He joined him when Sezan clandestinely returned to the ongoing project and sought help from his loyalists.

"My Lord," Samael addressed as he entered the quarters, "I return from Soleus-3 to bring you news of Jhowah's visit and his admonitions to its leaders."

"Samael," Sezan said, "take a seat." He waved his hand toward a chair nearby. "What have you been able to find out for me about my most hated Hivanian?"

"He doesn't plan to join the creations with us, at least not right now. The plan to bring them into our society and introduce them to the member planets of the Reticulum as well as reveal the elements of our space technology are not on the table. As you have heard, he has become dissatisfied with them so much so that he has considered destroying many or all of them. Then at the last moment He decided to give them a lengthy trial period, a second chance, and return later for his final assessment."

"That's not like Jhowah." Sezan muttered as he pondered the sudden changes. "He usually carries out his plans quite precisely and to the end. This requires that we must change our plans also, in order to accomplish our goal of taking over the project, and as you know we might very possibly even need to destroy him to make it work."

"You don't want to use our forces to take control of the project as we had planned?" Samael asked.

"The project as we knew it is over," Sezan barked. "We must yield to his changes. We may even be able to enlarge our forces in an association with those he wishes to destroy if we can accomplish it. You know they will never change their ways. I have seen to that.

"In addition to the small group of families who believe themselves to be The Enlightened Ones, there is a group of human individuals in power in an area very near the location where we placed our first creation who are ideal subjects for our efforts. They were disenfranchised from Jhowah many centuries ago, when the founder of their tribes, Ishmael, was exiled from his Hebrew father's family and sent into the desert. They have long been in control of the carbon-based liquid that the entire planet has used for many Earth decades to create energy for their primitive internal combustion engines.

"They call the carbon-based liquid, which results from the decaying of organic matter oil. This dominance over the control of the major supply of that energy source puts them in a position of control of a large portion of the economy of the entire planet. If they choose to lower the price that they charge for the oil it is advantageous to those whom they supply, and if they raise the price of oil it is very disadvantageous to the economy of those supplied.

"They believe that it is the wish of the god they call Allah for them to kill all the descendants and allies of Abraham who was Ishmael's estranged Hebrew father, especially those living in the country known as Israel. Because of our efforts, my dear Samael, Islamic religious leaders have been convinced that their Allah is not Jhowah. In fact, we have been able to convince them that Jhowah and his followers are the enemies of Allah. This division in loyalty has allowed us to create the kind of chaos that serves our mission and not Jhowah's.

"Over the past century, the Islamists have accumulated much of the wealth of Earth and used it to manipulate both their allies and enemies. They have bought decision-makers the world over and placed individuals who are beholding to them in the highest positions of leadership. Slowly, but surely, they are acquiring nuclear weapons and, with them, the ability to control the world. They have no fear of death. In fact, we have been able to convince their leaders that the surest way to the after-life paradise is to kill those who don't agree with them, in the name of their god, Allah. Our plan has worked. The greatest army we have, my loyal comrade, comprises those who hate anyone whose religion differs from their own. Do you understand where I'm going with this train of thought?"

"I do," Samael answered, still considering the implications of Sezan's statement. "I understand the premise but how do you plan to use it?"

"You will see," he said, "but there is much work to be done. When you were monitoring Jhowah's revelation on that island were these individuals a part of it?"

"No," Samael answered, shaking his head, "they were not. Only the most technologically empowered countries sent a delegation. There were a few third-world countries but none from the region and religions that you suggest."

"Well," Sezan replied with a wicked smile adorning his Dromedan face, "Jhowah, my most hated Hivanian, has given us a significant advantage, but we will need to keep an eye out for Metatron. You know the two of them are inseparable."

Over the Middle East
Aboard Sezan's Vessel

As Sezan directed the navigator of his starship over the arid lands of the oil-rich countries near the original site of the first human colonization, he studied the terrain below through the monitors that were positioned in front of them. He stood like the defiant commander that he had become with his thin arms positioned behind his back and his small black eyes focused like steel balls on the monitors. Evil though he was, he was a leader to be reckoned with. Samael stood nearby with the remainder of the five-man flight crew in their assigned positions.

"I'm looking for a large inland sea," he informed them. "It will be to the east and slightly north of the site of the Garden of Edena by about five hundred kilometers. When we see it we will find a very large population area a hundred kilometers south of it. That is the location of one of the centers of government for this nation.

"There are other governments in the area, but this particular one is led by a human that I have followed in the radio transmissions we receive. I believe him to be the leader who would be most receptive to our efforts, and he has infiltrated those countries who do not agree with him with an insidious army of followers. He has been a human of whom I am quite proud."

"There is a large body of water," Samael alerted him, his small Dromedan finger pointing to the monitor.

"I see it," Sezan confirmed. "Now we go south to find the city."

"My Lord," the brawny Janosian navigator said, "I am seeing the outskirts of a city but my sensors are picking up the reflections of several Solean airships headed in our direction."

"They don't have any idea who we are," Sezan instructed, a smile moving across his face. "I suppose this is not only a good way for them to get to know us, but a way for us to gain a little respect from them in our own way."

The Dromedan watched and studied the situation as the military jets approached. He certainly didn't want to destroy the possibility of negotiating with this group but he also wanted to demonstrate to them his power and invincibility.

"Put up our energy shields," he instructed the crew.

"Yes, my Lord," was the reply of the obedient crewman behind them. Obedience was ever present on this starship or anyplace where Sezan was present. It came out of fear of retribution from him which was established early after the assembling of this group of individuals who had fallen from the grace of Jhowah and vowed allegiance to the Dromedan.

"My Lord, should I return fire if they fire on us?" The question came from behind them and drew a swift answer from Sezan.

"No!" he called out. "Let them realize, first, the invincibility of our ship against their primitive vessels and weapons. It will give us a definite advantage in our negotiations and assure us of their complete cooperation."

Sezan cackled as the jets fired bullets and several rockets at his starship. He saw the missiles explode and the bullets bounce away as they reached the periphery of the defense energy shields.

Soon his crew, realizing the futility of the attackers, also began enjoying their efforts that appeared somewhat like a small child attacking a full-grown man with his small fists and tiny feet. The attacks continued but the Solean action proved to be useless. One of the planes flew into the shield in an effort of self sacrifice to protect his homeland but the ship exploded and broke up as it reached the impenetrable energy field surrounding the ship.

"If another one tries that, hit him with a shot from the particle beam weapon before he reaches the shield," Sezan commanded. In moments, another one attempted the same maneuver. When the beam struck the ship it exploded into thousands of minute pieces. The other vessels immediately turned and left with explosive bursts of sound as they reached supersonic speeds.

"Now place us in a stationary position over the base of operations of the ships that we just sent home," Sezan instructed. "We will sit there and listen for radio efforts to contact us. Be sure to monitor the Solean frequencies, all of them."

Within minutes the communications crewman alerted Sezan. "I believe they are trying to reach us, but they don't sound very confident about their wishes."

"Tell them we want the leader of their country to come here and we will then descend and land beside their ships. I want to speak with him on board this vessel."

After a few moments the crewman informed Sezan. "They say their leader will not be able to come but he will send a representative and, my Lord, they want to know who we are."

Sezan laughed aloud. "I'll bet they do, and you can tell them that we represent other worlds who wish to discuss an urgent problem. You can tell them that their leader WILL come immediately. If he does not arrive within the next fifteen minutes we will leave their base in ashes and do likewise with their leader. We will then find another country to do business with."

Moments later the crewman smiled as he told Sezan of the response. "I think they understand you, my Lord. All they said was 'Yes, immediately.'"

Sezan gestured toward Samael. "A little show of force can often create a very cooperative attitude, my friend."

Samael nodded and smiled at him, a look of fearful respect in his eyes.

Ten minutes later the navigator pointed to the monitor. "An airship with a large rotating propeller on top is approaching the field below and I see a large group of humans gathering on the ground there."

"All right, take the ship down, once they land, and place it as close to their air ships as possible without causing injury; then let down our entry ramp."

"Yes, my Lord," was the navigator's response.

In only moments after the starship settled into position, the egress ramp doors opened and as the ramp extended, two large and very muscular mahogany-skin Janosians walked, unarmed, down the ramp as it stabilized on the ground.

Janosians were very large individuals when compared to Hivanians and Dromedans. They were a warlike group before they were defeated on their home planet of Janos by the overwhelming superiority and technology of the combined forces of the other two species. It was centuries before the Janosians were able to join with the other two species in the manner that had come to exist at this point in time.

They motioned for the leader to mount the ramp to enter the ship as they stood guard on either side of the ramp. The human leader was an olive skinned and slightly built individual with dark and deep-set eyes, a short beard and a full head of shiny black hair. He began to walk forward, flanked on each side by two armed guards who appeared quite fearful, but the Janosians pointed to the guards, who began to raise their weapons, and wagged their fingers and shook their heads at the humans. The guards brought their weapons up, aiming at the aliens, but the leader, showing much of the white of his eyes, held up his hands toward them and motioned for them to go back, and they obligingly did.

The human leader began his walk up the ramp and was greeted at the top by a very jovial but definitely alien Sezan who invited him inside and to his quarters where the two of them along with Samael sat to talk.

"And how are you today, my friend?" Sezan asked the confused human.

"I'm not really sure right now," he answered as he released a nervous and hoarse laugh from his throat that caused him to cough to clear the hoarseness.

"Don't worry," Sezan promised him. "I'm sure we can get along just fine. I've brought you here to see if we can work together to the benefit of both of us. What should I call you?"

"You can call me Mister President, but what if I don't agree to do that?" The human asked.

Sezan grinned and motioned to a viewing window across the room. "Well, Mister President, walk over there and take a look out the window," he suggested.

The president, not used to being told what to do, looked back at Sezan with suspicion in his eyes.

"Go ahead," Sezan said. "I have no reason to do you harm, right now."

He walked over to the window and looked out. A stunned expression came to his face. Unbeknownst to the leader and to the dismay of the humans who had accompanied him to the base; the ship had risen and traveled out of the atmosphere to a position three hundred kilometers above its original position on the ground.

"Our inertial damper works pretty, well doesn't it?" Sezan mocked. "That's a long way back to your base, human. I don't think you would be able to walk that far, and I don't see any wings attached to your back," the Dromedan said as he sidled up to him and looked out the window back down at the planet.

Realizing his predicament and accepting the dominance of this extraterrestrial, the human took his seat again. Looking over at Sezan, he finally gave a short-lived smile. "I realize that right now you have me at a considerable disadvantage. May I ask who you are and where you came from, and what do you want with me?"

"I'm afraid that I will always have you at a considerable disadvantage, my human friend. I understand that you carry a bit of weight on this planet in that you and others around you control a large amount of oil and wealth, and at the same time you have developed nuclear weapons, AND that you have let it be known that you won't be pushed around, especially by a group of humans you refer to as Zionists."

"It is true, on all of those accusations, especially the last one. I don't like them. I have pledged to destroy them, to wipe them from the face of Earth, and I will."

"Not so fast," Sezan cautioned, "all things in due time. Right now I need to let you in on something that is important to everyone on this world. A few nights ago an event occurred for which many have long waited. You see, I am a representative of the powerful being whom you call Allah."

The president suddenly sat erect in his chair and looked at Sezan. It was obvious to him that this was no human who sat in front of him. If he were not from this world how would he know of Allah? Could he really be a representative from Allah?

Sezan watched as he absorbed his statement no matter how false it had been. "Allah has put me in a bad situation," Sezan began. "A few nights ago he revealed himself to your world or, at least to the leaders of certain governments. It just happens that the other leaders of the world didn't invite you, and it has now become my duty to inform you of his plans in hopes that He may include you."

"Allah would have wanted me there," the human leader yelped, "I and my people have been loyal and obedient servants. I wait for my place with Allah and my seventy-six virgins. I deserve my place."

"Aah," slipped from the throat of Sezan as he heard the claims of the human. "Actually the virgin claim you have made is probably a fallacy spread by someone for a purpose for which I am unable to explain, but there are things which Allah has asked for me to request of you."

"I am His servant. What does He ask?"

"Only to lead the followers of Mohammad all over the world and help Allah gain control of the Christians and Zionists," Sezan answered.

"Even of the great Satan we call the United States?" He questioned.

Sezan smiled. "I do feel we will be great friends some day, if there is a need to do so," he answered.

"And how will I be able to do what he asked? He is the all-powerful one. I can only do as He says to do."

"Yes, and it seems that your stature in this part of the world places you in a position to gain the help of others who also have a plentiful supply of these fossil fuels. This can be a very helpful thing to Allah if you can cooperate. He feels that by reducing the output of the liquid energy source you call oil to the rest of the world and convincing other followers of Allah to do the same, it will make these infidels a bit more vulnerable. We MUST do something to free the world of this unholy scourge."

"Tell him that I will begin immediately," the president said.

"It is something that he wishes to be done in increments," Sezan continued, "and, of course, as the supply diminishes, the price shall rise. It's a rather universal law. I'm quite sure that you have no objection to that, nor should any of the other members of your societies that produce large amounts of oil. As you know, there are countries out there that use very large amounts, but whose political leaders have been convinced by the promise of financial favors to themselves not to produce it. It sounds crazy but you are one who has reaped the profits of such short sightedness and personal ambition for fame and fortune and this will only improve when you begin your restrictions."

"Allah should have already seen that we have done this in the past," the human reminded him, "and that we have regular meetings to decide on such changes in production. An alliance of oil-producing countries already controls many of the political leaders throughout the world. Our next cartel meeting is in five days and I will present this effort to my Islamic brothers and our allies."

"You will find that some will be against this move," Sezan warned, "but I would suggest that if they are, you should take them aside individually in a private area and explain what has happened to you and your military today. I would think that the mere fact that the non-Islamic countries left you and your Islamic brothers out of his revelation would be enough to cause them to wish to gain His favor. Exert your influence over them. If you have any problems with the local leaders that show disbelief, I will approach them."

"Will you be returning?" the human asked.

"Yes, I'll be back soon after you meet with your partners in the cartel to see if there are any who I need to speak with. You might warn them that I wouldn't like it if I have to go to them individually. By the way, I'd appreciate it if there were no explosive receptions when I return to meet with you."

The human, appearing a bit agitated, smiled. "I assure you there will be no hostility. What should I call you?"

"My name is Sezan, but you should address me as my Lord."

"Yes - that is what I will do, my Lord. Have no fear. We will not be attacking you on your return. I am the president of my country and they will follow my orders."

"Oh, I will hold no fear," Sezan said with a chuckle. "My defenses are impenetrable, even to your nuclear weapons. Have you not yet realized that?"

"Yes, my Lord," the human replied meekly.

Sezan watched as the human leader turned and followed his escort to leave the ship. He turned to Samael with a look of victory as he savored the moment.

One Month Later
Aboard Sezan's Starship
Monitoring the News

Sezan and Samael sat across the table from each other at in the ship's conference room listening to the daily INN broadcast.

The INN reporter spoke sharply as she summed up the recent world news and followed up with an attempt at a fair and balanced commentary.

"Oil prices have reached two hundred and thirty dollars a barrel in the recent run up that seems to be originating from the OPEC nations of the Middle East and certain of their South American allies. Political observers are suggesting that much of this new crisis might be based on the remnants of the policies imposed during the last years of previous Republican administrations in the U.S., particularly in the way they handled these countries, and America's dependence on foreign oil. Some have also said that much of this has been happening as a result of the associations of previous administrations' ties with the oil-producing nations."

The reporter continued: "Representatives of the American oil industries deny any part in causing the rise in prices as certain leftist spokespersons have implied. The issue is having astounding affects not only on the United States economy, but worldwide, and anger is mounting. Fanned by America's enemies, class warfare is running rampant, and division of Americans into ideological camps is further dividing and polarizing the once-united peoples of this country. The politics that are developing in the United States has separated citizens into even more partisan camps than in the recent past.

"The now dominant Democrat Party is saying that the confusion is caused by the Republicans in Congress who continue to call global warming a clever hoax created by the One World initiators, or Illuminati, and embraced by the Democrat Party in an effort to gain them even more control over world affairs.

"The political left sees the global warming debate as a way to further liberal causes by creating new taxes. This same group is preventing drilling for domestic oil deposits in the states by tying the use of carbon-based fuels to atmospheric changes that, they say, cause global warming. They do however er continue to purchase oil from the oil-producing countries.

"Without tapping into the U.S. reserves, the price of fossil fuels will continue to skyrocket, resulting in an even greater amount of wealth redistribution away from the people and to America's enemies.

"Conservative Republicans insist that the radical environmentalists and anti-capitalists must be reckoned with if the U.S. is to remain a viable nation with the standing that it has always held within the global community. The data presented by free-thinking scientists shows that global warming is not the work of man, but is caused by shifts in the world's temperature that have been occurring for millions of years. It has been shown and accepted to be caused by the sun as well as a slight wobble in the planet's axis. Also, this is a result of natural events on this planet and on other planets throughout the solar system. Erupting volcanoes and rampant forest fires that incinerate thousands of acres of foliage also emit large amounts of carbon dioxide into the atmosphere every year.

"The Republicans also claim that the leaders on the left, with the cooperation of their friends in the world's media, are out to discredit the scientists who know the truth about the planet's temperature.

Sezan looked over at Samael. "This is interesting. I do believe we have chosen the right tool for our purposes."

"It is having an effect," Samael replied.

"The record cold winters of the last two years and the recent decade-long decline of average world temperatures is, however, making it more difficult to perpetuate their claims," the reporter continued. "This whole global warming campaign may have more to it than meets the eye. Critics claim that the climate change debate is an instrument being used by powerful insiders to gain more control of every aspect of people's lives

"Opponents of the global warming theory are quick to add: if saving the planet is the true concern, and if eliminating carbon emissions would save the planet, rather than taxing and controlling those who release byproducts of combustion, why aren't lawmakers and environmentalists advocating doing away with energy sources that contribute to the problem? Why aren't lawmakers spending taxpayer's monies in building cleaner and more efficient alternatives that are already developed, especially modern nuclear power plants -- large ones that could power major population areas, medium-sized ones, like those aboard Navy aircraft carriers, and compact ones, some of which would be capable of powering automobiles and other combustible engines? The Republicans have suggested that the billions of dollars spent on solar and wind energy would be more efficiently spent on harnessing nuclear energy.

"Other former leaders on the left are quoted as saying that these frigid winters are just a result of a massive summation of what happens when mankind's contributions to the problem allows weather to run rampant. They warn that the heat may return soon in a destructive frenzy, but since changing their predictions more to "climate change" rather than global warming, some are even predicting a new ice age.

"Through the global warming campaign, children and the very gullible all around the world have been frightened into believing that they and their families are in immediate danger of being swallowed up by the rising oceans caused by melting polar caps. They are told stories that the melting ice is causing polar bears to drown at sea when scientists have shown that they can swim from as far away as a hundred and fifty miles to return from icebergs to get to the mainland. The polar bear population has also been shown to be stable. Several studies have even shown that there has been an increase in their numbers.

"The president of the United States has had very little to say about problems related to the increase in oil prices since his return from his talks with the oil-producing countries of the Middle East and South America. One might even think that he desires an increase in oil prices.

"China and Russia are also silent on the matter, while continuing their economic growth, and are beginning to cash in on the rise in oil prices and the current downfall of the American economy. The average citizens of Russia and China, however, are not enjoying the fruits of their countries' profits. Only the high-ranking members of the Communist parties in those countries seem to be lounging in the luxurious effects of the windfall. Incidentally, although both countries rely on nuclear power for supplying much their domestic energy needs, neither Russia nor China has signed on to the global warming movement, nor have they made any effort to reduce carbon emissions created by their industrial plants and the fossil-powered machines used by their massive populations.

"While Western governments are gaining more control over their citizenship, the latest INN poll indicates that there is a developing distrust by the populace of the governments of all nations and it isn't seen to have any chance of improving in the near future. Those in the field are suggesting that within three months oil prices will probably hit twice the level of today's figures. A growing number of governments are concerned that as people learn more about the previously undisclosed connections between the global-warming movement, powerful socialists, and OPEC, they might take matters into their own hands, especially the Americans, who have a history of rising up when they have had enough.

"Stay tuned to this INN station. As we learn more, we will bring it to you."

Sezan leaned back in his chair and raised one of his fingers toward the ceiling. There was an evil grin on his face as the evening INN newscaster completed her summary of the day's news.

"Samael, we have chosen a very effective method to spread havoc throughout this planet, especially in America. We shall continue to be patient.

"I'm glad we were able to configure our communications to receive these transmissions from the Solean news media," Sezan commented as he drummed his small fingers on the table in front of him and watched the report. "In a way, some of them seem to be quite helpful to our cause. My ideas are slowly but surely taking shape the way we had planned them and, surprisingly, some of the reports from the American media seem to be enhancing our efforts. Peace and harmony among mankind is dying. Chaos is on the rise, a perfect setting for the kind of revolution that will allow us to gain a more complete control over the people of Soleus-3.

"I understand from some earlier reports that the human leader we are working with has received assurances from sympathetic high-ranking officials in the United States and other Western countries that they will not intercede should Tehran deem it necessary to protect its interests. Since American leaders have abandoned concern of any threat from Iran, the Iranians are no longer worried about assaults from them. It seems that the current American administration must have been satisfied after their conversations with the Iranian leader.

"The Iranian president tells me that he is building up his forces and acquiring newer and more high-tech air ships and weapons from the northern nation they call Russia. I just assume that this is in preparation for an attack which he so strongly desires on the small Zionist country to the west of him. In our last meeting he kept going back to his plans to attack them. I suggested that he wait a bit longer before actually doing it and, at that time, he agreed. However, he was still quite eager to get on with his foray into their country."

"I imagine," Samael replied, "that the Zionists are aware of the potential attack and are also preparing for it. The Iranian leader has certainly announced his intentions to the world. The Zionists would be fools not to realize it. And with the assurance that the United States will not intervene, they will have no alternative but to retaliate with all the weapons that they have in their arsenal."

"Oh yes, I'm sure they are preparing," Sezan agreed. "The human tells me that he has a secret weapon that will wipe them out if ground and air assaults fail. I'm sure it is some form of the nuclear weapons that were used on the planet sixty or so Solean years ago. They certainly don't mind how they dirty up their world that we made for them. And, it is thought that the Zionists also have an arsenal of such weapons buried in silos throughout their tiny country. The war they have long called Armageddon will be at hand."

"This certainly won't help in being at peace with Jhowah," Samael concluded. "This is diametrically opposed to his wishes and what he made very plain in the island speech before he left for Paradon, His beloved hometown on Hivania."

"Yes, my dear Samael," Sezan replied smirking. "Now you're getting the idea. We're seeing my plan developing as we have hoped for. Have you been able to determine what Metatron is doing these days? We have to keep a watchful eye on him too, you know."

Tehran, Iran
Moments later

In the city south of the great sea the human leader, the president of the country, stood before his most trusted ministers and revealed his plan to them. Also present were emissaries of his Western sympathizers.

"During the last month I have sent the most armed vessels in our navy in quiet maneuvers down south and around the Cape. They are now making their way toward the Mediterranean and within the week they will be off the coast of Israel. The rest of the world may or may not realize what has happened. I believe that the Great Satan could spot our actions from the eyes of their satellites in the skies above us, but they will be of no concern to us."

Whispers and questions arose from the ministers. "Have we cleared this through the Ayatollah?" one of them inquired. The ministers seemed surprised, but at the same time excited at the prospect of destroying their old enemy.

"It has been cleared with him and we really don't expect any reaction from our friends in the UN or the current administration of the United States. We have our sympathizers and surrogates in place among several governments who will not respond until after we have destroyed this scourge on our world.

"We are now holding one of the strongest and most well-trained and well-armed military forces on this planet with the exception of our allies in Russia and China. We outnumber and even out arm the United States since our friends in power there have seen to it that their military might has been reduced to such low levels during the past several years. When they agreed to the Treaty of Guantanamo recently, they did away with their nuclear capabilities. In fact, they have destroyed all of their nuclear weapons and demoralized and emasculated their intelligence networks. We have the strength and the capability to destroy our enemies and make this a better world."

A mumble of thankfulness met the human leader's ears and he nodded in return.

"We should be ready to launch our attack in eight to ten days and once it begins, the forces of Allah will overcome the Zionists and we will destroy their homeland and rid the world of these dogs. What might remain will be gathered up and removed. We will wipe them from the face of the Earth."

"Allahu Akbar, Allahu Akbar!" The praise resounded from the ministers who sat before the human leader. Now the plan was set and the time would fast approach. Would there be anything that would stop this planned genocide?

A Week Later In
Jerusalem, Israel

The prime minister of the nation of Israel, in an unusual move, called for a completely closed and secret session of the Foreign Affairs Committee of the Knesset and held it in an undisclosed meeting place near Jerusalem where he stood before them surveying the members and their demeanor.

"We are at a grave point in the history of our nation," he announced as he watched their faces. "Our intelligence has confirmed a set of circumstances that I and a few others construe as an imminent act of all-out war on our country. Today a fleet of Iranian ships sits a considerable distance off our coast in the Mediterranean near Gaza with their missiles pointed in our direction.

"The Iranian army is poised near the Iraqi border awaiting orders from the Ayatollah and cooperative forces in Al-Qaida and Hezbollah that the way is clear for Iranian troop carriers to cross that country and through Lebanon and into Syria from which they can attack northern and eastern parts of our country. They have just completed a revamping of their air force and have purchased the latest and most sophisticated jets and weaponry for their planes. I have called the United States to ask for that country's help and they tell me that they are unable to provide it because recent talks between their country and the Iranian government leads them to believe that there is no real danger that will come to us from Iran. And, even if they agreed to help us, it would be difficult for them to bring enough ground troops and supply lines into play in time.

"I also called the prime minister of Britain. He was more sympathetic, but told me without the support of the United States, his Parliament would not agree to provide assistance. We are on our own." He paused to allow time for his words to sink in. "I will accept any questions you may have."

"Mister Prime Minister, why is it that you feel that these are events that create an act of such severe imminent danger to us? We have seen their ships out there before and none of us met the events with apathy, but we didn't begin rattling sabers." The question came from the head of the Foreign Affairs Committee.

"We have more than just this," the prime minister replied. "We have internal intelligence from inside the government of Iran that we will be attacked within the week. Satellite Intel that we received from our own intelligence within the United States, believe it or not, confirms there are hundreds of vehicles gathered near the western border of Iraq that may well be moving at this time. The U.S. knows our plight even though they deny concern. Many of the vehicles are loaded with supplies and many are ready to carry ground troops to clean up after they strike from the sea and air.

"There are thousands of troops camped near the sites of the transportation vehicles. We've never before seen this kind of build up and activity in all three areas of their military at the same time, and all pointed in our direction. It is clearly in preparation for an aggressive military action against our homeland."

"Have we received word from anyone in the United States intelligence community to confirm this?" Another member asked.

"As you know, we have received less and less intelligence from United States security sources in the past few years. It has become a real problem at times to even confirm our own intelligence that we have in place there. Some of our people are beginning to feel nakedness in Israel's reliance on that country, even though in years past it has been a dependable ally for us. The comments from America today affirm that the winds of change are blowing in an adverse direction, and it appears that they will be siding with the radical Muslims. We might even be reaching a point in which to contact the U.S. government, might be counterproductive, if you understand my meaning.

"You are a part of the group that I look to as my advisers in a situation like this. Earlier I met with military and technical experts whom I trust and who agree with the conclusion that we have reached. If we sit back and wait for an attack, we are inviting the destruction of Israel. If we use our readied forces we might prevent this destruction. Whatever we do we have no time to waste. We must act now. They are truly readying for an attack on us."

"Before we decide," another member added, "would you tell us about any information regarding the possibility of a nuclear attack? Do we have any Intel regarding that situation?"

"We just can't say how ready their nuclear capability is at this time," the prime minister answered, "but we feel that it is very possible that it might be ready for the offensive purposes for which they have been creating it. Most think that they will only use this if it appears all other actions are failing. However, I do not believe that they will hesitate to use nuclear weapons to achieve their stated mission to destroy us. They have not been shy about their hate for us. That puts urgency on the matter of a pre-imminent attack. We should hit them before they can hit us."

With that the committee chairman stood and asked for a vote. All members voted for an immediate preemptive strike and that no information should be given to any other country, including the United States, prior to the attack.

Tehran, Iran
The Next Morning

"I stand before you with the full support of the state behind us. The Ayatollah gives us his blessings and I have assurances from abroad that we will be able to complete our challenge without interference," the president announced to his ministers and to a group of his military leaders gathered to hear the final plans before their attack was to begin.

"To our military..." he turned to face his generals and continued. "You have made your plans and we are all in agreement that if these fail we will fall back on a larger and more destructive method." The military commanders nodded. The plans were what they had been anticipating for years.

"Then let us go forth, destroy these dogs that pollute our lands, and take back Ishmael's birthright, lands that are rightfully ours. Allahu Akbar!" And with those words still lingering as an echo in the great hall of their meeting, he reached and took the gavel lying nearby bringing it down on the table.

As the gavel met the table top the entire room exploded. The walls and roof came down on the group, killing them all. Outside there were F15s and F16s swarming like a disturbed hornet's nest, firing missiles at every government facility that came into their sights. There was little or no resistance from the Iranian air force or ground forces, which were in place readying for a strike on Israel on the western borders of Iran. The element of surprise had been taken by the Israelis whose planes adorned with the Star of David and their own unique emblem struck the capitol with the precision of surgeons and maintained dominance in the airspace above Tehran.

Meanwhile military airborne robotic drones were over the uranium enrichment facilities at Natanz, the uranium conversion facility at Isfahan, the plutonium production facilities at Arak, and the nearby storage facilities which housed the nuclear material intended for future warheads. Within a period of twenty minutes the drones had found their targets and released their lethal payloads. The entire operation took only about thirty or forty minutes from the arrival of the drones and jets over their objectives until the last missile was fired in this preemptive strike.

During the attack one of the F15 pilots in the Sedeh area spotted an ominous circular construction on the ground. The pilot had been trained in observing from above and in the identification of nuclear missile sites. What he saw was a poorly camouflaged missile silo that he recognized as being of Russian design and used in that country specifically for the class of rocketry created to carry nuclear warheads. Having already exhausted his missile supply he called for a backup attack on the site.

Very shortly an F22 Raptor stealth fighter, the most advanced fighter in the world and armed to the hilt with a battery of missiles and onboard high-tech sensors and computers, moved in and unleashed a destructive bombardment on the site. The plane had arrived a month earlier from Australia just in time to be readied for this action.

Selling of the new fighter to Israel had been canceled by Congress when they had cut off the program in July of 2009. One of the fighters out of the initial order from Lockheed-Martin was, however, scheduled to be sold to Australia. Even its release and shipment had been delayed by congressional hearings and interference from a very pacifist-leaning executive branch of government in Washington, D.C., which had gotten wind of Israeli-Aussie talks. Nevertheless, refusing to sell the F22 Raptor to Australia would have been looked upon as a widening gulf between the U.S. and another of its traditional allies. In order to realize future aspirations, the U.S. administration didn't need to alienate any other members of the United Nations. So, it agreed to support the Australian sale.

Members of a secret group known as *Operation Shield* in Australia had been working diligently and quietly to procure the Raptor so that it could be used by Israel, if necessary, to defend itself or *Operation Shield* against its enemies. Now the time had arrived and it had performed as expected.

The explosions that emanated from the Raptor attacks were enormous. There were three silos identified and three silos destroyed. There would be a definite search by the Israeli for the telltale circular signs of other silos that might exist throughout the country.

Back near the Israeli coast another group of jets was pounding the Iranian ships that had failed to receive any orders to strike and release their missiles. Several of the ships were able to avoid a direct hit by the Israelis, and the jets, having fired the full load of their missiles, had to return to their bases for reloading.

The night before the attack several Israeli patrol boats out of the port of Haifa had carried an elite group of underwater Flotilla 13 commandos to the Iranian vessels. After the air bombardment, the commandos planted charges which were remotely exploded from a Dolphin submarine that had moved into the area from its normal recon position off the Libyan coast. Those ships not destroyed by the air attack were taken out by the remote activation from the Dolphin.

The prime minister proclaimed victory and revealed the destruction of the nuclear capability of the Iranian military. He announced that there had been reports of only minor loss of civilian life when the government buildings in Tehran had been destroyed. The reaction of the world would most certainly be forthcoming within a mere few hours.

CHAPTER TWO

THE UNITED NATIONS: A FAILED
INSTRUMENT OF CHANGE

March 23, 2013
Return to Bimini

Doug Bradley and Hank McConnell, acting as spokesmen and agents of the Majic-12 group from the United States, stood outside the temporary Bimini facility that had been constructed as a place of meeting and contact between the leaders of Earth and the representatives of the Reticulum Alliance. The Alliance was made up of the extraterrestrial species that had created this world and its inhabitants known as humans.

"Has the Israeli military occupied Iran?" Doug asked.

"It has never tried to occupy Iran," Hank explained. "They were only defending their nation. Anyway, there is very little left to occupy after the strike as far as remaining military or government facilities. The major government leaders, including the president, are all dead and the military is in shambles, what's left of it. Their navy and air force were completely destroyed, and the army is in a state of disarray that will take a while to rebuild. Israeli jets continue to fly sorties over Iran and they fire anytime there is military activity or they see a possibility of troops trying to resupply, congregate or regroup.

"Metatron has acted rapidly trying to get all parties here to try and calm the situation so that something can be done to handle this in a permanent way. He remembers the words of Jhowah and the fact that he has been left here to monitor our activities. Jhowah won't like this. We have the strong possibility of a global outbreak of war and I guess you could say an interstellar incident if Sezan gets involved. The United Nations is not very sympathetic to the Israeli cause and has been reported as saying where its loyalties and the majority of its votes would go if it is brought to their chambers. Our own U.S. administration has made similar statements. The future of the world is in the crosshairs."

"Sezan may already be involved," Doug suggested. "He seems always to be around when trouble arises. This alien is the same individual that we have always called Satan. What can we expect?"

"Metatron, of course, will be thinking of Sezan," Hank reminded. "There's not much he can do about him, though. The Reticulum Security leader, Admiral Pazon, has been trying to capture him for many thousands of years. He seems to be able to keep a step ahead of Pazon with his commandeered starship. One day he'll make a misstep and Pazon will nab him."

As they walked toward the temporary assembly area, the two looked over at the early signs of construction for a permanent building to accommodate these meetings. Jhowah had sent a set of plans for what he wanted to be built.

"Let's get inside the temporary," Hank urged. "Metatron will want the meeting to get underway as soon as possible."

As they entered the building they noticed the Israeli prime minister seated near the front row of the chamber. He was studying documents and was alone and not in conversation as were many of those present.

"I see the prime minister from Israel there," Doug noted.

"Yeah, he doesn't seem like a very happy guy, does he?"

"He's all business," Doug said. "I've watched him for years. He received some of his early military training in the U.S. and is one of the sharpest minds on the planet. He led the attack on Iran from his office and I'll bet his hands were on every phase of that operation. The Majestic group said Iran was only a few hours away from bringing down its entire arsenal on Israel and that would have meant nuclear strikes if they had needed it. The prime minister must have been following every Iranian move like a hawk after a young rabbit."

"I don't think the current U.S. administration thinks too highly of him," Hank offered. "They lean more toward the Islamic countries. That's a shame. Israel is like an island, sitting out there all alone among the Islamic states and it seems like they can't depend on us anymore. We have always backed them until this latest group took over at the White House and in Congress. For the last four to five years they have fought against every effort the conservatives made trying to keep Israel armed so we can have a reasonable balance of power over there. I heard someone saying that they almost prevented the delivery of the high-tech F22 Raptor that we have been trying to get for them. The administration fought it tooth and nail, and the liberal congressman running the House Finance and Banking Committee was right in there also trying to stop the shipment.

"Had the Australians not stepped up, had the United State's economy not been so bad, and had the aeronautical union workers not put such pressure on Congress, the administration would not have allowed the sale even to the Aussies. Fortunately the Raptor arrived just in time to join in on the attack on the nuclear silos. Just imagine what would have happened if Iran had launched its nuclear missiles. It would have set off a chain reaction around the world. Israel's action may have not only secured its existence, but it has given the world one last chance for peace."

"I think Metatron is about to speak," Doug cautioned.

Metatron, as before, was dressed in his toga wrap and had a stern look on his face as he approached the podium. Metatron, like Jhowah, scanned the audience and since he had already ascended or had been taken to Hivania, he had been given a newly cloned body by Jhowah that was capable of being treated with Sezan's age-arrest therapy, which also made him telempathic. He read the thoughts and emotions of the audience and discerned the mixed emotions and thoughts of those in attendance just as Jhowah had done at the first contact meeting.

"It has come to my attention," he began, "that a warlike state has erupted in certain areas of your planet, and, if you remember the words of Jhowah that he spoke before he left for his home world, you should understand that this will not stand. We must attend to this today or this planet risks annihilation by a decision from Jhowah. He is a being who does not speak unless he has thought out the situation. Once he has fully evaluated it he carries through with His warnings.

"Now it is my understanding that the country of Iran was in the process of making war on the country of Israel, and Israel, upon finding out, made severe preemptive attacks on Iran in an attempt to stop the assault. What I intend to do is hear from each of the countries. I ask first for a statement from the country of Israel. Have I been advised wrongly, sir?"

Metatron stepped back and took a seat behind and to the left of the podium, and the Israeli prime minister, a highly respected leader in his country, took to the podium in almost a soldierly approach, setting his notes to the side for later reference and looking forward at the audience. There was a virile and foreboding sternness in his voice.

"Yes, you were properly counseled, my Lord. I am a man of peace. The action that I led against the forces of Iran were not done without deep consideration of what it may mean to the status of world peace and to the commands made to us earlier by Jhowah. We were careful not to attack civilian populations or compounds. It was precisely directed at the weapons and those who were preparing to create or use them to annihilate my country, my people and our way of life. Peace is all we want; all we have ever asked for. We have no interest in invading the countries that surround us. We only want to live our lives as we wish, as Jhowah has directed our ancient ancestors through the laws He passed down through Moses. Yet, there are those who hate us and who have pledged to destroy us as did the Iranian president, and as he has done on many occasions.

"Our intelligence sources were alerted by those who care about world peace that Iran was amassing troops on the border of Iraq, sending armed warships to anchor off our shores and had readied their newly purchased jets for combat. These initiatives were confirmed by satellite reconnaissance, and sources inside the country of Iran had assured us that we were in imminent danger of attack. It is my duty to protect and defend the nation of Israel and I was left no choice but to attack those who would rain down the weapons of war upon us and perhaps set off a great world war." With that he stepped back awaiting questions from Metatron or the other member nations.

"It is my understanding," Metatron said, "that you have an organization here on Earth that is called The United Nations, and that they have the duty to take situations like this and hold hearings that prevent such catastrophes. Why did you not use this international resource?"

The prime minister's countenance was pensive as he responded. "This organization, to which you refer, my Lord, is known to spend much time in verbal activities which they call negotiations and dialogue, thus delaying or preventing justice to those most urgently needing it -- to impose economic sanctions on resolution violators rather than take corrective action. And with the decisions rendered by this body over the past four years, to depend on them for rapid action and to expect them to take such action designed to protect my country is unrealistic to say the least and would be insane to say the most.

"The power base within the United Nations has been anti-American at times but, more currently, anti-Israeli. There was no time to present my case and expect a suitable response unless I was willing to accept the sacrifice of many of my countrymen and the destruction of our country and our way of life.

"It is of the greatest importance to the cause of world peace and to the challenge which Jhowah made to us that the countries of Russia and North Korea be shown to be equally guilty in this case as was the country of Iran. Both Russia and North Korea have aided and abetted Iran and the enemies of Israel by training and arming them with nuclear weapons while trying to appear to be helping them to develop nuclear power plants, ostensibly for peaceful energy purposes. They have also armed them with their most technologically advanced jets and missiles.

"It is also important to mention that the country of Iran has been in the lead in the run up of oil prices causing the current global crisis in fossil fuels, which has led to a deepening of the world's financial problems. All of this is designed to create a new world order and a shift of wealth and power away from predominantly Judeo-Christian countries toward Islamic or agnostic nations, sworn to Jihad, a universal war intended to eradicate Jews and Christians from the face of the Earth."

"What say you?" Metatron asked as he pointed to and addressed, from his seat, the Russian representative.

The former president of Russia, who represented the current regime, approached the podium passing the prime minister who was returning to his seat. The Russian glared at the prime minister who maintained a stern countenance.

"My Lord," he said as he looked toward Metatron and then took a position at the microphone, "I take great offense at the remarks of the prime minister of Israel that my country was complicit in a planned action to destroy Israel. I suggest that no such plan had been formulated and that the country of Iran was merely setting up its usual and expected defenses as any prudent country would do. My country is an ally to Iran and will be in place to assist in their return to recovery and normalcy, and to assist them in defending their borders or even retaliating if they feel that it is necessary."

With the mention of retaliation Metatron came to his feet and drew near the former president. "Mister President, I would like for you to return to your seat, and would the representative of Iran now approach the podium?"

The Russian representative abruptly stopped his return to his seat and turned back to respond for Iran. "My Lord, Iran is in such a state of disarray that they were unable to find a knowledgeable representative at this time."

"I see," Metatron responded, "what about North Korea?"

"My Lord," one of the U.N. staff members who was seated behind the podium said, "North Korea chose not to send a representative."

Metatron nodded in disappointment. "Then, perhaps someone from around the border or near Israel would give us their opinion as to what happened and what they plan to do about it," he said.

The Syrian ambassador from the United Nations stood and commented from his location. "Syria and all of the nations around Israel and nearby are planning the possibility of discontinuing oil and any other necessary supplies to Israel, which we feel made a non-provoked attack on our neighbor, Iran."

Metatron shook his head. He next questioned the Germans and then the French, both of whom had no specific remarks and no threats. China was not in the least upset, as this event would probably add to its profits from oil which in the past few years had led to a booming economy.

Finally, Metatron reached out for the opinion of the United States whose representative responded in an impotent fashion saying that, since there had been no communication with the Israeli prior to the attacks, it knew nothing. The representative said that, in fact, the president had been in recent contact with the late Iranian leader and condemned the attack. "Our president," he said, "knew of no thoughts or plans of an attack by that country on Israel, at least that he could ascertain."

"Listen to that," Doug whispered as he leaned over toward Hank. "What the hell could we say? We have been gutted defensively and offensively by the agenda of recent administrations and their liberal counterparts in Congress. Against the advice of his chief-of-staff and to appease the United Nations, they even signed the Guantanamo Treaty which, besides returning the land and military base back to the Castro group, has resulted in destroying all of our nuclear weapons, even the nuclear defense system developed during the 1980s, a technology that we had never used, but always had in place. We were kept strong and protected by its very presence."

"Yes," Hank agreed, "they wanted to make a show of good faith to the world, to bring about what they called 'change.' They thought if everyone liked us everything would be OK. I have long thought that some in our leadership have their sights on a bigger plum, one hanging at the top of the United Nations hierarchy."

"We have change, all right," Doug added. "We can or won't do anything to help Israel, or ourselves for that matter. As a nation, we are broke and unarmed. The plan to borrow and spend ourselves into prosperity failed miserably. China owns more of America than Americans do. It controls the only trade route from the Atlantic to the Pacific Ocean, the Panama Canal. We have been gutted as a superpower, by our own leaders. Iran, before Israel took the initiative, could have taken *us* out."

"Who is that guy over there?" Hank asked as he leaned toward Doug and nodded into a row of seats near the wall. "He's been watching us rather intently."

"I'm not sure," Doug replied looking at him.

The observer, a large man with short blond hair and with a black eye patch, gave a nod toward them, confirming Hanks assumption of his observation.

"If he wants to talk, he'll find us," Hank surmised.

As the dialogue began to terminate, Metatron stood before the earthly representatives and announced that he would be in contact with Jhowah, and based on recent world events, was not expecting a very pleasant response. He told the body that, although he would plead for clemency and more time, he could not assure them of Jhowah's reaction to what had just occurred. He admitted that he had impressions of who were the wrongdoers and who were the people who were trying to live and rule as Jhowah had commanded, but it would be up to him to move in any other direction. No matter who was in the right or wrong, he advised strongly that there *would be* an immediate cease fire followed by serious peace talks that would lead to an agreement with teeth in it.

After they were dismissed by Metatron who ascended in his usual way, the two Aquarians moved outside following at a safe distance behind the individual who seemed to have such a keen interest in them. He moved over into a spot that was not very well seen by the leaders who were exiting the meeting and heading for the Alice Town Seaport or the airstrip on South Bimini to return to their homelands.

"What can we do for you?" Hank asked as they approached him.

He reached into his coat and brought out a leather bound folder and exposed the contents to Hank and Doug. He was CIA.

"My sources tell me that you two have known our extraterrestrial friends for many years," he advised in a low but distinct voice as he returned his CIA identification to his pocket. "They also say that you have no compassion for the agenda of the current U.S. administration." He waited for their response. He had not identified his own leanings but he had stated a well-informed knowledge of their position.

"If you know this, then you know the organization which we represent," Hank responded, testing the true knowledge of this man.

"The Majestic-12 group," he correctly answered. "The Aquarian group would more exactly label your position within the organization."

"And what do you need from us?" Doug asked.

"Since the treaty signed at Guantanamo, a group of people in high places has been in the midst of a dilemma that is requiring help from many sources... and how do you like the car that I heard you bought last month?" He asked a confused Doug.

"What?" Doug asked. The two were stunned by the remark, but soon realized his ploy and continued the small talk while one of the visiting dignitaries walked quite near and past them.

"As I said," the CIA agent continued when they were alone, "it is the duty of my group to protect our nation -- and in doing so -- the world; but the current leadership of our country is making it a difficult job. In fact, we are baffled by the recent decisions coming out of the White House and Congress. We are currently in talks with the Israeli and Australian governments that have given us hope to be able to make some progress in our efforts to stabilize the world economically, politically and militarily. My superiors are in a very untenable position as we all work behind the backs of the current administration to make some attempt to protect our way of life."

"And where do we fit into this picture?" Hank asked.

"Beside my duty in the CIA, I represent a group of puissant, yet unknown, world leaders devoted to God, or as you call him, Jhowah, and who have taken on the idea of leading a protectorate movement of the entire planet. We need someone to be our liaison with Jhowah and Metatron. Although the founders of this movement knew Metatron, they are no longer alive. Those of us, who are carrying out the covenant which they created, need to meet with Metatron. It is very possible that there is a connection between the radical Islamic groups and the one they call Sezan, or at least the Israeli intelligence feels that way."

"I hope not," Doug replied. "He would be a dangerous adversary. By the way, who or what do we call you?"

"Just refer to me as 'Prophet,'" he said as he shook their hands, "and you will hear me refer to this alliance with Israel as *Operation Shield.* This is why we need you as liaison. If this connection with the extraterrestrial known as Sezan is true, we have a serious complication in handling our sworn duties and what help we might need from Metatron and Jhowah in restoring order in the world. We hope that this can be mediated by you."

"Should we inform him now?" Hank asked.

"He already knows. We need to get all of our ducks in a row, first, and see if this most recent military incident is a real threat to our ability to control the economic and military events on a global level. We also need to penetrate the powerful sub-rosa group known as the Illuminati. They, and their ancestors, have long controlled the flow of global capital and, many times, the leadership throughout the world. We need to know how they stand on this current crisis. The good news is that we, and I mean *Operation Shield,* as the keepers of The Covenant are known, have the capability of a high-tech defense system that could render short-, medium-, and long-range nuclear missiles impotent once we learn to use it properly."

"What?" Doug mouthed with very little sounds coming from his throat.

"Yes," Prophet resumed. "It seems that during the 1980s there was great concern not only about the defenses of the United States, Europe, and Australia but that of Israel as it sat in the middle of an ever-increasing philosophy of Jihadism among the radical Islamists. The American and British leadership had a considerable arsenal of nuclear weapons secretly placed inside the borders of Great Britain, Israel, and Australia and we are sure that this was not known by any of the recent administrations. As suspected members of the Illuminati group, they would not have been informed. There have been public speeches by some that were very much along the lines of the philosophy of the Illuminati.

"The original operation and secret transfer of weaponry was referred to among the operatives as *Operation Big Stick,* named after the defense policy of the early twentieth-century president, Teddy Roosevelt."

"What about the current administration, does it know? Did any of the earlier administrations know?" Hank questioned.

"As I said, we feel quite sure that they never found out. The leadership at the time The Covenant was created kept this under wraps; even the cabinet members were kept in the dark," Prophet answered. "We knew before the most recent elections that the current administration and those who engineered its rise to power had an agenda that was not compatible with America remaining the world's preeminent military superpower and having a workable defense for our country. With China and Russia back in as economically and militarily powerful nations, and now Russia standing behind Iran and North Korea, we must be able to protect the people of the United States and our trusted allies. It seems that this cache of nuclear weapons, along with other powerful defenses, and it is a large cache, are our aces-in-the-hole, if we can make it all work, to preserve world peace.

"Our current efforts are under the title of *Operation Shield* and, considering what the world has at stake, we must make it work for all free nations and for the sake of Jhowah's project and his plans for our future. We intend to do as *the first* president Roosevelt advised: 'Speak softly, but carry a big stick.'

"There are several powerful Jewish and Christian leaders around the world who are working with us to inform world leaders that we control nuclear weapons in silos under the sea and in other strategic but unnamed locations scattered about both hemispheres. There are also many loyal military leaders from the United States who saw this coming and are secretly helping us to initiate these plans. We will also let them know that we have a fully operational SDI or Strategic Defense Initiative capable of destroying nuclear-armed missiles in their silos – or in the air anywhere in the world.

"We also have several high level Aussie and British officials who are in on it. Our mission at this time is to create plans for the activation of these weapons and to decide where the most strategically effective targets for their deployment might be. Except for the Islamic radicals who believe that death should come while carrying out Jihad, knowing these targets would be the key to the continuation of life on Earth should help shift the current world order toward preservation rather than destruction and compliance with Jhowah's covenants."

"If the current administration and the majority members of Congress find out," Hank suggested, "they would do nothing militarily but they would spread the news through their own political connections that could put an end to *Operation Shield* before you could even get it moving. I'm sure you remember how they released details of interrogation tactics used by our intelligence agencies against the 9-11 perpetrators. That was the beginning of the end of U.S. superiority in the intelligence arena. I don't believe that we can trust this administration, nor those who supported its rise to power, to stand up against those who have their own agenda for America, which is total economic and military collapse."

"There is very little chance that the left has that information," Prophet added while touching his eye patch. "We have been watching the same actions that you have observed about their loss of a sense of protecting the country. When will you two be ready to join me, if you are receptive to this?"

"We are definitely in agreement," Hank answered. "Am I right, Doug?"

Doug nodded and added, "I think we have to get back to Washington to turn in our report of this meeting, and then we should be able to join you, if Majic-1 gives us the go ahead. They have certainly been dismayed, as have you, about the defensive posture and declining capability of our country, especially with its relationship to the efforts of Jhowah. Stay in contact through Hank; as you know, he is my superior."

"I will give you about four days and then get back with you on where you two can meet me. Only give Majic-1 the basics of our conversation and talk to as few of the members as you have to. We can't take any chances. There is just too much at risk."

"Understood," Doug replied. "We know how to keep a secret. You forget that we kept the existence of extraterrestrial space craft from being believed by much of the world for decades. So, you can feel free to tell us more about who is running the operation. Do we have a good man in charge?"

"Do we have a good man? Yes. Who is in charge? I could tell you but if I did I would have to shoot you." Prophet never cracked a smile. "You will possibly learn when we get to our meeting place which will, in all probability, be in Tel Aviv. Hank, I'll be in touch." And with that Prophet turned and exited around a caterpillar grader at the site of the new contact building construction.

Hank looked at Doug and tilted his head. A puzzled look was on his face. "Doug, did you hear what that man just said to you? Did he say he might have to shoot you?"

"Yes Hank, he did and he did it without a smile. I don't know whether he was joking or if he was for real."

"Well, remind me not to turn my back on him," Hank advised. "I'll have to learn more about his personality first."

The two men looked at each other, smiled, turned and left for their waiting jeep to be taken to Alice Town where they would be flown to Washington, D.C., and then driven to their office in the U.S. Naval Observatory.

Ben Gurion Airport
Lod, Israel

Nine Miles From Tel Aviv
April 1, 2013

As Hank and Doug disembarked from their plane they passed through Israeli customs and headed for the car rental, where they found a good deal on a Fiat Grande, and began their drive toward Tel Aviv on Highway 1, the main Jerusalem-to-Tel Aviv highway.

"Well, getting out of there was easy enough," Doug said as he looked over at Hank who was doing the driving. "Have you ever been here before?"

"Yeah, I had to come over one time for a rather serious UFO sighting about ten years ago. Our fellow employee, Zach Donovan, came with me; in fact, it was his first actual duty event with us.

"The airport here is near the city of Lod which is about nine or ten miles from Tel Aviv and is located out near the Mediterranean coast. The land is rather flat here but it gets a little hilly back to the east of us."

Hank squinted as he looked up into the rear-view mirror. "Uh oh," he said. "There's a red Mazda that has been following us since we pulled out of the car rental at Ben Gurion. He may be just headed for Tel Aviv like us but I'd better check him out to be sure. We don't want to run into any problems."

Doug got a view of the vehicle by looking into the passenger side mirror as Hank increased his speed by a good fifteen kilometer per hour. "He seems to be picking up speed as you do," he warned.

"We're getting closer to the city," Hank said. "I'll take a side street. We have a GPS so we won't get lost and we don't have a definite time yet to meet with Prophet." He took the next right turn and maintained his speed but the red Mazda did the same and continued to follow at a fair distance, thinking that he was not yet noticed.

"I don't understand this," Hank explained. "We haven't even gotten into the operation yet." He pressed his lips, but continued to drive and even increased his speed. He took the next left turn, then an immediate right turn that took him into a fork in the road where he took the left branch. The Mazda stayed behind him.

"That settles it. Hang on, Doug. I haven't been able to drive like this since I was a teenager." Not having a stick shift to deal with, Hank took another right turn and floored the Fiat's gas pedal; then another right, passing three cars and almost being hit by one that was approaching from the opposite direction. Then another turn caused him to almost careen into a parked vehicle on his left. When he made the next high-speed right turn, his left wheels momentarily left the highway, but he saw the red Mazda just going out of sight around the turn in the distance. Hank kept the pedal as close to the floor as he could without taking the chance of losing control' and as he rounded the curve he could easily see the Mazda in front and he was sure he had been spotted.

"We'll see if he likes being chased as much as he likes chasing," he said.

Doug took a swipe with his sweaty palm across his hairless scalp and looked toward Hank. "Do you do this often?" he asked. "You seem to be pretty efficient at it."

"Never driven like this before," Hank replied and just as he approached the intersection, another car was crossing and there was a stop sign that loomed up in front of them. He pressed hard on the brakes and the Fiat went into a spin, doing a 360, and ending up sitting as it should, facing forward, behind the stop sign. He could see the Mazda disappearing in the distance.

"Well, at least he's in front and not behind us now," Hank remarked as he drove across the intersection and on down the road. "I never was able to see into the vehicle. There was too much tinting. Are you all right Doug?"

"I may have chewed a hole in the seat but otherwise I think I'm good."

Hank laughed. "You have to have teeth to do that, buddy. I guess we should set the GPS and get on into town."

Tel Aviv Israel
In The Private Office Of The Israeli Prime Minister

"Gentlemen, please be seated. Prophet is in an adjoining room and he'll be with us momentarily." The prime minister spoke English with the preciseness of a language-trained Ph.D. "So he tells me your job is to search out UFOs? Have you seen many?"

Hank being the chief of the Aquarian group cleared his throat and explained. "Yes sir, we have seen many of them, but mostly we have been sent in to debunk serious sightings or the ones that are the most difficult to explain without admitting their true existence. For thousands of years these UFOs have been visiting Earth to monitor Jhowah's project and provide counsel to selected world leaders, but since Jhowah has revealed himself we now let the sightings go without debunking. Our main effort since then has been to act as liaison between our leadership and the Creators - or Designers, whichever you might wish to call them."

A door behind them opened and Prophet came into the room. He shook their hands without a smile and took a seat beside them. The prime minister was seated behind his desk looking across at Doug and Hank.

"You know, we had to bring you all the way over here to explain our plans for *Operation Shield*," he explained. "We just can't handle any of this using a telephone or even encrypted email. As you can imagine, our communications are regularly monitored by the Palestinians and others on a minute-by-minute basis. We never send out sensitive information over email, telephone or any method other than by face-to-face discussion. We do, however, send out much misinformation using those methods.

"We want you on board to help us keep Jhowah and Metatron informed of our efforts and to make sure that they understand that we have no offensive plans. We have none at all. Our objective is defensive to protect our country and a way of life that actually arises out of Jhowah's direction in the "Book of Laws" or the Sefer Torah scrolls, which contain the laws handed down in the five books of Moses.

"Our plans, as you have been briefed in a small degree by Prophet, include conducting a mock launching of the strategically placed defensive system of nuclear weapons that were moved into Israel, Australia and also in underwater locations around the world. The project, *Operation Big Stick*, was carried out clandestinely and co-jointly during the 1980s by the U.S. and Britain. The U.S. dealt with us directly and not through underlings. They, like us, did not want any leaks to occur. Prophet's chief was one of the ones who worked with our people to get some of the weapons into Israel after all of the legalities and logistics were sorted out by the leaders. It was, primarily, a CIA operation.

"I have always been awed by the foresight of the American and British leadership back then; not just in this affair, but in many of the other avenues that related to the defense of the world. They were not afraid to look evil in the eye and call it what it is. The statement of 'Trust but verify' that came from one of your presidents has become a part of the standard operating procedure of the security branches of most peace-loving countries. I think those leaders really cared about the 'Shining City on the hill' and the people who lived there. They proved that peace through strength is the most effective way to maintain a true peace and that 'In God we trust' was more than a motto on your country's currency. Now it is up to people like you and Prophet, and the group he represents, to take the reins and keep the elements of the Covenant protected, to keep the whole world protected. The group of politicians that has recently been sent to Washington has no intention of creating an acceptable defense; they had rather appease and disarm than create strength.

"In some crazy way we have allowed a group of leftist and anti-American sympathizers to take control of many of the world's governments, but, most regrettably, yours. Until the American people wake up to what is happening and throw the current administration and its lap-dog Congress out, we have to do what we have to do, and that is to set up the defenses that were given to those 1980s leaders by a group possessing super-human intelligence that the leaders would only refer to as *The Covenant Makers*. After what I have learned over the last two weeks, I suggest that *The Covenant Makers* were the extraterrestrial intelligence represented most recently by Metatron and Jhowah. The top of the leadership back then had the foresight to install the system and put it into our hands. I do not know if they were advised to do so or not by Jhowah's group.

"I have some surprising information for you. It shows how incredible the intelligence and preparation abilities of those leaders were as they planned for the protection of the world, not just the free world, but protection for all of humankind. They had to know even more than they let on. Several American presidents, you know, were aware of the extraterrestrial presence and even tried to imply that fact in speeches to the United Nations.

"The majority of the countries represented by the UN, however, couldn't see past their greed and hunger for power to understand the message. At the same time *Big Stick* was moving nuclear weapons here, the human representatives of *The Covenant Makers* were learning about space-age defense technologies and developing the one that came to be known as SDI, the Strategic Defense Initiative. Some called it the Star Wars Initiative, and after the end of the Cold War most thought that it had failed or was shelved.

"We believe that to direct later attention away from SDI, after it was perfected, the U.S. leadership acted as if the disrupter beam that was photographed knocking out a missile over the Pacific was not real and that trick photography was used to fool the Russians, which helped to lead to the end of the Cold War. This, for some reason was what they wanted the world to believe."

"We know a bit about disseminating misinformation," Hank injected.

"Well," responded Prophet, "it was no failure. It is a real and an effective weapon to control world peace. It is an x-ray laser-beam weapon that has the ability to disrupt the very molecular structure of its targets. The 1980s leaders were concerned that their political systems and future leaders would allow for anti-American forces to gain influence and affect the creation of future policies. This was probably a caution from the extraterrestrials, who for thousands of years had dealt with the one called Sezan, or Satan as we call him.

"A few of these leaders had been face to face with the extraterrestrials, probably Metatron, who had seen great nations fall into the hands of inept leaders. The Covenant leaders knew that Israel had to survive and could be trusted to keep the Star Wars project from being exposed until the time was proper.

"We have a technology so efficient and so accurate that if the location of a missile is known before launch, SDI can detonate it as it sits in its silo. If sensors don't find the missile until after ignition, this x-ray laser-beam weapon can reach out and destroy it as it leaves its silo or launching pad. This weapon can handle short, medium or long-range types, and if the missiles make it out of their silos and into the sky the beam can knock them out anywhere from the silo to their targets, putting the possessor of such weapons at great risk.

We, of *Operation Shield,* have SDI capabilities strategically hidden in many of our communications satellites and they can strike anywhere in the world. It was a trick getting the links on the satellites up there without the missile experts realizing the presence of the SDI. With the advent of high-speed and miniaturized computers, the satellites have video and sensors that can take the point of origin of a missile, its flight arc and speed and compute its target before it gets to fifty miles in altitude.

"It takes this information and sends it to our computers while it uses the same information to bring down the missile. All the time the satellite is bringing us the evening news and as many phone calls as we can make. Isn't technology wonderful? At least it is when it is used to promote good over evil? Just imagine what wonders are available to humankind if only we would listen to the messages of the higher intelligence to which we have just been introduced."

"All this had been planned in the eighties," Prophet added. "Why has our country strayed so far from the principles of those leaders and that small group of conservative Congressmen and women who had actually proven that their agenda would work? Not only did they later give us a 'Contract with America,' they gave a 'Contract with the World of the Present and the Future.' Now, however, we are in lock step with a group of national socialists who want to grow their own power and wealth."

The mid-twentieth century novelist, Ayn Rand, had warned Americans that this would happen. Because she had grown up in communist Russia, Rand, a proclaimed atheist, knew how their system robbed people of free will and made them slaves of their system of socialism and communism. Doug and Hank had read her book, *Atlas Shrugged,* as young men. However, with all the top-secret material that they had to deal with, they had forgotten its prophetic message. They had let slip from their minds the symbolism portrayed by the mythological god whose job it was to stabilize the earth in space, but who became perplexed with the world's growing love affair with socialism and found the change more than even he could bear. Even as far back as Thomas Jefferson and our country's Founding Fathers, the arrival of people who would attempt to interpret The Constitution to further their own secular-based political agendas had been predicted.

"The integrity of the greatest democracy the world has ever known is in jeopardy," the prime minister explained. "Free enterprise advocates, not only in the United States but the world over, are allowing socialist constructionists to try and convince them that capitalism is bad and socialism is good, that slavery to government is better than freedom from government.

"Where in this world has socialism been successful until capitalism is added to the mix? The entrepreneurial spirit is a major reason for early mankind coming out of the caves and creating the modern society in which we live today. It is why my people were able to transform much of the barren land here in Israel into an agricultural and technological oasis.

As of a month ago, we have begun the inspection and maintenance of underground and underwater missile silos designed to hold defensive-class nuclear weapons. We have them placed all around the world in sympathetic countries that have helped us to keep them secret. As you have been advised, we have a sky filled with satellites that contain a weapon so high tech and so lethally intelligent that, once it is activated, no missile fired anywhere on this planet can escape its destructive force.

"I want you to advise Metatron that you now know these facts. He knows that we have them, but I want you to let him know that you are now aware of their existence and that you will keep him constantly in the loop of our intelligence. Be absolutely sure that he knows we understand the purpose of these weapons and that they, in no way, will be used offensively or in an aggressive fashion unless we are the object of an attack. As he directed in a previous visit to Earth in the 1980s we will use them to 'keep the peace' and 'save our planet.'"

The prime minister looked at the two Aquarians who sat in awe of their recent knowledge. "Do you two have any questions about all of this?" He asked.

"This is not a question," Hank said, "but a point of information for you. Today as we drove in from Ben Gurion airport we were followed by a red Mazda. I don't know the year or any other specifics other than it was a late model, but they got behind us and tried to stay there until we were able to out-maneuver and get behind them. They fled and went out of my sight when I had to stop at an active intersection."

"I wouldn't worry about them. They were probably trying to find out information that they have been unable to obtain from their own sources," the prime minister suggested. "We will announce most of these facts in a non-specific way when the installation of the silos and other weaponry is completed. Until then we will see much posturing among the countries such as Russia and those in the Middle East. Well, what do you think about our plans and hopes for the future? Will you be a part of *Operation Shield?*"

"We will be presenting these facts to Majic-1," Hank informed him. "He is the current leader of our organization that has the duty of controlling the outflow of information regarding UFOs and extraterrestrials. We will certainly recommend our being a part of such a devoted group, and knowing that Jhowah is aware of it, and actually helped us develop it, will probably assure his agreement to cooperate. It is part of our duty as liaison between our government – at least the one created by our Founding Fathers – and our Creators."

Doug rose from his chair and addressed Prophet. "Now that we know the man who leads this is a 'good man' and that we now know who he is, I hope you won't still have to shoot us."

Prophet held a straight face for several moments, enough to make Doug a bit nervous, and then a bit of a smile showed through on his face. The men all shook hands and Doug and Hank left to return to Washington.

July 4, 2013
INN Broadcast

Sezan and Samael were again listening to the INN broadcast to follow the extent of the changes happening around the globe as a result of their manipulations and to gain insight into the minds of the Soleans.

"I hear that the economies of the non oil-producing countries are in trouble," Samael said.

"That's our plan," Sezan added.

The INN broadcaster sat before the camera as she returned to an increasingly common subject that was affecting people all over the world.

"In only a matter of three or four months the price of oil has reached three hundred and eighty dollars a barrel and is touching off the worsening of a world recession and economic uncertainty in many parts of the world. Gold is selling for $4,000 per ounce when it can be bought. Most third-world countries are feeling the impact and several are collapsing economically. Countries like China, Russia, Venezuela and the Middle East, along with Canada and Mexico, are quite happy with this predicament.

"While tightening a 'choke-hold' on the economies of many struggling nations, the economies of the oil-producing nations are doing well. The income from their oil leadership brings their citizens a cheaper fuel and less taxation. But countries such as the United States, which still refuse to drill for their own domestically located oil or build modern nuclear power plants, seem to be facing bankruptcy.

"The president of the World Bank has said that the situation in the United States is without an explanation. 'Why,' he asked, 'do they not drill for their own oil? There are areas in Alaska that contain as much or more oil than all of the OPEC nations combined?' He referred to a report issued by the governor of that state that the lands of the coastal plains of northern Alaska, which are desolate stretches of unusable arctic tundra, Gull Island, and the recent finds in North Dakota and Colorado are all accessible to drilling using modern high-tech drilling techniques that would have no real effect on the environment or local ecologies. This network has discovered that when these new areas of fossil fuels are located, the U.S. congress inexplicably turns them into public lands and bans the drilling of oil, an action that might worsen an already fallen economy. Many experts are asking: 'What good will it do to save the planet and destroy mankind?'

"The current U.S. administration, despite the severe inflation and growing economic depression, responded that there will be no drilling in their country. They are quoted as saying that their intention is to sit down and talk with OPEC leaders to try and resolve the growing crisis in the world. In the meantime, they added that the U.S. can depend on Canadian and Mexican oil until it is able to get entirely on alternative fuels, which they estimate taking place in about ten to fifteen years, a number that has not changed in any speeches or releases from that administration or Congress made in the past. This policy has been backed by a Democrat president and a Democrat-controlled congress beholden to multiple fragmented ecological environmental and anti-capitalist groups.

"With the new aggressive drilling policies of Mexico, it is seeing a tremendous influx of capital. The standard of living has risen to the point that no longer do Mexicans cross the border into the United States, and the Mexican government has closed its borders and made it virtually impossible for Americans to enter its country, legally or illegally, except for travel and tourism. The penalties for breaking immigration and deportation laws there are a deterrent for anyone choosing to break them.

"Change has come to America, but it does not appear to be the change that many Americans expected. The United States is rapidly becoming a second-rate power and the dollar is becoming a second-rate currency on the world market. According to sources within the United Nations, there is even talk about removing the United States from the UN Security Council and giving its seat to Mexico.

"In other news there have been many recent rumors that official confirmation of the presence of intelligent extraterrestrial life will soon be made by the United States government in cooperation with Britain, Brazil and Australia. These same rumors contain claims that a large interstellar vessel has already been seen in the sky over North Bimini Island in the Caribbean, and that the occupants have dialogued with members of many of the larger countries already possessing limited space technology. INN will continue to follow this story."

In The Office Of The President
SORGE Headquarters
In The City Of Paradon On The Planet Hivania

Welcome home, Metatron," Jhowah said. "How are things going on Soleus-3?"

"Not well, my Lord," he answered. "The leader of Israel, a country whose people are very special to you, had to attack one of the nearby countries, Iran, to avoid an all-out war that could possibly have spread into a war throughout the whole planet."

"Had to?" Jhowah asked.

"Yes, it was a preemptory-type strike that only hit governmental, military and political installations that were being used in the Iranian leader's promise to destroy Israel. The leader of Iran has been a real bully when referring to the nation of Israel. He is quoted as saying that Israel and its entire people should be wiped from the face of the Earth, or Soleus-3 as we know it. He began massing troops and setting up his navy and air forces. He was only hours from the destruction of Israel when the Israeli leader took the only action that I think he could have taken.

"The move was swift and made with pinpoint accuracy. It was so accurate that very little collateral damage occurred and very few civilians were killed or injured. Military vessels and personnel, government structures, nuclear and non-nuclear weapons were targeted and probably ninety-five per cent or more were destroyed. The president of Iran, his generals and cabinet officials are no more. They were killed in the initial strike."

"So, it's good that Israel did not have to use the Strategic Defense Initiative that we had provided for them. Peaceful coexistence has always been a real sticky situation in that area with the two opposing religions," Jhowah observed. "If they could only understand that Allah and God are the same. I am both, and I care greatly for all of them. That's why we made provisions for them to have a system to destroy nuclear weapons before they fell on Soleus-3 and its people. Well, what do you think the future holds, Metatron?"

"My Lord, I think we need to wait to see. If we are to remain consistent with our challenge to let the humans choose their own destiny, we have to see how it will play out. You have given them your final ultimatum.

"The Israeli leader is a reasonable man and, I feel, a peaceful one, but he had to do what he did to protect his country, his people and the planet. He did this in spite of a lack of cooperation from the current leadership of the United States. The Israelis were always a strong ally of the U.S. until things began to change politically in recent days. Now they seem to avoid seeking U.S. help. It's like they are suspicious of its leadership. In fact, it is hard to tell whether the current leadership is committed to saving itself, or the United States, or making itself a pawn to the radical Islamic countries.

"If there is any hope that the people on Soleus-3 will come to their senses, Jhowah, I'd like to see you give them a bit more time. Surely, the good men and women there will see the dangers of the times. My Lord, would you consider holding off on their judgment for just a while longer?"

"If you still think there is a chance that the people of the world will make the right choices, I will." Jhowah responded. "We'll give our probation period a bit longer to see what else is taking place. It seems that the Israeli leader has handled one of our problems for us -- the one agitated by Sezan. We now need to see how the rest of the world goes."

"Yes, my Lord, and there may be more positive happenings from this leader from Israel. He is one who believes in peace backed by the strength of a powerful defense, much as the way we have held Sezan at bay. That is how he vanquished the Iranian leader, and, as I monitored the exiting from the meeting on the island called Bimini, I sensed conversations from our Aquarian liaison agents and the CIA individual from the United States who are working with *Shield*. I sensed covertness to their conversation. It centered on a global defense initiative using the weapons moved into Israel during the 1980s. It seemed proven to me that the current American administration knows nothing about it so far."

"Metatron, this sounds very positive. We had to take similar measures when we were in combat with the Janosians." Jhowah thought back about those ancient times. "It was before your first time on Soleus-3 or even the beginning of the Challenge, but they were a formidable enemy. I'm glad we are at peace today and that they are a part of our project. Perhaps, there is a possibility that our Soleus-3 experiment will turn out as we had hoped."

"I feel that Sezan may have had a part in the actions of the Iranian leader," Metatron observed, "and maybe the actions of other neighboring countries."

"Do you now?" Jhowah asked as he looked up from his desk toward His trusted one. "What makes you feel that way?"

"It's not the battle that he provoked but the recent increase in the price of the planet's most precious energy source that is occurring. The Middle East is demanding too great a price rise. It is not reasonable for several countries that have a product that has kept them in such luxury to place such a price on their product that it could price them out of business or destroy the economies and existence of those countries that are almost parasitically dependent on them for the need of their product.

"When you gave mankind dominion over all of Soleus-3 and free will, you didn't intend for it to use them to divide those created in our image. By the way, the Syrian leader suggested that the Islamic countries might stop selling oil to Israel. Some have said that oil is the fuel of freedom, and to not be able to obtain it would allow Israel to be destroyed easily."

"I have put a lot of thought to a possible solution for the current crisis on Soleus-3," Jhowah said. "It is my recommendation that it is time for us to give mankind, those loyal to our laws, the kind of energy that we have long known. Our primordial energy technology may be their one last hope for survival. We need to instruct them in the way that it is available everywhere, even in the void of space. As we know, it is the most available form of energy that exists in every nook and cranny of the universe, even in interstellar and intergalactic regions of space. And, when they are ready, it is the form of energy that can be most easily converted in the appropriate engines to eventually create faster-than-light-speed vessels. In the meantime, it will allow them to heat and cool their dwellings, power their modes of land and air methods of transportation and provide artificial light.

"When humankind is no longer dependent on fossil fuels, the power base, or World Order as they prefer to call it, will change. All we have to do is to give those who are loyal to our laws the ability to build the energy collectors and converters, and train them on how to use it for the sake of good.

"Hopefully, they will eagerly do the rest but, at first, we have to become more involved in their activities and make sure that this technology does not come under the control of some of the same people and countries that might use it to create more division and unrest among the people of Earth. Except for the anti-defense missile program that we gave to the Soleus-3 leaders in the 1980s, virtually every other technological advancement that we have passed down to them has been used to foster a greater divide among the neighborhoods we have created there. In the future, we will need to become more visible and show a display of support for the ones who have chosen us over Sezan.

"Do you have a plan in your mind as to how we could introduce our knowledge of primordial energy to Soleus-3 so that it could be available to our followers in all nations on an equal basis?"

"That will be a challenge, my Lord," Metatron responded. "I haven't given it any thought before this discussion, but I will try to have the details worked out as soon as possible. Sezan's influence on the planet has recently been on the rise."

"I know," Jhowah responded. "Did the oil-producing nations not have anything to say in your last conference? Did they seem suspicious or give any unusual responses during your dialogue?"

"I don't believe they have been invited to either meeting, my Lord, except for the ones aligned with Iran who were at the meeting after the assault by Israel. Because of their radical views on how the world should be they were not among the countries you requested to be invited. Perhaps we should get our liaisons to make the appropriate invitation. Since the Iranian leader was killed in the Israeli strike, there was no representation from that area at the meeting I called, except the

Russian leader, who vowed to protect and back the Iranians and any other country attacked by Israel or its allies."

"Yes," Jhowah said as he reached for a pen and rolled it in his thin gray fingers, "you must certainly do that. Although the Russian government has long promoted atheism, without contact with us they might feel that we have no concern for them or that we might have removed them from our plans for the future. If they haven't already, they will surely be contacted by Sezan, who will try to convince them to side with him.

"When you return to Soleus-3, you must visit the Russian and Chinese leaders and make them realize that we created the planet on which they live and that we also hold the power to continue or to destroy it. In their case, the possibility of complete and utter annihilation may be the only way we can gain their cooperation. With them, we'll have to exercise the tried and true method of peace through strength. At least, in the case of Russia, it worked in the 1980s.

"Have you been able to meet with the Illuminati Council?" Jhowah continued. "Since they currently brandish so much power on the planet, they need to know that we are aware of their methods and will not allow them to use primordial energy for the group's personal gain. It is they who will have to deal with the oil-producing countries when the world no longer needs fossil fuels."

"Not yet," responded Metatron. "But I intend to do so when I return to Soleus-3. This group may finally reap what they have sown. Their Inner Circle seems to control much of the flow of wealth and influence on Soleus-3, and has done so for a very long time."

"You must convince the Illuminati," Jhowah interjected, "that they must turn away from their mission to rule the world and become part of a world order that, from this time forward, will be directed toward the survival and welfare of all, and not just a few. And, given how the group has functioned in the past, that's a tall order.

"I'm sure you have some personal business or need that you have to attend to here in Paradon, so take a few days for that and, afterwards, return to Soleus-3. It is a four-week trip at our normal travel speeds but I do believe it to be very necessary and you will need to be there to monitor their activities."

"Yes my Lord, I shall return and I'll send a report back to you as soon as I have accomplished this mission and receive a report from Mister Bradley or Doctor McConnell regarding the answer from the Islamic leaders."

Four Weeks Later
Somewhere In A Private Chateau In Rural Switzerland

Tension filled the room where many of the most powerful men and women in the world had been instructed to gather. The meeting was called to receive a direct message from Jhowah. The attendees were told no more.

The group, considered to have been in control most of the monies of this planet since the 1700s, waited patiently for Jhowah's messenger to enter the room, but the knock on the door announcing his or her arrival never came.

Suddenly, there appeared before them was a tall handsome man with long brown hair dressed in a white toga wrap. His countenance was unmatched by any whom the humans in that room had ever seen. Clearly, he was of an extraordinary origin and place.

One of the three French members sitting at the table leaned over to a U.S. representative positioned to his left and said, "This is a trick, a hologram. I have seen it used many times."

Overhearing the conversation, the other U.S. representative said to the two, "I'm afraid not, my friend, one of my companies developed our most advanced holographic technology. This is not the work of our scientists. It is far superior to anything I've ever seen here on Earth, but he is real. I have no idea how he might have been transported here."

Metatron moved gracefully to the head of the long table, a position from which he intended to address the group. He glanced at the faces of men and women who prided themselves in being above most other men and women. What he saw were expressions ridden with shock and awe.

Those he had come to address were descendants of The Committee of 300, a very old secret society founded in the early 1700's by the British Crown. These powerful families and their emissaries had controlled the world for more than three centuries. It was they who determined where and when wars would be launched, and when it was in their best interest to end such conflicts. As had their familial predecessors, this group gathered around the table controlled the financial systems of the world. They drove the international markets up and down all the time, creating chaos in order to bring even more of the world's assets under their control. They fabricated recessions, booms, and depressions as necessary to further their own self-serving agenda and had controlled many heads of state for centuries.

A small core of families, known as the Inner Circle, directed and expanded this secretive worldwide organization known as the Illuminati or Moriah. By whatever name it was called, the group represented the epitome of greed and nepotism. They alone determined who would sit in the seats of power in the nations of the world. Although they had gone to great lengths to hide their identities and operations from the public eye, the presence of this "Shadow Government," as they have sometimes been called, was felt in every corner of the globe.

Since the thirty-nine founding members of the original "Steering Committee" were called together by the Inner Circle in 1954 at The Hotel Bilderberg, a ritzy hotel located in The Netherlands, many others had been invited to join their ranks. Although thirteen families represented the governing body, more than 120 members make up sub-groups, organizations such as The Trilateral Commission, founded in part by the late New York mogul, David Rockefeller. the Trilateral Commission was an international outgrowth of an existing semi-secret organization, The Foreign Relations Committee, comprised of Americans and Canadians.

Anxiously awaiting the words of Metatron were representatives of just over a dozen wealthy and powerful families, committed to creating One World Order, their world order. These were powerful leaders and members of well-known, even famous, families of today. Although they had no voting rights within the order, some new blood lines that had come into great fortunes were "invited observers."

Never before had someone with more power than the men and women around this table appeared before them. But this was different. The group had received good intelligence that a new kind of energy was being developed which threatened to unravel their One World Order – the one controlled by this so-called illuminated group. It was possible, they had been told, that no longer would the world be dependent on fossil fuels. If this were so, the Order that the Illuminated Ones had created would be turned upside down. And where would that leave them? The stakes were high. They were anxious to hear the words of Jhowah's Messenger.

One of the members was looking about the room as if he was looking for a specific person. He turned to the woman beside him.

"Have you seen Timothy Geithner, the U.S. Treasurer?" he asked. "So far, he doesn't appear to have shown up this year. I definitely remember him being at the meeting back in May of 2009."

"I imagine he is back in Washington getting ready for the next election," the woman answered.

"Yes, I guess you're right," he said.

Within each member's head was reverberating the question: "How can we gain control of this new energy and use it to our advantage?" What they didn't yet know was that Metatron was telempathic and that he knew their thoughts and picked up on their self-serving mental ruminations. They would soon learn, however, that their clandestine motives were futile. Sooner than they could imagine, their grip on the world was coming to an end.

Metatron's words were firm, yet soft-spoken. "I have come to deliver a message from Jhowah," he began. "The true ruler of the dimensions that you call Heaven and Earth has sent me. I am his messenger. I know what it is like to be human. I have returned to Earth many times with different names. Each visit was meant to show mankind how Jhowah wanted you to live and to treat one another.

"Shortly before the Great Flood, my Hivanian father, Jhowah, or God as you know him, sent me to this planet to live as a human being and to serve as an example of how life here should be lived. He then took me in human form to a place in a distant star system known as Hivania. There, as I have been on many occasions, I was transformed back into a creature capable of existing as both a physical and meta-physical being, capable of transcending a tiered order of realms you know as dimensions. I have lived among the Creators of this world and many others similar to it for thousands of your years. The rest of what I am going to reveal to you will seem unfamiliar to many of you. That it may, however, is no excuse for your not doing whatever is required to familiarize yourselves with the revelations contained within my message.

"I was imbued with a technology known as age-arrest therapy, which means that I shall never age and never die due to aging. I was given the power to sense the thoughts and emotions of others. I have telempathic abilities and the ability to ascend, descend, or to move about from one dimension to the other upon my own free will to represent the Godhead throughout the universe. This is why some of your scriptures have referred to me as 'The Comforter.' It is through these special powers that I have come to you today to fulfill the mission for which I was commissioned. When I am finished, you will truly be enlightened."

The members looked around the room and at each other. This being spoke with a believable authority.

"However, what I have to say to you today will not comfort many of you. Nevertheless, I have been instructed by Jhowah to inform you of his displeasure with the New World Order that many of you and those you control are attempting to create. I have already heard your thoughts in my mind, so put aside any ideas of deception and listen to the message that I bring.

Jhowah has instructed me to tell you that he is unhappy with the world that you, who have been swayed by Sezan, Jhowah's adversary, have played a role in creating. You have had a hand in creating a world that has turned away from what Jhowah and his team of Creators intended. I know that you have been informed about His visit to Earth and the admonitions He gave to political leaders from around the world while here.

"Unfortunately, his admonitions have not been heeded. And, that is why I am here to tell you – first hand – that because of the power you have amassed you now hold the destiny of Earth in your hands. Jhowah knows of your influence over your fellow men. He has asked me to inform you that he expects you to use all the influence that you have mustered over the centuries to put an end to war, once and for all. He expects you to put an end to violence and terrorism. He expects you to instruct the media and entertainment industries, which you control, to stop glorifying the worst of humanity and report the truth about the things occurring in the world.

"You are to tell the political leaders, over whom you have the power, to rescind laws aimed at diminishing His presence in your society, and replace them with laws that will bring his ways back into the schools of education, the board rooms on Wall Street and Main Street, and into the homes of people the world over, regardless of religion, creed, or race. You must confess that there is one God and only one God, and his name is not Sezan."

A muffled chuckle could be heard by those in the back of the room. Metatron pause for a moment but then continued his message from Jhowah without responding to the unwanted reaction.

"You have to put an end to your quest to control the minds of men and allow God, or Allah, as Jhowah is known in the case of Muslims, to regain the intended place of prominence in the lives of all people, as it was with the original man and woman he and his team created in our image.

"You have to stop promoting chaos and lying to people about the things that influence their decision and actions. You must refrain from stealing from them, making them slaves to your ways, and return the wealth you have stolen to its rightful owners, the people who earned it.

"In short, you are advised to denounce Sezan, the fallen angel from our hierarchy, Jhowah's adversary, the deceiver you call Lucifer, and voluntarily relinquish the power he has urged you to assume over your fellow man. If you do these things and cut off all support to regimes who oppose these principles, Jhowah will give the world a bit more time to right the wrongs He sees and you will be a part of this promised society.

"If, however, you do not use all of your accumulated resources to carry out His wish, that good prevails over evil, the time you know of as Armageddon will soon be at hand. And, none of you who have been involved in bringing about that fateful day can expect anything but the kind of misery and death you have imposed on others, the condition of a living hell, and the total absence of Jhowah. Staring you in the eye is the worst kind of retribution, absolute and eternal nonexistence."

With that, Metatron paused and looked into the minds of every person in the room. He gave the illuminated ones a moment to ponder what they had just heard. Then, he asked, "Are there any questions?"

The silence that filled the room was deafening. No one uttered a word, moved a muscle, or dared allow an opposing point of view to enter his or her mind. They knew that the Messenger before them knew their thoughts.

For the first time, the so-called "Illuminated Ones" were truly enlightened with truth. It was different from the revelations of "The Secret Doctrine" Sezan, or Lucifer as they knew him, had led them to believe. Today they had heard from the source of all power and intelligence that their reign over mankind had come to an end. All they could do, now, was to try and save themselves. The ones among men who had come to believe that they alone were anointed to wield power over planet Earth, and all of its inhabitants discovered Who was truly in charge.

Once again, Metatron studied the thoughts and emotions of every person present and peered into their eyes with a resolve that none had witnessed from any earthly man. When he was convinced that each of those who had heard his words clearly understood his message, he raised arms and ascended, disappearing from their sight into a higher dimension, where he went to meet with Jhowah. Now, his task was to inform his lord, the Ruler of the Universe, of what had transpired in an out-of-the-way chateau in rural Switzerland.

CHAPTER THREE

ISRAEL HOLDS ALL THE CARDS

April 2013
INN Special Alert

"Have the INN broadcast sent to us, Samael. Let's see what Jhowah and Metatron have been up to since our last broadcast."

"I suspect they are becoming quite active since the first contact occurred," Samael suggested as he contacted the communications officer. "Here it comes across the video link."

The video screen lit up and the audio started.

"It was reported today from a private and unnamed group of globally influential people that a part of history, as we know it, has been revealed to be untrue.

"In the 1980s nuclear weapons creators were challenged to develop a new defense system using, among other methods, a new x-ray-laser technology. It would become known as the Strategic Defense Initiative, or SDI, designed to use ground- and space-based systems to protect the United States from attack by land- and air-based nuclear attacks and essentially make nuclear missile attacks obsolete. At one point we were shown Department of Defense videos of such a counter attack by the newly developed x-ray laser beam on a friendly launched missile over the Pacific Ocean which was highly successful. The missile's demise was visible on the video.

"Later it was said that the video was created by special effects experts and was more propaganda than reality, thus leading the U.S. Congress to be quite chagrined by the deception. The action, however, is said to have been a significant factor in leading to the end of the Cold War, thus enhancing the call to protect peace by using a strong defense.

"Today the unnamed group has announced that the SDI defensive weapons were real and effective, and that American and British leaders of the eighties held such concern for the future of world safety and peace that they sent a large cache of SDI defensive weapons and technology, as well as nuclear weapons, to Israel and to other strategic locations around the world. It is said to have been done for the protection of Israel and possibly the world. The leaders were satisfied that Israel was a safe place for their storage. The U.S. Congress stopped the development of the new technology more out of embarrassment than out of denial of the need for such a weapon.

"As expected, the Islamic nations and their allies are enraged with the deception by the United States. The American administration's press secretary has promised a press conference within the next hour to apologize for this error of the country's past. Sources say that the administration considers the action an arrogant and clandestine action that threatens the stability of world peace.

"Since this administration has taken office they have been able to remove all nuclear weapons and greatly reduced supplies of other weaponry from the United States' arsenals. They have dramatically shrunk the already small total of military personnel by fifty percent. Their leadership has tried to show people everywhere that they are out to bring about a change over the entire globe.

"A spokesperson for the top secret group coalition has said that these weapons came under their realm of influence through an interstellar covenant known as *Operation Shield.* This previously unknown coalition, owing its newly realized status to the administration's modification of American defensive and offensive capabilities, appears to be the strongest militarily capable group that now exists on this planet. Yet, the identities of its members remain a mystery. Furthermore, the president has said that he has no control over the group's actions, nor, at this time, does he know who has."

Aboard Sezan's Starship

"What is going on, Samael?" Sezan asked his close associate as the correspondent continued with the news. He was seated at his desk in the ship's conference room with Samael seated nearby. The commandeered starship was temporarily parked in a geostationary orbit above the planet in order to monitor the news media.

"I thought we had our eyes and ears on this planet and had some semblance of control," Sezan said. "According to this report all of our Solean allies are poorly armed when their armamentarium is compared to that of this covert group that calls itself *Operation Shield*. At least we still have the cooperation of those nations that the human leader of Iran helped us obtain before his death allowing us to still maintain a control of the major sources of oil. They absolutely can't do without it to keep their military and motorized vehicles and weapons ready for action."

"I hope that is the case, my Lord," Samael interjected. "There is a rumor that Jhowah may be planning to share our long held knowledge of primordial energy, a source that the Soleans have theorized but have not been able to develop. They do realize its universal presence and that it can be obtained anywhere for very little expenditure of financial and natural resources. A now-deceased scientist planted the seed of its existence but, thus far, it is only an idea, and they have developed no method to identify, collect, or convert it so that it can be put to use."

"But they don't have the technology for creating the collectors or the energy converters," Sezan barked at Samael.

"If Jhowah actually decides to intercede in their technological evolution, he can do what he wants," Samael reminded him. "It is his experiment. He'll set them up with the collectors and converters and the technology to put them to use."

"True, but you don't have to remind me. I hope we can change that premise."

"If he does it will remove our greatest advantage," Samael suggested.

"Yes, maybe we should somehow get into this organization and find an informant so we know, definitely, if he makes such a move."

"I have some sources," Samael said. "I'll see what we can find out but I believe the newest leader from the land known as Iran will have the best intelligence that we could obtain."

"I hope so. We may lose our greatest hold on this planet without having current knowledge of Jhowah's activities. The United States has said that it wishes to go to alternate sources for energy, but much of their economy is just too dependent on fossil fuels to change any time soon. They have dabbled in developing collectors to absorb and utilize the energy of their parent star. They have tried to capture the energy within the wind and waterways, and they have tried to create an efficient source for electric energy, but because the Illuminati group and its allies have such a grip on the world's economic machine, they are unable to break the ways of their past.

"They continue to fall back on oil. To protect their investment in the OPEC cartel, they have politicized using nuclear energy and water power to create electric energy. Backed by the oil-producing nations, their environmentalists have a strong hold on them and that's fine with me. It helps us to gain the upper hand and hopefully we will one day take control of this experiment. We absolutely cannot allow the inhabitants of Soleus-3 to harness primordial energy. We have to stop Jhowah from giving it to them."

"What good will it come to?" Samael asked. "You are a fugitive from justice back in the alliance. Jhowah and his followers wouldn't just allow you to take over like any other being."

"You never can tell, Samael. Many millennia have passed since I escaped from them. There could be changes among the Alliance politicians that might allow me back; especially if things go bad for Jhowah as its leader, or if he is out of the picture."

Sezan cackled as he turned to Samael. "If you know what I mean by that."

Samael smiled back at him. Sezan had long said that if it were necessary, and if he could, he would do away with Jhowah. He thought he had killed him when he attacked one of the colonies where he had intelligence that Jhowah was residing during the infancy of the project soon after his DNA alterations had been discovered.

"I think you need to get a shuttle and move down to the planet, Samael, so you can see what you can find out about any unreported happenings. We have to be alert to Jhowah's efforts to keep his creations under his wings. I sure hope this energy sharing doesn't take place."

"I'll contact you when I gather the needed information," Samael said as he moved through the door toward the shuttle bay.

The Next Day
North Bimini Near The Meeting Facility

Prophet cautiously entered the SSV Command shuttle behind Metatron, as they readied themselves for the short trip to the mothership in its parked orbit behind Luna, or the moon.

"Do you have any idea what Jhowah wants with me, Metatron?" Prophet asked as Metatron handled the controls taking the shuttle up and headed for the SSV Command

"I believe he wishes to discuss this energy situation that is wreaking havoc on the planet. The economic and political consequences are devastating, creating the kinds of chaos that leads to wars around the world until you ultimately destroy yourselves. You and your kind have evolved to the point that you now hold your destiny in your own hands. That is why Jhowah and I decided to reveal ourselves to your leaders and give you one final chance. But your people will never be able to come through your probationary period under the financial and social pressures that the current conditions of Soleus-3 place upon you."

"I certainly agree," Prophet noted as he looked around at the inside of the shuttle. It was his first shuttle or starship experience. "A major portion of our monies go to buy fuel for transporting supplies, running the cooling and heating systems in our homes and getting food. We actually are unable to do little else. Our enemies now control much of the world's flow of capital. We seem to be slaves to the oil producers. The agenda of the leaders of my own country is aiding and abetting these fuel extortionists. I cannot understand why they would sell our country out to those who have sworn to destroy it and Israel, unless there is another agenda being propagated by people in high places."

"Now, you are beginning to see the light. It is because of an overabundance of greed that Soleus-3 has reached this critical point in its evolution," Metatron suggested. "We had hoped that your kind would see the wisdom in following the laws that Jhowah gave you to live by, but the passion for power and wealth has blinded many of your leaders. The oil-producing countries have long passed large sums of money in secret bank accounts to U.S. leaders and media moguls. It is part of a master plan for radical Islamic nations to take over the world and destroy Judaism and Christianity, an economic Jihad that augments their terror-based military one.

"When they accumulate much of the world's wealth, they will have to put their money in banks for safekeeping. And who stands to gain most by their success? The answer is so obvious that we have been amazed that Soleans haven't figured it out. The people who control the flow of money throughout the world win, no matter whose money they are playing with. It doesn't seem to matter whose name is on the bank account. As long as the so-called 'enlightened ones' can control the availability and value of money, they may as well own it.

"This Illuminati group feeds on conflict. And the one that exists between the radical Islamists and the Zionists started many millennia ago after Isaac, the ancestor of the Israelites of today, was born. Abraham caused to be exiled from his house Hagar, his concubine, and Ishmael, her son by Abraham. That was the beginning of a conflict between the descendants of Isaac, Abraham's son by Sarah, and those of Ishmael, his son by Hagar. It is a conflict that has lasted for almost four thousand years, and, the Crusades didn't help matters. The slaughter of both Muslims and Christians in the name of religion was a hard thing for us to witness.

"We also were saddened by a similar crusade that occurred in South and Central America and in Mexico. Under duress, thousands of native Americans were forced to abandon the ways and beliefs of their forefathers and convert to the religion of the conquistadores. A similar event occurred in the homeland of these same conquerors during the Spanish Inquisition, when Jewish citizens were forced to denounce their religion and convert to Catholicism. Jhowah has always been more interested in the fact that you recognize him and follow his ways than how -- and where -- His creations do it.

"Have you ever heard of a fellow by the name of Sezan, or Satan as many on your planet call him?"

"Yes, of course," Prophet answered. "What has he got to do with it?"

"Based on some of our information we think he has been involved in a modern-day version of the events I just mentioned, the evolving Islamic Jihad designed to annihilate the Jews and Christians from the planet. He is using this current manipulation of oil prices as a means of economic warfare and to create chaos among nations to start a military initiative that would destroy Israel and weaken its Christian allies in the eyes of the remainder of the world. The price rise began within the oil-producing nations. Iran, in particular, was the first place to start the hike. This was just before the planned Israeli incursion which resulted in the death of the Iranian president who was very probably the one in this generation of human beings who had first contact with Sezan. He then contacted the remainder of the OPEC group."

"But why would they raise their prices to such levels?" Prophet asked with a perplexed look on his face. "The current prices, even if you can get the other oil-producing nations to go along with you, will devastate the economies of your customer nations. If the price doesn't drive the customer away he becomes economically a third-rate nation and unable to purchase your product. Then there is no more wealth to be transferred, only debt."

As they talked the auto pilot banked the shuttle starboard toward the Command.

"You mean like the U.S, your own country? Because the current administration and Congress have orchestrated and guided the government takeover of the U.S. financial, automotive, healthcare, and insurance industries, a once-great capitalistic country has gone down the path of nations strapped by socialism. By doing so, the United States has fallen to the level of a second-rate nation and headed rapidly to the next lower level.

Its enemies are forcing it to borrow its way into a debt that can never be repaid, at least not with money. They want more than wealth. They want to rule the world, and if the U.S. and Israel are out of the way, they will have smooth sailing. And I am confounded by the fact that your liberal leaders are willing to go along with this. Do they have no loyalty to the country that gave them the freedom to choose their own style of government? I am reminded of the moral within the fairy tale: 'When one kills the goose that lays the golden eggs, there will be no more eggs.'

"They continue to borrow money to purchase energy from people who don't like them. They still won't go after your own natural resources and release the U.S. from its dependence on foreign oil while it at least has the ability to drill and refine its own natural resources. There have been multiple sites where oil and natural gas have been discovered...some places haven't even been told to your citizens."

"What places?" Prophet quizzed him.

"The ocean floors surrounding the United States contain a wealth of natural gas and oil. Then, there is a location in Alaska which is an island just north of the Prudhoe Bay oil facilities there that has been shown to contain as much oil as the United States would ever need to get you through until the change into other alternative fuels can occur. It is known as Gull Island. This information can easily be found on the Internet with a simple search but you won't hear your leaders telling you about it."

"But if all of this is true," Prophet questioned, "why would the OPEC people start such a ballooning of their oil prices and an economic rape of their customers? It seems that this would put them out of business if the other countries didn't join them."

"Sezan is a very evil individual," Metatron advised him, "and he has many convincing ways to gain the cooperation of this group. More than any other living creature, he understands how to use greed and deception to get his way. He has convinced radical Islamic leaders that they are the chosen group to control the world, and that whatever means are required to achieve this end is Jhowah's desire, though they prefer to call him Allah. They think Sezan is an agent of Jhowah or Allah."

Metatron completed his explanation and Prophet watched as he guided the shuttle into the shuttlebay of the SSV Command and toward the front of the bay where he could see Jhowah standing and draped in his formal toga-like dress.

"My Lord, I have brought you Prophet who is our liaison between us and Majic-12 and also the newly revealed group known as *Operation Shield,* the coalition that we established on Soleus-3 in the 1980s. Both of these groups are friendly to us and, in many ways, devoted to our cause. Majic-12, of course, is usually represented by Doctor McConnell and Mister Bradley, but Prophet is in constant contact with them and will keep them apprised of this meeting."

Jhowah turned toward Prophet. It was the first time Prophet had seen the extraterrestrial face-to-face rather than from a position in the audience at the Bimini meeting place. Those large glistening eyes were quite disarming. It was obvious that he was seeing into Prophet's very soul and reading his thoughts. Just then Jhowah placed His hand with such long spindly fingers onto his shoulder.

"Prophet? No last name?" Jhowah asked.

"No, my Lord, it is a code name which is part of my identification within the *Operation Shield* group."

"I understand. Let us move up to the command conference room and talk. I have an interesting proposition to put before you."

In The SSV-Command Conference Room

Jhowah extended his arm in an inviting gesture toward the entry door. "Metatron, Prophet, please take a seat, both of you, and we can get started."

Prophet was still in awe of the trip he had just made, seeing the backside of the lunar surface from the shuttle at such a close proximity and now sitting down at a table with Jhowah, the Supreme Being of the known universe in outer space. Now he realized how vast and wonderful the universe might be and that there could well be many other civilizations, not only in this galaxy but in the myriad of galaxies beyond ours.

"I'm honored and privileged, my Lord, to be before you as I am, an honor that I suspect few, if any, of my fellow humans have experienced, at least not for thousands of years."

"I understand, Prophet," He replied. "The reason I have had Metatron to bring you here is to discuss your group and the current crisis on Earth. I know that there seems to be, as I would expect, a group of our creations who are slowly aligning themselves with my professed enemy and an enemy of this planet, Sezan Lucefed, even though they aren't aware of it. They, by their actions, are choosing to disobey my laws, resist my commands, and ignore the very spirit of my "first contact" speech.

"Metatron tells me that there is an energy crisis that has developed, one that is more profound than any of your previous ones. He says that the demands being placed on your primary energy source, the fossil energy you call oil, by the nations of the Earth who control it have risen to a level that is creating unrivaled political chaos and destroying the way of life that we had hoped you would choose for yourselves. This is calling into question the survival of the entire world. I cannot stand by and allow this to happen to so many people whom I love and consider my children."

"My Lord," Prophet interrupted, "I can see no rhyme or reason for this occurrence."

"Oh yes, Prophet, there is good reason for this happening and it is not just a recent event orchestrated by Sezan. It has been a long time in the making. I've looked into this recently after Metatron advised me of the severity of the developing crisis. There is, and has been for a long time, a very deceptive sequence of events that has taken place, especially within the United States, a nation that I have followed so very close since its formation.

"Metatron may have already told you that individuals from the current oil-producing nations and especially their allies have penetrated the inner circles of the government of the

United States and the national information sources of that country. Over several generations this shadow government has hindered not only the truthful flow of information to the peoples of the world but the fair and equitable distribution of energy sources under the lands and seas they control. These same power-thirsty individuals have achieved the support of much of the populace by using the tools of environmental, ecological, and climatic protection to instill fear within that country.

"More recent fear tactics associated with biological pandemics have allowed them to create additional uncertainty and unrest. Biological terrorism is just another example of creating chaos in order to provide a solution that allows them to gain more control over the people.

"By using these tools they have created unlimited amounts of power and wealth for political purposes. In the process they have created a powerful group of those who produce this most precious energy source. This fossil fuel that is created below the surface of your planet by the evolutionary and cataclysmic changes that take place there is a weapon of Sezan. He knows that humankind has become dependent on it. He has seen its potential and is taking full advantage of the situation.

"I was pleased to hear of the formation of *Operation Shield* and that you have contacted and are working with the Majic-12 group to try and bring stability to a growing, and potentially apocalyptic, military crisis. It is for that reason that I have called on you.

"In 1980s I communicated with the leadership of the United States. It was then that we designed the plan whereby they and the British, in cooperation with certain military leaders, scholars of human behavior, and some within the American Central Intelligence Agency, designed and completed a plan to secretly set aside a considerable cache of nuclear weapons and secretly move many of them into Israel. The remainder of the weapons was relocated in strategic places around Soleus-3, known to only participants in The Covenant. Using technology that we shared with them, the American and British leaders were also able to send a cache of x-ray laser beam weapons that have been incorporated into many of your communication satellites."

"Yes, my Lord, I am familiar with these efforts," Prophet assured him. "We were briefed by the Israeli prime minister."

"Prophet, we plan to give you a gift of great value in the form of knowledge, and at the same time we would like to have you agree to certain principles. As we have sat here and discussed the energy crisis that exists on Earth, we both realize that there is no way to change the agenda of these humans who have been working to create this situation. It is an attempt at a power grab that to this point has been quite successful. So what is the best way to handle it?" Jhowah asked, posing a question to himself as well as to Prophet and Metatron. "I believe that to really put an end to this we need to remove the need for fossil fuels on Soleus-3. In this time in the planet's evolution, it seems to be the cause of much evil."

"But my Lord," Prophet pleaded. "Our whole economy is based on this carbon fuel energy source. Remove it, and the world will literally stand still. Gasoline, diesel, kerosene and propane, even asphalt, all of these are products that are derived from oil or in the obtaining of oil. There are many other byproducts that come from it. Our government claims to be working on alternative methods of energy but the conversion will take a few decades. That is what makes it impossible for many of us to understand why we aren't allowed by our government to drill for this known vast amount of oil in our own country to help us get through until the transition occurs. While the U.S. has massive reserves buried in caves and caverns underground in the western part of the country, for yet unexplained reasons we allow our nation to slide backwards in the global arena. The 'rainy day' for which these reserves were intended has long come and gone."

"That will no longer be a problem, Prophet. There is a form of energy that all interstellar space traveling beings discovered many thousands of years ago. We call it Primordial Energy. It is a very basic energy that exists everywhere, even in the vacuum of space. It is all around us and all we have to do is to collect it and convert it into a useable form.

"Metatron tells me that you and some of your friends may be familiar with a book written by a woman who claimed not to believe in me. Even so she described herself as an atheist, and she wrote about lifting the human spirit and mankind's gift of free will, conditions that we built into our creation experiment. In one of her publications -- the one she released in the 1950s -- she wrote of a form of energy that was very similar to primordial energy. Not knowing the things you know, today, Ms. Rand called it 'inertial energy'. There is a reason why your politicians decided to ignore these early hints to divert the world's attention *away* from non-replenishable forms of energy. For more than fifty years large sums of the commodity you call 'money' has been used to suppress less costly and more efficient forms of energy. The people who were behind censoring this technology are from the same families responsible for the chaos that exists on your planet today."

Prophet could understand the concept that the term primordial seemed to connote but not enough of the specifics for it to be clear. "What actually is this form of energy, my Lord?"

"As you might know, Prophet, interstellar space is not a total vacuum. It contains gases, dust and even energy in the form of electromagnetic waves. Your scientists have already learned this. The gas is ninety-nine percent ionized hydrogen and the EM waves are in a wide distribution of bands. There are several wave lengths of EM waves that can be readily concentrated and utilized to interact with the hydrogen ions creating a cold fusion that can be used to energize interstellar engines to travel at faster than light speeds. Hydrogen is also readily available on Earth, in the air and water, and, by using EM converter chips, you will be able to power individual vehicles or develop energy centers that create and can wirelessly transmit energy to properly authorized receivers."

Prophet definitely appeared to be impressed but still had questions. "This will require us to develop expensive engines and batteries that can use this form of energy," he insisted.

"No," Jhowah replied, looking at Metatron with a slight twist to his small mouth which he was able to interpret from past knowledge as a knowing smile, "it is combustible, but the combustion is internal. There are no toxic emissions. It will serve you even more efficiently than fossil fuels. And, converting your present-day energy sources to primordial energy will require only a small modification. There will be only minimal modifications to current battery construction. Electricity is electricity. You've already developed and refined a way for engines to generate electricity. You only need to convert to primordial methods as the primary energy source for your engines and, as a secondary benefit there will be no emissions injurious to humanity or the planet in any other way. Large amounts of energy can be stored in tiny power cells that can hold much more than one of your analog batteries, and it can be configured to fit into almost anything that currently uses electricity in any voltage or amperage.

"As we have said, in addition, this energy source will be convertible to a form that can be used to produce cold fusion in faster-than-light-speed vehicles when you reach that level of technology. It is different from fission, the process that creates the next best source of nuclear energy.

"All of the necessary fuels are available in the interstellar and even intergalactic regions. All you have to do is have the appropriate collectors and converters, and we will help you make this conversion to primordial energy."

Prophet realized the tremendous importance of such a gift. As Jhowah said, it would make fossil fuels unnecessary and remove the need that had created such a devastating blow to the economies of the world and to the environment. Now he needed to see what was required in return for such fantastic knowledge.

"So, Jhowah, what will you require of us so that we might receive this knowledge?"

Jhowah smiled again. "You do realize, Prophet, that you and all of humankind are my creations, or the creations of my project members. As I have explained on Bimini, you have been a part of an experiment that has lasted many millennia. Prophet, you and all humanity are my children and as my children I don't require anything but your love, appreciation and obedience in return. Also, as my children, I like to give you advice. Like any father, I want to see you prosper and to be happy.

"It pains me when I see you fighting among yourselves and causing harm to your brothers and sisters. Every time you have asked for my help, and believed it would come, I have given you what you have asked. Sometimes it hasn't come so quickly or in the form you have requested, but I and my team of Creators have never abandoned you.

"Because I realized that unrest was growing on your planet, I decided to challenge you face to face and give you one last chance to follow the teachings that my messengers have brought to you throughout the millennia. I knew that my visit would send shock waves throughout the so-called Illuminated Ones, their shadow government, and the New World Order that they have attempted to create. Although they have come quite close to achieving their goal, even as we speak they are frantically meeting, trying to decide how to counter act this new energy form which they have already learned I am giving to you. And, I suspect that Sezan is using all the contacts and influence he has within this group to try and sway them to his ways of thinking.

"Our current challenge is to convince the self-anointed power brokers of Soleus-3 that they now have a rather simple choice, to bring order out of chaos, or to sit by and watch me destroy their organizations, their wealth, their power and the world they have created. They must, now and forever, choose between Sezan and me, a clear choice. For the sake of one of the most beautiful planets and most promising creatures that occupy it, let's hope that the groups who claim to be 'illuminated' can see the light.

"I have destroyed much of civilization before, when the Great Flood covered a large part of the planet. I have destroyed evil cities with fire, like Sodom and Gomorrah. I have sided with those promoting good when they stand up to evil. But never before has such organized corruption, greed, and subversion exercised its grip on civilizations across the face of the planet. The human species has evolved to the point of being able to destroy not only those whom they identify as their enemies, but themselves in the process. This is a concern that SORGE had when we decided to launch this project. We have seen similar conflicts within the Reticulum Alliance.

"You, Metatron, and I, simply have to identify those who have been loyal to our laws and cause. We must arm them with the thoughts and words to persuade their fellowman to turn to us for direction. Prophet, this is why I have chosen Metatron, a beloved son, as my emissary. Metatron has been a man. He has experienced how it is to feel detached, and connected, to me and our ways. We have shown him good and evil and instructed him to share what he had seen on Hivania with his fellow humans."

Jhowah turned to Metatron and spoke directly to him so that Prophet could hear his words. "You saw then, how they disbelieved what you had experienced in other worlds and turned away. Several thousand Soleus-3 years later, I sent you back as the babe, Joshua, to once again, demonstrate that it is possible for a human being to be like us, like me. Now, as I promised to John of Patmos, I have asked you to try one final time to bring our great experiment to a successful conclusion even if it takes a thousand years.

"As you did in previous missions to Soleus-3, you are meeting resistance from the power brokers, who view you as a threat to the world that they have tried to create. What they haven't yet realized is that Soleus-3 belongs to me, to all of us who planned and created it and every living thing that inhabits it, even today. As our messenger was shown, and wrote in the book that has come to become known as The Revelation, there will be a final battle between Sezan and the Alliance. My patience is wearing thin and I am ready to settle this thing once and for eternity. Are you up to the task? Prophet, are you with us or against us?" He said, focusing on the agent of *Shield.*

"My Lord," Prophet responded with an agreeable smile on his face, "as an obedient child I would like to hear your advice. What would you have me do?"

"We feel that the power over people," Jhowah responded, "the kind that has been gathered by the Illuminati and its allies, both Islamic radicals and non-Islamic, will be very difficult for them to lose. I foresee a very militant counter attack once you have learned this new technology, this new energy source. The stakes will grow even higher when you put it to use. We must do everything we can to interfere with our adversary's ability to effectively make war. We have to strip them of their power.

"You *will* have a more efficient energy system. Since the current American leadership and their political allies have destroyed the defensive and offensive capability of the greatest peace-keeping nation on this planet, that leaves only a few defensive nuclear weapons among the allies of the forces of those following Sezan. If you follow my plan, none of the missiles, those belonging to the troublemakers or those belonging to *Operation Shield,* will be needed.

"These Sezan-allied nations, even though they signed the Guantanamo Treaty, have also put aside a few nuclear weapons. Deception just seems to be a part of their very nature. The American and British leaders of the 1980s knew this to be true and took the appropriate measures to neutralize their efforts.

"It was a real challenge to keep the project from the Bilderberg Group and its emissaries, the Trilateral Commission. Both are controlled by the thirteen most powerful families on the planet. They have a firm grip on the flow of information, resources, and capital throughout your world. When we shared our ways with the Bavarian priest, Father Weishauph, two hundred years ago, he and the other founders of the group were committed to assisting us in promoting good over evil and in creating another Hivania on this planet. But, as he did in the early days of the Solean experiment, Sezan got to some of their leaders and began to insert his own influence over them and their offspring.

"Rather than directing our project *toward* the outcome that I anticipated, Sezan has convinced the illuminated group that we created Soleus-3 for their benefit. In turn, they have attempted to create their own self-minded hierarchy, eliminating anyone who refused to cooperate with them, including heads of state. In their own minds they are gods; at least they enjoy playing God. They start wars for their own purpose. They create financial crises for their own benefits. They create epidemics for their own benefits. They are even engaged in population control, so that it will be easier for them to hold power over people and the leaders they elevate to office.

"Now, we have to strip this oligarchy of its power. It was never intended for them to enslave their fellow human beings and make them subjects to their own self-serving ways. Their founding members were given the keys to many secrets. They were shown scientific ways to enhance life on Soleus-3 as a way to carry out our wishes, here – to help us create a peaceful existence among all nations and see your kind evolve into a species and civilization much like our own.

"What the Illuminati have done is to want more, to be Gods. Sezan has convinced them that he is more like me than any other and that he can give them the powers they seek. He has shown them some of his own tactics: create a problem, initiate a reaction, and provide a solution that complies with their own agenda.

"Sezan, too, wanted to be a god. Though he was once my trusted ally, his own lust for power caused him to turn against me and our project. Since the oligarchic shadow government of Soleus-3 has adopted Sezan's ways, we must now take drastic measures and prevent them from indoctrinating all human beings who are not of their bloodlines and coercing them into destroying each other and all of Soleus-3's living creatures with them.

"What we propose, or what we advise," Jhowah said, "is that we make all energy, weaponry and communications under the control of *Operation Shield* to be functional only with a highly secretive and encrypted code. The mere fact that they are available to be used for our purposes will be enough of a deterrent for many nations. It's the others who will present a greater challenge. We will develop codes that, even with Sezan's help, they will be unable to break. They will lose much of their satellite communications, which will block their abilities to access their wealth and to use the secret communication systems and networks that they have developed. We will also attempt to interfere with land-based communications as well.

"This is part of a new covenant that I made with the Soleans in the 1980s who understood my involvement in the Solean Experiment. Now, only you and your team, the group that is involved with *Operation Shield,* will be able to access the x-ray laser beam weapons since you will be the only ones with the codes. While Metatron will be conducting the Soleus-3 operations, I will remain in close contact with him."

CHAPTER FOUR

PRIMORDIAL ENERGY: THE GAME CHANGES

U.S. Naval Observatory
Washington, D.C.

Prophet sat with Doug and Hank around Hank McConnell's desk.

"So, Prophet," Hank injected, "you feel Jhowah is concerned enough to come to our aid in the operation?"

"Yes," he replied, "He is quite concerned with the current state of our world and the power seized by the Illuminati group. There have been many conspiracy theories about them here on Earth and he has been able to ascertain that they are more of a threat than any of us thought."

"In what way?" Doug asked.

"They are among the big players in our current economic crisis," Prophet answered. "Jhowah feels that some of their leaders are directly allied with Sezan along with the OPEC nations. Of course the Venezuelan and the Cuban leaders have quite similar political leanings and have also joined in with them."

"What does the Cuban leader have to do with this?" Doug asked. "They aren't considered part of OPEC, are they?"

"Not technically." Prophet answered. "However, it has been said that in the agreement cut with the Russians during the Cuban missile crisis, the U.S. agreed not to drill off the shores of southern Florida or in the Caribbean, signing over all U.S. claims to oil in the region to Cuba in return for Russia removing most of their missiles from the Cuban mainland. The Castros and their regime have controlled huge oil and gas reserves, reserves that the U.S. could have used to offset its foreign dependence on fossil fuels. And they are quite cozy with the Venezuelan leader."

"What does Jhowah feel we should do?" Hank quizzed.

"We are about to embark," Prophet explained, "through *Operation Shield*, on a new version of the new world order, not the one that the New World Order, as we have known it, had planned for us, but one that Jhowah planned."

"What do you mean?" Hank asked.

"I mean we are about to be given the most wonderful and empowering gift from Jhowah. He is in the process of setting up a training program using His experts in the Reticulum Alliance group to train personnel in *Operation Shield* on the basics and theory of the use of primordial energy, a form of energy that seems so simple that we can convert to it with minimal difficulty. It will take a little time but we only have to make what Jhowah and Metatron say are minimal modifications to our existing electrical and internal combustion powered systems.

We'll need collectors and converters and when we are through we will be able to use the most plentiful and inexpensive energy in the universe, and it is everywhere. We can also create energy storage cells for use in mobile engines or for any form of mobile power users, even battery-driven devices. We'll even be able to use it in the future to move among the stars like Jhowah and his arch enemy, Sezan."

"I wonder what the oil producers will have to say about this." Doug added.

"They'll fight like Hell to stop it," Hank responded. "This technology will be a threat to the world order that they have created. They'll lose their power, and all that goes with it. The Illuminati, who have wallowed in their wealth for nearly two and a half centuries, will use every remedy at their disposal to stop it. Our leaders and their environmental advisers should be happy with such greening of the entire world taking place with this energy transfer. It sounds like it is environmentally friendly. They will, of course, surely find a way to tax it."

"No, they won't be happy about this," said Prophet.

Hank turned toward him. "You think different?"

"Much of the Muslim extremist world is in bed with the Illuminati," Prophet answered. "In fact, they helped those countries get started. Don't you recall that U.S. oil companies did the initial drilling in the Arab countries, built the refineries, and then turned them over to those countries? That was, unknown to most, an Illuminati sponsored plan. Both they and the radical Muslims, through banking and oil-delivery cartels, have enjoyed the profits of oil, and even more so since the price has risen to such heights. These groups are known by the U.S. administrations both personally and politically.

"Although it is not the kind of energy that they and their supporters had in mind, this new alternative energy source will also place the nation of Israel in a commanding position. Since many of the controlling individuals in our operation are Jewish they will actually be a large part of the management of the new energy power base. Israel will certainly become a prime target for leaders like the Venezuelan and OPEC groups but, since Israel and its allies will hold the reigns of the 1980s nuclear transfer and the SDI group of satellites, they should do well."

"So where do we go from here, Prophet?" Doug asked. "What's next?"

"To make a statement to the world, Jhowah will bring his starship, SSV Command, to the Middle East and park it in a geostationary orbit over Tel Aviv within the week and begin the training sessions. Those involved will be shuttled up to the ship, which has all the conference areas and meeting and training rooms that will be needed. It will be a college in the sky," Prophet said.

"In this galactic university, Jhowah will also have the machinery and monitors needed to give hands-on labs for the lectures that they will be giving. After the education of the first wave of future technicians is completed, construction of energy centers and modifications of analog power plants and engines will begin first in Israel.

"He estimates only a couple of weeks before power plant conversion will give at least one plant capable of producing electricity from the primordial source. Then, the Israeli instructors can begin training its allies on how to convert to this new alternative energy. Additional equipment is now on its way to us from manufacturers on the Reticulum planets."

"This all sounds wonderful," Hank said. "Maybe I'll soon be able to take my wife out to eat without worrying whether or not I'll be able to fuel my car to get to work the next day."

"Ahh," Prophet added smiling, "You'll be able to afford to take her to the finest restaurant in the area, and exquisite meals at less expensive prices."

Tel Aviv
A Week Later

The huge triangular SSV Command starship hung motionless above the ancient people's capital. It was a cloudless day with the sun high overhead. The vessel cast a visible shadow over the buildings. A shuttle from the Command moved upward from the city and entered the back of the mothership. The prime minister remained seated as the shuttle settled on the floor of SSV - Command's shuttlebay.

"You've been on board before, haven't you, Prophet?" he asked before they moved out of the shuttle.

"Yes, a couple of times with Metatron and I'm more and more fascinated each time I come up here. The first time I was here Command was in orbit behind the moon, what a ride and what a view."

"And what have they been doing up here for the past few days?" The leader asked.

Prophet stood up from his seat and followed him as he exited through the side door.

"Well, so far they have set up the lecture and lab areas, as well as teams and teaching plans. I believe this evening will begin the first classes in the concept and basic theory of the primordial energy and its uses. I think I see Jhowah and Metatron entering the bay up ahead."

"Mister Prime Minister, Prophet, welcome aboard," Jhowah hailed. "You have seen our ship in the past on your news programs, or at least our safety lights that show up from the corners of it. It was the only way that we could aid in the desensitization program. Now you can see what you have come to know as a UFO looks like up close and personal.

"I'll be able to show you the command position from which I directed your creation and that of your world. There were many others involved but they are back home at SORGE considering plans for new projects on other worlds where we are considering taking the lessons learned here and applying them to new civilizations if our problems here can be solved. Things should go better then because we don't have to deal with the Sezan effect on the sexuality of the creations."

"My Lord," the prime minister responded, "I was at your first contact address on Bimini and I understand the background related to Sezan. My people have long dealt with him and his followers. We have stood between his teaching and Your Word, passing along your commands to our ancient ancestors.

"I regret the actions that I had to take to protect my country from the hateful efforts of the late president of Iran. I felt there was no other choice except to take the defensive action that I did."

"Mister Prime Minister, have no regrets. You did what you had to do to protect the people and nation to whom I first passed my written laws and into whose society I chose to have Jesus, my only son, born into humanity.

"Iran's president ignored my dictum as if I had never spoken. He will spend eternity on Sheolos and under the supervision of a ruthless Sezan, and he will quickly learn that there are no virgins waiting there for him."

"Speaking of Sezan," Jhowah continued, "I have some Intel that he might be in the area. I usually have an armed starship nearby but they have gone for routine maintenance at the space station near Alpha-Mensae-5 which leaves us a bit exposed here. I've sent word to Admiral Pazon, the commander of the Reticulum defense fleet, to send us some help but it will take a while for him to arrive. He was in the area of Tau Ceti. He may not be here in time to be of much help.

"Well, Prophet, you have worked hard since we arrived and your efforts have been appreciated."

"No more so than the appreciation that we hold for you for giving us this wonderful gift of primordial energy, my Lord."

"I had no choice, gentlemen. I came to you at our first contact and ordered you to follow my laws and gave you an ultimatum. As soon as I left for Hivania, the Iranians and Sezan, I'm sure, went into an offensive role in an attempt to destroy Israel and her allies. And if they could neutralize the political and fiscal conservatives of the United States, they would then be in a position to control the economies of a world of their own making."

Jhowah finished his explanation and beckoned to the two. "Let me give you a tour of our ship," he offered and strolled away knowing they would follow.

Moments later the threesome stood at the bridge of the starship as Jhowah was introducing them to the workings of the bridge and its crew. The navigator turned to Jhowah.

"My Lord, our long-range sensors are showing a starship entering the Soleus system. It carries the profile of the vessel in which Sezan travels. It is still in the position of Soleus-8 and does not appear to be in a hurry."

"Contact Admiral Pazon, and find his present location," Jhowah ordered the communications officer.

"Are we in trouble, my Lord?" The prime minister asked.

"We'll soon find out," he answered. "Our guardian star-ship left us a fully armed Viper-STG starfighter with our own advanced version of the SDI system, similar to the type we gave *Operation Big Stick* in the eighties and a trained pilot, but the last time we encountered Sezan he still had several Vipers aboard. He has been leaving a couple of Vipers in the vicinity of Sheolos to protect his growing ground population there but they are no match for Pazon's pilots. Have you been able to find the admiral?" He asked as he turned to the communications officer.

"Yes, my Lord, he is actually well on this side of the Tau Ceti system and he says he is jumping into his highest SAMSL engine speeds. He's not as far away as we originally thought"

"He could use the worm hole near Tau Ceti that leads to an area near the Soleus System," Jhowah said, "but I doubt he'll try it. It is not dependably stable."

"I believe he is well past the wormhole," the navigator informed him. "We lost a shuttle in it not too long ago and, since Admiral Pazon is a cautious man, I doubt that he would use such an unstable route."

"My Lord," the prime minister asked, "I'm not much of an astronomer. Where is Tau Ceti?"

"It is the nearest of the Reticulum star systems to Earth. One of our species is from there. They are known as the Janosians, who are from the planet Janos which orbits Tau Ceti. They say the admiral has already passed there, but I'm not sure how far on this side he is located. We will just have to wait to see how things work out. Keep me informed," he ordered the navigator.

"Mister Prime Minister, Prophet, please come with me to my conference room. It's just through this door and to the left."

Jhowah led them into the room and offered them seats which they took. The walls were covered on three sides by images of early humans and views of the planet Earth before and after the initial atmospheric alterations. There were also images of the earliest primitive humans who were present before Jhowah's genetically cloned humans were placed on Earth. Some of them looked very much like computer images of the Neanderthals that once lived on Earth before SORGE arrived; in fact, that's what they were, it became obvious to the two humans as they studied the details of their features. View windows were on the fourth side through which the city of Tel Aviv could be seen below them.

The prime minister rose and perused the images until he stood before the image of a handsome male and a beautiful female, both scantily and primitively clothed, standing in a forested surrounding. "My Lord, this young couple, is it who I think it is?"

"Yes," Jhowah answered, his face expressing the pride he held for his creations. They are the product of a challenge that I issued to a team of creative experts within the Reticulum Command many thousands of years ago. This Adamite and his mate thrilled our hearts when we realized that she was pregnant with the first Solean child to be born on this planet, even though with Sezan's interference they mated sooner that we had planned. The creation of the first 'natural' offspring of our genetically engineered creations caused us to have to change our plans and have them take on responsibility for themselves and their offspring before we were ready for them to do so. Back then we called them Adamas and Evon. I know you call them by somewhat similar names that have evolved over the years through verbal tradition."

The prime minister smiled as he felt compelled to look at each image while he had the chance. Farther along the museum-like wall, he stopped again as he saw the image of a young woman who was clothed more than adequately and who seemed to be pregnant as suggested by the bulge that showed through her draped clothing. He turned to Jhowah. "And who is this?"

"That is the woman who is known on your world as Mary, the mother of my son, the only one who lived and died as one of you. At the time, his people, your own ancestors Mr. Prime Minister, called him Joshua. In your modern language, you call him Jesus."

"I see," the prime minister explained. "As you know, my Lord, I am of a different religious upbringing, but I do respect the beliefs of others, as many of my Christian friends respect mine. I am very curious and have been so since first hearing of the belief of a virgin birth. How is it possible? I mean, I know all things are possible for you, but surely there is a logical explanation?"

"You are right, Mister Prime Minister. "While the answers may not be clear to you at this time, I assure that one day quite soon the mysteries of the universe and of my kingdom will be revealed to you. I am aware of the fact that the birth, life, death, and resurrection of my son have been misunderstood by many humans. We are far more technologically advanced than you are on this planet, and have been so since long before that couple you saw back there was created," he said pointing to the previous images. "To us the human birth of Jesus was a very simple procedure; actually, your scientists are now able to create the same scenario if they decide to do it. We knew that in those times there would be no knowledge of our methods and that a virgin birth would certainly be a miracle. The procedure itself is a miracle, just to be able to perform it.

"We used what you refer to as a fiber optic instrument and implanted an embryo cloned from my tissue cells into Mary's womb. It had to be engineered to our genetic profile of

Solean humans, but from this procedure Jesus was born after a normal gestational period and, so you see, he really is my son. Because he is of my own genetic make-up, he and I are as one. Likewise, his life energy, which you call the spirit or soul, is shared. It belongs to both of us. He was sent to you so that you could see me in human form, like yourselves, and to see him live as I would prefer that all men live."

The prime minister smiled as he realized the simplicity of what Jhowah was telling him. "My Lord," he said, "I may have some additional questions about this miracle, and some of those our Hebrew Scriptures describe, especially the one involving Elijah. I will also be interested in learning where your son is today but that discussion can wait for another meeting."

At that moment the navigator leaned inside the door and motioned to Jhowah. "My Lord, the starship I have been monitoring is moving less than at SAMSL-1 speed. I will continue to monitor but, at the sub light speed at which he is traveling, he will probably be here in about an hour and a half."

"Thank you," Jhowah responded. "Keep me apprised of his whereabouts."

The prime minister chuckled. "My Lord," he asked, "May I ask one other question?"

"You *are* full of them," Jhowah said, smiling. "Of course you may."

"What is meant by a speed of SAMSL-1?"

"Our faster-than-light starship engines' speeds are categorized as to how fast they are moving in relation to the speed of light. SAMSL-1 means that it is going at the speed of light. SAMSL refers to Speed at Multiples of the Speed of Light but expressed logarithmically; thus SAMSL-2 is ten times the speed of light, or SAMSL-1. SAMSL-3 is ten times the speed of SAMSL-2, and so on. And this is done using engines that function using primordial energy, the very thing that we are here to discuss. Please, have a seat."

"One more question, my Lord, if you don't mind."

Jhowah laughed a hardy laugh. "Talking with you today, Mister Prime Minister, I wonder if Sezan might not have augmented the gene involved in an individual's curiosity. Please, ask all you want."

"This primordial energy we are about to discuss. You say that it is what you use in interstellar travel. How is it collected in the void of space?"

Jhowah remained standing as he answered him. "It is collected with a scoop like mechanism that is located on the underside of the starship. One of your television programs used to mention such a device on its fictional starships several years back. It was the Star Trek series and they referred to it as a ram scoop. Doesn't that make sense?" He asked.

"Yes it does, my Lord," the prime minister responded. "It makes it totally understandable and makes me wonder if you had ever had conversation with Gene Roddenberry while he was writing."

Jhowah grinned in his Hivanian way and left the two visitors wondering if it had been true.

"I want to give you my schedule for energizing *Operation Shield* and its allies with the new energy sources," Jhowah said as they seated themselves.

"As we said earlier, I feel we can have, at least, one of your analog power plants producing power from primordial sources within two weeks from the initiation of this conversion project. Then we will follow as fast as possible with conversion of the remainder, but in places other than Israel we must know that the leadership of each country is a true ally of *Operation Shield* and will follow my laws and not aid in pirating the energy source to unauthorized countries or individuals. To do so would remove them from the list of authorized users.

"By the way, I plan to make these converted power plants capable of wireless transmission of energy to those who are authorized to receive it. I really feel that we can make the conversion within the next ten to twelve weeks and in doing so we will be training Solean-3 personnel in the theory of the technology and the methods of conversion.

"After power plant modifications are completed, the conversion of individual, business and residential power units will be next in line, and, I believe, we can complete those within another three months. In fact, by putting every worker currently involved in the fossil fuel industry here in Israel on this project we can set up a planet-based manufacturing plant to produce self or home modification kits that could be used by anyone to perform their own conversions. That would speed things up tremendously and keep our allies, the world over, engaged in the project."

"These individual and residential power units," changed, "do they create their own power or do they receive the power wirelessly?"

"Either or both," Jhowah answered. "Each unit can have a self-contained power-producing primordial cell or it can contain only a wireless power-receiving cell, or it can have a primordial-power producing cell with a wireless receiver to be used as you would use a spare tire on your Earth vehicles. In time I will also tell you about the nuclear booster that we insert into very small solar power plants. But that is a subject for another day."

"My Lord, you leave me in awe of this new primordial Energy that you give us," the prime minister said as he shook his head.

"As you use it," Jhowah advised, "you will be in even greater awe. It is a much more efficient and environmentally friendly fuel than what you currently use. I'm not talking from the position that you have heard from extremist environmentalists, but purely based on a technical evaluation of the fuel itself.

"I have monitored your television and radio transmissions and I have heard the claims of global warming. I have also watched as these same hypocritical climate prophets themselves profit from their doom-and-gloom scare tactics. They profit personally and also politically in the taxes that they create to 'correct' the 'rapidly deteriorating' problem, a fantasy problem that they created for their own motives. It is a problem that doesn't exist.

"As many of your scientists have tried to tell your people, this is a fraud that is developing into the greatest scam that I have witnessed since creating this world. You have rightly been informed by unbiased scientists that any climate changes that occur on your planet are due to a wobble or cyclic changes in the axis of Earth and the energy arising from Soleus, your sun. You do not have the technology or ability to change it. In fact, your planet has experienced total polar shifts in the past.

"I should also warn you, if you haven't already realized it, that within six weeks after we complete the conversions you will have a real problem on your hands coming from those who have benefited from the elevated prices of your current energy sources."

"Yes, my Lord," the prime minister agreed, "we have already anticipated the possibility of trouble and we now even plan on it as a probability."

After an hour of explanations, planning, and decision making, Jhowah stood before the other two. "I believe we have the most important plans in place for the conversion," Jhowah said. "I'll need to see you again, probably several times, before the conversion is complete. Prophet, if you'll stay in the Tel Aviv area it will make it easier."

"Yes, my Lord."

"My Lord, we need you on the bridge," the navigator informed him.

Jhowah followed with the prime minister and Prophet following close behind. When he approached the bridge he noted the sensor display was active.

"My Lord," the navigator instructed, "as you can see, the sensor shows the ship that we presume to belong to Sezan, and it is now slowing and near the orbit of Luna. I'd predict that he'll be here within the next twenty to thirty minutes."

Jhowah looked over at the two visitors. "I don't want you to go right now. If he sees you leaving Command he may try to take you out just to prove he can." He turned to the communications officer. "Tell the Viper pilot to ready himself and his vessel to do his duty if Sezan approaches Tel Aviv. I'll let him know when to leave. Make sure he is armed and ready."

Jhowah and his visitors watched anxiously at the developments. As the starship moved in it was heading straight for the Middle East. The navigator began to appear apprehensive and Prophet stood with his good eye open wide. The prime minister, however, stood beside Jhowah like a military general ready to command an attack.

"You seem too comfortable, Mister Prime Minister. Even I am a bit tense over the possibilities that exist here, and I have already dealt with Sezan in the past in a combat situation."

"I have been unfortunate enough to have been in this situation many times, my Lord," he replied. "You see, my neighbors don't like me." He grinned.

Jhowah returned the smile. "Let's hope we can deal with that in the near future," he said.

The navigator who had been leaning over the sensor display in front of him suddenly sat up. "My Lord," he said, "Sezan has put down in the country of Iran near the capital city."

"Tell that Viper pilot to get over there and try to take out his SAMSL engines. He needs to move in stealthily and rapidly."

"Yes, my Lord," he replied.

As soon as the message had been sent, those standing on and near the bridge watched as the sleek Viper-STG starfighter left its berth in the shuttlebay and came into their view. The long, pointed nose piece filled with sensors pierced the sky as it rose upward, rolled and banked into the direction of Tehran. In a sudden burst of speed it disappeared in that direction.

The Viper pilot closely observed his sensor array screen to be able to recognize the energy signature from Sezan's starship. His speed and the stealth design of his starfighter made it highly unlikely that he would be spotted by any Solean radar before reaching Tehran. Sezan's vessel, however, might spot him and so he stayed low, just above the roof tops. He knew the houses below were being shaken violently and losing their windows as the sonic boom that followed him passed over them.

As he approached Tehran he saw Sezan's ship lift up and move rapidly away. He charged his weapons and tried to get as close as he could. He was able to get off one blast from his particle beam weapon, but he didn't have time to get a good aim at the SAMSL engine. He did see an explosion in the rear of the ship in the vicinity of its shuttlebay a fraction of a second before the starship broke into light speed. Time would tell whether or not he had created serious damage to the ship.

He moved the Viper in position to return to the Command but didn't fail to notice that there was no response from the Iranian fighters located at their bases outside of Tehran.

"Viper-STG to SSV-Command. Are you receiving me?"

"Go ahead Viper, we've been monitoring you."

"I was unable to make a hit on the SAMSL engine but I did get off one particle beam that struck somewhere near the shuttlebay. He broke to light speed then and I know no more after that happened."

"Viper, what! Wait! Viper? We see why he left so rapidly and refused to respond to you. Admiral Pazon and a couple of the ships from his defense fleet are coming into view. Sezan must have spotted him on his sensors and didn't wish to join a fight. Return to Command."

"Yes sir, Viper out."

Tehran, Iran
Later In The Day

Samael sat before the council that had been quickly created after the Israeli preemptive strike months earlier. He was
addressing the group led by the newly appointed Iranian president, Jahid.

Samael, the Dromedan and a representative of Sezan, had
been delivered to Tehran by Sezan in his ship earlier in the
day. He had come at the request of the new president through
a communications with Sezan's ship that had been set up with
the late president prior to his death during the Israeli attack.

"Mister Samael," the president said, "it seems you had a
precarious landing and debarkation from your starship. We
were all anxious for you."

"Thank you, mister president," Samael offered, his small
dark Dromedan eyes glistening in the subdued light of the
room. "My commander did a fine job in getting the ship out
of here. We needed to make contact since there seems to be
much activity centered on the starship above Tel Aviv. Do you
have any intelligence as to what might be happening there?"

"No," the president answered. "We should be there. We
have been loyal and obedient followers of Allah. Why are we
being left out? Isn't that Jhowah over there?"

Samael heard voices in agreement with the president and
responded. "You won't be left out. There are preparations
being made to bring us all together, and Lord Sezan wishes
you to be patient and be aware of what is happening. He
would also like for you to obtain all of the information that you
can about the infidels in Israel and the starship that rides above
the city to the west. He wants to be able to send any important
information that you can gather for him back to Jhowah. It
might be helpful in the end."

"And what information does he wish from us?" The president asked.

"No particulars, just what might be taking place over there
in Tel Aviv."

"That we will study. Will you be returning to your starship soon to be with Lord Sezan?"

"Uh, no, I imagine it might be a little while before he'll be able to return. I believe I'll have to impose myself upon you for lodging and food until he can return. It shouldn't be too long. I'm sure he will be working for Jhowah in some way to bring us all together."

"We will try to get some of our intelligence people over there. They'll be able to work their way in under the Palestinian border. We have access methods and friendly contacts on the Israeli side who have allowed tunnel entry through their houses."

"Very good, Mister President," Samael replied. "And how are you doing now that you have the price of your fossil fuels so high. Are you reaping the rewards?"

"Not as well as you might expect, my Lord. With the price so high it has a reverse effect. It has thrown the economies of our customers into disarray and the demand has dropped. We control the world's oil, but only a few countries now have the money to buy it from us. In fact, we have been lending money to other countries so that they can purchase our oil. None of us can account for where all the money has gone. Much of it appears to have vanished from the face of the earth.

"Rampant inflation has devalued our financial reserves. Even after we abandoned the U.S. dollar as our currency standard, the currencies to which they were converted are worth a fraction of their original value.

"Even after draining the treasuries of one of the so-called superpower countries, trying to prop up their economy, we are probably creating no more wealth than we did before the price was raised. We did appear to attain considerable wealth immediately after the rise, but when one factors in the loans and defaults our true profits have slowly dropped to earlier levels and below. We don't have to sell as much oil but we create the same wealth, at least on paper. Would you agree to let us lower our prices?"

"No," Samael answered, "Allah has told Lord Sezan that things should stay the way they are. This is part of his plan to render the infidels powerless so that we can destroy them."

"Why does Allah not come to us himself?" The president asked with a bit of confusion and anger in his voice.

"Mister President, you must be patient. It will all work out and you will see him, but things have to be done a certain way. Allah himself has said this."

The Iranian president did not respond other than to call the meeting to a close and order his assistants to care for Samael.

"The meeting is adjourned. Please see to it that Lord Samael is taken to his lodging, and set up a meal schedule for him. He might upset some people if they see him on the streets of Tehran."

On The SORGE Science Vessel (SSV) Command
2 Months Later

"Gentlemen, I have called you all here to give and receive progress reports on the status of *Operation Shield*," Jhowah advised.

Prophet, along with all of the Aquarian members out of their branch of the Majestic-12, the Israeli prime minister and two of his cabinet members, were seated in Jhowah's conference room. Five of the members of the group representing the foreign and Israeli military and the Jewish members who had originally come together to form the group that became *Operation Shield* were there.

"Mister Prime Minister," Jhowah said. "Israel is the nation that should be nearing completion of its conversion from old or analog power sources to the new primordial energy source. Have you noticed any differences in the efficiency of the new power source?"

"Definitely, my Lord," he answered. "We are right on target and all is going well with the presence of the expertise of the Reticulum technicians that you have left here with us. Do these beings represent the images from which we were created? I have to say that it took a while for my Israeli technicians to accept the appearance of the variety of species you have, and I am amazed at the large size of the Janosians. They are a species of huge individuals."

Jhowah gave a Hivanian smile that was barely noticeable and pointed a long gray spindly finger at him. "Mister Prime Minister, do you not have *Star Trek* on your television down in Israel? And, have you not seen the movie, *Star Wars?* We're giving it to you in small doses, Mister Prime Minister. Small doses. That has long been our method of revealing ourselves to you."

"Touché, my Lord," he returned.

Jhowah dropped the smile and looked over the entire group, allowing time for the seriousness of the next subject to be recognized. "I have intelligence from Prophet and you, Mister Prime Minister," he said looking through his large black eyes at him, "that the decline in sales of crude oil in the surrounding nations has only just begun to be noticed and that Sezan or his top adviser Samael, as we have also learned, have discovered the fact that primordial energy is slowly being introduced globally to acceptable nations.

"This would be an opportune time to announce to the world that the conversion is actually occurring and that there will be a group of energy satellites placed in orbital positions to wirelessly distribute energy to those with the proper authorization, and that the authorization and energy will be under the authority and control of the energy committee of *Operation Shield.*

"I suspect that initially you will hear nothing from the oil producers and that they will continue to use their own product but as the use of your new energy source receives greater distribution they will be hit by considerable reductions in their sales and revenues. In a very short time they will realize their inability to make a change and we may see problems developing."

"What benefit will it be to us," Prophet asked, "to keep this energy panacea away from them?"

"They have followed the agenda of Sezan," Jhowah answered. "They have taken the teachings of all the prophets, not you, Prophet," he corrected, "and twisted the meanings of the writings of all of them. Killing Christians just because they believe in the Solean or earthly visitation of my Son is nowhere in the teachings that I gave to all of you.

"The Israelis have an accepted respect for the beliefs of other religions and there is a general respect from all religions for the beliefs of others except for these radical Islamics who resort to such violence. I hope that they can realize what I am doing and have done as their Creator, and how they are treating their non-Islamic brothers and sisters.

"I also see others taking advantage of the entire world using natural resources or financial and political powers as tools to conquer or influence the lives of others. I have been shocked to see the value that you humans place on shiny stones retrieved from the ground, the ones that you call diamonds, rubies, emeralds, and the like. Your values system has always puzzled me. The Illuminati are among the worst of the power brokers, creating a market for the natural resources and fruits of the vines they control. They seem to have a genetic memory of the expertise in wielding their power and taking whatever they want from their fellow human beings.

"No, Prophet, I don't plan to extend to these mongrels of war, greed and power the use of primordial energy."

"My Lord," the prime minister interrupted, "does Sezan not possess the secret of this energy source? What is stopping him from giving it to our enemies?"

"Me," Jhowah answered. "We will be watching closely and if he tries to help them convert, it will take considerable time, as you can tell from the time involved in this operation. That would give Admiral Pazon just the opportunity he would need to apprehend the most wanted fugitive in the history of our alliance. I don't believe he would want to take that chance, Mister Prime Minister. He risked apprehension by Pazon early in the creation of this planet and he was only seconds from capture when he was able to break light speed and disappear. He has managed to keep his distance since that time. No, he won't try."

CHAPTER FIVE

THE RATTLING OF SABERS

Tel Aviv
November 2013

"Prophet, what may I do for you today?" the prime minister asked. "It's good to see you again."

"You may, hopefully, tell me that my information is incorrect, Mister Prime Minister," Prophet answered as he entered the room.

The Israeli leader leaned across his desk using his hands as a prop. "If you are referring to the increase in rocket attacks on our country it is true. They began again last week, and, as has been the case in the past they are coming out of the region of the Gaza strip that has long been a Hamas stronghold. There have been no casualties so far, but we expect it will happen sooner or later. They try intimidation at first, hoping that by dropping them into lightly populated areas they will draw us into conflict. They do that to avoid bad public relations. I've always tried to ignore their initial efforts like an aggravating fly or mosquito, but they usually hurt someone and, after a while, I have to bring out our bombers and jets."

"I just came in from Washington," Prophet explained as he and the prime minister took their seats. "Do you expect any attacks to come in this direction? Into Tel Aviv?"

"We never can tell," he answered. "They have hit us before but when they do, the missiles are usually coming from Lebanon and they are a larger and more powerful weapon."

"Well, I spent some time with the Majestic-12 and then later I talked with Hank and Doug of Aquarius," Prophet explained. "The whole group is a bit worried that the administration there will get wind of their cooperation with us. They say Washington is not a very happy place right now. The White House could very well back any moves by the Palestinians; whereas, in the past they have given political support to you here in Israel."

"We've been aware of their lack of loyalty to us for several years now," the prime minister acknowledged. "The group of politicians that run the U.S. now is quite different from those of the past and we are not only learning to live with it but we are ever more cautious of any information leaving here for fear that it will be intercepted by them.

"The Majestic group shouldn't have to worry about any leaks from us but it is a shame that they have to be afraid of their own government. They have long been unattached to the executive branch and more intimately attached to the higher echelon military leaders, but the chiefs of staff are coming under tremendous pressure to expose us and torpedo *Operation Shield.*"

"Times are different," Prophet agreed. "The changes in our government make me feel like we are living in the old USSR as it was back in the sixties. I think I feel more like I'm in the U.S. that I knew so well in the past when I am over here."

"Now, Prophet," the prime minister jokingly extolled. "I remember four or five years ago when enough of your fellow citizens were crying out for 'change' that those with the current political agenda gained power. Have they changed their mind rather than their politics?"

"Sir," he answered, "there is nothing we can do about it – at least not for a while. I am far from being alone with these opinions and the feeling back home is that we have placed a dragon in the chair that should be occupied by a servant. Our new government has taken us so far away from the dreams of our founding fathers that I seriously doubt that we will ever be able to return to the country that they gave us. Many of us believe that our president has aspirations of becoming Secretary General of the United Nations and creating a world government system that could impose the kind of 'change' that has occurred in the United States on all nations, including yours, assuming you can withstand Jihad."

The prime minister gazed understandingly at him and slowly shook his head. "I do understand, Prophet. I have watched with dismay as this evolution has unfolded over there and I always remember what happened to Rome and many of the great sovereignties that reached a pinnacle and grew corrupt decaying from within. I sincerely believe that we are witnessing that in your country. I always hoped that you, or your people, would learn from history and not have to go through what I see happening."

"As would I, Mister Prime Minister, as would I." Prophet's eyes dropped to the top of the desk where the prime minister's hands were folded together.

"Mister Prime Minister, may I interrupt?" It was his secretary. "This is of the utmost importance."

"Please do, what is it?"

"We have monitored the launching of several larger rockets from the northeast out of Lebanon. We need to get you into the shelter."

"Have we located the origin with our satellite?" He asked as he stood up from his chair.

"Yes sir, but you need to get into the shelter now."

"First things first. Get those coordinates over to *Operation Shield* and let them get some x-ray lasers into the launch areas. We are accurate to within ten feet with the SDI weapons. That should send a message to them that we weren't joking when we warned them earlier about the capabilities of the *Shield* group."

At that moment a rocket hit and exploded three or four hundred meters away, breaking the glass in the office windows and shaking objects off the shelves in the room. They had to grab for the sides of the desk to maintain stability.

"Please, Mister Prime Minister; let me get you to the shelter. That strike was too close."

"I'll get me to the shelter," he ordered. "You get that information over to the *Shield* group right now so that they can get a strike down on the launch site. It will very probably save lives. Prophet, you come with me. You and your duties with *Operation Shield* are more important than I am right now. We can't risk losing you." He moved out from behind his desk and headed out the door with Prophet close behind.

"Yes, sir. For the moment I don't wish to argue the importance of my duties."

As Prophet spoke he stayed close behind the prime minister but had to stop to hold against the wall as another rocket struck less than a hundred yards away from the building. The explosion was of such force that ceiling tiles and supports fell toward the floor and the interior lights flickered down the hall.

Both men entered an elevator which began a quick descent as soon as the doors closed.

"How deep do we go?" Prophet asked realizing that they had started at ground level, but before he could get an answer another explosion could be felt bringing the elevator to a halt.

"Uh oh, what'll we do now, sir?"

The prime minister moved over to the control panel and pounded the RESET button. The elevator started up again heading down. "It has a safety brake," he explained. "A jolt like that could break the cable and send us uncontrolled down the remaining eight stories."

"This is ten stories deep?" Prophet exclaimed. "What a getaway!"

When the elevator reached bottom the doors opened and Prophet could see a dimly lit, comfortably large, well-stocked and furnished apartment. He meandered over toward the middle of the room and saw other areas off the main foyer section. In some rooms were beds with the walls lined with boxes that appeared to be placed there as storage of necessities for long-term survival. In another room he saw a refrigerator, tables and chairs, a sink and cabinets for more storage.

He watched the prime minister head for a closed door, which he opened going inside. He heard a motor start up and suddenly the lights in the cavernous apartment brightened as he came out closing the door to the room firmly. It revealed a much larger area than could be seen in the subdued light.

"We have a 15 KW generator that can keep us going for a couple of weeks if necessary," he explained. "We haven't, yet, had time to power this area with primordial energy. There's a powered ventilation system in there and within the complex to keep us safe from bad gasses, and a slow-release oxygen supply controlled by a monitor to keep the generator going."

"What a place to spend a lost weekend with your sweetheart," Prophet suggested. "All we need is a television for a little extra entertainment, or propaganda, depending on which source we would watch."

The prime minister grinned and winked at him as he walked over to a desk in the main room. "This is my entertainment and my mistress," he said lifting the phone from its stand on the desk. He looked at the phone and punched a button on the face and after a second he had someone on the other end.

"Who do I have here? The sound is terrible on this piece. Okay, what's happening up there? It's like a tomb down here."

Prophet saw a look of satisfaction come to his face as he listened to the reply.

"Okay, I'll stay here for another hour and if I don't hear from you we'll be heading back up. By the way, has there been any damage assessment?" He waited for a moment as he listened with no change in the expression on his face.

"Well, we can deal with that soon enough. Tell the *Shield* group that we appreciate their initial show of force. I'll see you in an hour."

As he hung up the phone he laughed. "They hit the Leb-anon launching site and the Gaza launch site from one of our communication satellites. After the x-ray laser strikes there were no more rockets from either location. They want me to stay here another hour to be sure that they don't start up again. Prophet, it looks like we have initiated the SDI in a real way. I know there was a name change from your political left in the 1990s but I like SDI. It sounds better, maybe because I liked the man who led its creation."

After the wait and with no call from the surface, the two men returned on the elevator. When the door opened, Prophet was surprised at the damage he saw inside of the building. It had been a relatively short rocket attack. When they went outside they saw that every window was either cracked or broken out.

"We'll have to get those repaired right away," the Israeli leader said. "We can get a good bit of rain here in November and December."

They also noticed that the north wall of the building was severely damaged by a strike that had landed after they had left the surface probably the one that had set off the emergency safety brake in the elevator.

They returned to the prime minister's disheveled office where Prophet finished giving him a detailed report on his meeting with Majestic-12 and Aquarius.

Moments Later
Aboard Sezan's Spacecraft

Sezan pounded his fist against the table. He had just managed to get down close enough to the surface near the city of Tehran to pick up Samael and they were back in his confer-ence room monitoring the Solean-3 newscasts.

"How did they put an end to the attacks?" He asked. "This was to have been the beginning of an action that could have put this new group out of business. What do they call them, *Operation Shield?* This will not stand. I'll have them start again."

"I'm sorry, my Lord," Samael explained. "I was already in the viper shuttle when they started the attacks. They attacked from the west of me from a place called Lebanon which is on the northern border of Israel. I never had knowledge of the results."

"Yes, I'm quite familiar with the geography," Sezan replied in an exasperated voice. "I want to know why they stopped. They were right on target with their rockets."

"I need to talk to that Iranian human, what's his name, Jahid, and have him kick some butt as he refers to it. I want a larger-scale attack and I want it to continue and not stop if they run into a little trouble."

"I believe we need to handle this as soon as possible, my Lord. Jhowah may well spot us down here from his orbit beyond Luna. I'm sure he has been monitoring the rocket strikes, so even if you have approached Soleus-3 from a sensor-invisible direction, you are now exposed."

"I agree," Sezan said. "Get me that Iranian on the communications system."

Samael jumped to the orders of Sezan and soon had Jahid on the speaker for him.

"What happened to the attack? It stopped before you even got started." There was anger in Sezan's voice and Samael could see his Dromedan eyes shine in an almost sparkling glow. This meant trouble for the Iranian leader or anyone else if the attack failed again.

"My Lord, the team in Lebanon reports that they got off three or four of our larger rockets, and just as they were about to launch the next one, the whole launch area exploded. When the flash and smoke cleared, there was nothing there except an indentation in the ground. We received a report from the team in Gaza that the same thing happened there. They had been firing the smaller rockets into southern Israel for about a week but they were disintegrated at the same time as the Lebanon team."

"Well, what happened, Jahid? What caused the disintegration that you describe? "

"I don't know, my Lord. We have heard that they may have some type of new weapon, and I guess this is the results of that weapon."

Sezan was quiet for a moment and then responded. "You had best find out what happened and what this weapon is able to do or I'll make that country you have there that you call Iran look like the craters you described in Lebanon."

"I will try, my Lord."

"No, you won't try. You'll do it, and you'll take the army, tanks and weapons left by your last leader, whatever he called himself, and lead an attack on the country of Israel where we think the *Shield* group is positioned. Get some of the armament and military units into Gaza and the major elements into Lebanon. I'll have to leave now, but when I return I don't want to be listening to a bunch of excuses again. This time, you had better not fail. Israel must fall."

"Yes, my Lord." Jahid said, and he became silent. He had been present the day that Sezan had introduced himself to the former Iranian leader. He had seen the results of the initial attack by the Iranian jets, and he knew he was not able to match the weaponry of Sezan.

December 1, 2013
On The Lebanon-Israeli Border

Jahid, having been anointed by Sezan as the leader of the attack on Israel, stood on the ground south of Tyre, Lebanon, watching his tanks and truck-drawn howitzers as they got into position for the military incursion into Israel from their position in the north. Meanwhile, his generals in Gaza were lining up for an attack from the southwest.

The Iranian military commanders had spent the week getting their armies and weapons together and transporting them into the two positions. Thousands of military men and women were gathered and waiting. Many were from countries other than Iran and Lebanon who were a part of the radical Islamic military conspiracy against Israel. Terror groups from the hills of Afghanistan and Pakistan had come to wage what they called the "final battle" for the seat of Zionism. Some back home were prepared to join in the attack by launching recently confiscated nuclear weapons from the previous Pakistani government. All along the Israeli borders men, women, and children who had been preparing for more than a decade for such a showdown were poised to launch their own kind of Jihad. Those who didn't have sophisticated weapons were armed with crude sharp objects, clubs and explosives. None were afraid to die for their cause. They had been convinced that it was for this reason they were born and that treasures were waiting for each of them, if they could kill just one Zionist or die in the effort to do so. Tens of thousands of Mohammad's extremist warriors were poised to be martyred. All this activity, and nothing had been heard from an Israeli response.

Where are they? Jahid wondered.

As night descended over the Middle East Jahid entered his command tent to make plans for the next day. He was expecting an Israeli resistance. After all, there were satellites up there that should be watching them, knowing their every move, and then there was the new weapon that the *Shield* group had. He knew all of this, but it was as if nothing was happening in Tel Aviv or Jerusalem.

Operation Shield
Southeast Of Nazareth
Under The Mound Called Har Megiddo

In an underground facility packed with electronic equipment, a group of military leaders watched as hundreds of monitors displayed images from all over the globe. Other personnel were focused on control panels positioned against the rear of the building.

"General, what seems to be happening," the Israeli prime minister asked.

"This appears to be a significant invasion," the general answered. "There are probably military elements from countries other than Iran involved in this also."

He stood with a commanding countenance as he explained. He was a slightly overweight man more than six feet tall. His uniform was that of the U.S. military to which he had belonged before joining *Operation Shield*.

"The troops are massing on your northern border with Lebanon and appear to have several thousand armed personnel and considerable numbers of tanks, howitzers, and troop transporters. There are many women and children among them. There is another group of a lesser number that is assembling in the Gaza Strip region. It appears they are planning a pincer-type attack on your country. I am amazed that they are so open in their movements, but I'm not surprised that they have brought women and children into the fight. They have long used them as human shields or to carry out unsuspected acts of terrorism in public places. Now they appear to be openly engaging them in the attack."

"They are either entirely overconfident," the prime minister said "or they are desperate in their goal. Do we see any evidence of an air force?"

"We've found a force of Russian jets armed to the hilt with missiles in the Beirut International Airport. They're clustered in one corner of the airfield. There is another group at the old Mazzeh Airport in Damascus. It is normally a military airport but these are the same missile-armed Russian-class birds as the ones in Beirut."

"Do you have any idea when can we expect an attack, general?"

"They haven't even begun to fuel the jets yet, and they would be the first wave if these military leaders are planning a standard attack. I strongly suspect that they won't be attacking until before sunrise tomorrow," the general informed him.

"Good," the prime minister replied with a sound of relief in his voice. "This will give us a chance to map our enemies' coordinates. That way, in the morning, we can strike each one at the moment the incursion begins."

"It isn't that simple, Mister Prime Minister. The problem is in the numbers. As you know, the SDI weapons are designed to handle several nuclear-capable missiles, one at the time, but here we have a hundred or more armed jets in two different areas and massive numbers of military personnel and vehicles. SDI can't handle all of these at once."

"I didn't expect to hear that," the Israeli admitted. "Do you have any advice for my military leaders?"

"I won't be abandoning you. I can hit these jets one at a time but some will get through, unless you start now before they take off."

"No, I can't do that. They would deny any plans to attack us, and that would put us in a bad light internationally," he explained. "You know that our enemies have convinced the United Nations to hold us to a different standard than they hold those who would destroy us."

"Yes I left a similar political situation among the media in the U.S. Then I'll wait until they expose their hostile intent and begin then. Your people can take on the stragglers and I'll hit the jets out front. Our control computers here will be able to lock on and avoid hitting yours but I'd rather keep SDI as far out in front as I can."

The prime minister looked pleased that there would be some support from the *Operation Shield* team but he had been expecting a more complete "wipe out" at the beginning of the attack of the opposing forces by the x-ray lasers as in the earlier attempt to hit Tel Aviv. His own generals would have to become intimately involved along with the SDI support.

"Thank you, general. I'd better get with my military now and make plans for the morning. If I understand you correctly they can plan on SDI strikes from the lead planes back. What about the ground-based vehicles?"

"I'll monitor the air war from here," he replied, "and if I see your forces getting dominance in the air, with SDI help of course I'll move to the ground vehicles. You'll have to handle the individual personnel without SDI assistance. It wasn't made to handle that. We'll be doing well to handle the air force. It is a nuclear-deterrent weapon, designed to destroy ICBMs, but we'll try to improvise and use it in a classic twentieth-century-type action."

"Thank you, general, I'll be back in touch later in the night. If they appear to be moving any earlier than expected, I'm sure you'll let me know."

"Will do, Mister Prime Minister."

The Next Morning
4:30 AM
Damascus, Syria
At A Military Airbase

The Iranian general stood before his men gathered near their jets who were in their flight suits after having been briefed as to their missions in this planned Jihad into Israel.

"Today we are gathered in the name of Allah before entering the air and land of the Zionist infidels. Our duty and our mission from Allah and from the prophet Mohammed is the destruction of Israel. We have been ordered by him to seek out and kill the Jew Zionist where ever we can find him. When possible he should be beheaded.

"Our war machinery is fine tuned and well oiled. We are committed to this, the greatest of all Jihads, to rid the world of the Satan who has taken our land and seeks to destroy us.

"Go out and fly with the wind and send your missiles into the heart of Israel, into Tel Aviv and Jerusalem, destroying the leaders of the Satan. The Great Satan of America will not stop you for we now have allies there who will prevent this.

Go forth, and if you die, Allah will reward you in the next life. Allahu Akbar, Allahu Akbar."

With those words the general thrust his fists into the air challenging his men to enter the battle, the Great Jihad.

Moments Later At
Hatzerim Airbase
Near Beersheba, Israel

"Hello,"

The prime minister held the phone close to his ear as he sat up and slipped out from under his cot covers. His mussed hair and squinted eyes revealed a restless sleep.

"Mister Prime Minister, I can see increased movement in both airports from our satellites. I believe they are fueling for the attack. We are ready here and I already have SDI set and focused in preparation for the attack. You can inform your generals that we will begin our SDI strikes on the lead jets when they cross the border and move toward the rear until we feel that it might be too great a risk to the Israeli pilots who will be attacking from the rear."

"Thank you, general I'll be back in touch as we proceed. Good hunting."

"And thank you, Mister Prime Minister."

The Israeli leader eased off of the army cot and looked back at it. *Not too comfortable, but it served its purpose for the night,* he thought as he hyper-extended his spine and stretched his arms. There were not many more comfortable places in the military hangar that he had rather have been than that cot.

Heading for the war room at the other end of the building he could hear the echo of his footsteps coming back at him as he walked across the floor of the large, hollow facility. The floor was filled with electronic telemetry devices and monitor screens to follow the progress of the mission. There were high-tech jets with clusters of rockets hanging from their wings. They were being fueled and readied for the mission ahead. He nodded to several of the personnel as he passed. He was a highly respected leader and admired by his commanders on down to the lowest echelons of the military.

When he reached the war room he saw that his commanders were all gathered around the map table with their pilots refreshing their memories about the locations of the air fields and discussing the strengths and weaknesses of the Russian-made Iranian jets.

The prime minister headed for the coffee brewer and motioned for his top commander as he began filling his cup with coffee. "Is everything going off without problems so far, commander?"

"Yes sir, I assume you have spoken with the *Operation Shield* leaders this morning."

"Yes, I did, and he will notify us as soon as he sees the first bird headed out on the tarmac. I do want to speak to the pilots after you finish briefing them. They will need to be familiar with what might be happening from *Shield* during the air battle."

"That I will, sir. I am ready to speak to them now. I'll turn them over to you just before they are ready to take to their planes."

The commander gave the pilots final briefing instructions and handed off to the prime minister who stood before them.

"Gentlemen and lady," he sternly smiled and nodded toward the female pilot who had made a name for herself as a top gun in the earlier pre-emptive attack on Iran when the Iranians were attempting to pull a sneak attack on the nation of Israel.

"I come to wish you Godspeed and to inform you that you'll be witnessing the use of a very unique and special weapon during this confrontation. It is known as SDI and is under the control and operation of an also special group located in a secret location. This weapon is guided from Earth by that group, and satellite technology is used in the guidance and the firing of it. What you see will convince you right away that it is very powerful, so you'll not want to be mistaken for an Iranian jet.

"In order to prevent an accidental friendly shoot down, those who are guiding and firing the SDI weapons will start with the lead Iranian planes and move to the rear as they take their shots. The plans are for you to come in from the rear and attack toward the lead plane. You'll want to restrain your aggression as you near the firing zone of the SDI beams.

"Yes, I said beams. It is a modified x-ray laser weapon and when they strike their target you'll see total disintegration. We used them a few weeks ago during the rocket barrages from Lebanon and Gaza. After the strike there was nothing much left of the rocket launch areas but an empty, scooped-out crater. It took only one shot to each launch site to wipe them from the face of the Earth."

"If the old Iranian president was alive he wouldn't like that," was a response from one of the pilots, followed by a restrained level of laughter from the rest of the group.

The prime minister smiled and raised his hands high and clutched his fists. "Godspeed, gentlemen. Do this for Israel, the future of our planet, and for the glory of God."

With that the pilots dispersed, heading for their planes where they began going through their system checks.

The prime minister heard a voice and turned to see his top commander approaching.

"The *Shield* group has notified us that the Iranians are beginning to head down their runways for takeoff. We are about to do the same. Thank you, Mister Prime Minister, for your explanation and your inspiration."

"Certainly, Commander, keep our pilots safe and bring them home."

"I shall do my utmost."

"Commander, I'll be remaining here with you to monitor the war," he advised.

In The Air Over Beersheba

The skies were still dark as the young lions took to the air in their planes heading north. In order to avoid the barrage by the SDI weapons on the lead planes the plan was to move out low over the Mediterranean as they traveled toward Lebanon and move back in behind the Iranians who were arriving from the north. Since the Iranians were flying from Beirut and Damascus, they would need only a short time to reach and cross the Israeli border where they needed to be before they would be called aggressors.

Lior Rozin was a young pilot who had graduated into the Israeli Air Force only two years earlier from the training fields near Beersheba. His close friend who graduated at the same time was Yoni Caspi. They often flew together on missions.

"Yoni, are you ready to take down a few Ruskie jets?" The two were piloting their own separate jets and flying near each other in formation. They could almost see each other's silhouette through their canopies from their positions in the cockpits of their planes.

"Yes, my good friend, and I'm quite eager to see that new weapon. I have heard that it is actually a gift from God."

"I heard something like that, also," Lior added. "Our prime minister seemed to have great respect for it. Sounds a bit like Star Wars or Star Trek. I wonder if they have Picard in that secret location to push the firing button."

Yoni chuckled and added another piece of information to the legend. "I heard that they actually locate the targets from a satellite camera monitoring system and the killer beam comes out of the exact same satellite to strike it."

"No, Yoni, that sounds unreal. Are you sure?"

"You know how these things get embellished. It could all be rumor, but the prime minister didn't doubt its capabilities."

"Yeah, he said it was used to knock out the rocket launch sites a couple of weeks ago in Gaza and Lebanon," Lior added as he looked through his canopy and saw that they were moving out over the Mediterranean.

The moon was low and to the west, sending out a light reflection band on the water toward him. He was a young clean-cut Israeli with his hair covered by his flight helmet. His chestnut-brown eyes were complimented by his olive complexion.

He wondered what his parents were doing. It had been several months since he had been able to see them. The Air Force kept him busy, always practicing maneuvers or going to class to learn the profiles of enemy planes and new instrumentation. He needed to see them and keep that love in him that they had instilled along with a love of the God of Abraham and Isaac. He had been an active child when he was growing up and he knew he had given his mother lots of worries. *I guess I should apologize for some of my old ways,* he thought.

"We're coming up on our turn to the east in sixty seconds." It was the wing commander giving a heads-up on the next change in the flight path. This meant that they were getting in a position to move in behind the Iranian planes. He hoped that group in the secret command base was watching the enemy and not confusing him for the Iranians.

Light would soon be breaking into the horizon from the east making it easier to see the land below. Lior could see that they were approaching the coast line right at the Israeli Lebanese border. As they began to make a tighter turn toward the south, in behind the enemy, he looked down at the border area. It was active with Islamic and Hezbollah troops, trucks and tanks. He could see smoke rising where the enemy had struck border guard stations and the Israeli residential guard posts. He so wished that he had authorization to leave the wing and wipe out those tanks.

"Enemy ahead at two o'clock," his commander warned through the comm system. "Remember to strike the rear trailing planes first," he reminded them.

From their position and flight direction, normal direct eyesight vision by the Iranians was minimally impaired by the brightness of the early rising sun. Their position put the Israelis between the sun and the port or left side of the enemy. Lior hoped that would help, at least a little. Then he saw Yoni roll to starboard and begin an attack run. He followed close behind and headed for the next Iranian jet to the right of Yoni's target. Yoni's first missile took out the enemy and at the same time Lior locked onto his and fired. The rocket exploded and took off the left wing of his target. He saw it begin a spinning action toward the ground as he passed.

By this time the enemy was in full alert of their presence and was beginning to take evasive actions, but ahead they all saw an extremely bright explosion. The explosion was so bright that the pilots brought their arms up to shade their eyes from it. Moments later a shock wave could be felt passing through and shaking the jets as if they had been grabbed by an invisible hand and jerked about.

"Did you see that, Yoni?"

"How could I miss it?"

"That had to be the SDI that the prime minister described. Wow, I wouldn't want to be in a Ruskie jet right now. There wasn't enough left to fall to the ground."

Then again another bright flash and powerful explosion occurred, and moments later it happened again. Neither the

Israelis nor the Iranians had time to strike and the wing commander called the group back as they watched SDI slowly take the remainder of the Iranians out of the air even as they twisted and turned trying to avoid the beams that were locked on them by the satellite-based computers.

The commander turned his attention to the ground action. "Caspi, you and Rozin go back and get that group of howitzers that we saw just below our border. The rest of you follow me down to put away as many of the tanks and ground troops as we can. We can shower them with tear gas canisters. That might disperse the women and children. I doubt they have gas masks. We'll hit the military forces after sending the women and children off the battlefield with the tear gas.

Yoni was able to take out three of the howitzers with one missile and Lior finished off the other two leaving the pilots free to head back to join the wing to destroy the ground activities, but as they turned Yoni received a hit in his tail section from anti-aircraft fire that had gone unnoticed as they were making the strike on the howitzers. His jet immediately went into a spin and headed for the ground.

"Yoni!" Lior yelled over the com system. "You've been hit! You have to get out of there! Eject!"

"I will. Get me some help, Lior. I don't know what might be down there. It looks like there are still a good number of Iranian and Hezbollah troops in the area. See you at dinner tonight."

Lior watched as his friend was propelled from the falling jet. He was able to see his chute open just as he lost him from his vision in a turn. He circled the area as Yoni settled onto the land below. He flew by him and tipped his wing giving him encouragement and letting him know he would be calling for help.

Lior knew that if there were any enemy troops in the area they would have seen the crash and would be headed for his friend as fast as they could. He called his leader who was leading a strike just south of him.

"Yoni was hit and went down in an area near enemy lines. We need to get help to him."

"I'll try to call for help but I'm sure Rescue has their hands full right now," his leader replied. As Lior heard the call for help going across his radio he circled back to see if he could see his friend.

The chute was gone, hidden by Yoni for sure, in order to hide his position, but Lior could see him hiding among an outcropping of rocks on a nearby hillside waving at him with his flight helmet. Again he tipped his wing and as he leveled off he saw a group of Hezbollah troops headed toward him. He looped and dove toward them, firing a missile into the center of the group. It was a direct hit. On his return loop to the site he saw no movement among the bodies that littered the field.

"Lior to squadron leader."

"Go ahead, Rozin...did you see Caspi?"

"Yes sir, but I had to knock out a contingent of enemy troops that were headed for him. Were you able to get help from Rescue?"

"Yes, but I'm afraid it will be quite a while before they can get to him."

Lior gritted his teeth, "Sir, I'm going back to the air field and get a chopper with some armament. I know the enemy won't allow him to stay there long enough for Rescue to get to him."

"You Go ahead, Lior; we have things pretty well under control here. You be careful, carry your sidearm and don't let yourself get captured."

"Yes sir, and thank you, sir."

With that Lior headed straight for the nearest military airfield in hopes that he could get to Yoni with help, and he soon found some. As he landed he saw an Apache battle chopper that was just landing in front of him probably to rearm, and after a short time he was able to gain the pilot's cooperation. The two soon left in the freshly armed Apache to save Yoni.

"Did your friend have a weapon?" The pilot asked as he guided the Apache forward.

"Only his sidearm," Lior answered. "There, look over there near that rocky hillside. There are some enemy troops around him."

Not seeing Yoni, he directed the pilot to fire into the enemy. The pilot filled the air and the ground with fire from his 30mm gun located on the underside of the chopper. The enemy fell like flies as he unleashed the weapon, and soon there was nothing evident but the agonal gasps and spasms of the dying troops.

Setting the chopper down a short distance from the bodies, the two men jumped from it with their handguns drawn and headed for the place where Lior had last seen Yoni. They ran among the rocks and the bodies looking for him. Lior saw two legs protruding from behind a large boulder and ran toward them. He recognized the uniform, but as he rounded the rock his greatest fear was realized. Yoni was dead, but he had been brutally beaten and tortured before being given the final death blow of the Hezbollah. He had received the symbolic Islamic beheading, the cruel, life-ending blow that these merciless extremist killers are taught to bestow slowly on what they call the Zionist Infidels.

"Oh, my God. Yoni."

Lior stood at the feet of his friend. Tears filled his eyes for his dead friend, lay dead before him. He gritted his teeth as he remembered the happy days they both had enjoyed with each other as they went through their training at the airbase near Beersheba. They and their families had become close friends during this time as they celebrated their love and allegiance to Israel.

The stare of agony that remained on Yoni's motionless and bodiless face told Lior of the pain and fear that he had experienced as the enemy took his life in their slow and methodical slicing of his neck. His body was covered with blood that had been released as they took the life from him.

They had known this could happen but they were willing to fight for Israel so that their family and countrymen and women could live in safety in their homeland. Lior remembered how once they had listened over the Internet to a Lebanese woman who spoke of the atrocities of the Hezbollah and how it had affected her childhood and the rest of her life.

Her name was Brigitte Gabriel, a Christian woman who had written several books describing events she had seen similar to what had just happened to Yoni. She had lived her childhood in a cave with her family in Lebanon, hiding in order to stay alive. She said that she had been unable to travel in her country because the Hezbollah would set up checkpoints along many of the routes, where vehicles would be stopped and their ID cards checked. Since the cards gave the religion or ethnicity of the individual, the Islamist would take any Christians they could identify in the vehicle and kill them. She said she had found more compassion among the Israelis for Lebanese Christians than from her own people.

As Lior stood there remembering, the pilot approached him. "I'm sorry," he said. "I wish we could have made it sooner. We could possibly have saved him."

Looking up with moisture in his eyes, Lior smiled. "I doubt it. Those people are insane. They would have risked their own lives just to complete the beheading. Yoni was a good man and a good friend." Picking up his friend's bloody headless body in his arms he headed for the chopper. The pilot followed behind him with Yoni's head. Blood dripped from Yoni's neck as he walked toward the helicopter.

"Take me back to my jet," he said. "I need to do something to avenge my friend. Later I must take the bad news to his family. They are good people. It will be the hardest thing I have ever had to do."

With the airways now dominated by the Star of David, the ground forces out of Gaza and Lebanon were constantly being bombarded by missiles from the Israeli jets and constant SDI strikes from the satellites, which caused violent explosions as they struck the ground, leaving empty craters. By the end of the day the Jihad had collapsed and the northern and south-western borders of Israel were filled with enemy infantry and vehicles in disarray retreating toward the surrounding borders as rapidly as possible.

The ground in some areas appeared somewhat like the surface of the moon where SDI had struck tanks and howitz-ers, leaving a field of craters so dense that it was impossible for military trucks and mobile weapons to negotiate. Many vehi-cles and weapons, because of this, had been left on the field amongst the craters as the troops retreated. Neither of the ex-cursions had advanced further than five or ten miles into Israe-li territory, with only a few exceptions.

The large number of undamaged trucks, tanks, howitzers, and other weapons that were left behind would be useful to the Israeli army once they were gathered.

Back At Hatzerim Airbase

"Give me a report, Commander," ordered the Israeli prime minister. They were still in the large hangar near Beer-sheba where Command Central was located and where the prime minister had been throughout the day monitoring troop movements and the progress of the battle.

"There seems to be a full and complete retreat taking place into the Gaza strip and north into Lebanon. The ground forces that had penetrated deepest toward the south are retreat-ing east into Syria and then back toward the north. None of the troops out of Lebanon made it as far south as the Jordani-an border.

"We have a large number of their military vehicles and equipment that they have abandoned as the retreat began. They are strewn around the border areas where they entered our country. It seems that they had planned this as the Great Jihad to end all Jihads. They were coming at us with everything that they had and more, and I believe that if we hadn't been able to use SDI they would have put us away. It has now saved us twice.

"Mister Prime Minister, the way they began their retreat leads me to believe that they may have had some Intel that would have come from satellite surveillance showing them our positions. It makes you wonder if this came from someone who was in bed with our enemies, a source from within the U.S."

"Commander, get someone from *Operation Shield* on the phone for me. I need to know their status."

"Yes sir, in fact we already have them. They were calling to see what your plans are from here."

"Let me see the phone," the prime minister said reaching out.

The commander handed it over to him and went back to his monitors.

"How are things there at *Shield,* General?" the prime minister asked as he pressed the phone to his ear.

"We're getting a bit of expertise with these SDI x-ray lasers. They are quite effective on the Russian jets," he answered. "There were several Iranian naval combat vessels that approached Haifa during the encounters with all the intentions of attacking but when the lasers hit them there was nothing left but bubbling, steaming sea. It just seemed to vaporize them."

"Very good, general, you are getting some real hands-on experience with SDI."

The prime minister heard a chuckle over the phone.

"Yes sir, we sure are. What are your plans from here? Should we make any other preparations?"

"I believe we will require less of you and your machines for right now, general, but please stay alert and available. I will chase these Jihadists back to their bedrooms if we have to, and try to put an end to their display."

"Very well, we will be here if you need us."

The prime minister hung up the phone and turned back to the commander. "Are you ready to follow these troops back to their homeland?"

"Yes sir," the military man answered, turning from the monitors. "Are we going into Lebanon?"

"We'll follow them into Lebanon, Gaza, and, if we have to, we'll strike them in Syria and Jordan. We'll even take it to them in Iran if they try to retaliate in any way."

"Excellent, Mister Prime Minister. That we can do." With those orders the commander turned to his leaders and ordered a seek strike against the retreating armies.

A Month Later
Above Tel Aviv
Aboard The SSV COMMAND
In Jhowah's Conference Room

"Jhowah, it is complete."

The chief engineer of the SSV Command, a Dromedan, spoke as he stood before the conference table in the presence of Jhowah, Metatron, the prime minister of Israel, the members of the council of *Operation Shield,* and its operative, Prophet. Doug Bradley and Hank McConnell, who represented Aquarius, the clandestine branch of Majestic-12, also a clandestine or secret branch of the U.S. Government, were present among the attendees. All were seated as the engineer pronounced the completion of the installation of all the facets of the project to bring primordial energy to the people of Earth who had lived up to the Commandments of Jhowah.

The group from MJ-12 and Aquarius was acting in its own capacity, since the current executive and legislative branches of the United States government were not a member of this project and had no knowledge of the group's participation. The more recent actions and goals of the United States were not acceptable to the wishes of Jhowah and the council of *Opera-*

tion Shield. The once great "Shining City on a Hill," had been high jacked by those to whom it posed a threat.

The Illuminati and those in political power in recent years in control of the development of a one world government had made poor choices in their mishandling of the fortunes that they held. They, however, replenished their own accounts with clandestinely devised electronic transfers from many of their OPEC friends. Even in the highest branches of government there was a scramble to overcome rampant inflation that was cutting into the value of currencies the world over. For the past few months, fortunes, not just in the form of monetary riches but as natural resources, were also used for personal gain and to dominate the citizens of their domains. But everything was about to change.

"Today is a day that will be noted in the history of the Reticulum and possibly in that of Planet Earth if its society is allowed to exist and continue as a living part of the universe," Jhowah said as he watched the expressions and experienced the thoughts and emotions of those present.

"You now have a clean and inexpensive form of energy that can carry you into a new economy and later into the age of interstellar and even intergalactic flight if we are able to handle that barrier. You have all of the wonders of our universe waiting for you if you can learn to live within the laws of the universe as I have interpreted them for you. My laws should dominate your lives and the way you live and interact with others.

"Once the others see that all of their efforts to control the wealth and natural resources of the Earth are for naught, and their income from the sale of their energy forms to you cease, there will be massive changes to take place, and you will have to handle the reaction as you best see fit. The way you handle this and the lives you live will determine the future of this planet and will play a large part in how we handle the creation and habitation of other star systems with planets."

Jhowah looked about the table waiting for questions, but it seemed that his words had been received and accepted by those at his conference table.

"The country or countries that you have recently crushed, Mister Prime Minister, are going to rearm, and when they realize that you and those under the umbrella of *Operation Shield* are in charge of the cleanest, the most efficient, and affordable form of energy in the universe, they will want to get in on the, shall we say, management. You will not allow this or you will lose your status as the part of *Operation Shield* that you share."

"Yes, my Lord, I understand." The prime minister was aware of the respect and privilege that he had earned from Jhowah. He was also aware of the anger and hate that he would soon have to handle when the reality of the recent energy conversion struck home in the fossil fuel industry.

"My Lord," he questioned, "There are those in the United States who have been faithful to you and your laws. They will want to be a part of this new age. Will they be allowed to use this new energy source and become part of the world order that we are out to create?"

"I'm afraid that I have to say no to that," Jhowah answered. "Australia should be allowed among those participating, but the United States, in its beginnings, was created as a nation that existed under the laws which I passed down to Moses, and for years it honored those laws. In recent decades it has moved away from these laws and even more recently it has voted for leaders who have deliberately allowed the removal of references to me and the laws that I handed down. No, until the citizens of that nation take their lives into their own hands, make sensible choices and clean up their political leadership, they will continue to suffer the consequences.

"I have learned to trust and respect Prophet as the representative agent of *Operation Shield* and I would like to see him as the general controller of the codes and participants in the use of this primordial energy.

"I am honored." Prophet bowed his head in acknowledgement of the command of Jhowah. "My Lord, there will be those who will wish to be a part of this. Should I reject all, other than these whom you have already mentioned?"

"Any requests should be forwarded to me through Metatron and I will make the needed assessment and get back to you. There will be others allowed in but they may have to make significant changes. Great Britain, for instance, has been inhabited by a large number of radical Islamists and therefore allowed itself to be guided by the misguided laws of some of the same radical groups who control the current energy producers that surround Israel. Changes will have to occur before we let them into the operation."

Jhowah smiled as he looked around the room to find anyone with questions on their minds. "Gentlemen, this meeting is adjourned."

With that, the participants rose and exited the room to be shuttled to the surface.

Riyadh, Saudi Arabia
June 15, 2014

It was a usual hot, dry, and sunny day outside as the secret Council of Riyadh was in conference inside the comfortable palace of the Saudi king, who was acting as moderator and as the Saudi representative. Ambassadors from Jordan, Syria, Iran, Lebanon, Sudan, and Yemen were present. There were also two agents from Al Qaeda present. The atmosphere was solemn and official as they all sat on the floor around a low table in traditional dress and turbans.

"My country has attempted to bring down the price of fossil fuel to encourage a resumption of sales, your majesty," the Iranian representative stated. "After lending them billions of dollars, we are able to sell oil to the United States, but there are very few other non-oil-producing nations that are buying.

The new energy that is under the control of the *Shield* group is a fierce competition."

"What happened to this representative of Allah who started our energy war?" The Jordanian representative asked. "He said this was Allah's desire when he ordered us to raise our prices. Where is he?"

"He has not returned since his agent, Samael, visited us five or six months ago," the Iranian answered.

"Our sales have fallen by seventy percent," the Sudanese added, "and they are continuing to fall."

"And we have lost eighty percent of sales in Yemen," the Yemen ambassador wailed.

The Saudi King raised his arms. "It seems we have been receiving inaccurate information from your leader in Iran," he said looking into the eyes of the Iranian ambassador.

The Iranian sat there, momentarily speechless, but he soon gathered his courage and replied. "You will remember the sudden appearance of the agent of Allah, or the one who claimed to be His agent, in the air space above Tehran. We had no defense against his vessel. His weapons were like none we have ever encountered. Such magnificent and advanced weapons and vehicles led us to believe his assertion of being an agent of Allah."

"You mean like the weapons that Israel used on you recently," the king reminded him.

"Yes, they were," the Iranian replied, looking back at the king with sudden realization.

"Perhaps Israel has this agent of Allah on their side," the king suggested, "or perhaps he is a fake." He tightened his jaw as he completed the sentence.

The members of the Council looked about the table at each other as they considered the words of the king.

The ambassador from Sudan spoke up. "We, all of us, are being economically destroyed, and our wealth and prestige are rapidly being lost. Without the ability to sell our product we will collapse as the individual sovereign nations that are and

I feel that we should not just sit back and let ourselves be trod upon. I suggest that we watch our efforts for one or two months, then reassess. If our futures continue to appear to be doomed as they are at this time, we should all join in on a final and complete attack on the *Shield* group and the nation of Israel and remove that scourge from the face of this Earth. We should make nuclear armament our weapon of choice and also encourage the Nation of the Bear to continue to be allied to us."

As he finished his statement the other members were heard mumbling among. They all were beginning to realize the position in which they were finding themselves. The stability of their governments and societies, their very way of life, was about to disappear and they would have to do something.

They pondered aloud as the Iranian ambassador tried to give encouragement. "My president tells us that the Promised One, Mahdi, will be arriving as soon as word reaches him of our failed Jihad. It is the prophecy that he will come in time for Last Judgment in order to save our world." With those words the Iranian rose and left as the remainder of the Council turned toward the king.

"I don't believe a thing that comes from his mouth," the Sudanese ambassador said when the Iranian had left the room. "He didn't even seem convinced of his own words. I believe we must place this problem in the hands of the United Nations. We should demand that Israel and this *Operation Shield* group share the new technology with us. If they refuse we should use our friends in the United Nations to have the whole new form of energy banned from the planet."

"There is much we must find out about this new source of energy," the Yemen Ambassador advised. "We know very little about it. We would certainly need to understand how to collect and store it and then how to use it. The UN could force Israeli compliance if we push it."

"No," the Sudanese warned, "This won't help us. We have been the producers. What good would come of this if we are merely users or purchasers? There is no wealth in that. We would never again experience the way of life that we have known for the past fifty years. And the world wealth that we have seen come into our treasuries would begin to leave."

"Then I agree," the Sudanese added. "If we are unable to get the help we need to become producers we should make it worthwhile to those of our friends in governments around the world to have this force banned."

"That shouldn't be too much of a problem," the Jordanian ambassador said. "Those environmentalists seem to be able to handle that type of a problem with ease. They have been a good investment. We should also use the college professors we have helped gain important positions within universities throughout the United States to start protests and add a few agitators. The current administration in Washington loves that type of anti-capitalist activity and they have the media over there in the palm of their hands. They'll help also."

"If it comes to that," the Saudi king said, "we can consider that as an option. Tonight, I will brief my ambassador to the United Nations as to what we are thinking and ask for a hearing on this energy war as soon as possible. He will contact our friends on the United Nations' Security Council and ask for their support."

The room was silent as the members of the secret council of oil-producing countries considered the ramifications and consequences of such actions. After a few moments the king looked about the room with evilness added to the smile that adorned his face. "Remember, those who are in control of such matters have always been kind to us, and we to them."

CHAPTER SIX

CORRUPTION AT THE HIGHEST LEVELS

The United Nations Security Council
New York, New York
August 2014

"Mister Secretary General, I come before the members of this prestigious assembly today to discuss a crisis that is building on this planet. It is a crisis that has implications involving countries from all of our continents and with global consequences." The United Nations ambassador from Saudi Arabia, himself an Islamist with extremist tendencies, looked about at his peers as he spoke. He had taken a position at the podium of the Security Council.

"Never in the history of our world," he continued, "has such a criminal activity that affects the lives of so many been allowed to continue to fester within the ranks of the members of this esteemed organization."

The Saudi ambassador had dark eyes set deep under thick black eyebrows with a prominent forehead, and was dressed in his traditional wrap. He spoke in a solemn and reserved voice as he began his planned assault. He was taking the position of first in line to complain of what he seemed to feel was a tragedy.

"Mister Secretary," he said, "I am only one among many members of this august body whose countries have been unfairly attacked economically by another country that has removed our ability to live as usual and to continue to create a national income based on our natural resource of fossil fuels or crude oil. This is unfair to our people. It is an inexcusable example of arrogance and greed.

"The nation of Israel has developed an energy source that is produced and sold in that country, and they have conspired to under sell the energy sources produced by my country and the other oil-producing countries of this globe, an industry in which we have invested all our resources and energies. Not only have they created a product with which the remainder of the world cannot compete, they refuse to reveal the origin or methodology of the development of this energy source.

"Our inability to compete with this product causes much harm and discomfort to the way of life of my countrymen. For years we have served the comforts of humanity by delivering a most precious product. Ours is a product that not only can be turned into energy, but can be converted into other materials and byproducts that make for a more comfortable life for the peoples of Earth. We help to cause the production of many polymers that enhance our lives today. We also cause the improvement of our roads and highways with the use of oil products to pave them.

"I stand before you asking that you condemn this action and its effect on this globe. It most surely will throw my country and others into bankruptcy and even poverty. This cannot stand. This new technology gives the country of Israel an unfair advantage over the rest of the world's nations. They must be forced to share it with all the members of this august assembly, or to face the most severe sanctions this body can impose upon them.

"We insist that the energy source and the methodology of collection and storage be revealed, first, to all of the oil-producing countries so that we can share in the opportunities which it creates. When we have perfected it, we will share it with our friends throughout the world."

The Saudi ambassador turned from the podium and strode back to his seat as the Secretary General moved to the speaker's position and spoke.

"And who is next on the agenda?" He asked.

"The United States ambassador," was the response from behind him.

"Will the ambassador from the United States please respond to the gentleman from Saudi Arabia?"

The U.S. ambassador, remaining at his desk area, leaned forward toward his microphone and began to speak. "Mister Secretary, I wish to agree with the gentleman from Saudi Arabia. This new method of energy creation has hit us all by surprise and what surprises me most is that the nation of Israel has decided to keep it for themselves and their special friends in other parts of the world. If we only had the plans for the technology of its creation then all countries could share in its use. This won't help only the economic problems of the members of the oil-producing nations, but we who purchase our sources from them and other members of this assembly could achieve many things and it would be very beneficial to the world's economy."

Then, the U.S. ambassador said, "Unlike nuclear energy, this new energy source could go a long way to solving the global warming problem that this body has long been concerned about. Israel owes it to the world to help us."

He continued, "In the past we have allowed the nation of Israel to purchase some of the highest technology we have, in terms of weapons and machinery of war, from the United States since it gathered there again in Israel as a nation during the 1940s. It is hard to understand why they now refuse to share, with us, this new technology that they have developed. Do we have to beg to receive from our friends that which we would normally expect them to freely give?"

"Israel, do you wish to react to these charges?" The Secretary General questioned. There was much chatter and talk in the background related to the U.S. response.

"Yes, we would, Mister Secretary, there seems to be some confusion of the facts among some of our members about the origins and source of our technology." The Israeli ambassador walked to the podium and looked toward the Saudi ambassador then toward the ambassador from the United States, and then to the general audience.

"Gentlemen, I will tell to you the facts as I am allowed to reveal them by my country and those who represent the recently disclosed Reticulum Alliance." He cleared his throat and reached out to take a small notebook.

"As you remember, the Reticulum Alliance, represented by Jhowah, made first contact with many of us in this assembly in December of 2015, an event that was accurately predicted by the Mayan civilization many centuries ago. The morning after first contact, Jhowah and Metatron met with us to explain their presence and express disappointment, no, even remorse, at the choices we have made since they placed our ancestors here on Earth and created such a paradise for us to live and raise our families.

"During his most recent visit to Earth, Jhowah challenged the leaders of this planet to change our ways and seek higher and more moral ground, but after he left many chose to revert to the ways of the flesh and the poor decision-making of the past.

More importantly he has been informed by Metatron of the ways of some groups of men and women who have for generations controlled and directed the use of the wealth of this planet and the many sources of this wealth. Banking and fossil fuels are among the instruments used to create greed and the wealth that often follows in its path. This is one of the deviations from his original plan that has most concerned him. The group that has been called the Illuminati and those whose efforts are to produce a One World Order are most disconcerting. The order they are out to create is not in keeping with the one Jhowah had in mind.

"It is his opinion that these people are destructive and are causing more damage to society than he has ever dealt with in his own world, the one He calls Hivania. The ideals and political agenda of these sub-rosa groups and individuals produce an economic system that would best be described as one of 'shadowy socialism,' a system that robs man of free will. He feels that such a system suppresses the spirit of man and the basic freedom given to man by him when he and others like him created our planet and our species of people. This manmade top-to-bottom system gives those few who control government the power to control the entire human race.

We have long realized the corruptive capabilities of power. Our history books teach that the Dark Ages robbed the masses of knowledge and hope. Only the elite were allowed to learn to read, write, and think for themselves. Power was held by a monarchal family. And, the results were devastating to the human race. Based upon what is being advocated here today, this body may well add to creating the darkest time in the history of the world. There are those who say 'Power corrupts; and, absolute power corrupts, absolutely.' And, ladies and gentlemen, if you attempt to interfere with my country's participation in a covenant between Jhowah, Allah, or God, and those whom he has chosen to help him bring this incredible energy source to this planet, I believe that dire consequences will befall you.

"After listening to the comments made by those who spoke out against Israel, realize that those who controlled the sale and distribution of fossil fuels are, currently, wealthy pawns of the most selfish and destructive individuals who are affecting man. The plot, under consideration here, today, has been strategically planned by the group known as The Illuminati. OPEC's recent production and sales methods were destroying the economies of the world. And that means that their "investment" in oil is in jeopardy. This clever attempt to have you, the UN, to do their dirty work plays into their mission to control all the people of this planet.

"There also appears to be some interplay between the countries controlling oil production and the one called Sezan, or who we have always referred to as Satan, the exalted leader of the Illuminati and its chief adviser. Allow me the privilege to remind this body of the words of an Irish political philosopher by the name of Edmund Burke, who once said: 'All that is necessary for evil to succeed is for good men to do nothing.' For that reason Jhowah has attempted to help those among us who have followed his laws, and Edmund Burke's accurate interpretation of our role in keeping them.

"In recent months, we have learned from Jhowah and his messenger, Metatron that throughout our great universe there is a basic energy that is available to all. It is something called primordial energy and it is used on all of the Reticulum planets by those who created our planet Earth. It is an energy source that is found everywhere even in what we have previously referred to as the void of interplanetary and interstellar space. In fact, the Reticulum Alliance planets use this source to power their starships, collecting and using it as they travel along in space. It was what allowed Jhowah to travel to this planet and reveal himself to some of us. When he is ready, it is what will allow those of you who wish to see Him, do so on His return.

"Jhowah has given this to us as a gift to be shared with those who have followed his laws and admonitions. He has also instructed us not to share it with those who are filled with the greed for money or hate for his or her fellow human, be it for political or religious reasons. The matter of manmade religion concerns him as he watches those who hate merely because they have been taught to despise the heritage or religious beliefs of others.

"It is for that reason that I say to you that this energy source was not created by Israel but it was given to us by Jhowah who is the same Supreme Being that we have worshipped over the millennia as God. It also has to be stated that Israel has no say in who is able to use this form of energy. Those of us who were given this gift are merely servants, emissaries, of the one whose laws have governed our people for centuries.

"Only Jhowah can say who will use this source, which he has protected with encrypted codes. He has placed these codes and their distribution in the hands of the group you have come to know as *Operation Shield* and has given them specific instructions as to whom he will allow the privilege of using primordial energy.

"If those who have presented these complaints to you, Mister Secretary, wish to share in the use of such a God-given gift; then they should seek out the laws and rules that Jhowah gave to us thousands of years ago and abide by them. These laws have been available for centuries. And every nation represented here in this assembly has made a choice either to follow Jhowah's laws or to reject them. I have been instructed by Jhowah to tell you that any nation that wants to share in the gift of primordial energy should, immediately, stop with the suppression of the natural freedom that exists in the soul and hearts of human beings and recognize Jhowah, the entity most of us know as 'God' as our creator and the ongoing supreme ruler of the universe. Metatron, whom Jhowah left to work with humanity, is always available for purposes of guiding us, but unless we cease the ways of the past, Jhowah has promised that we will not see a future on this Earth or in his domains.

"Thank you, Mister Secretary. That ends my response to the gentlemen from Saudi Arabia, the United States and anyone else who feels that Israel is holding back technology from them." The Israeli ambassador returned to his seat and waited for further debate, which failed to materialize.

For more than thirty seconds, no one dared speak or make a move. The representatives present in the assembly hall on that day had been rocked on their heels. Quickly, however, the Secretary-General changed the mood. He said, "All that being said, the problem of economic decline in the countries represented here, today, must be addressed, swiftly and decisively." With his usual commanding voice, the Secretary-General said, "The vote as to whether or not we should instruct Israel to share this new technology with the world will now take place." The Secretary-General looked toward the assembly of the nations of the Earth as he called for the vote.

As the vote accumulated on the boards it was plain to see that all of the Islamic and socialist nations voted "Yea" to force Israel to share in the use of primordial energy. Even the United States was now voting right along with Russia, Cuba, Venezuela, and the Islamic states.

The Israeli ambassador turned to his assistant at the desk beside him with a look of amazement on his face. "Do they think they are greater than God? Clearly, they don't know what they are doing. They don't understand what Jhowah is doing, or they don't wish to know."

"Mister Secretary-General, may I approach the podium and speak to the Security Council again?" The Israeli ambassador asked.

"Most certainly," was his answer.

As he started to speak he scanned the assembly and saw many smug smiles among those members who were his geographic neighbors.

"Ladies and gentlemen," he began, "you have voted to force the nation of Israel to give you something that it does not control. I was clear in my response to the Saudi and U.S. ambassadors that Israel does not have any responsibility toward primordial energy. My country is merely a conduit of a higher power's wishes to save the world from itself. Jhowah has placed the management of this gift which he has given to us in the hands of the group you have recently come to know as *Operation Shield.* This group of faithful men and women receive specific instructions from Jhowah through his Earth emissary, Metatron.

"Let me repeat, Jhowah will not release the use of this gift to any nation who does not live by the codes of Moses or the commandments given to the world as Moses traveled those many years from Egypt to what we call the Promised Land.

They are simple rules that we must abide by as we live and interact with others. We are in the phase of life on Earth that we have all referred to as 'End Times.' Jhowah has come to us from his home in the city of Paradon on the planet of Hivania. He has returned to this planet according to prophecy recorded in the Scriptures accepted by most of us, here today, as the word of the Most High.

"I stand here to warn the world of nations which you represent that Jhowah is angry at us for the decisions that we have made over the eons. He means for us to live by these rules he has given us or he will release his wrath upon us. The future of the human race hangs in the balance. We will not only fail to exist on this planet, we shall never be able to visit or live in Hivania or any of the Reticulum planets or take part in the creation of other civilizations on other worlds unless we make changes in our own lives and the governments that we have allowed to rule us. Unfortunately, this body has spoken. The decision you made will not be well-received by the One I and other like-minded inhabitants of this planet serve."

He stood erect and turned toward the Secretary-General. "You have made a grave mistake with this vote and in the way this body has chosen to attempt to rule Earth and there will be severe consequences to these actions from the mightiest One in the known universe."

With that he returned to his seat hearing soft chuckles as he sat down.

Tehran, Iran
September 2014
In The Office Of The President

"I have been briefed by my United Nations ambassador, sir. Please do not take me for the fool that you apparently think I am."

"But, Mister President," Samael begged, "you must believe me. There has been a misunderstanding. Jhowah would gladly give you such power if he had the control that your ambassador described."

"No, Mister Samael, there is no misunderstanding. My ambassador appeared to be perfectly clear in his understanding of the Israeli ambassador's response to our complaint. The Israeli is not a man who would make up stories. Although I don't like him and I would like to destroy him and his people, I also know him to be a man who speaks no lies."

"Then I will have a conference with Sezan, my leader, about this bizarre suggestion that Jhowah is holding the energy source for only special countries."

The Iranian president threw the pencil he was holding onto the desk and looked up at Samael. "I suggest you not come back here with more fairy tales," he warned. "The members of the oil-producing nations of Earth have given me strict orders to obtain from you the same energy source that the Israelis have. If you are truly a representative of Jhowah as your leader has claimed, you should be able to convince him to give us that power."

"Mister President, I feel your ambassador has been misinformed by this Israeli, as you call him, but I will give your message to my leader and I know he will respond to your satisfaction."

"Don't fail me, Samael. I have a keen distrust of people with small beady eyes like yours and I hope you don't confirm my feelings."

Washington, D.C.
The White House
The Oval Office
November 20, 2014, 10:00 AM

The chief of staff, Dick Anderson, addressed his leader. "Mister President, we must do something to change our polling results. You now have dipped to the levels of the polling data of the last Republican president and you know it took immense assistance and cooperation from the media to get his numbers down that low. The recent backlash to our policies and the changes in the results in the election of two weeks ago will change the makeup of Congress.

"This resulted from the so-called 'Silent Majorities' awakening and will make us almost insignificant in so far as future legislation creation is concerned. How can we cause any legislation to pass with seventy percent of the House soon to be made up of representatives from the new Constitutionalist party, and eighty percent of the newly elected Senate also will be from that party? These are not Republicans whose arms can be twisted. They are true Conservatives and Constitutionalists who are committed to giving power back to the people and they will take on their positions in the halls of Congress in January."

"I know, Dick," the president acknowledged. "We are losing the hearts and minds of many people who had supported us from the beginning. I have continued to campaign for our agenda throughout my presidency, preparing the way for the real prize that I have always wanted as leader of the United Nations.

What I can't understand is why we are being shunned by those of our own party who were so eager in the past to support our policies. The most recent election was surely a change in the political climate of this nation. I hope we can regain our control and, again, cause a shift in this turnabout."

In the middle of the president's statement the door opened and the energy czar, Charles "Chuck" Boyd, entered. When the president finished his statements he looked up to see him.

"What can I do for you, Chuck?" he asked.

"Mister President, I am receiving word that those countries from which we normally purchase our crude oil have ramped up their prices by thirty percent. Their prices had fallen earlier this year but because of their reduced profits since then and since the development of the new energy being used in Israel, Australia and a few other countries their sales have begun to drop. As new countries are added to the virtual grid of the new power source the price of our oil will be increasing. Our friends within the OPEC group have asked me to come to you and ask that you use all your influence to see that the United States continues to buy their oil and not initiate drilling in the oil fields in and around the United States."

"That puts me in an even deeper bind," the president said. "It means there will be more problems to add to our economic depression. We need to contact a few effective and long-term party strategists and get their opinion on how to put the best spin possible on this. No matter what crisis occurred in the past, they have always been able to turn public opinion in our favor. I need to get my approval ratings up so that I can put pressure on this new Congress that will be seated within the next eight weeks or so, a Congress that won't be so easy to give us what we and our friends in high places want. We must have public pressure and opinion behind us to get anything through this group of right wingers."

"We also need to get our bill through to terminate the limitations of the president running for only two terms," Dick added. "We may need that in a few years. On the other hand, with the changes in the political climate I wonder if we can pass anything in your agenda."

"Perhaps, we can use the 'America's-at-war tactic,'" Dick added. "It has worked in the past. Americans don't like to change presidents when we are at war. What if we focus on a theme aimed at Israel and accusing them of pirating the new replaceable energy source. How does the mantra: 'The War on Energy Piracy' sound? It's just an idea, but 'Global Warming' worked. Let's get with our strategists and take on what to do, and what to call the campaign. We are at risk in losing ground that we had gained in replacing capitalism with social-ism in the United States."

The president looked back up at him. "We'll talk about this later. Is the Secretary of State still in Iran?"

"Yes sir," Dick replied.

"Get in touch with her, Dick. I need to talk with her be-fore she has her last meeting with President Jahid."

The chief of staff turned and went to his office to make ar-rangements.

"Mister President, as your energy czar I have wondered why we have failed to solve our energy needs considering all the money we have poured into it. It seems that our plans should be showing a significant reduction in our need for fossil fuels. Perhaps we should have earmarked less for social pro-grams and more for ensuring energy for our people. A lot of people have jobs, but the gross national product has been down for several years. People who have had their jobs creat-ed by our efforts can't afford the cost of gas to drive to and from work, or to heat their homes."

"For God's sake, Chuck, you're my energy czar. If you don't know, how the hell am I suppose to know?"

Boyd was a bit stunned by the president's response. He had never been spoken to before by his boss in that fashion.

"I'm sorry, Mister President, it's just something that isn't going the way we had planned. I have my own evaluations based on the data that we have accumulated, but there are so many variables that it makes it difficult to assess."

"What variables do you mean? We need to handle them, not complain about them. A lot is riding on my legacy as pres-ident, a lot more that you can imagine, Chuck."

"The major stumbling block," Chuck answered, "of course, is the cost to develop the new alternative energy sources that we have all referred to during our campaigns. Once we add the costs of developing them and the cost to make alterations to the machines that they will operate, it adds a tremendous additional cost to the purchase of mechanisms using alternative energy sources. The American people are beginning to see what we have long known, that many of the alternative sources are not that efficient or desirable and are costly to produce. The American people are beginning to ask why Israel was given this new energy source and not us. They also want to know why Israel is refusing to share it with us. There are a lot of questions in the minds of the electorate."

"We have also found, Mister President, that what many of our opponents said during the last campaign is true. Wind energy is not as functional as we were told by your political backers that it would be. Wind is predictable only a few days ahead and there is not a constant source of wind, which limits the amount of energy derivable from that source except in a very few places. Also, the storage of energy from the wind has not been shown to be a well-developed technology. Solar energy has the same disadvantages and problems associated with it, including the high cost of installing solar panel receptors and converters.

"We have similar problems associated with geothermal energy collection and storage. Some of the most ideal places to achieve success in the production or collection of this form of energy seem to be in national parks and you know the problems raised by the environmentalists who have backed us. If we tried to install geothermal plants, they would scream bloody murder, just as they do when our political opponents suggest drilling for natural gas and oil in these regions.

Another ideal location is near volcanoes, which isn't necessarily a worker-friendly environment. Some members of Congress representing the new Constitutionalist party are beginning to make headway in convincing our own power base that they have been misled. Perhaps, we should offer up a bill to allow limited drilling for oil and gas offshore and in Alaska, as they have wanted for years. This might bring some of them around and show the electorate that we are trying to do something about the energy crisis and the rising price of oil. "

The president pondered the assessment of his energy czar and added. "If we move quickly, we could throw the Constitutionalists a bone and add some tax credits to purchasers of the alternative sources. That would make them more attractive items."

"But, Mister President, when companies are not making money, cutting taxes on the profits that don't exist will not provide resources for government-run operations. Furthermore, you have advised against any form of tax reduction, which that would be."

"Yes, well, we won't be doing any drilling. I believe we are ultimately going to find it necessary to join some our OPEC and Trilateral Commission friends in putting even more pressure on the U.N. to force Israel to share the wealth of their new energy source. That would elevate my approval ratings and perhaps allow me to push my plan to eliminate presidential term limits through Congress. We'll show the so-call Constitutionalists who is really in charge of this government, and who is the one destined to lead the world. And, as far as Israel is concerned, we aren't going to continue to be the same suckers that we have always been. As much as the United States has given them over the years I just can't understand their refusal to help."

"Mister President, this has just come before the United Nations Security Council and it was found that Israel has no control of who gets use of this new source. It is Jhowah, or God, or Allah, or whatever you may want to call him who says who does and who doesn't get onto the new power grid."

"Well, you're right Chuck. Israel does claim that these extraterrestrials are actually controlling its use."

Just then, the president heard his chief of staff return to the room.

"The Secretary of State is on the phone from Iran, Mister President."

"Very well," he answered, "I'll take it in your office if you don't mind, Dick."

"No problem sir," he answered and watched as the president exited the room.

Aboard Sezan's Starship
Admiral Pazon In Pursuit

"Pazon is gaining on us," Sezan observed as he watched through the stern monitors. "We have to make these SAMSL engines give us more speed. Can you get us out of here any faster?" he asked the navigator. "If you can't we'll be headed for Sheolos by the end of the month and I've never been very pleased with the thought of spending eternity in that place."

The navigator of Sezan's starship had never seen such a degree of concern in his commander's face. "My Lord," he responded, "I can go down and readjust the hydrogen-radiation mixture, but we have to be careful, sir, or it will ignite at an explosive rate and blow us out of the sky."

"Just go do it, whatever it takes. This bothers me. Pazon has never gotten this close. We usually lose him when we hit light speed but they jumped to light speed about the same time as we did, which was good anticipation on their part."

"I believe we stayed a little long over Iran this time when you were there to get me," Samael suggested.

"I know that," Sezan barked back in an angry voice. "We can't relive our mistake now. We have to get ourselves out of here before Pazon gets close enough to take us."

"My Lord," the navigator reported over the comm system, "I am completing my changes here, but I had to increase the radiation containment field. We were getting too much radiation scatter and I was afraid it would reach the bridge. You can try to pick up the speed now if you want to try."

"I'll be happy to do that," Sezan said as he moved to the control panel and hit the button that sent them rapidly out of range of the sensors on Pazon's ship.

"Excellent work," he said as the navigator returned to the bridge. "Now make a ninety degree turn."

"Yes, my Lord," the navigator answered as he made changes to the navigation system.

"Now drop to half standard speed," Sezan ordered.

The starship decelerated rapidly dropping out of light speed. This would assure them that Pazon would pass them and be light years out in front of them futilely searching with his sensors. The navigator turned and was going to the engine room to reset the SAMSL engines mixtures to their normal and safe ratio when Sezan stopped him.

"Before you go, please set course back for Soleus-3."

"Are you sure, my Lord? Admiral Pazon might turn and come back to the area in hopes to find us."

"No," Sezan countered, "I know him well, and I've jousted with him on many occasions. He'll be headed further out thinking we were lost from his sensors due to the increase in our light speeds. Go ahead set the course as I ordered."

"Yes, my Lord," the navigator responded.

"That was too close, Samael," Sezan said. "Let's go to the conference room and see what your meeting with the Iranian president brought forth."

The two Dromedans moved into the room, where Sezan pointed to a chair across the table from Samael for Samael to seat himself. Sezan sat on the edge of the table peering down at him.

"And what do you have to report to me, Mister Samael?"

"We have a real problem on Soleus-3, my Lord."

"What's happening? I thought you had made everyone happy down there," Sezan said as he stood and made his way to a nearby seat.

"No, Jhowah's energy conversion is complete, and its efficiency and affordability are very noticeable not only by all who are using it, but also by those to whom it has been denied. He has gifted them the technology of mobile energy cells, storage units, and the whole technological gamut of primordial energy. It is in use and the Soleans have trained technicians among them who were trained by Reticulum experts to maintain and repair as needed."

"So?" Sezan asked spreading his arms wide. "All of this new non-polluting energy should be appreciated by all of the fossil-fuel-haters down there."

"Not at all," Samael answered. "Jhowah has some complex form of a code system which restricts the users of all modalities of the energy to only those who are in possession of the codes, and he controls who has the codes."

"I guess that does present us a little problem. Doesn't it, my dear Samael?"

"It presents a very large one, my Lord. Since you have assured the Iranians that we are representatives of Jhowah, they demand the same service, but the competition is destroying their sales of crude oil, a product which has given them a rich and luxurious life style. They have used it as their primary source of income for decades. And with the dollars accumulated from the sale of oil, they have been able to buy weapons and have long had influence on the world stage."

"What do you suggest I do, Samael? Can't we find someone who can be paid enough money to defect? It has always worked in the past. If we promise them great wealth and power among their fellowman, these human beings will do almost anything. In the meantime, we are up against Jhowah's demands."

"You have no choice but to see that our friends acquire the energy source. I see no other way. We have the same technology as Jhowah. We can show our friends how to make it work for them."

"Well, that presents a rather sticky problem, doesn't it my friend?" Sezan placed his small fingers against his chin and tapped gently. How was he to go about this new plan without risking capture?

Focusing on trying to set up an energy grid would surely make him more vulnerable. Sezan realized that if Jhowah was in the area, Admiral Pazon and his security starship, Protector, would also be making frequent trips to Soleus-3 region.

"It looks like I need to visit Jahid and instruct him in the expertise of primordial energy production. Let's head back there and you take a trip down to the surface, pick up Jahid and bring him back up. We'll leave the area and I can brief him as we leave the system. Tell the bridge to get us back over Iran, and you prepare a Viper to be ready to leave to pick up Jahid as soon as we get within a reasonable distance of Soleus-3. Pick him up and return as fast as possible."

"Yes, my Lord," Samael answered as he left the room heading for the bridge.

At The Airbase Outside Tehran

"Why are we in such a rush?" Jahid asked as Samael pushed him into the back seat of the Viper-STG Starfighter. Several starfighters were on the starship many millennia earlier when Sezan had commandeered it in his escape from incarceration on his way to the penal planet of Sheolos. He had used them immediately after his escape in his attack on Soleus-3, but had since found them helpful to act as shuttles. However, they were limited in that capability to only one or two occupants.

"Lord Sezan is waiting on us, Mister Jahid, and I have learned not to make him wait around on me," Samael answered.

The Viper rose from the Iranian tarmac and headed for the starship. Sezan was standing on the bridge in front of the forward observation window awaiting their approach.

"Be prepared to leave the system in any direction," he instructed his crew. "I just want us out of here. Pazon just might turn back after he fails to find us in the other direction. I don't want to be here if he returns."

"Samael has landed in the shuttlebay," the communications officer reported.

"Very well," Sezan said, "get us out of here immediately and have them to report to the conference room as soon as they can."

The three met just as Sezan reached the conference room. "Welcome, Jahid, sorry to rush you like this but we need to move things along so we can get your country some of this new energy. Have a seat," he said, extending his hand toward a couple of empty chairs as he took a seat also.

"And why have we been made to wait so long?" The Iranian president asked in a somewhat agitated voice. "The infidels were given the gift and then told to keep it from us."

"That was a mistake," Sezan answered. "Jhowah didn't mean for you to go without it. He sent me back to get you set up also."

The Iranian wasn't buying Sezan's explanation. "We have seven or eight countries that have been refused power from Jhowah's grid and they are all followers of Allah. If Allah and Jhowah are one and the same, why is He making it so difficult for us to get the new power source?"

"He's not. Allowing it to fall into the hands of the Israelis was a mistake, one that we are in the process of correcting. It will take a little more time to get this all handled in the right logistical manner," Sezan said, reaching over and patting Jahid on his shoulder. "And now you'll be able to help your fellow Islamists to get this power source. Allah does not want you and your allies to lose the ground and influence that you have gained over the past few decades."

As they left the Solean star system, Sezan laid out a plan for Jahid and instructed him to gather a group of mechanically and electronically inclined Iranians to be able to come aboard his starship on his return and be trained in the creation, use and maintenance of the new energy grid. After plans were laid

Sezan had the starship set a course and cautiously returned to the space over Iran sending Jahid back home.

"Well that should keep him satisfied for awhile," Sezan muttered as he looked out the window at the planet as it grew smaller. He turned to Samael and smiled.

"Do you not plan to go through with the plans you presented to him, my Lord?" Samael asked, amazed that Sezan was even considering such a thing.

Sezan looked pensively back out the window. "I'm not really sure. He was pretty upset about not being able to get onto Jhowah's grid. I wonder what he might do if I never returned."

"He's just been through a war and lost thousands of soldiers," Samael responded, "and billions of dollars worth of sophisticated war machinery including high-tech jets. He'll probably be very upset."

"Do you think he'll be upset enough to go to war again?" An evil smile adorned the Dromedan's face.

"Well, he knows he can't defeat you, my Lord," Samael reminded him. "He might go to war against the ones he calls infidels but they are the same ones who recently destroyed his army, navy and air force when he attacked them. According to the history of these infidels, they have almost always been the victors when they were attacked. They truly believe that Jhowah is on their side, and the way their wars usually end it seems like he is."

"But Jahid now has seven or eight other countries he just mentioned that he might gather with him as allies. Maybe they could together defeat the infidels and pave the way for us to influence more of the inhabitants of Soleus-3."

"My Lord, where will this all lead?" Samael asked. "These countries, as you have just grouped them all, have been warring for over three thousand Solean-3 years. Now the infidels are truly being backed by Jhowah and are in possession of an inexpensive power grid. They have all of the war machinery confiscated from the Iranians in the recent war. The Iranian told me that they also have an alliance with a group known as *Operation Shield* that is in control of a satellite-based beam weapons system given to them by Jhowah over thirty years ago. Well, it was actually given to the United States when it was under the control of a capitalist government. That government has changed to a socialist nation now, but the leaders back then sent a considerable amount of nuclear and beam weapons to the infidel country, feeling that this very scenario might one day happen. How could they have anticipated the events of these times?"

"You have gathered quite a bit of intelligence, Mister Samael. It does seem like our Iranian leader is between a rock and a hard place, but it is a place that sounds familiar to him. We will see what happens here. All that I desire is that someday I can take over this planet and the project that we started over thirty eight thousand Solean-3 years ago. If the perfect set of circumstances ever develops with Pazon far away protecting the Reticulum planets, I will do away with Jhowah and take my rightful place as the leader of this project.

I have decided - I will let the Iranian leader sit in his squalor. I suspect we might see some action happening sometime in the future. It may be necessary for you to make one more trip to visit him to seal his fate."

Samael looked at Sezan, who was still peering through the window into the blackness of space. What was he thinking? What was his warped mind cooking up now?

Two Weeks Later
Tehran, Iran
December 5, 2015

"Mister Jahid," Samael explained, "Sezan is just unable to get your energy project started right away. He is very distracted right now with other business. Allah has him very busy in Hivania working on the other planets where we are hopeful that you will be able to go when the time is right, the worlds where the seventy virgins await you and your martyrs who eliminate the infidels from the face of the earth. This is the place you know as heaven, and when you and your friends arrive there we want it to be everything that you expect it to be.

I hope you can understand. He has been trying very hard to work your project here into his schedule and he feels that perhaps by next month we can all get together and get something started. Do not worry, my friend, Allah intends for you to have the new energy source."

"Mister Sezan is filling us with lies," Jahid scolded. "I have intelligence that tells me he is Satan, not an agent of Allah as he told my predecessor and as he has let me continue to believe. My information is that he is the enemy of Allah. The anger of my people and those like us in the region has reached its limits. I want Mister Sezan to come here and defend his honor. In fact, I want you to defend your honor today as you sit before me."

Samael's right eye began to twitch and he opened his mouth to speak, but nothing came out of it except a deep sigh.

"So, what do you have to say for yourself, Mister Samael?"

"Your information is erroneous, Mister Jahid. Mister Sezan is very close to Allah."

"I'm afraid that I have the utmost confidence in the people from whom I received this information. I also intend to have Mister Sezan bring Allah here to confirm this relationship. As you know I not only represent Iran when we have these little meetings but the neighboring countries and those from abroad who support our efforts, as well."

"Yes, I understand Mister Jahid but Allah, as you might realize, is so very busy working on a greater plan for you and your Islamic brothers. That is why he may be unable to make the trip here, at least for a while."

"What could possibly be more important than this? I believe that he would do it if he were asked," Jahid suggested, his eyes staring stone hard into the eyes of Samael. "I wonder if it might make it more probable if I were to keep you here as sort of a hostage. Perhaps one of my best air force pilots could learn to fly that spacecraft that brought you here. It would be a great addition to my air force."

As Jahid spoke he rose from his seat on the other side of the table and began to move around the table toward Samael.

"That would not be good," Samael said. He stood up in front of Jahid, raising his hands wide apart and high above his head, vanishing from sight.

"That was a nice trick," Jahid said aloud. "I must get him to show me how to do that next time he is here, if he returns."

Jahid walked over to the window to see if Samael's ship was gone, as well. It was.

At The Gaza-Egypt Border
About Two Miles North of Rafah
Sinai Peninsula, Egypt
December 15, 2015

It was a Monday about noon when a raggedy twenty- to twenty-five foot truck with a tarp covered bed, and appearing probably thirty or forty years old pulled up near a cluster of donkey-drawn hay wagons. The sun was high in the sky, the air dry, and a fine dust still lingered above the road that the truck had traveled. The donkeys, covered with dirt and heads hanging low, stood almost motionless under the heat of the Egyptian sun.

The driver side door was pushed slowly open and an Arab in traditional but tattered body and head wrap stepped onto the running board and then down to the ground. He looked out at the hay wagons and the people with them. He could see the poverty written on their faces. One by one they lined up near the rear of the truck and pushed the hay toward the back of the wagons.

Only moments later the passenger side door of the truck swung open and another Arab, similarly dressed, jumped to the ground and walked toward the rear.

"Hassan, what would you like for me to do to help?" He asked.

"Get inside the truck, Abdul, and slide the crates out to me," Hassan answered with a gruff voice. "I'll help them with the placement in the wagons."

Hassan was a tall, dark-skinned Arab with black curly hair and rugged facial features. His physique was right out of a body builder's book of photos. He was lean with sinewy, well-defined muscles. He had been at this for many years as many as he could seem to remember. It was an endless task, thankless, and with very little pay but enough to help pay his bills.

Abdul began to grab the crates, which were about five feet long and heavy enough to cause him to struggle moving them. He would slide them backward through the opening in the tarpaulin truck cover to Hassan who would help the wagon driver carry them and place them in safe and hopefully unnoticeable positions in the wagons. When each wagon was loaded, the two men would pull the hay over them until they were fully covered and bring up the next wagon.

"That's the last one," Abdul said as he threw back the tarp and stood at the end of the truck bed. "When should I return?"

"I should be back by noon tomorrow." Hassan answered as he reached into the back of the truck and pulled out a full canteen of water and strapped it to his side. "Don't be late; the sun is hot that time of day."

"I will return," Abdul said jumping down from the truck bed and heading to the front of the truck as Hassan reached up and pulled the tarp together, placing a single rope tie to hold it closed while Abdul drove back. When Hassan reached up to make the tie, part of his garment opened up revealing an eighteen-inch-long curved cutlass.

He watched Abdul drive off toward the depot where he would load and return again the next day. Turning his attention back toward the wagons, he walked along beside them stopping at intervals to adjust the hay in the wagons and speak with the drivers. When he reached the front of the hay-wagon line he walked beside the first driver as the rest of the drivers began to lead their animals along an ancient and well-traveled path across a barren flat area. They traveled the path for a couple of hours.

It was a slow and weary trek toward the border and the Gaza Strip. As they neared the border they could see the town of Rafah Gaza on the other side. Several old buildings that looked to be abandoned were just inside Egypt. Hassan guided the caravan in the direction of one of them. When they reached it he walked to a door, which was leaning against the front and off its hinges. He pulled it over and went inside, where he found a broom and swept aside the hay on the wooden floor. After sweeping over a part of the floor, he reached down and pulled open a trap door, and then walked around and opened the other side of what could be seen to be a double door. It was the entry to a tunnel system through which the caravan entered while Hassan went outside. He dragged the door of the building back in place after the last wagon was inside.

Back inside the building, he scattered hay and debris and checked for donkey droppings before entering the tunnel and pulling the trap doors down behind him. The tunnel went down at a rather steep angle for about a hundred and fifty feet and leveled off. The coolness of the ground around them made this the most pleasant part of the journey so far. In about twenty minutes the tunnel turned upward. Hassan soon saw light coming through a crack at the end of the tunnel. He pushed the doors open and they came up inside a large warehouse.

"Welcome to the Strip."

Hassan recognized the person speaking as the agent he had been dealing with for several years. He was a man of few words and a suspicious mind. Once he had been ready to cut Hassan's throat when he thought he had been shorted on a delivery. He was dressed as Hassan in the traditional Arab wrap and was surrounded by workers and weapons of war.

"We are ready for you to inspect the shipment," Hassan instructed him. "I'll return again tomorrow with another one. My helper has gone to reload the truck at the depot. They tell us that you are going to be receiving a much larger than usual shipment. Are you planning some activities larger than you usually do?"

The agent looked at Hassan and didn't answer. It was a hard glare that made him uncomfortable.

"Okay, bring the crates over here as you unload," Hassan ordered the wagon drivers. "I'll open them for inspection."

When he opened the first crate he found it filled with Russian AK-47 rifles. The next one contained long banana clips for the AK-47s filled with ammo. The next crate was filled with Russian 40.6 mm fragmentation grenades. He looked at the Palestinian agent and wanted to ask another question, but he thought better of it when he saw the glare again. In the remainder of the crates, some fifty of them, he saw more grenades, rifles, machine guns, mortars, mortar rounds, and a whole host of handguns and ammo.

"That looks like the last one," he said. "I'll return tomorrow. They said there would be no payment from you."

"True," the Palestinian answered.

Hassan glanced down at one of the crates as he was about to leave. On its side were the words: "Product of Iran."

Outskirts Of Damascus, Syria
December 15, 2015

A World War II "deuce-and-a-half" military truck drove past a group of Quonset hut-type structures inside the airbase abandoned after the last skirmish with Israel. Behind the vehicle was a convoy of jeeps and more trucks, some dragging howitzers. Large gasoline tankers trailed some of the trucks. They all were headed for a large hangar building nearby.

The commander of the group was riding in the "deuce-and-a-half" and he was talking to Damascus Command over the communications network.

"We have reached our destination. We'll get our weapons and support equipment into the hangar before setting up camp here. The old airbase looks pretty good despite having had no care or maintenance for two years and the destruction wielded by Israel during the retreat of the last skirmish." After hanging up his phone he had his driver to pull to the side. He got out and directed the convoy into the hangar.

"Commander, we have a rather large supply of weapons here." It was a captain speaking who commanded one of the howitzer groups who was stating the obvious. "Are we planning an invasion or some similar action any time soon?"

"We are acting on orders from Damascus, Captain. I have been told nothing else but I could speculate, and that would be that this might have something to do with recent military actions by Israel, the developments around this new energy form and the fact that Israel has refused to turn over certain areas to the Palestinians that they were considering to do at one time. These weapons came in from Russia within the past forty-eight hours and we were sent to move them to a safe and accessible location. Here we are. Get back to your post and get this delivery offloaded into a protected location in the hangar."

"Yes sir," the captain answered. He saluted, did an about face and left.

Port City Of Beirut
Dora Terminal

Beside the Russian Cargo Ship Kapitan Konev

"Kaleel, what are you soldiers planning now?" The Lebanese civilian asked as he dismounted from his forklift.

Kaleel, a member of the Hezbollah, turned from his position at the receiving platform.

"Why do you ask?"

"This is a very large delivery, and I have heard there are more weapons on this ship than the small rockets that you usually receive. I even see crates that are large enough for small or medium trucks."

"You had best ignore what you are seeing," Kaleel warned. "I am doing that, and I have no idea what this is all about but it must be something big that is about to happen."

"Kaleel, you had better be careful. If this gets too big America will be getting into it to protect the infidels over in Israel."

"Don't worry about that. They have people running that country now who are one hundred percent behind us. Israel has been on its own for quite a while."

"How could that be, Kaleel? They have supported Israel for decades."

"I don't know. I don't ask questions; I just do what I am told."

Kaleel turned back toward the crane that was lowering a load of crates.

Tehran, Iran
The President Speaks Before The Majles (Parliament)
December 15, 2015

"I come before you today in the presence of the worst economy in the past century. I have asked for the utmost in secrecy and trust from you. For years we have economically thrived on the profits of our abundant supply of fossil fuels.

We have only had to drill and store the crude that comes up from the depths. Sale of this product has enriched our society and vaulted us onto the world scene as a force to deal with. It has allowed us to enjoy the life that Allah has given us as an indication of the one to come.

"Until recent days we have lived without the fear of poverty and with the respect and fear of most nations. We've accumulated great wealth and trusted the New World Order and its banking system to keep it secure and provide us with a reasonable return on our investments. In current times, however, the world's financial collapse has eroded much of the wealth that our country had accumulated. We did not lose it all, because we were alerted by high-ranking officials of the West that they were in the process of orchestrating a financial reversal of the capitalistic government over there. We shifted as much of our wealth to Swiss banks as possible.

"While we do not yet know where some of our money went or who is directly responsible for its disappearance, I have good intelligence that many of the perpetrators were one-time allies of Islamic nations. Others have ties to Israel. And, I have appointed some of the best minds in the world to find what is rightfully ours and return it to us. The infidels will pay a high price for this. Our friends in the U.S. government have questions to answer as well.

"Today, with the world's economy in shambles, we wallow in our own fears while the nation to our east, filled with infidels, has conspired with extraterrestrial beings who claimed to be our Creators and led by one who calls himself Jhowah and claims to be Allah. They have brought to Israel and certain other countries a form of energy that may very well replace our fossil fuels as a desired form of energy. This could make our product obsolete forever. This must be viewed as an act of war. It cannot stand."

Jahid looked around at the members of his Majles and watched their solemn faces sadden more. Before the meeting they had anticipated some positive news that they could carry home, but this was to no avail. Jahid had now confirmed the fears that they all had been realizing in current years.

"We have great things to do," Jahid continued. "It has been said that there will come the end of times, and when that comes, our messiah, the Mahdi, will rise from his veiled location to protect the followers of Allah. There are millions who wait for the time when he will arrive but until he, the Mahdi, believes that the end of times is near he will remain where he is today.

"It is for that reason I have come before you. Those days appear to be not far into the future, but we must not let that time come before we remove the country and nation of Israel from our world. We have been taught by our religious leaders that the very act of destroying Israel will bring Mahdi to our aid. At long last the followers of the Prophet Mohammad and his chosen counsel will rule the world."

The mention of the destruction of Israel brought back painful memories of the last two efforts by their military to attack that country. A quiet chatter began among the Majles members, and was heard by President Jahid who, expecting such a reaction, called out for a verbal response to his plans.

"What is the commotion? Is there a better plan to accomplish the arrival of Mahdi to care for us and give us dominion over others?"

"Mister President, we have twice within the past two years attempted to crush and remove the infidels from our midst, but we suffered greatly during these actions. Should we attempt the same activities again? Some say that Allah may be behind their victories over us."

"It is a different time now, and we are doing it for a more divine reason. Allah will come to our aid. This will not be a simple military action by Iran and our allies. It will be an all-out effort to cleanse the Earth of a scourge that has existed for over four thousand years.

"There are parts of this effort that I cannot disclose to you at this time, but these elements will become clear as we go forth into this, the Mother of all Wars, a Holy War to avenge Ishmael and Hagar and to return us to the type of lives that we have always lived."

"During the last effort on Israel, there was a new weapon that was able to essentially disintegrate jets in mid air and ships on the sea," the same member reminded him. "Also there was no United States intervention needed, but if the severity of our attack is as intense as you are portraying, the U.S. may well enter the conflict."

"No," Jahid responded, "there is no need to even consider such an alliance. We have seen to it. The United States will not be there to help their former allies. Even the Israelis realize that the new regimes over there are more committed to our cause than theirs. We have invested heavily in their political system and have friends in the highest levels of their government. We have great numbers of martyrs living in their cities and in training camps throughout the United States. No, their leaders know what could happen if they raise a hand against us. The events of September 11, 2001, will pale in comparison.

"To add to the immediacy of our dilemma, they, the infidels of Israel, have become more aggressive in their own intelligence efforts during the last several years. They have been without the aid of the U.S. Intelligence services that they had depended on in the past. The Israelis have been very active in their intelligence efforts into our nuclear program. You, of course, know that they failed to stop us except when they hit us with the high-tech Raptor jet. We tried to get the U.S. to prevent that jet from getting into the Israeli air force but there were just enough members of Congress who could not be swayed by our lobbyist and friends in Washington to push the sale through of one of them to Australia, which had also been in line to obtain one of them. The Aussies, then, immediately sold it to Israel. We'll have to deal with them later.

"Our time will come soon and the Mahdi will come to us. I will keep you informed."

Jahid raised his hand in a fist and shouted the Islamic chant, "Allahu Akbar, Allahu Akbar!"

Port Bandar Abbas, Iran
Near The Straits Of Hormuz
Late Evening A Week Later

The setting sun had brought some tolerability to the working conditions at the port facility. The temperature had been one hundred and twenty degrees Fahrenheit and the humidity had been unbearable earlier when the sun was high overhead. During that time of day the port workers would lie on the grass resting from the exhaustion they had experienced even before the heat of the day began.

Mahmud had worked the port for about ten years and had seen many ships offload their contents onto the wharves. Today his curiosity was piqued when a Russian ship arrived alongside. But the first event that caught him by surprise was the sudden arrival of three military jeeps from which a total of twelve armed Iranian soldiers stepped out onto the wharf and moved into what appeared to be prearranged positions to guard the ship as it was being unloaded.

"Ali," he asked of his friend who had worked with him most of his years on the dock, "what's going on?"

"I don't know Mahmud. There must be something of extreme importance on this ship."

The two workers went onto the ship and were shown the part of the load that was to be crane-lifted to the dock below. As soon as they reached out to examine the crates they were stopped by two soldiers who had moved up to watch them as the two went about the preparations to attach the lifting mechanisms.

"Ali, I think we could be in trouble if we get too nosy about these containers."

Mahmud looked at the nearest container, noting how large it was. "I don't ever remember working with something this long and this large, Ali."

"Shut up and get to work," one of the soldiers yelled at them. "I want these containers removed to the dock immediately. There is a long-bed truck that is pulling up as we talk. Place this on the truck bed and we'll have personnel there strap it down. There will be two more trucks arriving behind this one to carry off the remainder of them. Get busy."

"Yes sir," Ali said.

As the two went about their jobs, which they were both well-trained to do, Mahmud noticed an unusual sign on one of the containers that was large but smaller than the rest. He nodded his head toward it so Ali would see it.

"What's that symbol?" He whispered. "It looks a bit like a three-blade propeller."

"That is a bad symbol, Mahmud. It is for some kind of radiation. It would be dangerous if this container were to burst open as we crane it down or if we drop it."

The offloading went along without incident and soon the flat-bed trucks with their loads tied down and covered with tarps were rolling north. Twelve hours later they were being moved into a large, very high, hangar-like building near Sedeh, Iran.

Outside there was a very large rectangular piece of ground that was covered with camouflage netting.

Washington, D.C.
White House The Oval Office
December 22, 2015

"Bob, as my Secretary of Defense what is your understanding of our obligations to Israel when they are under attack by anyone else?"

"There are no contractual obligations, Mister President," he answered. Until Iraq became a democratic country, Israel was the only democracy in the Middle East. Previous administrations believed this to be important for America's interest. The United States has always helped supply them with weaponry because they are located geographically in the midst of those who declare them as infidels and wish to destroy the State of Israel. Many influential Americans have ties with Israel and have put great pressure on previous administrations to support Israel in its struggle to survive as a nation.

We have always voluntarily given them political support but in the last weeks of the George W. Bush administration there were a couple of agreements. One was that the U.S. and Israel would share intelligence; as you might remember this was during the time of the Israeli military drive into the Gaza Strip after seven or eight years of tolerating small and medium rocket attacks by Hamas and the Palestinians. About that same time there was another agreement in which we agreed that Hamas would not be allowed to rearm. This was agreed to only days before Bush left the White House. We have always been committed to ensuring that Israel has the weapons to prevent being overtaken by the radicals and terrorists who are all about them. And, many Jewish people and organizations in the U.S. and throughout the world have raised money and resources for Israel's survival."

"Well, Bob, things have changed. I want you to help me gather a force to be sent to the Mediterranean. Israel has refused to share in the use of the latest alternative energy source even after the matter was presented to the UN and voted on. They have the energy in Australia, but that doesn't seem to matter. The Australians won't share it with us, either. I'm still miffed that the Australians conned us into selling them one of the supersonic Raptor jets and then let Israel have it. We might have to go up against one of our own high-tech aircraft. I just hope our pilots are better than theirs."

"Mister President, what type or size of force do you want and what is our mission? I don't really understand."

"I want at least two of our top carriers loaded with air power and at least thirty-thousand ground troops with the technical and usual supporting infrastructure sitting in the Mediterranean on troop ships within the next two weeks."

"What are our plans, sir? I need to know how to present this to our military commanders."

"You just get the generals and admirals together and tell them that I am their Commander-in-Chief and I want this to happen. No mission is to be stated at this time."

The secretary stood dumfounded before his president, unable to speak and totally in the dark as to what he was about to do other than blindly carry out his orders, and without consultation with the Joint Chiefs of Staff or the consent of Congress."

CHAPTER SEVEN

A GATHERING STORM

Canberra, Australian Capital Territory, Australia
Office Of The Australian Prime Minister
December 24, 2015

"Mister Prime Minister, developing intelligence from London is quite upsetting. They feel there may be a bloody war abloomin' in the Middle East and it may all be based on the lack of distribution of our new power sources." There was a look of deep concern on the face of the governor-general.

"And what is the source of this assessment, mate?" The prime minister asked.

"It comes from multiple sources: satellite photos, some of our people stationed in Washington, Israeli sources and even from an agent that we have in Russia. There has been movement especially within the Islamic countries among the radicals. We hear that the Chiefs of Staff in Washington have been ordered to send a sizable force into the Mediterranean. Our sources tell us that although the admirals of the vessels do not, yet, know their mission, they will be ordered to support possible attacks on Israel."

"This is remarkable; the U.S. has always supported Israel and not supported attacks on them."

"Change has come to the U.S. government," the governor-general said. "The recent administrations have been diametrically opposed to many of the policies of the past, especially those related to relations with Israel and the surrounding Islamic nations despite the radical actions that have involved Israel into relatively recent conflicts."

"True," the prime minister agreed, "but I never thought that they would be involved in an attack on Israel. Mister Governor-General, as much as I hate to suggest this, I feel we should be doing whatever is necessary to support Israel."

"You mean countering the efforts of the United States?"

"I mean doing what's right, mate. That's why we were brought into *Operation Shield* twenty or so years ago."

"Mister Prime Minister," he said, a pensive look on his face, "you are so right. What did you have in mind?"

"Well, we need to get the ADF into the conversation but I believe we'll need to be prepared to wait and watch the developments. I will suggest that we send some of our Adelaide-class frigates and some ground support to be sitting outside the Gibraltar Straits in case they are needed. They shouldn't be obvious and their deployment could be random in such a way that they might not reach the Straits all at the same time. They can be directed to arrive when our Intel suspects an impending attack."

"Agreed, and I am wondering what Jhowah may be thinking as he watches this happening."

"That is a good question. I doubt if this goes along with his wishes as he stated them to us at Bimini. However, I am sure that Metatron is keeping him informed."

The governor-general walked to the office window and looked thoughtfully at the surrounding buildings. He turned and looked back at the prime minister.

"Brian, have you ever read the Book of Revelations? It talks about a battle in which many countries descend on Israel as an act of war, a battle that the Bible calls Armageddon. I wonder how close we are to the End of Times. You hear a lot of talk about it lately, but I guess no one really knows. These next few weeks might turn out to be rather interesting, or should I say frightening."

December 30, 2015
On Board The SSV COMMAND

"Metatron tells me that you have serious business to talk about, Mister Prime Minister. I understand that there is trouble brewing at Israel's borders again. That is why I had you shuttled up." Jhowah looked for an explanation.

"Yes, my Lord, I believe my country to be in grave danger. In the past we have only had to deal with one country or government at a time, but recent information tells me that a conspiracy of many nations is taking place, and even a long-time ally, the United States, may be readying to take up arms against us."

"Yes," Jhowah said shaking his large Hivanian head, "I have been very disappointed in that nation in recent years. They originally were my pattern for future worlds. Trusting in me, their founding fathers placed a constitution in effect that rewarded effort and encouraged those who might fall behind to work and improve themselves. They were also advocates for a moral and peaceful life. I stood behind them in wars and helped to bring a sense of prosperity to their land, but because they have come under the influence of my adversaries they have begun to stray from my laws and there seems to be no effort, at least on the part of their leaders, to return to the ways that made them a great nation."

"I have one ally with a military structure that might be helpful in support of us," the prime minister said bringing the conversation back to his urgent concern. "Otherwise we are open to attack since it is coming from so many directions. There are forces poised at our northern, eastern, southern, and western borders."

Jhowah seemed to be in deep thought as he assessed the problems of the Israeli prime minister.

"How long do you think it will be before they will be attacking you?"

"I am not sure but I suspect it will be within a couple of weeks, my Lord. The activity in the surrounding countries is moving at a fervent pace with arms being brought into Iran in massive numbers."

"I'll be able to give you some help," Jhowah said. "My protector starship that the Reticulum has left with us will be here if I am here, but if Sezan arrives, its priority is this ship, the SSV Command."

"I understand, my Lord. My Australian allies will help also. I have heard from their new prime minister, Brian Cortella. I don't believe any of the other nations know about their support. This is about the only element of surprise that I might have."

"Use it," Jhowah urged. "You have always been a nation close to my heart, and you know that I will be there to help you in every way that I can help. I may even have a surprise ally, who will add much in an effort to assist you."

"I shall do that, my Lord. Thank you for hearing me."

January 10, 2016
Aboard Sezan's Starship

"Has the navigator used the ship's sensors to see if Jhowah, Metatron, or their security ship is anywhere in the region?" Sezan was thinking of his safety.

"Yes, my Lord," Samael answered. "Jhowah doesn't seem to be anywhere around right now. He is very possibly back on Hivania dealing with other duties, but Metatron and the security ship are most probably behind Luna. We'll keep an eye out for him."

"Good, now tell me what you have found out."

"As you know, my Lord," Samael explained, "and considering that, under the present political climate, I am unable to return to the Iranian region, I have nevertheless managed to visit some of the other Islamic nations and the country in the north called Russia. I believe them to be armed and ready to join in the attack on the country that our Iranian friend, Jahid, was so eager to destroy. I believe he will get his chance. I was able to get information that as a result of a relationship with the northern part of a place called Korea, Jahid might have missiles and possess the nuclear weapons to arm them. The missiles should be adequate to reach their objective."

"You bring us excellent news, Samael. If Jhowah is around when it happens, I might take advantage of this conflict to take my rightful position in the project. I'm sure Jhowah will have his attention focused on the Israeli group. I've heard he is a bit partial to them. That will be fine with me.

"Samael, with our sensors and video monitors, do you think we have the capability to check the progress of these nations and see how far along they are with their preparations for war? Do you think we can move into viewable positions?"

"Yes, my Lord, they will pay no attention to us even if they see us. Since Jhowah's first contact, the world accepts that what they have called UFOs in the past are now identified and not worthy of too much curiosity."

"Then let's do it."

Samael moved with Sezan to the bridge where they had access to the monitors and control of the sensors.

"Take us over the eastern border of the country called Syria," Sezan ordered, "but stay alert for Jhowah's ship and its shadow ship, the Protector."

They watched as their monitors and sensors found explosives in the midst of a large number of military vehicles. Most were trucks and jeeps, but there was a long line of medium-caliber howitzers with many neatly stacked piles of shells beside each of them that were capable of reaching a significant distance into Israel. Back behind the howitzers was a tent city capable of housing tens of thousands of personnel who could be howitzer teams as well as infantry or other combat troops.

"Now let's move over Iran in the area where they used to have missiles," Samael suggested.

"Excellent," Sezan replied.

As they moved out the navigator found an unexpected sensor reading in a very unpopulated desert region of Syria.

"I'm getting sensor readings that indicate nuclear material located under the sand beneath us," he noted.

Sezan thought for a moment and a twisted smile came to his face. "Yes, I remember that an earlier regime in the country of Iraq buried nuclear material out here to get it away from some of the inspectors from the United Nations group. No problem here. Move on out to Iran. If necessary, we can show them a few tricks on how to use this cache of nuclear material against the so-called infidels."

"Yes my Lord," the navigator replied as he began to search the surface for evidence of the missiles near Sedeh that Samael had heard of in reports, missiles that been replaced after the attack earlier by a Raptor jet during preemptive strikes by Israel.

"There they are, and the sensors are picking up nuclear radiation from inside that area," the navigator called out.

Sezan smiled and looked at Samael. "This could get interesting," he said. "Get out over the large sea to the west of Israel and let's see what's going on out there."

As Sezan's starship moved out over the Mediterranean there was noticeable military and naval activity in the eastern region of the sea.

"Look at that," Sezan said, chuckling as he pointed toward the gathering of the navies of many nations that were converging on Israel, obviously poised for a huge offensive action. "This is hard to digest. It's been sixty or so years since I have seen such an armada. Many of those ships are from superpowers."

"This is what the world has come to, my Lord," Samael informed him. "Our presence and influence has been effective. Over the millennia, the allegiances to Jhowah and his teachings have slowly turned to us. His teachings had been the dominant force in the codes, laws and canons of many people.

Some have referred to him as God, some as Jehovah, and many call him Allah, but all have encompassed the commandments that he laid down several thousand Solean years ago into their own legislature and laws.

"In recent years these rules or commandments have come under attack by our activist friends, who worked their way into different religions and high-ranking positions within governments throughout the planet. Many have made their own rules and attracted large groups of followers. There used to be ethics among the politicians and leaders of all nations, but they have also been altered.

"Down there are many ships of many nations but the one country I have been most surprised to see is the United States of America. It was once a mighty nation that trusted in the sovereignty of the individual and gave them the freedoms that they were born with. They were once a country that had little tolerance for us and those who supported us. In recent years, all that has changed. They have now become a nation of pawns who are literally controlled from a central government that takes their fortunes and uses them to run government programs that seem most interested in controlling every aspect of its people's lives.

"They gave up their civil rights without much of a fight and are almost like slaves. Only a couple of decades ago they were the richest country on the planet, had the most powerful military, and controlled their own destinies. Today, the country operates more like a dictatorship. It is essentially owned by China, which bought much of its debt during the financial crisis of 2009 and 2010. Its currency has been devaluated and inflated to the extent that the world no longer recognizes it as the standard by which all other currencies are measured. Its leadership seems to be campaigning for an even more global agenda.

"I am amazed that the population was so eager to give up their freedoms and become a second-class nation." Samael shook his head. "The black population fought with their very lives for their freedom in the sixties, and now they eagerly throw themselves into a socialist enslavement from which they may never escape. The country has lost its superpower status. Even so, it still has enough military might to be a force in world affairs. We can be thankful that they have come over to our side."

"Well, Samael, what do you think I have been up to all these years? From the very beginnings of the creation of Soleus-3 I have worked toward shaping the destiny of these people to be under my leadership. Jhowah caught on to my plans sooner than I had expected, and with the aid of the courts of the Reticulum Alliance had me ostracized from our society. His efforts were quite successful. If it were not for my successful escape, that would have been the end of me.

"I like it, Samael. This situation that is developing is very possibly my chance to take over the Solean-3 project as I intended to do so many thousands of years ago. These are my creations, too. I am pleased to see them coming together to destroy the country named Israel, the race Jhowah calls His 'chosen people.' They are 'chosen' alright, chosen to be wiped off the face of the planet. Yes, I like it."

The Same Day
Tel Aviv
Office Of The Prime Minister

"When will the U.S. president be ready for our teleconference?"

"He is about to come online now," the prime minister's assistant answered.

"Excellent, I need some answers to all of the intelligence that is coming in. I can't tell rumors from fact."

"Mister Prime Minister," the president said as the teleconference opened up, "I hope you are feeling well today. Please forgive the video. We're having a few technical problems here. We'll have to do without it for now. What can I do for you?"

The United States president was a congenial and very well-spoken individual who had made little effort to help Israel, and the prime minister knew it. He could probably care less about speaking to the prime minister. As for video technical problems, this was hardly true from such a high-level office, especially one that depended on the use of such technology during every address to the masses. This could very well be an effort to avoid betrayal by his body language. The prime minister was known to be well-trained in the interpretation of body actions and movements during conversations and speeches.

"Mister President, I'm sorry that we have not had any closer relations than we have had these past few years. I have often questioned members of my Knesset regarding our loss of contact."

"I'm sure it is related to the stress and incessant duties that they throw upon both of us, Mister Prime Minister. I would like to get to the point of our conference, though, and see what problems you might be having."

That is a very abrupt and impersonal response to my statement, the Israeli thought, *not what I would expect from a leader with such charisma and communicative skills that have been praised to such a high degree.*

"Yes, Mister President, it has come to my attention during the past few days that many of the countries surrounding us are building their arms and air power. This seems not to be in the usual defensive fashion but more in the form of plans for an eminent offensive action. Are you aware of any such efforts?"

"I've heard some talk of war games in the works, but I do doubt any overt military actions are being planned by any of them. They may be all cooperating over there in a larger than usual war game strategy."

"Mister President, is your country participating in any of these games? I have reports that ships flying U.S. flags are part of the armada anchored off our shores."

"As you may have learned about me and my people, Mister Prime Minister, we abhor war. I have pledged to change the world and make it a more peaceful place for people of all nations."

"I'm not sure of your answer, Mister President. Is that a Yes or a No?"

A video feed would have been quite revealing at this time but there was enough strain in the president's voice for the prime minister to know that his first response was veiled to avoid giving away the truth.

"Mister Prime Minister, war games are just what the name suggests: war games. Many years ago in my country there was a saying, 'Loose lips sinks ships.' If I give away any of our possible participation in this effort, it might affect the outcome. So, I am not at liberty to answer that question."

"Yes, Mister President, I do understand. Is there any other information that you are aware of that might be of benefit to us?"

"No, I don't believe so," the president answered. "It has been nice talking with you. I've been hearing good things about you since you came into office from your liaison here in Washington. I hope we can get together soon. We must make plans."

"Yes, Mister President, we should do that. Thank you for your time."

As the conference ended a click could be heard and silence followed that was broken loudly as the prime minister slammed down his fist against the table shaking the blank video monitor violently.

"Damn," he exclaimed. "That narcissistic socialist liar couldn't tell the truth if he had to. That cinches it. The U.S. is against me also. The reports of their ships off our coast are real. And, they aren't there to protect us. I hope Jhowah is watching all of this. I pray that he will come to our aid."

"Get me on the phone to our defense minister immediately," he ordered to his assistant and only moments later he reached out and took the phone.

"I have talked with the U.S. president and his response has confirmed our concerns. I feel sure that we are being surrounded by a heavy offensive buildup on land and that there are ships from Russia and the United States moving into position in the Mediterranean that are fully armed with jets, missiles, and manpower. What our intelligence has learned is that we are not, I repeat, not witnessing war games. We must make preparations to defend ourselves. This battle will not be a battle like the last two incursions by the Iranians and their radical Islamic friends in Gaza and Lebanon. This will be a battle for our very survival as a people and we are greatly outnumbered."

"The U.S. is actually joining them?" The defense minister asked in amazement.

"Yes, from his response to me and from my Intel from *Shield* I am quite sure of it. The only superpower that might not be against us is China. I'm not sure of that, but we have Australia as a committed ally in this. I don't yet know where the British stand. If there is any silver lining it is that we have Almighty God, Jhowah, in our corner.

"I want you to be sure that we have all of our radar units, both the X-band and the Green Pine systems, online and covering all points of the compass. Make sure *Operation Shield* is tied into our reception from the radar units. I want special attention on Iran. We've been convinced that they have their nuclear missile silos repaired and armed again, probably with help from Russia. Jahid is quite eager, I'm sure, to send one of those nuclear birds our way."

"Yes, Mister Prime Minister, right away."

The Israeli leader returned the phone to its cradle. As his hand remained on it, he thought: How would he protect his beloved Israel? Never before had they been so outnumbered by so many nations, at least not in recent history. He was reminded of the battle of Masada, where his great ancestors had withstood the Roman legions for longer than anyone believed was possible. He was in hopes that Jhowah would not allow the upcoming battle to end as did the one at Masada.

The most perplexing turn of events in the current challenge was that, of all countries, the United States was siding with Israel's enemies. It was a country that Israel had relied on for support for decades. Now they were being led by a different group or type of people than before. Now, should it become necessary, even the Australians were ready to defend Israel against their American allies. The United States was clearly caught up in political change. It was betraying all of its old friends. What a different world it was! How could this have happened? He clasped his hand into a fist.

One Week Later
Aboard The USS Gerald R. Ford
Somewhere In The Mediterranean

"Captain Johnson, have you opened our orders yet?"

"No, Commander Mayer, I have been given a specific time and place where I'll be doing that, but I assure you that you will be at my side when I do. That's why I invited you into my cabin for coffee."

"Thank you sir," Adam Mayer replied, smiling at his commander who was seated across the table from him with cup in hand.

This was the first military mission for the USS Gerald R. Ford, itself the first in a new class of carriers for the U.S. Navy. It was commissioned in 2013 and was planned as one of three carriers of this new class to eventually replace the older Nimitz-class carriers as they were deactivated. Construction of the other two carriers had been stopped and their completion canceled by the current administration in Washington. Their explanation was that newer VTOL jets, such as the F-35, would have the capability of vertical lift-offs and landings and would not require a runway. This would allow for a much larger number of planes on the carrier, making it unnecessary to construct any more of this new class than the Gerald R. Ford.

Commander Adam Mayer was a rising star in the U.S. Navy, having been placed as next in command to Captain Grayson Johnson on the USS Gerald R. Ford. Mayer had been instrumental in directing the improvement of the nuclear converters that powered the Navy's aircraft carriers and several other craft. The nuclear plant that powered the Gerald Ford was his most prized accomplishment.

The ship's crew had been on shore leave and the ship had been in dock at Norfolk, Virginia, where it was undergoing routine maintenance and having a few minor repairs when orders came from Washington to proceed to the Mediterranean at top speed. They were to be accompanied by the Nimitz-class carrier USS Ronald Reagan. Both had a full complement of aircraft. The Ford was carrying two F-22A Raptors along with F-16s and the newer vertical take-off jets. Only a few Raptors were constructed before the administration and Congress of 2009 cancelled construction.

"I wonder why they needed us over here so fast," Mayer said. "I know this whole area has been at war for, some say, three thousand years, but it usually is something that is handled here and usually by Israel."

"Maybe they just want us to make a show of force, Adam; after all, this is the most advanced carrier in the world and I'm sure it might make these smaller countries have second thoughts about attacking."

"I hope you're right, Captain," Adam confided. "I am Jewish and I would like to see situations like this to be ended rapidly. I have family living southwest of Nazareth and I tend to worry about them when the Hamas or Hezbollah start acting up."

"I can see where you would. Family is family, especially with them being so far from you. Perhaps we'll know more as we open the orders. A few minutes shouldn't matter," he suggested as he walked over to a cabinet, opened it and then turned the combination lock on a safe inside. Reaching inside the safe he pulled out an envelope and took out the piece if paper from inside it.

"Now we shall know, my young commander," Captain Johnson said with a smile on his face as he opened the orders. When he looked at the paper his smile melted as he read. He looked up at his next in command, then back at the orders with a look of alarm.

"Damn them," he said. "What the hell has happened to our country?"

"What's wrong, sir?"

"Adam, you won't believe this. The commander-in-chief, through the chain of command, is ordering us to anchor in the Mediterranean off the Gaza Strip in support of an all-out attack on Israel."

"What! But Captain, those are my people. I can't fight and possibly kill my own people, my own family. It is my religious heritage. As much as I love the United States, I cannot be a part of an assault on the nation of Israel." The young commander's voice almost broke as he considered the implications of the orders.

"I understand, Adam. Let me talk with someone and see what this is all about. I would never have predicted this in a thousand years. I knew the current administration was anti-military and had sympathies toward the radical Muslims, but this makes no sense at all to me. What could they be thinking? We have very little time to work something out. These orders indicate that something will be happening soon, maybe within the next couple of days."

Adam Mayer stood before his commander with a tear on his cheek. "I must go to my people, Captain."

"I know, Adam, and if there is any way, I'll get you there. Israel has always been our friend and I just can't understand these orders. What is the world coming to? Could we be witnessing Armageddon? Is it possible that you and I will be part of conducting the final war of the world as adversaries? I have some decisions to make. I'll get back to you as soon as I can."

Later

About ten thirty that evening Adam Mayer was in his quarters sitting at his desk trying to deal with the orders that his captain had read to him earlier when the door opened and Johnson came in shutting the door quietly behind himself.

"Adam, don't ever tell anyone what I'm about to do for you. If you do, I'll deny every word of it, and don't ask how I did it."

Captain Johnson leaned forward and put his hand on Adam's shoulders looking him in the eye. "You have a big and quick decision to make, Adam. In ten minutes an Israeli fishing trawler will be pulling alongside the Gerald R. Ford. The captain of the trawler will wait 20 minutes and if you aren't on board he will leave. If you choose to go he will take you and help you get ashore near Haifa. There you will be met by someone from Israeli intelligence who will carry you to your family near Nazareth."

"But, Captain," he replied as he rose from his desk chair, "how..."

"No, Adam, don't ask. My career is on the line and I don't want to leave any information around that might destroy it. What I am doing is not right, at least not according to military rules or regulations, but I would hope it would be judged right in God's eyes. I am doing this because I have serious misgivings about what is happening in my country."

"Thank you, sir. I'll be there and I thank you for what you have done. I imagine I'll lose my commission, no matter what, but my own relationship with God, and doing what is right in his eyes are more important to me than a military position."

"Adam, I believe that if you contact the Israeli military you could find that you might fill a redeeming position in the Israeli Navy."

A smile cleared the serious expression on the young commander's face as he took his captain's hand and shook it, and then he took one step backwards and delivered a short and snappy salute which was returned by the captain.

"Good luck. And God's speed, Adam."

"Thank you, sir. I hope we meet again someday and not as adversaries. I believe I need to pack up a few things real quick. I'll leave all of my navy clothes for the next man who gets the job."

"Don't leave your shoes, Adam. I don't think I could get anyone to fill them as well as you."

The Next Day

It was still early in the morning and quite cool as Adam walked up to the door of his paternal Uncle David's small house near the Jezreel Valley. The sun was not yet up but he could see a light coming from the kitchen window as he reached up and knocked on the door.

"Who is that at this ungodly time of the morning?" He heard from behind the door. It was a woman's voice.

"It's me," he answered.

"And who is me?" she barked as she jerked open the door with a look of anger on her face that changed rapidly to a grin when she saw him. She opened her arms.

"Adam Mayer, what are you doing outside my door this early in the morning?"

"I heard my Aunt Sarah was about to disinherit me and I didn't want to lose all that money." Adam took her in his arms and gave her a loving hug.

"Where is Uncle David?"

"He's in Nazareth and might possibly have to travel to Tel Aviv. There has been talk of more war. Take a seat, Adam, and let me fix you some coffee." Sarah gestured toward a seat at the table and went to fix him a cup.

"It's more than talk, Aunt Sarah," he said as he sat down. "I'm not here on a simple family visit. I had to leave my ship during the night and I was able to get here through Haifa with the help of an Israeli intelligence agent. When I left my ship it was loaded with the most technologically advanced instruments and jets in the history of the world. Our orders were to anchor off the Gaza Strip and support an all out-attack on Israel. I don't know what other countries are involved but as only a support group we brought along two carriers and many thousands of troops and support personnel. I saw Russian military ships as we approached through the Mediterranean, and they aren't usually around to protect Israel. They were also armed to the hilt."

"My God, Adam, we need to get this information to your Uncle or someone who can get it to Tel Aviv."

"The agent who helped me get here will do just that, Aunt Sarah," Adam assured her. "I think it would be best if I stayed with you until we hear from Uncle David. After that I need to get to Tel Aviv and see what I can do to help."

"I can't believe America is about to be at war with us. We have always depended on it so completely. What has happened to it?"

"In recent years," he explained, "they have elected governments that lean far to the left and with ties to extremists of all types, possibly even to radical Muslims. Well, you see the results. The olive doesn't fall far from the tree.

"I have elected to leave, give up my career and, if you'll have me, I'd like to make Israel my home."

"We certainly will have you, and we wouldn't have it any other way. I wish your parents were alive to see you now, Adam. They would be so proud."

Jhowah's Conference Room On SSV COMMAND
In Stationary Orbit Behind Luna
January 19, 2016

"Metatron, when was your last contact with Prophet?"

Jhowah and Metatron were seated in the conference room discussing the events taking place on the surface of the planet below.

"I spoke with Prophet only yesterday, my Lord. He is still monitoring and policing the use of primordial energy and reports that Israel, Australia, and the other smaller countries on the new energy base are reaping the economic and environmental rewards of such an inexpensive and convenient energy source.

"We haven't seen the kinds of leadership coming out of Soleus-3's shadow government, the Illuminati, which we had wanted. We had hoped that following my visit to them, they would see the error of their ways and help bring stability to the planet. Although they seem to have enough power to influence the decisions of the planet's superpowers, they are bent on destroying the countries that possess primordial energy technology and protecting their assets.

"There is still discontent among those countries that are not a part of the ones who are authorized to use the new energy form. Many are beginning to question if the Illuminati group has somehow confiscated the fortunes that many countries had accumulated over the past century. A lot of Soleans, and governments, are missing huge sums of currency. And, no one seems to be able to explain where it went."

"What of the rumors of global war that we have been picking up?" Jhowah asked. "I had the prime minister up here recently and he was in fear of a war with severe consequences for his country."

"It seems that since the Israeli prime minister last talked to you there has been an even greater build up of offensive forces in the area." Metatron was pessimistic. "I believe that another great war such as occurred on Soleus-3 in the 1940s is about to happen, but all forces seem to be directed at Israel which is as an island surrounded by many Islamic nations with many radical and extreme elements. What would be different with this war is that Soleans have now developed the capability to destroy not only those they consider enemies, but themselves and everything else on the planet."

Jhowah shifted to a familiar topic. "Have we heard from Sezan recently? This should fit right into his plans for an attempt to remove us and take control of the Soleus-3 project, assuming there would be anything left for him to rule. The last I heard was that he was having difficulty keeping the allegiance of the Iranian leader and his allies."

"My Lord, Sezan seems to slip down to the surface and leave just as clandestinely as he arrives. I believe he may be leaving his emissary on the surface to deal with those on Soleus-3 who have chosen to trust him, but more recently they seem to be rebelling at his inability to assist them. There is growing concern that high-ranking American officials are in close contact with Sezan and his disciple, Samael."

"Do you think Sezan is playing a very large part in the offensive build up around Israel, Metatron?"

"Not directly, but I have learned that he has met with the self-anointed One World Government Group, the Bilderbergs, and tried to convince them that he can give them what they want. He is using their influence to get what he wants. When the action that appears to be about to occur begins, he will get right into the middle of the battle to assure himself that those loyal to him will be victorious."

"We will have to be sure that he will not be able to do that," Jhowah said. "We have to display a show of force that the people of Soleus-3 have never seen. Perhaps the only way to keep them from destroying themselves is to strike fear into the hearts of every nation. The challenge will be dealing with those radicals who follow Mohammad's teachings. We have to convince them that dying to destroy the planet will not gain them the afterlife that they were promised by their religious clerics. We must also make them understand that I am God and I am Allah. They need to know that I do not approve of this so-called jihad agenda. The radicals will refuse to believe it, but those who believe in the true Allah will understand. We can deal with the extremists later."

Damascus, Syria
The Same Day

The Syrian leader stood before OPEC.

"I have called together the leaders of all of our OPEC nations to determine the status of our planned action against Israel. As best I can tell from my location here, you are all prepared to strike. The greatest concern we have all had is whether or not the superpowers might take up arms against us in order to protect Israel.

My last briefing by both the Russian and U.S. ambassadors were quite acceptable. We expect a total support from both of them; in fact, they are already in position to support our attack. There is a question with regard to China's involvement but even though we aren't sure of its support we have been assured that it will not interfere with us, which in a way, is support. And, with the breakdown in the United States-British alliance, and the numbers of martyrs we have moved into their country, and the destruction and death that they are capable of causing, the UK has essentially been neutralized.

I'm confident that the British will not interfere with our actions and create more conflict. They have enough going on within their country."

Tel Aviv
The Next Day
Office Of The Israeli Prime Minister

"We are ready for them, Mister Prime Minister." The voice on the phone was from the general in command at *Operation Shield*. "Only time will tell if we will be able to handle the numbers that are amassed to attack us. We have good responses from our satellites and yesterday we test-fired the beam weapons at dummy targets. They were all direct hits. We plan to take them offline tomorrow for a period of no more than thirty minutes to make some final adjustments to our transmitters that will correct a few small errors that we found yesterday in our tests and after that, let them come."

"Excellent, General, our lives and the very existence of the State of Israel hangs in the balance, perhaps even more. Please contact me when your adjustments are completed."

The Next Day
Near Sedeh, Iran

The desert like land just above Sedeh, Iran, was heating up under the January sun. A lizard scurried across the ground seeking a safe place to rest and warm in the sunlight. Sedeh, located about a hundred and fifty miles northwest of Shiraz, Iran, was just waking for a new day.

As the lizard scampered it stopped and stood still in its tracks, its tympanic membrane alert to a rumbling sound building in the distance.

Suddenly a rectangular piece of ground nearby, three hundred feet wide and about two thousand feet long with a small metal building at one corner, began to move. Inside the building was located a disk-shaped control booth manned by one Iranian soldier. As he worked the controls, the piece of ground raised slowly from one side. As it rose, like a lid on a box, hydraulic lifts could be seen under it pushing it upward. The controller, in his chair in the disk like control unit, remained in a normal upright position as the disk rotated on a pivot under the pull of gravity.

Soon it was standing in a perpendicular position and the Iranian controller could be seen sliding down a ladder in the rear of the control unit to the ground below and moving quickly to a near-by truck covered with camouflage netting. He removed the netting, threw it into the back of the truck, and drove quickly away from the site.

The open area revealed at least three silos that had been beneath the covering lid. They were now open to the sky, and showing the gleaming tips of the metal of the nuclear warheads mounted on the rockets positioned within them.

A blaring sound came from speakers positioned on the underside of the upright cover that alerted anyone who happened to be nearby that a launch was about to occur.

Soon the deep rumbling sound began to build and the ground shook so much that the lizard had to squat lower on its abdomen in order to stay upright. The sound became louder as smoke began to boil out from one of the silos and the rocket inside began to rise, moving slowly at first then accelerating as it gained altitude.

Many of the people of Sedeh looked outside and saw the long column of smoke trailing from the missile that had begun to arc gently toward the west. Its destination would be the beginning of a historical battle that had been prophesized many millennia in the past.

Tel Aviv
Moments Later

Residents outside the city of Tel Aviv heard a sound and looked up to see a gleaming missile. For many it was the last image to reach their minds because suddenly there was a flash high in the sky above the capital and its many government buildings. It was followed by an ominous mushroom-shaped cloud that grew larger and larger. An act of barbarism and genocide was occurring. Those who had lived there had read and experienced over the years many acts of hate such as this but none to this degree of modern destructive force. It was an act so severe that it could, potentially, equal in destruction of life, the combined death total occurring in Nagasaki and Hiroshima in 1945. Beyond immediate death, it would likely maim and leave internal bodily changes that would ultimately kill millions.

Operation Shield Headquarters
Near The Jezreel Valley
Not Far South Of Nazareth
Deep Under The Mound Called Har-Megiddo

"General, we are about to complete the adjustments on our satellite uplink. You may want to advise the prime minister." The general was working near his desk on a map hanging from the wall as the captain reported to him.

"Get his office on the phone."

The conversation was immediately interrupted by a strong shaking of the ground beneath them. The general had to grab for the wall to keep from falling. His grip took hold of the map he had been using. As he fell, the map went down with him.

"What the hell was that? Have we been hit?" he asked.

"Sir, our seismograph is recording heavy activity centered in the region of Tel Aviv. It is still rising, so I can't give you an estimate of the strength yet. It must be an earthquake."

"Okay, Captain, get me the prime minister's office on the phone," the general ordered.

Moments later the captain returned.

"General, I can't make contact with his office and we had a contact call in saying that there was a nuclear explosion over Tel Aviv."

"My God, our entire government has been attacked and if that was a nuclear device, our prime minister is no longer. The Knesset may have time to get to their underground shelter in Jerusalem but due to the radiation they will have to be there for quite a while before they can be taken out."

"Sir, there is a call from the prime minister on the phone."

"Give it to me," the general ordered reaching for it. "Mister Prime Minister, are you all right?"

"Yes, General," he answered. "Our radar groups saw right away what was happening and contacted us soon enough for my office personnel and me to get into the underground bunker. We are ten stories below Tel Aviv and we are all set up and ready to lead us out of this mess. I want to get an immediate alert to Jhowah. He said he would help if we were attacked. It came out of Sedeh, Iran. They said they would do it and they did."

"I'm sure the sensors on the Command have already picked up the explosion and the radiation, but I'll send an alert to him anyway."

"Very well, we'll be looking out for him. This was the first strike of a war that could leave deep physical scars on the face of our country and also in minds of our people. We nor the universe in which we exist can allow the enemy to win."

Immediately after he stopped speaking the Shield facility began to shake and the floors rolled much stronger than they had when the nuclear explosion occurred over Tel Aviv.

"Mister Prime Minister, our enemies are many. May God be with us."

"General, he is and he always will be. He has assured us of that, and he has assured me personally."

CHAPTER EIGHT

THE WAR BEGINS

January 25, 2016
Aboard The SSV Command
Jhowah On The Bridge

"Mister navigator, please take us down to a position near enough to the surface to get an idea of what humanity is doing to itself. The way I understand *Shield* is that a strong nuclear weapon has been exploded over the city of Tel Aviv where the Israeli government offices are located and another over Har-Megiddo. Call Metatron to the bridge; he talked with *Shield*."

"Yes sir," the navigator responded to Jhowah. "There are definite sensor readings of nuclear radiation from that city, my Lord, and from Har-Megiddo."

"This is an event that I have known would occur since the beginning of our Soleus-3 project," Jhowah said. "I have dreaded for this day to come. We are about to witness the breakdown of the human civilization as has been predicted in all the messianic prophesies to these people. We need to prevent it if possible.

"Let's study our monitors and sensors of the area for awhile and see what the situation is. Can you make out the results of the nuclear strike on the city?"

"Yes sir," the navigator answered. "There is considerable damage and the life signs are weak. It leads me to believe there could certainly be a lot of death and many injured individuals down there. This doesn't even consider the long-term effects of the radiation that will be sickening and killing most of those around the city that survived this initial blast, and -- if it was a high-grade bomb - these effects will be happening for some time to come. That's a nasty dirty weapon that they used, even in its purest form. This will make the Holocaust look like an accident. Sir, I wonder what happened to the Israeli prime minister?"

"He made it into his underground bunker," Metatron said as he came onto the bridge. "He is safe and is readying his defenses to respond but the same type explosion took place over the *Shield* location as he was talking with the prime minister. Their facility is well protected also. They are many stories underground, and they're located, my Lord, just south of Nazareth where your son grew up."

"I know the area very well," Jhowah added. "I monitored it closely while he lived there. What does the sea beside Israel look like?"

Jhowah's large black eyes scanned the monitors and the sensor panels with deep concern. His project for the creation of a new being to be permanently added to the universe seemed to be disintegrating rapidly. The centuries-long efforts by his project personnel (the beings that the Creations called "angels") were at risk.

"Metatron, we can't let all of our work be lost. We must at least salvage the faithful among them."

"Yes, my Lord, humanity has come a long way. And, there are many among them who have evolved to the point where they can be taken to Hivania or another one of our planets if we desire. We have to save the ones who have lived their lives on Soleus-3 as we have directed. We have too much invested in the experiment to just let them destroy themselves."

"The explosions have started movement among the invading fleets down there, my Lord," the navigator informed him. "I can make out many ships but most of them are from only two countries."

"That would be Russia and the United States," Metatron reminded Jhowah. "I would have never thought that those two countries would have allied themselves against Israel especially the United States. I wonder if our gift of the primordial energy helped to form this unexpected alliance."

"No, it was developing several years before we set up our power grid," Jhowah told him. "We saw the possibility of this alliance from the very beginning, but we gave them a chance to choose a different destiny. The people of the United States, instead, chose leaders who changed what their founding fathers had created. The *new* government has refused to recognize and include me. They have sided with Sezan's emissaries. Now, they must pay the consequences of those choices."

Jhowah studied the large carriers and troopships with soldiers from the two superpowers. The carriers were filled with jets with advanced technology for satellite communication and were armed with the latest laser-controlled missile weaponry.

"These carriers from the U.S. are set to do considerable damage to whomever they might attack. That larger ship has some of the newest jets on this planet."

"Those new high-tech jets are called Raptors, my Lord," Metatron informed him.

"Unless we stop it, this battle will be like no other we have witnessed on Soleus-3. Let's lower the Command to about two hundred yards above the two fleets and hover," Jhowah ordered. "Once we get there, if you will activate the SAMSL engines and let them run unengaged, it will release a broad and very intense electromagnetic frequency that will neutralize all electrical power in these ships along with their main engines, including the power to the jets and the firing mechanisms to the weapons on the aircraft and ships."

Soon the engine room reported, "We are in position and the SAMSL engines are active and disengaged."

"Keep them running," Jhowah said. "The naval fleets should now be dead in the water and we will keep it so until we get this hostility under control."

On Board The Gerald R. Ford

"Captain Johnson," his next in command advised, "I'm getting runners from the lower decks reporting that we are suddenly without power after that massive space vessel settled over us. Even our guns are without the ability to position or fire. Outside, it is as though a massive dark cloud had suddenly appeared in an otherwise clear and sunny sky. There's not a computer that is working on this ship and I suspect that it is the same for the rest of the fleet, but we have no communication with them to know."

Johnson looked out from the ship's bridge at the deck of his ship and up at the huge triangular craft above that was so large that it blocked out the sun from ninety percent of the American and Russian fleets.

"This loss of power means that the jets can't fly or fire their weapons either," he said.

"Yes sir," the commander agreed, "we are unable to participate in the attack and we are even unable to send out any communications or even a small emergency craft to report our problems to the leaders in Gaza, which is less than a half mile from us."

"Why is that?" He asked.

"The rafts are powered by a simple outboard motor. They have been working fine but we still have to get the spark plugs to spark to make them go. Even they are without electrical energy. All we can do is sit here."

"As much as I would like to see that happen, Commander, I have been given orders to participate in the attack. We can't just sit here. I'm sure that something about that ship above us is blocking our power," he said. "I've read that about UFOs since I was a child."

Johnson reached for the ships intercom trying to make contact with the ship's chief engineer. After two attempts he realized the futility and slammed the mike back in its cradle and turned to one of the bridge personnel.

"Get down to engineering and ask the chief if he can create some form of lead shielding to mount over the motor of one of our emergency rafts? We need to see if we can block the neutralizing effect of that space vehicle that is floating above us. If that works, we can get word over to Gaza and let them know our predicament."

In a few minutes the chief sent word topside that it worked. The outboard had cranked immediately after he created the lead bonnet.

Aboard SSV Command

"My Lord, there is a small raft like vessel coming out from the big carrier and headed for land," the navigator reported. "I wonder how they make it go."

Jhowah studied the craft through the monitor. "He has a lead sheeting cap over the power plant," Jhowah explained. "It seems that we created some intelligent beings down there. The lead cap is blocking the neutralizing EMF waves originating from our SAMSL engines."

He shook his large head and chuckled. "But, I believe we can send him back to his ship before he can make it to land. Open the exhaust stream from the SAMSL engines and direct it in a constant, widely splayed burst between the small boat. No, between all of the ships and the Gaza shore."

The crew configured the exhaust and began the continuous release. As the stream flowed out into the sea below it began to create a long trough in the water that continued to deepen as the stream persisted. Within a few minutes there was a large linear water trench that was so deep that it exposed the sea bottom.

"Jhowah," Metatron reminded, "This is giving you the same effect as the parting of the Red Sea for Moses."

"Yes, that is the plan. I don't think he'll have the courage to try to get across that."

They both smiled as they watched the occupants of the raft stop and stare ahead at the deep trench in the sea. Realizing the hopelessness of their efforts, they finally turned and maneuvered the small craft back to the ship.

"Metatron, we have this part of the invasion under control, but the other participants in this attempted genocide are beginning to prepare themselves for a multi-country and multi-faceted attack on their target, the nation of Israel. The Australians are just outside the Straits of Gibraltar readying themselves for a rear assault on the Russians and Americans if necessary. As long as we interfere with the power and communications abilities of the Russians and Americans under us, they would be sitting ducks for the Australian carrier weapons. So, negating the attack from the west appears to be well in hand.

The entire world is about to be at war, a war to end all wars, and I won't allow this to continue. I have a job for you, Metatron."

"What is it, my Lord?"

"We'll need to talk this over," Jhowah said, getting up from his seat on the bridge. Let's go to my conference room."

The News Room Of Al Jazeera Television
Doha, Qatar
January 27, 2016
During The Daily Newscast

"Before we go any further," The television reporter said while placing his notes on the desk in front of him. "We have an Al Jazeera News Alert that we are bringing to you directly from our newsroom. This is a happening of global importance.

"We have in our studios a man who calls himself the agent of Allah and says that he is bringing to us a warning from Allah. Let me just turn our microphone and cameras over to him for his own explanation. He calls himself Metatron. Mister Metatron, what do you have to say?"

Metatron, with his long flowing hair, and dressed in his toga like drape, strode to the center of the television image holding the end of his drape looped over his right arm. Highlights in his hair reflected the intense light rays from the studio lighting above him as he stood near the announcer, who offered him a seat. Refusing the seating, he stood erect and looked sternly into the camera.

"People of the world, I come to you with a message from Allah. I must first inform you all that there is only one ruler of the universe, only one God and he is known by many names. Many of you know him as Allah, the God of Islam. He is the same God that others call Jehovah, the God of Christians and Jews. By all names, he is one and the same. You must understand this before I go on. Many of you already know this, but many deny the very idea. It is true, and unless you understand and believe this concept your remaining days on this Earth may be very painful.

"I have come before you to present a message that is meant for all people, but since the Arab nations are the ones who have allied themselves to destroy Israel I have chosen to present it over Al Jazeera and trust that other nations will broadcast it to their people as well. This way I will most assuredly reach the leaders of all Islamic nations.

"This warning is aimed primarily at the radical anti-Zionists among you and should be received as a fateful warning to all people on this planet. Those of you hearing me will soon realize that, no matter the language you speak, you will understand every word and thought that I present to you from this location. I hope that you will realize that there is no one on Earth who can communicate in this same way unless he has been gifted by God, or Allah, as I have been gifted.

"What I am about to say to you should be believed by you and considered as the Word of God coming from his heart through my lips. It is a serious warning of a global catastrophe of proportions not seen since the great Flood of over four thousand years ago. There are biblical predictions to the occurrences of recent history.

"At the same time John received the visions of the 'Seven Seals' on the Island of Patmos he received others. He was given these visions by the same God, or Allah, who has sent me to give you these words. Most of the signs of the Apocalypse that were given by God as visions to John when he was exiled on in the Aegean by Emperor Domitian have already occurred."

Metatron paused to allow those watching to realize the significance of his message. His telempathic abilities were receiving both positive and negative impressions from those who were hearing him, including the Al Jazeera reporter seated behind him. He could not allow the negativism he was receiving to continue as he had with the Bilderberg group.

"I will not permit the disbelief that I am sensing. You will remember that before Moses left the land of Egypt, he and Aaron demanded that the Pharaoh release the Israelites or he would place ten plagues on Egypt. This occurred over three thousand years ago. I tell you today that unless you turn away from your plans to destroy the Israelites, these plagues will again be sent to Earth against those attacking and seeking the destruction of the people of Israel and its friends."

The Al Jazeera commentator turned his head so that he could see his producer and spoke softly into his mike through a line that would not go out over the air. "Did he say he was bringing back the plagues that Moses brought down from God on Egypt?" His lips curled into a slight smile.

"The predictions of the Seven Seals are proof of the promises and knowledge of Allah," Metatron continued. "These prophesy should be studied by humanity closely at this time, for it is the promise of God that he will bring down the original plagues of Moses upon this planet if you do not heed this warning.

"As followers of a radical form of Islam you have attempted to convert the world to your religion, and if you are unable to convert them you call them infidels and feel that Allah has given you the right to behead, or in some other way kill them. That is wrong. You have been misled. Allah does not accept such treatment to his creations. The teachings I gave to your prophet, Mohammad, have been twisted by a radical-thinking branch of Islam. And, unfortunately, many of you have remained silent in quiet support of this group. This is the 'First Seal' which represents the conqueror going forth conquering or to conquer. The First Seal is opened.

"The 'Second Seal' is of wars, revolutions and bloodshed, as exemplified by your acts of terror on innocent people throughout the world. The ongoing war against Israel is but the latest example of such acts. The Second Seal is opened.

"The 'Third Seal' is famine, and, as shown by John on Patmos, this is when the cost of food reaches almost unobtainable levels, as caused by you as you have raised the price of oil so high that it has caused inflation in costs of food, making it unobtainable to many. Thus the Third Seal is opened.

"Pestilence and disease epidemics are present all over the world. The epidemic of AIDS is of significant importance but there are many newer viral diseases that are developing the world over that are killing the people of Earth. The Fourth Seal is opened.

"The 'Fifth Seal' is 'Souls under the altar' and shows the persecution of God's people. This is a sin which radical Islam has certainly been shown to practice, beheading those you identify as infidels, simply because they do not agree with your interpretation of religion. The Fifth Seal is opened.

"The 'Sixth Seal' contains celestial signs and events that John described as earthquakes, meteors, changes in the appearances of the sun and moon, and terror throughout the populations. The Sixth Seal is not opened but much about it will be occurring before you decide to follow the commands of Allah. The Messiah and the covenant he made with Allah to shoulder the sins of all who acknowledge him will not be revealed to this world before this seal is opened.

"The components of the 'Seventh Seal' are many and varied but the seal represents the happenings around the return of Allah, his protection of the faithful, and the sending of the unfaithful to the planet of Sheolos, which is where Sezan, whom you refer to as Satan, will be returned when he is finally captured.

"Allah is very close at this time, and Mahdi, the promised Messiah, stands ready to make our presence known to all the people of this planet. Many of the prophesies of the Seventh Seal will occur during these next few days if you persist in your efforts to destroy the State of Israel.

"As you may be beginning to understand, the 'End Days' are close at hand. Allah or God or Jhowah, whom I represent before you, has now been heard. Many of your leaders have already heard these warnings from Allah's own lips, but have failed to reveal his admonitions to you. You have now heard with your own ears what He expects. It is your decision as to whether or not you will accept this responsibility or the consequences that will occur if you don't.

Metatron could detect empathically the skepticism coming from the commentator, as well as from the viewers. He chose his words carefully.

"The great pharaoh of Egypt chose not to believe until he saw his country devastated by plagues and lost his own son. Don't be as foolish. Insist that your leaders comply with my words and Allah's demands. If necessary, take to the streets, as you have often done, to demonstrate as a show of support or displeasure. Make your voices heard. Demand peace.

"In the beginning of the plagues in Egypt, Allah turned Aaron's staff into a snake. The pharaoh's sorcerers followed by turning their staffs into snakes. Aaron's snake then swallowed up the snakes produced by the sorcerer's staffs. I call the lies of the radicals about Allah's wishes false witness. Their words are not the words of Allah, but those of Sezan, the Deceiver. Now, in the name of the one true God, or Allah, of the universe, I command you to stop with your attempted destruction of Israel or be swallowed up as were pharaoh's serpents."

With those words Metatron looked upward toward the ceiling and held out his arms. He vanished from the screen. The news reporter moved back into view of the camera watching the spot where Metatron had disappeared. There was a look of astonishment on his face.

Tehran, Iran

The day after Metatron's speech to the world, President Jahid of Iran stood before his Parliament, the Majles, and spoke.

"Yesterday we listened to a sorcerer put on an act on Al Jazeera. That magician put on a show to the Arab nations in an attempt to put fear in our hearts. I am convinced that he was not who he said he was but an agent of the Satan of Israel. The sorcerer's trick will not work. Today we shall continue our assault. The fatwa will be consummated. The city of Beersheba and the surrounding region, which includes much of their major air defense capability, will get the next nuclear strike. This should cripple the air defenses of Israel and allow us unimpeded activity through their airspace."

Sedeh, Iran

As Jahid spoke to his parliament in Tehran, the peaceful desert region just north of Sedeh was, again, about to see activity. As the warning blasts started, the large earthenlike lid over the missile silos raised, ever so slow, exposing two empty cavities and one nuclear tipped missile in the third silo. Countdown commenced and, at zero, smoke began to rise from the cavity around the missile. At first that was the only movement, but soon the shiny tip trembled slightly and then rose slowly to begin its journey to Beersheba. As it exited to one-half of its total length out of the silo, a sudden beam of light struck with a blinding flash and a thunderous blast and set off the nuclear warhead. SDI had responded this time. Instantaneously, the town of Sedeh was removed from the face of the Earth.

As the hot gases of nuclear fission and fusion expanded and spread across the desert region and the signature mush-room cloud developed over the area, a rumble began to develop that was unheard at first because of the building intensity of the blast. It soon began spreading and as it moved out from the area of the original explosion it became more and more audible. The ground began to shake so violently that a small truck that survived the initial strike and whose driver was trying to put a distance between him and the explosion was thrust completely off the highway and rolled over twice before coming to a stop on its side.

The shaking and rumbling continued to build and spread in all directions, and as it did the ground began to separate. Huge gaping cracks opened and on the road to Tehran two farmers on a wobbly old wagon drawn by a donkey and carrying produce to sell in Tehran were unable to stop as the road opened in front of them and they dropped into the chasm, disappearing forever.

Back In Tehran

Jahid was just finishing his speech before the Majles when the quake reached that location. He held on to the podium as the great building shook and plaster fell from the ceiling onto his head and clothing.

"May Allah protect us," he muttered.

The shaking persisted for another twenty or thirty minutes before slowly subsiding to a mild trembling of the ground, after which Jahid and the assembly went outside. To the northeast they could see a column of smoke rising above the horizon.

"Mister President."

Jahid turned to see one of the members of his Expediency Council approaching.

"Mister President, we have just received word that the last missile never made it out of the silo. We believe that it was hit by a particle beam from the *Shield's* SDI weapons. It was definitely destroyed and the warhead was detonated by some form of advanced weaponry. We have lost the entire town of Sedeh."

"Well, what is that column of smoke that is rising over there? Sedeh is toward the south." The president pointed to the northeast as he spoke.

"The nuclear explosion in Sedeh probably caused movement in a previously inactive fault in the mantle below us. The smoke appears to be coming from the region of Mount Damavand. It has remained inactive for ages but it appears to be venting now. The quake that we just experienced was almost assuredly from the explosion in Sedeh and also, I expect, caused the venting at Mount Damavand. It appears as if the blast was powerful enough to cause a huge crack in the Earth's crust. Let's just hope that things quiet down before more destruction is done to our country and our people.

"Mister President, do you think that this quake has anything to do with the warning aired on Al Jazeera yesterday?"

"Oh, I don't accept that," Jahid said. "We are considered to be one of the most earthquake-prone countries in the world. Don't worry about that magician."

"Sir," a voice called out nearby.

Again Jahid turned and saw that one of his Majles members was staring at him. His eyes were wide with terror.

"Sir, the earthquake and eruption of Mount Damavand are not the only strange occurrences. I was just told that both the Jajrood and the Karaj Rivers have turned red, intensely red, like blood, and that the fish in the rivers are jumping out of the water. Many of the fish appear affected by whatever is turning the water red."

Jahid froze, his mind flashing memories of the ancient history of the Middle East.

"Wasn't the first plague on Egypt that the rivers ran red with blood?" the Majles member questioned.

"It can't be," Jahid answered. "I want that water checked and I want to be informed what is causing the redness."

"Yes sir," answered the Parliament member.

Within the hour the answer came to him from the same Majles member.

"Mister President," he informed him, "the top man in our water department says that he is unable to find blood cells in the water but present is a pigment called hemoglobin that is found in the blood cells of animals, including us humans. Too much of it is toxic to life in its natural state. It could turn all of our rivers and water supplies red. He says that given enough money, time, and the appropriate materials, he can actually create such a situation."

"He said this could come from blood cells?"

"Yes sir, he explained to me that the fresh water could break down the cells releasing the iron-based pigment."

"This is ridiculous," Jahid said. "I don't believe this Metatron can make this happen. Order our generals to continue with our plans and for the attacks to continue. Have we heard from the Americans and Russians out in the Mediterranean?"

"No sir, those ships remain strangely silent out there," the Majles member answered.

"Nevertheless," Jahid continued, "get on with the attack."

Doha, Qatar
Later In The Evening

As the Al Jazeera reporter began the evening news, those who were watching the news saw Metatron slowly materialize in the background. The reporter touched his earpiece and swung around to see what had happened.

"Mister Metatron, you return."

"Yes," he said as the camera image centered him in the screen and zoomed to get a head and chest shot of the one who claimed to be an agent of Allah.

"To all who hear me, I have returned to reinforce what I said yesterday and which has gone unheeded. The countries of the Middle East are now experiencing what the people of Egypt experienced in the first plague placed by God on that country. Their rivers and water sources are running red with blood and this will continue unless the leaders of the campaign to destroy Israel agree to cease and desist in their efforts.

"Until they do, you will have nothing but bitter, red water to drink and to give to your children, water that will soon make everyone who drinks it sick. It will also kill the fish that are used to feed many of your people and all plant life with which it comes in contact. The iron in this chemical is present in toxic doses. Soon you will be facing the greatest famine that your country has ever experienced. People of the world take heed! Your future depends upon the decisions your leaders make. Time is running out. Insist that they make the right ones."

Metatron took one step back, raised his arms wide and disappeared as he had done the night before.

Shield Headquarters
Deep Under The Mound Called Har-Megiddo
Translated Armageddon By Some

"Mister Prime Minister," the general advised, "we are still safe in our bunkers here under Har-Megiddo. SDI is now functioning properly and we made a direct hit on the nuclear silo at Sedeh in Iran. It was the same launch facility that hit Tel Aviv and our site. Hopefully there are no more nuclear sites in Iran. The SDI hit on Sedeh caused the nuclear device to activate, and the following explosion seems to have stirred up some tectonic activity in the area. A 6.5 Richter quake began immediately after the explosion and there is a persistent movement of the plates even now."

"What's happening out in the Mediterranean?" he asked the general.

"Well sir, Jhowah seems to have both the Russian and the U.S. fleets stopped cold in their naval tracks. We are not able to detect any communications coming from the ships. We must assume that Jhowah has employed some way of neutralizing their communications devices. If that is true, they are also unable to fire a weapon or launch a weapon or even move their ground troops into Gaza for deployment. And a miracle similar to the one that parted the Red Sea in ancient history created a tsunami-like wave on the side of the trench made in the ocean by Jhowah's space craft, rocking the large vessels and capsizing some of the smaller ones."

"Good. We'll take all the miracles that Jhowah will throw our way," the prime minister said. "We can receive some television with poor reception down here, and we are seeing some reports that Metatron has begun, with Jhowah's help I'm sure, to replay the ten plagues that were used with the pharaoh in Egypt for Moses."

"It's true," the general advised. "They have already begun with the first plague of blood. I don't believe Jahid will give in right away. He is committed to destroying us. And, while the ships offshore may be quiet, our Intel reports that the troops out of Syria and Saudi are beginning to move across the deserts. I hope Jahid is convinced before they do much damage. We can monitor them and utilize SDI, but leaving this facility and going out into the radiation contaminated land above us is impossible as it is with you."

"Have we determined the radioactive fallout from the blast?" the prime minister asked.

"Yes, we have some preliminary information," responded the general. "I am in contact with our leaders in the Air Force and ground troops that are away from our locations and are not in any way bothered by the radiation. The good news is that the device that exploded over Tel Aviv appears to have been built with low-grade uranium."

The prime minister agreed. "That warhead must have been one of the earlier ones developed by Iran. I know that they have improved upon them recently. From all reports the one that SDI exploded at Sedeh must have been one of their later developments."

"Yes sir. It would seem so. To answer your earlier question, our Air Force and ground troops are setting up our defenses as best they can around Tel Aviv. They also have contact with our naval forces. However, that branch of our military is unable to mount any offensive since they are greatly outnumbered. I know the minds and hearts of these men and I can assure you that they are ready to put their lives on the line to defend our country."

Tehran, Iran
Moments Later

As Jahid visited the banks of the Jajrood River he was able to see the unbelievable redness of the water. He looked out over the river and saw the dead fish that were beginning to float on the water's surface.

"It's killing the fish," he said.

"Yes sir," the Majles member answered. "The pigment is probably stealing oxygen from the water. In the blood, that is its purpose, to take up oxygen from the lungs and deliver it to all parts of the body. The iron in it is also toxic to life when swallowed in large doses.

"We'll have a bad smell around here by morning," he added.

As he stood close to the water, the Iranian leader heard a splash in the water near his foot and looked down. A frog squatted beside him. A few seconds later another splash and another frog came out of the water onto the river bank nearby and it was soon followed by more. In a few short minutes there were literally tens of thousands of frogs that could be seen from his viewpoint and they were continuing to come up out of the river hopping everywhere.

"Why are the frogs coming out like this? I didn't know we had this many frogs in all of Iran."

"Sir, the second plague of Egypt was frogs."

Jahid look at him in disbelief. "No, I can't believe this is happening. Is this Jhowah really Allah, as Metatron said?"

The two men left and as they returned to the president's office they drove over thousands of frogs that covered the roads and ground in the capital. When they arrived at the office building the steps were covered with the frogs. They could not move without stepping on them. The creatures were appearing at unheard-of rates. They were everywhere, even getting into the building.

"You get in touch with Al Jazeera and tell them that when Metatron next contacts them to send him here as soon as they can."

Within moments, as Jahid walked into his office, he looked up to see Metatron appearing before him.

"That was too quick. There is no way that you could have been told to come here by Al Jazeera. Nevertheless, you are here."

Jihad sat down in the chair behind his desk. And with a smirk said, "So, you are Metatron, the man who has been playing tricks on me. How did you get in here so quick and how did you know I needed to talk with you?"

"I have special ways to do both, Mister Jahid. I am a man, but I am not the kind of man you are used to dealing with in your daily routine."

"Are you something special? And where did you learn such trickery?" Jahid asked with a chuckle.

"I am a man who is the highest angel of Allah. In the place you call heaven I sit to his left at his very table. For thousands of years, the God, you call Allah, has sent me to this planet to appear in human form before the people of the world. Each time my mission has been to demonstrate how Allah meant for your kind to live here.

"Because of the circumstances at hand, I have returned and given you fair warning to stop this obsession of yours of destroying the nation of Israel." Metatron looked deep into the eyes and soul of Jahid. What he saw was darkness, evil personified.

"You must understand," Metatron continued, "that the being who has claimed to be helping you is Sezan. He is not an agent of Allah. He has been cast out of the Alliance of our Reticulum planets for using deception and causing harm to your fellow human beings in the early days of the creation of this world. The conflict between him and Allah is intense and ongoing."

"That's interesting. I wondered about him, anyway, him and that Samael, who always spoke for him."

"Unless you cease your efforts to destroy Israel the plagues of Egypt will return, and the prophesies of the book of Revelation will be fulfilled."

Metatron looked again into Jihad's eyes and soul. There was no evidence that this human either agreed or disagreed to comply with God's wishes. The Iranian leader was quite capable of deceit.

"Then get this mess cleaned up. The dead fish are already stinking and by tomorrow the frogs will be adding to the stench. I'll go along with you."

"First, you order your troops and those of your allied countries to stop their advance," Metatron answered.

Jahid called his commanding general and gave him the order to call a cease fire, to stop all advances, and to give the same order to the generals of all the allied countries advancing toward Israel.

Seeing compliance with the wishes of God, Metatron performed a miracle of his own doing and caused the cleanup of the land and rivers of Iran. The rivers began clearing and returned to their pre-plague color. The frogs returned to the waters and those that had been lying dead on the highways disappeared as did the many dead fish that had left the creeks and rivers seeking oxygen that they could not find in the water. Having achieved this small step toward world peace, Metatron then returned to the SSV Command to report on the actions of Jahid.

Back On SSV-Command

"Jhowah, the Iranian leader has agreed to comply with your demand."

The Hivanian looked out the observation window in his conference room at the fleet below and nodded. Then he turned to Metatron.

"I sense that you don't feel very confident about the man. Is he being truthful?"

"I don't know," Metatron replied. "As much as I'd like to believe him, I could read nothing but darkness in his soul. I believe his dealings with Sezan have sparked even more hatred, causing confusion in him and affecting his ability to think clearly."

"Darkness in a man's soul will not allow him to negotiate in honesty," Jhowah advised. "Such a self-centered person is unable to distinguish fact from fiction. Truth, to such a person is whatever needs to be said to get past the current crisis. We have seen many leaders throughout history possess this unfortunate, narcissistic trait. It is something that has come about by making bad choices and decisions. It is a lack of loyalty to their Creators and to our laws.

"I think that it is best to reassess this situation in the morning. I believe we'll know better where we stand with this child of Sezan by then." Jhowah was a being of great understanding of his creations, and he also knew Sezan's soul and had long dealt with the actions of the Betrayer and his followers.

The Next Morning

By morning Metatron was able to tell Jhowah that reports from *Shield's* satellite monitors and sensors revealed that, against Metatron's highest hopes, Jahid had rescinded the order to stand down. The Iranians and their Allies were starting back in their drive toward Israel.

"I will not tolerate the impudence and disloyalty of these humans," Jhowah said in an angry voice. "I want the next three plagues to come down on them all at once. I must show them that I am the being they call Allah."

"Are you sure, my Lord? All three?" Metatron questioned.

"Yes, and immediately," was his answer. "This offensive is the work of Sezan. The time has come to send a message to his followers that, although I am a tolerant ruler, I will not stand for betrayal. There is no need to make this a long and drawn-out test of Jahid's endurance. Make it applicable to every country allied with him. No exceptions. This world will comply with my wishes, or I will allow humankind to destroy itself."

Washington, D.C.
The Next Day

It was the next morning in the White House and the American president was up early working on letters from Senators and Representatives, most of which were letters from his own party members who were protesting his recent State of the Union address and the budget he had sent down to them, one that contained more sweeping cuts in defense spending and border-patrol programs, virtually creating an open-door policy to anyone who wanted to enter the United States.

His latest initiative would provide entitlement programs to everyone living in the U.S., legal or illegal. Tens of billions of dollars of foreign aid were pledged to the United Nations to be distributed, at its discretion, to third-world countries, regardless of whether such nations had been traditional adversaries of America. Understandably, a growing army of Americans had tolerated this irresponsible and illegal use of its monies long enough. When the administration, with the aid of congress, rescinded the second amendment, outlawing the right of private citizens to own guns, the populace was pushed to the brink. Believing that the president was trying to remove guns so that the mounting number of murders and robberies would be diminished, the American people reluctantly swallowed another bitter pill. But this latest decision, to throw open the borders to "all comers" and further drain the U.S. Treasury to fund programs for America's enemies, was more than "the people" could take. A state of national unrest was brewing, but for now, there were more global matters for the president to consider.

"Dick," the president called out to his chief of staff, swiping at a gnat flying around his mouth, "what do you hear from our fleet in the Mediterranean?" Again he swiped at what he thought was one irritating gnat, but this time there was a small swarm of them in front of his face.

Just as one of the tiny insects bit him on the neck, he reached up and slapped it dead. "What's with all these gnats inside the White House?" he muttered in nearly a whisper.

"We've not heard a thing, Mister President. We think that a communications blackout occurred over there before any attack could be made. We will continue trying to make contact." Dick stopped and swatted at a swarm of gnats flying past the front of his face. "What is happening?" he asked as he swatted again at the insects. "Where did all of these gnats come from?"

"I don't know," the president answered as *he* swung out with his hands at the increasing swarms.

"I'll open the window and let some of these out," Dick suggested.

As he spoke he walked over to the window and raised it. As he did, literally thousands of tiny insects poured into the room through the open window. Looking out of the window through swarming gnats, he focused at some movement near the wall. As he unsuccessfully swatted away at the pestilent flying creatures, he was stunned as he saw a pair of feral tigers leap the wall that surrounded the building and lawn.

"Sir, there is a ninety percent absentee rate among the White House employees today." It was an aide to the president who had entered the room as the two were fighting off the insect swarms.

"Get someone in here who can get rid of these gnats," Dick ordered the aide. "We can't even think they are so thick. God, Mister President, I think I just saw two tigers come over the wall."

The chief of staff turned the aide. "Alert the Secret Service immediately."

Meanwhile, the president was looking sick. His face was pale.

"Oh Dick," he said, "I feel terrible. I have a bad headache. I really feel hot and I'm sweating profusely."

"Let me check you, Mister President," Dick responded and moved over and placed his hand on the forehead of the president. He *was* hot and his face was covered with beads of perspiration. Dead gnats, mashed to their death as he swatted, were caught in the sweat on his face.

"You get him to his bedroom," Dick ordered the aide, "I'll call the Secret Service and the White House doctor."

As the aide, a sturdy young man, left helping the weakening president to his bedroom, Dick stood in the midst of the Oval office, still filled with myriads of the small gnats, and now lice. He looked around.

"What the hell is going on?" he asked himself. His attention was caught by a tiger passing directly in front of the window.

Global Changes

It was happening everywhere. In every country that was allied to the Iranian attempt to destroy Israel, people were becoming suddenly ill, the skies and lands were filled with gnats and lice. Swarms of locusts were filling the air and beasts were roaming the streets. Domesticated animals were reverting to primal behavior. The fields that once were blanketed with waves of amber-colored grain and lush green stalks of corn reaching toward the heavens were now swarming with locusts. And with the past pressures from Greenpeace and the ecological and environmental extremists to have the government ban insecticides, there would be little chance to bring a fast end to the swarms.

Terrible beasts, cat-sized rats, and wild dogs were killing the livestock and occasionally attacking old people and small children. In Australia and Israel and in the few smaller countries that were willing to help the Israelis, there were no swarms of insects, no beasts roaming the streets. Domesticated animals displayed no signs of aggression or primal behavior. There was no pestilence and disease there, either. All this was occurring while large segments of the populations of the anti-Israeli countries were sick and some even dying.

In the advancing hoards of soldiers in the countries surrounding Israel and on the ships at sea, the military personnel were falling in their tracks with unexplained illness. Many seemed to have gone mad, exhibiting unusual behavior and turning on fellow warriors.

The American president remained ill as was a large segment of the American population. The recently socialized medical industry in America was being severely tested. The numbers of new doctors and nurses, as well as technical personnel, had shrunk since the conversion to a socialistic form of government.

Not only were many of America's brightest opting for professions other than medicine, doctors with established practices were leaving the profession. Many had appeared on television shows to explain their displeasure with a system that made them slaves to the government. As a prominent physician told a news interviewer, "Why spend half of your life training to work long hours, be away from your wife and children, and expose yourself to such horrible antibiotic resistant diseases to become a state-controlled medical technician or physician, one mandated to provide or prescribe *only* those forms of treatment handed down by a computer sitting in Washington, D.C.?"

The host asked the guest physician about the commitment to his profession, to which the doctor responded: "Why swap a life with a loving family that includes free weekends and nights to become a slave to a socialist form of medicine? Why listen to the complaints of hurting patients who need diagnostic tests that would direct the appropriate treatment, and be told that you could not order such a test, that doing so would cost too much money? And, even if the request to order testing was approved, even simple imaging tests that were done within a day or so before the destructive effects of government control would now take days or even weeks to complete. In some cases just to get authorization from some untrained individual without a single day of medical training would seem like 'an act of Congress.'"

The interviewer interrupted the doctor to ask, "How does such an untrained person gain so much authority?"

The doctor answered, "That's government. That's the way it is done. There is no push to fill positions with the most qualified person; it is all about quotas and affirmative action, whatever that is. Many obtain high-paying positions because of a friend or relative who knew someone who was able to get them their job in the medical field. The healthcare system in the United States is 'universal' all right, universally broken. Corruption in government was one thing, but corruption in medicine is becoming deadly."

"What about technology? We are told that electronic medical records have streamlined the healthcare system and helped prevent many mistakes that were common before such record-keeping was mandated?" To this, the doctor responded, "Installing the electronic medical record system was just a ploy used by the current administration to gain greater control over the medical profession and its records. Some bureaucrat can access any patient's record and see what treatment is being conducted. The same government employee can use a skillfully crafted software program to determine if patients visited their physician more often than the system allows, if they were referred to a specialist for more advanced treatment, or if they required more antibiotics or pain medications than the system allowed. If these so-called 'irregularities' were discovered, the physician would be punished. The costs of what the regulators of the Universal Healthcare System called 'overruns' would be deducted from the doctor's next paycheck."

The interviewer saw that the doctor was angered by the whole mess and let him talk.

"The money is not why I left the practice of medicine," he continued. "It was something much more significant. Over the past two years, my colleagues and I have had to watch patients die while waiting on some bureaucrats to approve a needed procedure, or be told that they could not prescribe the appropriate treatment. With the current administration's newly implemented Universal Healthcare Program, doctors no longer make decisions. American medicine has been delegated to a computer sitting in a multimillion dollar "stimulus bill" palace in Washington, D.C., and the technicians who have been hired to ration care. The current system is not only designed to ration healthcare, it was programmed to delay the appropriate treatment for as long as possible and to allow people to expire rather than expend expensive resources keeping them alive. The bureaucrats have realized that death is the most economical solution to massive demands on the U.S. economy. They figured out that a funeral is cheaper than three days in the intensive care units or three months in a nursing home.

The guest raised his hand and pointed a finger at the interviewer.

"The medical profession in America has been corrupted to the point of almost being a thankless job, one that requires anyone who could read instructions from a computer to act as a physician. Doctors have been relegated to technicians, carrying out orders from 'Big Brother.' The 'Art of Medicine' is no more. It has become just another government-run disaster, draining the country's treasury and getting very little return on the investment."

"Well, doctor," the host said. "You have certainly enlightened us about why so many people throughout the country are sick and dying. What about the recent crisis of pestilence spreading across the country?"

"Pestilence is not just a U.S. problem," the doctor answered. "It is a global problem. Gnats, locusts, beasts, and rodents seem to rule the Earth. It is particularly bad in the Middle East. But there is not much we can do about it, either.

"For decades, the U.S. has provided healthcare and medical supplies to poor and underdeveloped countries. Today, we do not have the resources to supply our own. The world is on its own. It seems that there is a 'New World Order' in medicine, as well. The question all of us are asking is: who among qualified physicians are in charge?"

The physician paused and the interviewer ended the session.

"I'm afraid that is a question for another program. Thank you doctor, we'll have you back soon."

* * *

It was a new world, but not one that was functioning very well. Chaos was mounting in every corner of the globe.

Because privately owned guns had been outlawed in many countries, it was impossible for many households to defend themselves against the huge rodents and wild animals that invaded their homes to consume the food that families had put away for difficult times.

Rodents were a particular concern because the fleas they carried were determined to be the cause of the Great Plague (or Black Death) that wiped out a major part of the population of Europe in the 14th century.

Once again, it appeared that mankind had delegated free will to the less knowledgeable, allowing to those who naively claimed to be committed to saving the world to have their way. Largely because of such groups, governments had taken over the responsibility of deciding what was best for its people. As a result of pressures from activists, tools such as guns, insecticides, and clean-burning energy had been banned by lawmakers who failed to see that the environment within a citizen's own household was safe. A price was being paid all over the planet. There would be famine and even more disease as pestilence spread and those who were supposed to be protecting citizens were disarming them in every way possible.

Tehran, Iran

There had been many aftershocks since the larger quake that had occurred immediately after SDI had exploded the missile in the underground silo near Sedeh. In the last twelve hours the aftershocks had been increasing in intensity.

As Jahid stood in front of his Parliament, the Majles, he was covered in clothing, wearing gloves, and a hat that had mosquito netting hanging down and draped into his collar. The insects swarmed about him. The Majles were dressed similarly. There were guards at the door to fight off the many beasts loosed on the streets. Many of the members were ill but trying their best to serve as they had been chosen to do.

"I am insistent on continuing our attack on Israel," Jahid announced. "I still tell you that what we are experiencing is a magician's trick."

"With all due respect, I don't believe so, Mister President," a voice said.

"Who said that?" The president asked. The anger in his voice couldn't go unnoticed.

"I did, sir." One of the members raised his hand and stepped forward. "Sir, these are the same plagues that were placed on Egypt, the ones forewarned by Moses, the one who they say led the Israelites out of Egypt. They are coming in the same order as they did back then. If we continue they will become worse and in the end it will take many of our children from us. We can't go on like this." There was fear in the voice of the member as he held out his arms to emphasize his point. His hands trembled and his head shook as if he had palsy.

Jahid looked at him with contempt in his eyes. He didn't speak a word back to him as he reached into his pocket and retrieved a small pistol. Aiming it at the member's head he pulled the trigger. The bullet struck the member in his forehead, leaving a clean entry wound with little bleeding. He immediately fell to the floor.

"Does anyone else, here, disagree with my decision? I will not have my Majles members fighting me," the president said to the rest of them. "The destruction of Israel is at hand. We must finish what we have started. It is what we have been taught that our people were destined to do."

As aftershocks continued, the constant shaking of the building began to increase, and the roar coming from the granite in the building as it was being ground against itself by the shaking became louder. Powdered plaster fell from the ceiling down onto the members. Later a Richter reading at the peak of the quake would be shown to have been measured at 10.4, a never before recorded reading.

The walls began to crumble and the members of the Majles rushed outside to avoid being crushed by the falling debris. When they were outside and away from the building they gathered near Jahid, but none uttered a word. Guards surrounded them to prevent injuries by the beasts and wild dogs that roamed the streets.

"Look!" yelled one of the members as he pointed toward the northeast and the pillar of smoke that had been constant since the quakes started. "Damavand must be getting more active. There is more smoke coming up."

As they looked in the direction of the great volcano, it suddenly exploded. Even though they could only recognize the top of Damavand, they could easily see the sudden explosion at its peak and the huge amount of material going upward. The air filled with ash and fire, and the land shook more violently than ever. As the ash and lava filled the sky it began to block out the sun, and day began to change to night. The temperature rose as the debris fell, pelting the crumbling buildings and streets of Tehran. Smoke and the smell of sulfur filled the air. The darkness that developed was as if midnight had arrived.

"Allah protect us," one member called out. The rest of them began to scurry, leaving Jahid standing alone. Even the guards left him as he trembled with the anger and disbelief that was building inside him.

Standing in the grassy area near the government buildings, Jahid held onto a small tree and watched as, one by one, the buildings crumbled and collapsed from the shaking earth. The air was blanketed with the plague of insects. It was only luck that he had not been hit by the falling rocks and embers from the eruption. He saw a leopard heading for him. He could barely believe what his eyes registered.

"Am I hallucinating?" he asked himself. "The smoke from the volcanic eruption must be getting to my head."

The animal before Jihad appeared to have seven heads with eyes like fire. A deafening roar came out of the mouth of each of the seven heads as the animal charged toward him. Was it an illusion, or was he witnessing a supernatural event. He was taking no chances. Frantically, he pulled out his pistol and fired shot after shot into the advancing beast until it dropped at his feet from the last shot that had luckily hit the spinal cord in the neck of the beast.

As he looked up to the sky, the fiery material fell all around him as the darkness increased. He raised his fist to the sky and shook it. From under the melting plastic of the mosquito netting he screamed out at the sky above: "Damn you, Metatron, damn you."

On The SSV-Command

On Board the SORGE starship Command in stationary position above the fleets of Russia and the U.S., Metatron talked with Jhowah.

"As with the pharaoh these people are resisting our efforts," Metatron noted.

"No, my son," Jhowah spoke, "I can sense a change, especially in the Iranian leader. In fact I will let up on our venting onto the sea so that they might be able to send a boat into Gaza, but we'll keep the SAMSLs going to suppress their power.

"Metatron, you need to make another trip to Al Jazeera television. We need to make a final plea before going any further."

Jhowah was interrupted in his conversation by a call from the bridge.

"My Lord, Admiral Pazon has just landed in our shuttle bay. He says he has a gift for you."

He looked out the window of his starship and saw the even larger starship of the Reticulum Defense Command Admiral that had arrived without his notice. Pazon had shuttled over from it.

"Very good," He said. "Send him up to my conference room. I have Metatron here with me."

In a few moments Pazon came into the room.

"My Lord," he said, "I have brought you a most valuable gift. It is something for which you have long awaited."

"And what would that be, Admiral?"

Pazon turned back toward the door. "Enter," he commanded. "I believe this is an old friend of yours."

Jhowah stood motionless as Sezan, handcuffed, ankles locked in leg irons, and accompanied by two guards, entered the room. Jhowah could hardly believe his eyes as he stared at the traitorous Dromedan that the Reticulum had been chasing for almost thirty-eight thousand years. The creature standing before him was the same Sezan that had been with him at the start of the project on Soleus-3 and who had made unauthorized changes in the DNA of the creations in order to use it as a tool to control them. It was the same Sezan who had tried to undermine Jhowah's challenge to create a new species of universal beings.

"I am proud to inform you, my Lord, that I also have his closest agent, Samael, on my ship. I left him there since I knew that this individual was the most important to you. The two of them had been sidetracked by the happenings on Soleus-3 and forgot to stay on the lookout for our vessels. This time we caught him." Pazon, the huge, hairy and mahogany skinned Janosian, chuckled as he finished talking. "And I have them both fettered with the newer incarceration bonds. They'll not be able to get away with any fancy moves."

This was the end of a long quest to harness the Prince of Darkness, the source of all evil. Now, Pazon could focus all of his attention on the crisis at hand on Soleus-3 and, when it was handled, return to his primary duties, protecting and defending the Reticulum planets that included the planet below. He had allowed the curious from other star systems and even a couple from other galaxies to observe the developing earth colonies from a distance, but if any tried to cause harm he would quickly escort them out of this system.

"So, Jhowah, do you wish to have him or do you want me to take these two back to Sheolos?"

Jhowah saw a grimace come to the face of Sezan at the mention of the penal planet of Sheolos.

"No, Dag, I want you to, first, do a fly-over of the armada located off the coast of Israel and create a blast that will shatter their eardrums. Let them know that there is more than one of our craft available to stop this attack.

"After you have performed this mission, I want to make sure Sezan makes it back to Sheolos this time. I have waited for this day as anxiously as I waited for the day our first creation was removed from the maturation pods on what used to be your vessel, the SSV-Human Lab," Jhowah said looking into the eyes of a being who used to be a trusted friend, or so He had been led to believe.

"Now, Sezan, I'll send you back to where you belong with Admiral Pazon, to the pits of the universe. There are people on Soleus-3 who have a saying that they use. They say 'I hope you rot in hell.' I know that is impossible because when you were an ally, and you gave us the ability to arrest the aging process with your brilliant manipulations of our DNA. That means you'll never die from natural causes. You will be there on that miserable planet that is so close to our star, Zeta-1 Reticuli, which stays permanently hot, and you will be there for eternity. You will live to smell your own burning rot.

Unfortunately, you will not be alone. I will send many of those who have followed your lead to be with you. It is a destiny that you and your followers have created for yourselves. And, you will at last have a kingdom over which you can rule forever, on the fiery planet of Sheolos.

Jhowah could hardly believe what had just happened. He turned to Metatron and smiled. He turned to Dag, the large Janosian he had come to respect, and reached out wrapping his long spindly fingers around the admiral's large hairy hand.

"Thank you, Dag, you did a good job. Please put this nemesis away forever. Now our creations are safe except for the damage already done by him in the past."

Pazon smiled as he grabbed Sezan's shoulders and proudly pressed him forward out through the door.

Turning to Metatron, Jhowah said, "I thought this day would never come. So now we can move on to other productive business. With Sezan out of the picture perhaps we can save Soleus-3 from those who would destroy it, but we must move quickly.

Doha, Qatar
Office Of Al Jazeera Television

As Metatron materialized at Al Jazeera, he was given the courtesy of having complete control of the video and audio going out to all Arab countries and even to the world. It seemed that they were now a bit more convinced of his genuineness than to the commands of Jahid.

"Today, I come before you to warn that Allah is angered by your continued refusal to believe in his power. He has created this great world and the people in it, and you have not followed the laws that he handed down many centuries ago. It is his love for you that has caused him to tolerate your transgressions this far.

"You have been experiencing the same plagues that Allah placed on the pharaoh in Egypt centuries ago. The blood in the rivers and water of Iran and the frog plague that they suffered were from Allah. The gnats, locusts, beasts, and pestilence of all of you were from Allah, as were what appeared to be natural disasters in the forms of floods, earthquakes, and volcanic eruptions.

"Your brothers in Iran have suffered even more as they attempted to destroy Israel by launching another nuclear weapon toward them. It was destroyed in its silo by weapons that Allah gave to those who trusted in him and followed the laws he had given them. This caused them to be in the midst of the strongest earthquakes to have ever visited this planet, which have reached so violently and deep into Earth's crust that they have released the power of the great volcano Damavand near the city of Tehran. This has blackened the skies over this part of the world.

"People of Iran, you have brought this plight on yourselves. You have allowed your leaders to misguide you and cause you to turn away from Allah's true message" one of love, tolerance, acceptance, and peace.

"These plagues will continue as they did in ancient Egypt until you accept that Allah, who is also God, who is also Jhowah, is the Supreme Being and Creator of Earth and that it was never his intent for you, the descendents of Ishmael, to avenge him by killing Abraham's children. Jhowah promised Ishmael his own nation, but it was not his intent to give him a nation of hatred and defiance. Jhowah and only Jhowah has the power to destroy this planet if he so desires. Although he has stood by and watched many evil-minded leaders take you to the brink of destruction, he alone will decide the fate of Soleus-3 and its inhabitants. No one individual, or group or nation, has the power to destroy this world other than Jhowah, the God you call Allah.

The eyes of the commentator were open wide and his head shook as if he had a case of palsy. This time Metatron could not sense any evidence of skepticism.

"It is also the command of Allah that you unconditionally accept the right of Israel to exist as a nation in the land of their fathers, which is all they ever wanted or asked to do, that you cease and desist from supporting acts of terror on innocent people around the world and harboring the perpetrators of such heinous acts.

"Because of recent decisions, the nation that calls itself the United States of America is also under the stress of these plagues. That nation has always had a warm place in the heart of God. It was born from the abuses of an intolerant British king who was self-serving in his treatment of that nation. Several men came together under their belief in God as the Supreme Being and Creator. With this common belief binding their thoughts, they formed a government like no other nation before or after them. They established a government 'of the people, by the people, and for the people.' They had seen what a dictatorial government could do: strip men of their dignity and unfairly take from them the fruits of their labors. They recognized the natural desire in humanity to be free, and how that freedom can release the best of humanity. They drew up a constitution that accepted God and that he created man to be free. They mandated that every session of their Congress be opened with prayer, in recognition of their Creators.

"It has been a great moment as we have looked down on the progress and success of that nation in just a few short years. Because we believed that they were committed to creating a world of peace and prosperity, a world in which Jhowah's laws came first, we guided them through world wars, economic depression and natural disasters. But in recent times the face of the United States changed. Self-rule was replaced with the rule of socialism.

"With the help of America's enemies, the people elected leaders who have an agenda that is diametrically opposed to God's laws. Because government has taken on the role of 'caring' for many of its citizens, a growing number have become lazy and allowed all forms of government controls and perversion of the laws handed down by God. They are thinking, not with their minds as did their forefathers, but with their hearts. They are slowly but surely destroying the greatest nation ever created by mankind.

"The United States is receiving this message also at this time. God commands you to take your lives into your own hands before all semblance of individualism is gone, before you no longer resemble the image in which you were created. Don't let those who seek their own power and your fortunes to be successful in changing you into something of their own making. If you give up free will now, you'll never get it back. Vote with your feet. Take to the streets, march on your capitals. Sit in the chairs and behind the desks of every branch of government. Bring the government that has taken away your freedom, your ambitions, your respect, your resources to its knees.

"Take a lesson from the early Americans who threw a Tea Party in the harbor of Boston and from the civil rights movement of the 1960s. Overcome what has been imposed upon you by those who would enslave you to a way of life different from the one envisioned by God and the founding fathers of your once great country. Resurrect the hope of the free world.

"From this day forth, act upon the premise that government owns nothing, most certainly not you. State and federal buildings, and everything within, are yours – the people's. They were built and paid for with your hard-earned dollars, your risks, your blood, and that of your forbearers.

"The liberties paid for by the blood of your brave young men and women have been stolen from you by those who contributed nothing positive to 'life, liberty, and the pursuit of happiness.' You were created free, free to take back what has always been yours: your pride, your honor, your freedom, your government, your country, your destiny. Act like what you are: children of the God that is known to the rest of the universe as Jhowah. These words are spoken from a messenger of God's lips to your ears.

"I speak not only to the people of the United States of America but to freedom-loving, creative people the world over. Rise up and be heard. The world has one final chance to comply with God's will. And, YOU, my brothers and sisters, are that chance.

"I leave you now but I hear your thoughts and feel your emotions. Many of you want to rise up and do Jhowah's work, but you are afraid. Do not fear, for he and I are with you. If you wish to join back into the kingdom of God or Allah, whichever you call him, just send me that mental message. When you do, you will experience a profound sense of strength and confidences come over you. That feeling is proof that we are with you.

"Let it be known, also, that today the enemy of Allah, known as Satan, has been taken prisoner and is at this moment being transported to the penal planet of Sheolos, known to you as Hell or Sheol. You should also remember that this event was prophesied in the book you call Revelation nearly two thousand years ago. The world as it was is no more. A new Jerusalem shall be forthcoming.

"I bid you farewell."

With that he reached out with both arms and vanished from the screen.

CHAPTER NINE

A NEW BEGINNING

Aboard SSV-Command

Jhowah stood before the forward windows on the bridge of the SSV Command as he observed the stillness of the fleet of ships that lay stagnant in the water beneath him. Metatron stepped onto the bridge.

"Do you still plan to hold their power?" he asked.

"That will all depend on your findings in Iran," Jhowah answered.

"I suppose so. Do you sense a change in the Iranian's beliefs?"

"Yes," Jhowah answered. "It has been two days since your address on Al-Jazeera but he is definitely under great stress. The quakes have settled down to mild tremors, and the volcano has begun only to smoke, but the skies are still dark and the effects of the plagues are still present. If he fails to stop this war and not believe that I am his true Allah, I will move on to the next plague, the incurable boils that will infest him, his people and even his animals. Change his mind, Metatron."

Tehran, Iran

Jahid was collapsed in a chair that he had found in a not completely destroyed part of a government building. He was covered in soot, ash, and debris that had settled on him as it fell from the sky. The drapes about his body were tattered, torn, and burned, and the expression on his face was one of total defeat. His skin was covered with blemishes and boils that resulted from scratching the intense itching from hundreds of insect bites. The pests still swarmed throughout the area. Metatron stood before him, materializing before his eyes.

"Did you come to gloat?" Jahid asked of Metatron.

"Gloating is not a useful tool," Metatron answered.

"Look what you have done to my country and my place of work. I'm destroyed as a leader. I have no place to go. Everything is destroyed."

"Jahid, this is what you have done to yourself. What you did to Tel Aviv, leaving them contaminated with radiation, you gave them no choice; but you do have a choice to go forward and live and rebuild with those of your country who have survived."

"What must I do?" he asked.

"Did you see my last transmission from Al Jazeera?"

"Yes, I did. It was brought to me on a device on which I could view it."

"Then you know the answer. It is up to you to call off the offensive that you created, and call upon all Muslims the world over to strike the word Jihad from their vocabulary, as it applies to destroying the groups that you have erroneously labeled infidels. You must now instruct all your radical Islamic brothers to make peace with their Jewish and Christian brothers."

"I don't know that I have any other viable choice, Mister Metatron. I will do as you ask."

"Be sure of what you say, Mr. President. I remember similar words of capitulation after the plagues of the blood and the frogs. I assure you, and you must know from these plagues, that you have angered Allah."

"I have always honored Allah," the Iranian said. "I have been taught since I was a small boy by the clerics in my country that the infidels were pigs, a scourge on the Earth, and that Allah wanted them eliminated. I was taught that it is Islam's duty to carry out Allah's wish to destroy the sons of Isaac. I thought that I was doing Allah's work and doing it well. And when that Samael character sent Sezan here, I was told that I had been chosen to become the new leader of the new world order that would result from annihilation of the infidels. He was an impressive man, who possessed some of the same powers that you appear to have and a flying craft that was unlike anything I had ever seen."

"If you watched me from Al Jazeera, Jahid, you know that Samael and Sezan were frauds, both of them, and that they have been captured and are incarcerated. You also know that many of your clerics and religious leaders have defrauded Islamic people into believing that Allah wanted them to kill their brothers, whom they, falsely, called infidels. These people are non non-believers. They believe as they were taught. Your hatred for Christians and Jews has been done in the name of power disguised as religion."

"Yes, I suppose you are right."

"Sezan and Samael will pay for their transgressions. Both have been sent off to the place you earthlings call hell. Some of the remaining leaders of radical Islam, terrorists, and confirmed atheists have been removed with them. You, on the other hand, have been given the chance of a lifetime. Like Saul, who, as part of the Roman Empire, persecuted the early Christians, you have a chance to become a disciple of Jhowah and right the wrongs of your past.

"The time has come for you to accept Allah or God as being your God and creator. You must accept that there are other religious beliefs than Islam and that other religions have a right to worship as its people may wish and live without fear. You have a right to your belief and you must be tolerant of those who believe differently, and promote peace and harmony among all nations."

"I have been a fool. I will do as you say, Metatron. Please get rid of these animals and gnats."

"Jahid, God has promised to continue his plagues upon you as he did in Egypt if you renege again. You promised last time to stop this attempt at genocide and went back on your word. If you make a wrong decision and cross us again you will evoke the final wrath of God on yourself and your nation. You can see from what has happened already that he has the power to ultimately change your mind or destroy you."

"I won't renege. It is over. What did you say was the name of the man who previously persecuted infidels, I mean the early Jewish-Christians?"

"The world came to know him as Paul," Metatron responded. "And because of your change of heart and the healing affect it will have on this troubled world you will call yourself Jaseed." "Jaseed," he said. "I like it."

Metatron nodded to Jaseed, opened wide his arms, and left.

Aboard SSV-Command

"Metatron, I have heard prayers from many countries under my name as Allah. They all sound as if they wish to accept the truth. I understand that Jahid, who is now called Jaseed, had promised to represent us among the religion known as Islam and that he has ordered the ground forces to lay down their weapons, stop their advance, and return to their homes.

"I am still worried about one group: the Americans. Their fleet still remains poised off the coast, next to the Russian armada. And the U.S. commander has orders from his president to participate in the destruction of Israel. There appears to be no effort to stand down. I stopped our SAMSL engines, so that they now have power, but I have continued to keep Command above them just as a show of our strength and the immensity of our vessels."

"My Lord, I am pleased to inform you that the Russians have left," Metatron said. "My meeting with their president was well-received. He was convinced that there was no future in continuing with the assault on Israel, especially with the Australians closing in from behind and Command overhead. Even so, the Americans are still poised to carry through, which is a bit strange. I need to visit them."

"You do that," Jhowah said. "I'll bring these other leaders up here one at a time and handle them while you are away."

White House
The Oval Office

The president was shaken as he looked up from his desk in what had been a quiet room with himself as the only occupant other than the numerous insects. Now, the gnats were larger, the size of wasps, and their sting was just as painful. His body was covered with bites and boils. Nevertheless, he was working on a speech designed to convince the American people that his administration had things well in hand, but that more money would be needed to implement his new agenda and to expand entitlement programs for those who had suffered as a result of recent events.

The giant gnats still infested the room. Secret Service could be seen on the outside ready to fire on any beast that attempted to get to the president. Everyone had on safety goggles and surgical masks or hats with mosquito netting to protect them from the insects.

"You are Metatron," he said looking up from his work. "I saw you on the transmission from Al Jazeera. What do you want of me? Can't you see that I am busy?"

"If you saw me from Al Jazeera, then why is your fleet still parked near the Israeli coast?"

"I've not moved them. I am waiting for word from Jahid as to his plans. I want you to leave me alone."

"Jahid is in no physical or political condition to be contacting you, and henceforth you will need to call him by his new name, Jaseed. It is one that Jhowah and I gave him when he agreed to become one of our messengers. He has agreed to cease from his efforts to ever again make war on the nation of Israel. Furthermore, he accepts its right to exist and live as he does. He also accepts Jhowah as his living God and has taken up the mantle to temper the anger of radical Muslims the world over against other religions. Mr. President, you now stand alone against Jhowah and Israel. And, as we speak, your people are mounting an initiative against you, your Cabinet, and your Congress."

The president looked shocked when he learned of impending uprising within the U.S. and the change of heart of the Iranian leader.

"Why has Jahid, or rather, Jaseed, changed his mind and stopped his advance?"

"Because he understands that the God of all mankind has given him no choice but to do so," Metatron answered. "If you witnessed my speech from Al Jazeera there is nothing else I need to say to you. You have already been told of the commands of God and what he expects. I must add that Jhowah expects the same of you with regards to the treatment and acceptance of Israel.

"In the case of America I must remind you that there are those within your government and of your political persuasion that have turned your Constitution into a document to change at will, making it useless as it was originally created. You are taking freedom away from the American people. You are falsely playing the role of Messiah and trying to convince many that you are *a* god. You, my friend, have been but a pawn in the hands of Sezan's legions. What you must believe is that Sezan, or Satan, is no longer a participant in the affairs of Soleus-3. He and his ardent followers are on their way to Sheolos, the planet known here on Soleus-3 as hell. And, unless you do as I say, you will be on your way to spend eternity with him.

"When your country was created, those great and God-fearing men who wrote your Declaration of Independence and Constitution gave you a document to give freedom and 'the pursuit of happiness' to all Americans. It has been considered by Jhowah, the one you refer to as God, as the finest crafted document in the history of your planet, because he was at its center.

"In recent years the very premise on which your Constitution was written has been swallowed up in new laws and in the interpretative findings handled by activist judges who agree with your way of governing people. As I informed your Iranian friend, your choice is simple. You make things right or God will very soon continue the plagues of Egypt and destroy this wonderful land. Return to God's laws the ways of your founding fathers or reap the consequences."

Before the president could answer, Metatron vanished in his usual fashion, which was a very impressive sight to the man sitting behind the desk where the fate of the world had so often been decided for more than two hundred years.

The president reached over and pressed his intercom to his chief of staff. "Dick what have you found out?"

"One moment Mister President, let me come in there."

As he entered Dick Anderson was shaking his head. He wore a hat with mosquito netting to keep the gnats away from his face. "We have real and serious problems."

"What do you mean, Dick? Is the right stirring up trouble again?"

"It's more than a partisan problem. It is the people and not the politicians. The evangelicals have rallied the masses. Almost our entire population heard Metatron on the transmission he made out of Qatar. Thousands have already descended upon Washington, and millions more are headed this way. They want just what God commanded through Metatron."

"I don't like the idea of other people telling me what to do. This Metatron, how do we know he's who he says he is, or if this Jhowah is really our God? I have always believed that it was I who was destined to save the world from destroying itself.

My birthright is being taken away from me by these beings from God knows where."

"Mister President," Dick called as he swiped at the swarming insects to be able to see the president, "if you just look around you, Metatron has left some pretty good evidence that he or whoever he works with has an unusual gift of power. The captain of the Gerald R. Ford tells an unbelievable story of a huge space vehicle, so large that it blocked out the sun from both the Russian and U.S. fleets. It was the same vessel that was over Bimini in 2015. The captain told me of the thunderous sound it made as it approached, and then hovered above the beach in dead silence. He said that during its approach, it sounded like thousands of foghorns blasting out notes of different pitches. The sound shook the walls of the vessels and created ripples on the water. And, when it parked above them, something happened to all of the power in both fleets. Nothing could be powered, not anything in the ships, not anything on the jets, and they could not get any communications off the ships.

"When he tried to send out a raft to get information into Gaza, the massive vessel that brought Metatron here parted the sea between them and Gaza, a gap that went all the way to the sea bottom. No one could pass. We thought that our fleet was running silent for an eminent attack, but that wasn't so. It was Jhowah, the one who calls himself our God. He stopped all communication coming from the fleet. It had no power of any type."

"Whoever they are, they sound like they mean business," the president observed.

"The people of America mean it too, Mister President."

The president, stunned by the remark, looked up at his chief, who nodded and gave a smile of concern.

"But Dick, what do you mean?"

"I mean we have lost. Our plans failed. Freedom means too much to most Americans. For years they have remained silent, but as we feared, the sleeping giant, as it were, has awakened. They have been moved by the words of God and those of Metatron and seem to be uniting behind leaders of the new Constitutionalist Party. I am afraid that they will no longer allow us to move our agenda forward.

"Our dreams of creating a worldwide socialist community, that we have yearned for, seem to be destroyed. Those protestors who have already made it to Washington have surrounded the White House, or they are peacefully sitting on the steps of the Capitol, Supreme Court, and every government agency building. Others are occupying every seat of the Congressional chambers, offices, and even in those on the benches of the Supreme Court justices, resisting anyone who tries to remove them. And there are so many of them, the minute the guards remove one, another fills the chair."

"Dick, we can go on with it. Yes, we can! We must! This is our last chance to bring to the United States the kind of social change that Robert Follette, the man who was instrumental in reinventing our party, advocated during his campaigns for the White House in the early 1900s. This is my last chance to eventually become the future secretary general of the United Nations. We've always been able to convince enough of the population to get our programs through," the president said. "Where are my strategists? Get them to help me write a speech. Then notify all the television networks that I intend to talk to the American people. I know that I can convince them to follow me.

"We have an army of our own out there, people whose loyalty we have bought with entitlement programs. We have a command force of community organizers who control community groups that would follow us into hell, and we have given them plenty of whatever they wanted to feel that way. We just have to tell them what we want them to do and mobilize them. We control many leaders of Congress and the new Supreme Court justices that I appointed. I have worked for a lifetime to be where I am. I am confident that we can with-stand this setback."

"Sir, if you continue with our plans they may have no choice but to march into hell, just to find you."

Dick Anderson motioned for the stunned president to follow him. He led him up to the second floor to a window on the north side of the White House facing Lafayette Park.

"Sir, look outside," he said, gesturing toward the window.

The president looked out. His eyes widened as he saw many hundreds of people swatting at the mutating gnats, seemingly growing in size and numbers by the hour. Large crowds of people were gathering in Lafayette Park and in any area outside the perimeter fence where they could stand. The park police had given up on trying to enforce the law that required a "permit" to demonstrate there.

The main street on that side of the White House was totally blocked with people holding signs and shouting in anger. One sign read "Give Us Back Our Freedom." Another read "Bring Back the Constitution," and another read "We are Capitalists not Socialists." One large sign held by two people read, **"Who Do You Think You Are?"** And one longer banner right next to it had the words "What Is It About a Command from GOD That You Do Not Understand?" printed in bold letters. Occasionally they could hear the shot of a pistol, fired by one of the law enforcers as beasts, huge rats, and wild dogs would try to come into the crowd.

He looked to his left, and there were protesters as far as he could see even as far as Seventeenth Street and further. They were continuing to pack themselves into the crowd. He turned to his right and the same scene met his eyes all the way up to and past Fourteenth Street. For once in his life, this president was speechless.

"Come with me, Mister President," Dick called. As he guided the confused and frustrated president through the halls of the White House toward the south side, he could see employees of the White House, their heads protected by netting, swatting at swarming insects and peering out of their office doors at him. The looks on their faces were solemn. Some appeared even to have tears on their cheeks. As the two reached the door, Dick Anderson opened it and led the president out onto the balcony under the south portico where the exterior walls were covered with all manner of pests. The White House shrubbery was being devoured by locust.

Standing against the banisters of the balcony, the two men looked out toward the Ellipse and the Washington Monument. The crowd was even more enormous than on the north side because of the largeness of the open areas in the Ellipse, the Washington Monument, the surrounding streets, and the Capital Mall. Not a single area of green grass or pavement could be seen. What the two saw was a mosaic sea of red, white, and blue. People representing all races and all regions of the country were waving the American flag and singing "God Bless America" to the tops of their lungs.

Even though they couldn't see that far, the word coming to them was that traffic throughout the capital city had come to a standstill, and that most of the passengers of cars that had been stopped by the protesters joined in with the protesters and the singing.

The president looked over at his chief and back out at the growing throngs of people. "Dick, what is happening?" He removed a handkerchief from his pocket, lifted his goggles and wiped a huge mosquito from his eye, taking a swipe at a dozen more before he covered his eyes again. His chief of staff walked him back inside and closed the door to the swarms.

"Mister President, the 'silent majority,' the 'sleeping giant,' has awakened from a long nap. The only conclusion that we can reach is that the people have rejected our agenda, our vision of government free from religion. The people are speaking. It is over. This crowd makes the King rally of the 1960s and the Million Man March of the 1990s look like exhibition bouts preceding the main event.

"There is nothing we can do but join them. You must issue an order for me to have delivered to the carriers positioned off the coast of Israel to stand down and return to international waters immediately. You must make peace with Israel and Jhowah and get this over with. You must abandon your plan to become the ruler of the world. Our social experiment is over. We thought we had a way to change the whole planet, redistribute wealth, and create a New World Order, but it is not to be.

The president gazed at the floor and back at his chief, "Let it be done, Dick. Issue the directives." He turned without saying another word and left. Moments later in the Oval Office he closed the doors, took a seat and bowed his head.

"Dear God, as your servant I have failed. Please show me the errors of my ways and show what you would have me do."

When he finished his prayer he opened his eyes and looked up into the penetrating eyes of Metatron, who had quietly reappeared. Metatron could see more than a man infested with insect bites, he could see into the president's soul where narcissism had been replaced with solitude and hopelessness.

"Do not let your heart be troubled. You've made a wise decision to turn to Jhowah," Metatron said.

The president was sad. "My whole country has turned against me. And I have let down the people who paved my path to the presidency. I tried so hard to follow my heart and I was doing what I thought he would want me to do, but along the way to realizing my field of dreams I lost my way. I became obsessed with the sound of applause and the resounding echoes for change. I was blinded by the promise of unparalleled power and intoxicated by the sound of my own words and the cheering crowds I addressed the world over. Now, none of that matters. I am a beaten man. I have failed."

"Mister President, your intentions are well-placed. The mistake you made was listening to people who used you to obtain what they wanted. They were the 'inner circle' of a global shadow government that had a more sinister and selfish agenda. You were also used by those whose own power was ensured by inventing and fostering premeditated chaos. You became an agent of those who thrived on hatred and greed. You got caught up in programs aimed at retribution and were convinced by those who knew how to control you by saying that you were the 'promised one.' You were enamored by those who would turn the tides and subjugate anyone indentified as their former oppressors.

"In your attempt to change the world, you have ignored Jhowah's original plan for mankind, to be self-sufficient and to make the world a better place for each succeeding generation. What you failed to do was remember the lessons of the Scriptures. You didn't initiate programs that complied with the parable of the talents, the one in which a master gave differing talents to three servants before he went away for a while. You will recall that when he returned from his journey, two servants had multiplied the talents given to them. Both were rewarded for their efforts. The third servant, who, you recall, hid his talent and did nothing to multiply it, was cast out to fend for himself in the wilderness. Neither, however, took a talent from the other, nor did the master take from one and give to another. That is a lesson that those who have supported your rise to power ignored.

"Mr. President, your administration pandered, in exchange for their votes and loyalty, to those who failed to expand the gifts given to humanity at the time of your creation. And that is why you find yourself sitting here today, a beaten man, alone in an office that once ruled the free world with a firm and just hand, the likes of Washington, Jefferson, Lincoln, Teddy Roosevelt, Truman, and Reagan.

"When this world and the people in it were created, it was Jhowah's belief that all would be created free and should be given the freedom of choice to live their lives. You have read that retribution shall lie with God, not with man, yet you listened to those who are driven by hatred and greed. Nowhere in Jhowah's mind or in his works was there a desire for other men, or governments created by man, to remove these freedoms. This is the legacy left by the president whom you have called yourself emulating, the 19th century emancipator and unifier, Abraham Lincoln, the man who toiled to preserve a union established by those who preceded him in the office that you have shared with him.

"Lincoln knew that it was never intended to take from one human being and give that which was taken to another without that person's consent. That, Mister President, is the part of Lincoln's ways that you failed to follow. And that is why you failed as a leader. You became that which you detested, an overlord.

"The plan we brought to this planet was intended to have men care for what we created and willingly help their fellowman, like Jhowah himself has always done, out of love, sometimes the kind of love that is best described as 'tough love.' Even when your country chose to declare its independence, the document stating this declaration made such an affirmation.

"In order to bring your people back into the heart of God, you will have to not only reinvent yourself, but your government. You must return the freedoms taken from them by your politicians and their legislation. You will have to go forward without the assistance of many of those who have orchestrated and supported your rise to power. Very simply stated you must abandon the failed policies of your past and take up a new banner.

"Rather than being buried by the revolution taking place around you, rise up from your chair and go to your people. Ask for chance to change America back to the one envisioned by its founding fathers, 'one nation, under God, with liberty and justice for all.'

"Take the original United States flag that stands outside this office out of its holder and walk out among your people with it held high above your head. Tell them to let you finish out your term and assure them that you will be the president of all people, a president of 'the American way,' God's way. Make this your new mantra from this time forth.

"Turn to your Bible and return to your Constitution. Both are the most properly designed documents ever penned by the hand of man. Both were created with our direction, Jhowah's and mine.

"You must also accept Jhowah as the God of Creation and the very source of the existence of your being, your world. You must denounce any religious or political leader who advocates hatred against a fellow human being and work toward the kind of unity that made your country one of the greatest to exist on the planet. You must go before your friends at the United Nations and tell them of your commitment to initiate a new kind of change, the kind that reflects your new covenant with me. That is, after you have heard me out, if you agree to what I have proposed.

"It has been painful for Jhowah to see his people hated and harmed, to see his name being banned from many important institutions during recent years. How can humanity understand the basic and essential laws that are so common among all civilized nations if you take away from them the Laws of Moses from which all other laws have arisen? Post Jhowah's Commandments in the courthouses around America and put prayer back into your schools.

"Challenge judges who have acted in an activist way and judged that your Constitution dictates freedom from religion, while, in truth, it states: 'Congress shall make no law respecting an establishment of religion, or prohibiting the free exercise thereof.' Only an activist who refused to seek the mind of the Creators could interpret this as removing God's names, laws or any reference to him from anywhere in the United States. How clear could 'prohibiting the free exercise thereof' be? Banning prayer clearly defies that provision.

"And, here's another condition. For as long as you hold this office, appoint only fair-minded judges, who are committed to seeing that Jhowah's laws are upheld as well as those penned by your founding fathers.

"It may be possible for you to achieve your dreams of being a leader who is revered the world over. Lead your people back to your roots, Mister President. Return them to the foundation laid by those who went before you who made yours the greatest nation in the history of humanity. These are my conditions. Do you accept them?"

The president looked up at Metatron, and with a sense of humility and resolve, said, "I will. I thought I knew the right way but I have been naïve. If I can convince the crowd gathering here in Washington that I am a changed man, I will bring my administration together and make your demands, and my new policies, known. I'll also meet with the Congress and do the same. I can only inform them. I can't make them do it. You know our form of government."

"I do," Metatron said. "However, you can do what you do best. Tonight, address the American people and tell them what you have told me. Tell them that you have become a party to a new covenant with God. Ask their forgiveness for the errors of your ways and tell them that you intend to begin anew, to be the president of all Americans, and to create the kind of change that will truly return this great nation to God and to resurrect the intent of the founding fathers. Tell them that you withdraw your proposed amendment to the constitution allowing you to hold the office of president, indefinitely, and that you will work for the rest of your days to return the government of the United States of America to its rightful owners, the people."

The president nodded in the affirmative.

Metatron now looked into the soul of a changed man, a president with a new sense of purpose and direction. He walked over to the president and laid his hand on the president's head. Immediately, the raised and draining wounds that covered the president's body were healed.

"Thank you, my Lord," the president said. "Tell Jhowah that I will serve him and no other."

Metatron nodded in recognition of the president's repentance. Without another word, he raised his arms and vanished from the room.

Back Aboard Command

"Jhowah, I have every reason to believe that the United States has decided to return to the policies that allowed it to become the greatest nation in the history of Soleus-3, and to let you back into their country and the lives of its people."

"It was the only reasonable thing to do, Metatron. With the newly enlightened president of the United States joining in the covenant to preserve the planet, with Jaseed signing on, and with the astral show of force that we demonstrated during the impending assault on Israel, I believe we have global compliance with our issues. In times of crisis, the good people have always rallied around the right course of action. It is only in recent years that they have come to believe that they were powerless. The events of the past few weeks have shown them that they still have a chance to control their own destiny. Let's make it known that we accept this and see if we can return Soleus-3 to a semblance of normalcy."

Jerusalem
The Dome Of The Rock
One Hour Before Sunset
July 2016

Metatron stood before Christian, Muslim, Buddhist, and Jewish leaders as well as the representatives of all other religious leaders of the world. The newest supporters of the covenant initiative, the U.S. and Iranian presidents, were in the front row. Religious leaders and many heads of state had been invited to come to hear the message of God or Allah. They stood just outside the entry into the place known to Muslims as the "Noble Sanctuary," where a massive crowd of believers had completed a pilgrimage to participate in the appearance of the promised Messiah. They had prayed for this day. From childhood they had been taught that the Messiah's or Mahdi's appearance would instill peace on Earth.

Metatron raised his arms to quiet the crowd and began to speak. "I stand before you at the place which houses our first covenant with humanity, the one that was sealed with Abraham. In this most sacred of places, we are here to affirm that there was a second covenant, one that we entered into with a small group of trusted men and women during the 1980s. It was designed to save the world from itself, just in case its leaders continued to take the nations of Soleus-3 on the path paved by evil.

"Over the past few weeks, you have witnessed the results of the covenant Jhowah established with a group known as *Operation Shield* through the American and British leadership of the 1980s. It appears that the technology and intelligence we passed along to this secret group has successfully averted global destruction. As the agent or representative of Allah or God, as you now know the two are in fact one and the same, I personally consummated the aforementioned covenant and returned to Soleus-3 with Jhowah who has been promised to see that its intent was carried out to perfection.

"The Creator of this great planet and its inhabitants has asked me to announce that, as of this day, he has received the assurance by all of the leaders of Earth that they accept him as their Supreme Being and the giver of life and love.

"When this day is ended, each of the religions represented will have seen the prophesy of your scriptures fulfilled. Peace on your planet will, at long last, be achieved, and the promised One will appear before you. When He stands before you, a new covenant will be made. The world will be saved. And, you will go forth to complete the challenge that led to your creation. You will establish a Hivanian-like civilization here on the planet you call Earth and prepare to experience new worlds in other parts of the galaxy.

"Each of the world leaders with whom I have personally met have agreed to become a part of the family of man – creating one world order, the one ordered by Jhowah in His commandments to Moses. All have consented to putting aside the many differences that have, for too long, separated the different religions. From this day forth, there will be *one* religion: Jhowah's. There will be at least a millennium of peace to the Earth and humanity will be allowed to enjoy the many gifts given by Jhowah as you continue to prepare yourself for the journeys ahead."

There came a crescendo of voices as the 144,000 realized the words of Metatron. The silence returned as he opened his arms and continued.

"In recent days it has become necessary for Jhowah to cause a return of the plagues of Egypt and in so doing most of the countries of this globe were under extreme stresses. Now, even the wake of those plagues is no more. Peace and understanding have come to the planet as he has brought the people and their leaders under his protection as their Supreme Being. As promised to you in the book you call Revelation, Sezan Lucefed, the being that many of you call Satan, has been captured and carried to the location that you know of as hell. He will no longer have any effect on the lives of your world.

"At this time the members of *Operation Shield*, the group to whom we awarded the ability to distribute primordial energy, who are physically located here in Israel, are, at this very moment, preparing an initiative to make primordial energy available to all people in every nation. There is much to be done in order to distribute this new energy form. With the assistance of the technicians whom we have already trained, we will only have to use some quite simple procedures to modify current engines and power-driven appliances to use it but it will be done.

"Our current mission here on Soleus-3 is done. We now leave you to return to Hivania. There we will monitor your progress. But Jhowah has an even greater gift for you. Before this day is finished it will be revealed.

"The mysteries you have witnessed, and those to come, were passed on to you in the Book of Enoch that I transcribed the day before I was taken back to the most sacred place on Hivania. These same laws were simplified when Moses was given the Ten Commandments on Mount Sinai. They were part of the ongoing bond with the children of a man whose name was changed from Jacob to Israel.

"You were also reminded of Jhowah's intent when His Son was on this planet in the form of a man the Scriptures refer to as Jesus, the deliverer of what became known as the 'Sermon on the Mount.' During that time 'the Golden Rule' was revealed: 'Do unto others as you would have them, and Jhowah, do unto you.' Against great resistance we attempted to convince all men of the responsibility that comes with the gift of life: 'Unto whom much is given, much is required.'

"Several hundred years later, as Jhowah's messenger, I met with the prophet, Muhammad, and directed him to transcribe Jhowah's, or Allah's, as the Muslim prophet chose to call our Hivanian Father, and create a religion for Ishmael's legions, one based upon peace and loyalty to the one God, the one that I represented.

"Unfortunately, the hand of Sezan intervened in the Jhowah-man relationship. The motives of the false prophet he influenced came close to destroying all that we have created and all that mankind has created as well."

Heads nodded among them. They knew what he said was true and had always been true since the escape of Sezan during the original creating of humanity and the planet.

Metatron continued, "Through it all I have attempted to carry out the missions to which I had been assigned. A special corps of angels was commissioned to assist me with some of your former leaders to create and oversee the plan that many of you came to know as *Operation Shield.*

"Given the turn of events and miracles that you have witnessed during the past several months, your species has been given a second chance to create a colony on this planet similar to the one that exists on Hivania, from which some of us come. Establishing a community of beings who had been made in our own image was a challenge that Jhowah issued to a team of us a very long time ago.

"And to those of you of the Muslim faith, when the one you know as Mahdi and I revealed Jhowah's challenge to Mohammad, we urged him to write down what had been revealed and share it with your ancestors.

"To those who have faithfully followed the teachings of the Buddha, you must know that I was sent by Jhowah to enlighten Gautama."

Those who heard Metatron's words for the first time were beginning to see the universal nature of the events that take place on Earth. Once they had seen, up close and personal the extraordinary being that stood before them, they understood the origins of their beliefs. They realized that many unexplainable miracles that they had learned of through reading The Scriptures were, in fact, the applications of advanced technology possessed by their Creators.

Among those gathered at the Dome, religious doctrines and practices differed. However, on this day, it was clear that their beliefs originated from the same source and that the fundamental message contained in each of the world's religions was the same. Differences of opinions and interpretation of the truth had resulted from the intervention of man. That they did was largely responsible for conflicts among people and nations. Now that Jhowah's plan had been revealed to them, a new challenge lay before them. How do people of different cultures, religions, and political persuasions put aside their deeply rooted differences and begin anew? The answer was about to be revealed.

Suddenly, and without fanfare, standing to Metatron's right were two figures who seemed to appear out of thin air. Some of those who had gathered at the Dome recognized one of the beings. Those had been present when Jhowah addressed the assembly of world leaders remembered him. The other being looked similar to Jhowah, but had a younger and more humanlike persona, similar to that they had seen in Metatron. And, like Metatron, both were draped in regal attire, reminiscent of that worn by ancient Greek and Roman people.

Jhowah spoke first. To the assembled group, He said, "While you are all my creations, there is one here today, who is of my flesh." He turned to the being standing to his right and said, "This, is my beloved Son, the one promised to your ancestors, the one who will ensure global peace. He has loved you before you were created. Although many of you know him as Elijah, others as Jesus, and still others as the Mahdi, throughout the Reticulum Alliance His name is called Immanuel.

"In the past, when your ancestors strayed far from my commandments, He came to me and pled to be among them, to personally show them our ways and shoulder the transgressions of your kind. His love for you is so strong that he chose to experience life on Soleus-3 as you do. He chose to be born as you are born, to live as you live, and to experience the same kind of death that humans experience. It pained me to witness some of the ways he was treated and the manner in which he experienced your kind of death.

"He did all these things to demonstrate that, although He was My Son, he understood what it meant to be human and to prove to you that the condition you call death is merely a transitional state from one of our dimensions to the next.

"All that Immanuel ever asked of you was to believe that he was who he said he was, and to follow my commandments, as did he.

"I agreed with his decision to live among you then. I went along with his wishes so that those of you here today could live as all of us who are part of the Reticulum Alliance live. Age arrest is now yours. From this day forth, none of you will experience death from natural causes."

While Jhowah spoke, no one moved. Everyone who listened to his words was spellbound. They were witnessing an event that millions had prayed for. Their God was, indeed, with them, and when he had completed his remarks, he raised his right hand and gestured to Immanuel, who was standing to his right, saying, "It was also in his likeness and in the images of those species which evolved on the planets of the Reticulum that your ancestors were created. More importantly, it is this same image and this likeness into which your species shall now evolve. Also, today you will assume our multi-dimensional capabilities of those of us from the Reticulum."

Jhowah paused, telempathically read the thoughts and sensed the emotions of those who had heard his word, and spoke. "Now, I have good news to all the nations of this planet. On this sacred site I now enter into a new covenant with humankind. Immanuel, the Messiah, the one who has lived among you, has returned as promised. When I leave you, he will remain behind. He will, once again, be one of you. The 144,000 of you gathered here today have been chosen to create a New Jerusalem -- a new city here on Soleus-3 that will be based on the design and ways of Paradon, our home on Hivania.

"You will become twelve new families, each consisting of 12,000 members. Immanuel will provide the details of your task. He will comfort and guide you as you tell your fellow Soleans what you now know. You have been chosen to complete the mission that was planned thousands of years ago, to create a world of your own making, yet one patterned after Hivania.

"There is another part of my promise that I reveal to you today. When some of you are ready, we will groom you for the next part of our plan, to go into the universe, where other planets similar to your own are being made ready for colonization, similar to the manner in which this one was populated. This, my children, is my covenant, the one that is sealed by having my Son live among you, as one of you."

With that, Jhowah issued a command. "Now, I say to you, people of one origin and one destiny, accept this gift and multiply it. Be all that you were created to be. Look deep into your souls and realize that you were made in our image. That part of us is in you. Exercise the talents instilled in you to create what has long been planned for your species: heaven on earth. And tell your children what you have witnessed. Teach them of my ways and warn them of the consequences that you have witnessed. Tell them to share the lessons of these days with their children and their children's children. The scribes among you must write down what has taken place here so that future generations can know what you have seen to be true. And know that you are one and all, our children."

"This is my challenge, the one that Immanuel accepted on your behalf during the previous times he has been on your planet; the one shared with the prophets of old, the one that Metatron, and the corps of angelic beings he oversees, have brought us back to Soleus-3 to consummate."

"Now, as I once told the prophet Daniel, let the wise among you hear these words and know the truth, that I am Jhowah, the Supreme Being, who sanctified you by My laws and commands you to kindle a light for those who have been lost in the darkness of their own doubt. By accepting this challenge you all become Adams and Eves, the bearers of future generations that will populate not only this planet, but others

Jhowah looked into the eyes of those present from the Majestic group, Doug and Hank, along with the one called

'Prophet' who was brought in from the CIA. These three had been entrusted to carry out the contract formed between Jhowah and a group of visionary world leaders in the 1980s. However, as a result of the events taking place at the Dome of the Rock, the kind of world order that was intended from the beginning would at long last be established.

Jhowah had one final order for those who had gathered to witness this momentous occasion. He said, "The prophesy fulfilled today, and the new ones revealed, will constitute a new promise between all Soleans and me. Because it is centered on Immanuel, who has chosen to live among you, it shall be known throughout the Reticulum Alliance as The Israeli Connection. Tell it to all peoples. From this time forth let it be known that I am, that I am. As it was in the beginning – and shall be for eternity, we are One; and you are one of us."

The Majestic group and Prophet had skillfully maneuvered their way to the front of the massive crowd. Jhowah's message was concise, yet profound. They knew what he said to be true. They had seen who he was, or rather is. Jhowah smiled at each of them in a gesture of approval for a job well done.

With his part of the mission completed, Jhowah motioned for Metatron to come and stand next to him. In their own special way, they bid Immanuel farewell. Simultaneously, Jhowah and Metatron raised their arms toward the heavens, looked upward in the direction of the mother ship above, and began their ascension toward it.

Once they reached the craft, its giant bay doors opened, and the two figures disappeared from sight.

The 144,000 faithful who had come to Jerusalem to see this awe-inspiring miracle were mesmerized. Each had been called to the Holy of Holies to be a part of the prophesized day of reconciliation, getting as close as humanly possible to their Creators, without knowing what was truly in store for them. Though most were familiar with the prophesy of Revelation, this was more than any one of them could have imagined. From this day forward a new God-man relationship would exist on Soleus-3.

The ascension of Jhowah and Metatron having been completed, the bay doors of starship SSV Command closed behind them. Like a soft cloud, the craft continued to hover for one brief moment. Then, in a flash, and without a sound, it disappeared into a brilliant Jerusalem sunset at a velocity that had to approximate the speed of light. Left in its wake was an indelible mark, forever imbued in the minds of all who had come to this sacred place to see the Scriptures fulfilled, and to meet face to face the welcomed prince of the Solean family.

As Immanuel began to move among the crowd, Doug turned to Hank and said, "Look at that sunset, would you please? Never has the western sky been so beautiful. In it must lie another message. Jhowah decided to go into the west for a reason. He wanted us to realize that as the sun disappears below the horizon, on this day, we can know with certainty that it will come back again tomorrow.

"With Immanuel among us, we can rest assured that we are not witnessing what so many have expected: the End Times, but an End of the Beginning."

EPILOGUE

The Revelations of Genesis

In the wake of a passing storm, things that once seemed obscure become crystal clear. And, so it is with the outcome of Jhowah's Solean Initiative.

With the dawning of its new beginning, humankind can look to the future, knowing that it has experienced both the Alpha and the Omega of the greatest cosmic experiment ever conceived.

At long last, previously hidden revelations contained in the first book of The Holy Scriptures have made their way from darkness, into the light. The wisest among the human race have come to realize that we are not alone in the universe, that we were created by beings from other worlds and other dimensions in their own image, and that they have never abandoned us.

After thousands of years of divinely engineered creative evolution, humanity has accepted the fact that the enigmatic beings that controlled the creation of our species are possibly involved in creating similar colonies elsewhere in the universe. Some of these new worlds are being created based on data and experiences collected here on Soleus-3.

The Israeli Connection that Jhowah entrusted to a long line of faithful disciples was consummated when peace and harmony was achieved on Soleus-3, at least for a thousand years.

The experiences gained during The Solean Initiative affirmed Jhowah's belief: mankind's mind is capable of being stretched beyond the limits of mortality, beyond the boundaries that some of the planet's self-anointed "gods" would have imposed had Jhowah not interceded.

After the Ascension the future of Soleus-3 held great adventures and life experiences for God's creations? With his tremendous curiosity, and with the help of Jhowah's primordial energy, mankind finally stretched its wings and reached beyond the Solean star system, outward to distances that skeptics had previously proclaimed "unthinkable."

Once oppressive, manmade governments were reigned in, the human species began to exercise the God given gift of free will. The spirit within was aroused and the potential for which mankind was created flourished. A new renaissance was ushered in. Imagination, thought, and action vaulted the human mind, body, and spirit to inconceivable heights.

As did their ancient ancestors, the newly enlightened members of the human race looked toward the heavens for answers. There, the evolved versions of the Solean Initiative discovered the source of their being and came face to face with their creators, and a destiny inexorably linked with worlds yet to be imagined and explored.

The wisest Soleans came to realize that it was never intended for a self-appointed few to assume the role of "gods" among men.

For a while on Soleus-3, the outcome of the experiment had been in question. The world became burdened with evil, to the point that Atlas himself had shrugged. Achievement and goodness were ridiculed – or worse, punished. The God man relationship and the free will that was imbued in the original partnership had been misdirected. The human spirit was shackled. It appeared as though the creature created by the omnipotent minds of the universe was bent on destroying itself and the planet upon which it lived. Then, biblical prophesies were fulfilled, saving their creations from themselves.

What are the lessons learned? What does the long-term future of Soleus-3 hold? What, or who, will rule the planet when the thousand years of peace comes to an end?

From what has been revealed, there is no way to know the answers to these, the mothers of all questions. Nevertheless, as long as mankind follows the words and spirit of Jhowah's ten simple commandments, the ones he passed to Moses, and looks to our Creators to guide us, one thing is certain: the road ahead will surely be paved with awe and wonder.

While humankind stands poised for a destiny of cosmic proportions and looks beyond the light, into the abyss of the unknown, it must believe that something greater than itself - the collective "us" of Genesis - fills the apparent void. Whatever emerges from The Solean Initiative must offer trust that the one true God, regardless of the names by which he is called, is there, waiting to place something solid beneath our feet, or that he and a hierarchy of celestial beings will teach the ever-evolving image of their likeness how to fly.

APPENDIX I

Star Systems of the Creators and their Planets

PLANET - HIVANIA
IMPORTANCE - Origin of the Hivanian species
STAR SYSTEM - Zeta-1 Reticuli in the Milky Way Galaxy
SATELLITES - two large natural satellites
DIAMETER - 13,800 miles
DISTANCE FROM STAR - 182 million from Zeta-1 Reticuli
SIDEREAL PERIOD - 703 days
AXIAL ROTATION PERIOD - 74 hours
ATMOSPHERE - Nitrogen-68%, Oxygen-30%, other gases - including
Carbon Dioxide-2%
SURFACE WATER - 53% of planetary surface

PLANET - DROMEDOS
IMPORTANCE - Origin of the Dromedan species
STAR SYSTEM - Zeta-2 Reticuli (Zeta-1 and Zeta-2 are binary) in the
Milky Way Galaxy
SATELLITES - one larger and two smaller satellites
DIAMETER - 9,400 miles
DISTANCE FROM STAR - 82 million miles from Zeta-2
SIDEREAL PERIOD - 212 ½ days
AXIAL ROTATION PERIOD - 36 hours
ATMOSPHERE - N-82%, O2-17%, Other-1%
SURFACE WATER - 75% of planetary surface

PLANET - JANOS
IMPORTANCE - Origin of Janosian species
STAR SYSTEM - Tau Ceti in the Milky Way Galaxy
SATELLITES: 1 natural satellite
DIAMETER: 18,578 miles
DISTANCE FROM STAR - 71,234,700 miles
SIDEREAL PERIOD - 252 days
AXIAL ROTATION PERIOD - 25 hours
ATMOSPHERE - N-80%, O2-18%, Other - 2%
SURFACE WATER - 68%

PLANET - MENSAE-5
IMPORTANCE - Location of colonization by the three species
STAR SYSTEM - Alpha Mensae in the Milky Way Galaxy
SATELLITES - 2 satellites (one capable of supporting life
DIAMETER - 14,500 miles
DISTANCE FROM STAR - 82,025,000 miles
SIDEREAL PERIOD - 320 days
AXIAL ROTATION PERIOD - 28 hours
ATMOSPHERE - N-76.5, O2-21%, Other-2.5%
SURFACE WATER - 78%

PLANET - SHEOLOS
IMPORTANCE - Location of penal colony of Reticulum Alliance

STAR SYSTEM - Zeta-1 Reticuli in the Milky Way Galaxy

SATELLITES - None

DIAMETER - 4,560 miles

DISTANCE FROM STAR - 65,150,000 miles from Zeta-1

SIDEREAL PERIOD - 220 days

AXIAL ROTATION PERIOD - 36 hours

ATMOSPHERE - N-78%, O2-16%, Other-6%

SURFACE WATER - No surface water; several sub-surface deposits

PLANET - SOLEUS-3/EARTH

IMPORTANCE - Location of the Challenge of Jhowah

STAR SYSTEM - Soleus in the Milky Way Galaxy

SATELLITES - Only 1 - Luna

DIAMETER - 8,200 miles

DISTANCE FROM STAR - 90 million miles from Soleus-3

SIDEREAL PERIOD - 365 ¼

AXIAL ROTATION PERIOD - 24 hours

ATMOSPHERE - N-77%, O2-21%, Argon-1%, Other-1%

SURFACE WATER - Over 70%

APPENDIX II

Chronology of Events

35,906 B.C. – The development of the SAMSL Time-Field Drive (Speeds at Multiples of the Speed of Light) occurs on the planet Hivania in the Zeta-1 Reticuli star system giving the Hivanians the capability of traveling interstellar.

35,904 B.C. – The planet Sheolos in the Zeta-1 Reticuli star system is established as a penal colony for incorrigible criminals.

35,903 B.C. – Initial contact by the Hivanians with the planet Dromedos occurs in the Zeta-2 Reticuli star system, a peaceful encounter.

35,902 B.C. – The Zeta Alliance is created to share the combined technology of the two systems for the betterment of universal civilization.

35,902 B.C. – Initial contact with the planet Janos occurs in the Tau Ceti star system, a hostile encounter.

35,886 B.C. – The Advancement of Technology agreement is created among all three planets.

35,350 B.C. – 37,100 BC – The Reticulum Wars begin with the Janosians taking up arms against the Hivanians and Dromedans. The Janosians were ultimately defeated.

35,216 B.C. - The Age-Arrest research is completed by Sezan Lucefed, and the Society of Reticulum Genetic Engineers (SORGE) is organized.

35,056 B.C. - The formation of the Reticulum Alliance occurs, which included the planets of Hivania, Dromedos, and the then occupied planet of Janos.

34,040 B.C. - The colonization of Mensae-5 in the Alpha Mensae star system by the three races of the over-populated Reticulum Alliance planets takes place, making it the fourth member of the Reticulum Alliance.

33,016 B.C. - The challenge is made by Jhowah to the members of SORGE to create a new world and genetically engineer cells from their own race to create new human life forms.

35,015 B.C. - The challenge of Jhowah is accepted and initiated. Soleus-3 in the Solean star system is chosen as the site to carry out the Challenge.

35,014 B.C. - The first genetically engineered cloned human embryo in the known universe is created and placed in a primitive humanoid host from Soleus-3 which is then transferred from the labs in Paradon on Hivania to Soleus-3 on the maiden voyage of the starship labs to their orbiting positions above Soleus-3.

35,014 B.C. - The 'birth' of the first genetically engineered clone occurs aboard the labs on the starship SSV Human Lab orbiting Soleus-3.

35,013 B.C. - The 'Sezan Effect' is noted in the first creation in the project, resulting in the incarceration of Sezan Lucefed and Yon Samael.

35,013 B.C. – The escape of Sezan and Samael, and destruction of the subcontinent colony both take place.

35,012 B.C. – The initial insertion of Zolan solution into new clones occurs.

27,500 B.C. – The construction of labs on Soleus-4 that are to handle all aspects of the cloning from the genetic engineering to clone maturation, birthing, and training of the human creations is initiated.

10,025 B.C. – An ecological catastrophe occurs on Soleus-4 leaving the Reticulum labs devastated and without an atmosphere. Remnants of the lab site as viewed from orbit appear somewhat like a face on the surface of Soleus-4.

7,000 B.C. – The SSV Human Lab is converted to an orbiting lab to seek out and monitor the fading degree of the Zolan Solution.

1,947 A.D. – There is an accident and crash of a shuttle resulting in the loss of Jon Dreel and two others on the western surface of Soleus-3.

1,956 A.D. – The SSV Human Lab is moved to a stationary orbit behind Luna, and movement of the remainder of the science fleet back to the Paradon docks to await the initiation of another project already in the planning stages.

2,012 A.D. – The SSV Command is relocated behind Luna to assist in the revelation at the end of the year. The SSV Human Lab is reassigned to Hivania until the plans for future projects are reevaluated.

2013 A.D. – Sezan interferes with the pricing of fossil fuels in the Middle East causing chaos, and further burdens the world economic crisis.

2013 A.D. (Early) – Israel makes preemptive attack on Iran in Tehran and on its nuclear weapons creation centers.

2013 A.D. December – President Jahid of Iran sets up an aborted attack on Israel.

2014 (Early) – The Reticulum Alliance makes the final adjustments on the newly installed primordial energy power grid.

2014 August – Complaints lodged against Israel at the UN that it is hoarding primordial energy and controlling it as a monopoly.

2016 January – Battle plans set for an all-out attack on Israel by Russia, the U.S., Iran, and all of the Islamic Middle East countries. Iran eventually sends nuclear missiles into Israel over Tel Aviv and the mound known as Har Megiddo (Also translated Armageddon).

2016 January 25 – SSV-Command takes a position above the U.S. and Russian fleets in the Mediterranean near Gaza immobilizing both to prevent the obliteration of Israel.

2016 January 27 – Metatron gives a warning to the world regarding war, loyalty to God, love and respect for fellow man. He warns of total destruction and issues warning that Jhowah (God) will reinstitute the plagues of Egypt. This eventually causes all parties to lay down their arms.

2016 July – Jhowah and Metatron speak in Jerusalem at the Dome of the Rock.

2016 to 3016 – One thousand years of peace

MEET OUR AUTHORS

E. Gaylon McCollough

Founder of the McCollough Institute for Appearance and Health in Gulf Shores, Alabama, Dr. McCollough is a world-renowned physician, facial plastic surgeon and author.

Author or co-author of seven books providing extraordinary insight into the behavior of human beings, McCollough focuses on the triumph of excellence over mediocrity and good over evil.

Dr. McCollough and his lovely wife, Susan, live on a small ranch with their herd of Tennessee Walking horses.

Symm Hawes McCord

Dr, Symm McCord is a co-author of *The Annunaki Enigma: Armageddon.* He grew up in th southern town of Augusta Georgia where he was educated and attended medical school. After medical school he was inducted into the U.S. Army where he spent two years – one in Vietnam and one stateside. After military service he spent the next forty years as a family physician; practicing in the mountains of North Carolina and then back in his hometown of Augusta. He retired in 2006 and returned to the mountains. He now lives in Waynesville, North Carolina with his wife Jacquelyn. They have six children from previous marriages.

As a child he witnessed the newspaper articles referencing the incident outside of Roswell, New Mexico which intrigued him immensely. His first novel, *The Annunaki Enigma: Creation,* introduced the concept of the Annunaki, the errant angels, and their relationship to our Creator. He may be contacted at smccord@live.com

Watch for more from this dynamic
duo and
A-Argus Better Book Publishers

Also in the Annunaki Enigma Series:

Book One: The Annunaki Enigma:
Creation

Book Two: The Annunaki Enigma:
The Oath

Other works by McCollough:
The Lords of Seduction

www.ingramcontent.com/pod-product-compliance
Lightning Source LLC
Chambersburg PA
CBHW051518260626
47170CB00003B/678